Make A Wish

ALSO BY HELENA HUNTING

SHACKING UP SERIES

Shacking Up
Hooking Up
I Flipping Love You
Making Up
Handle with Care

STAND-ALONE NOVELS

Starry-Eyed Love
When Sparks Fly
The Good Luck Charm
Meet Cute
Kiss My Cupcake
The Librarian Principle
Felony Ever After
Little Lies (writing as H. Hunting)

ALL IN SERIES

A Lie for a Lie
A Favor for a Favor
A Secret for a Secret
A Kiss for a Kiss

LAKESIDE SERIES

Love Next Door
Love on the Lake

PUCKED SERIES

Pucked (Pucked #1)
Pucked Up (Pucked #2)
Pucked Over (Pucked #3)
Forever Pucked (Pucked #4)
Pucked Under (Pucked #5)
Pucked Off (Pucked #6)
Pucked Love (Pucked #7)

CLIPPED WINGS SERIES

Clipped Wings
Inked Armor
Fractures in Ink

Make A Wish

HELENA HUNTING

ST. MARTIN'S GRIFFIN
NEW YORK

First published in the United States by St. Martin's Griffin, an imprint of St. Martin's Publishing Group

MAKE A WISH. Copyright © 2022 by Helena Hunting. All rights reserved. Printed in the United States of America. For information, address St. Martin's Publishing Group, 120 Broadway, New York, NY 10271.

www.stmartins.com

Designed by Devan Norman

Library of Congress Cataloging-in-Publication Data

Names: Hunting, Helena, author.
Title: Make a wish / Helena Hunting.
Description: First Edition. | New York : St. Martin's Griffin, 2023.
Identifiers: LCCN 2022037975 | ISBN 9781250624741
    (trade paperback) | ISBN 9781250624758 (ebook)
Subjects: LCGFT: Novels.
Classification: LCC PS3608.U594966 M35 2023 |
    DDC 813/.6—dc23/eng/20220829
LC record available at https://lccn.loc.gov/2022037975

Our books may be purchased in bulk for promotional, educational, or business use. Please contact your local bookseller or the Macmillan Corporate and Premium Sales Department at 1-800-221-7945, extension 5442, or by email at MacmillanSpecialMarkets@macmillan.com.

First Edition: 2023

10 9 8 7 6 5 4 3 2 1

Kidlet, you better never read this book past this first page,
but know that you inspire me endlessly.
You're forever my best invention.

Make A Wish

Prologue
A FUTURE TOO DISTANT TO REALIZE

HARLEY
AGE TWENTY

My eyes snap open at the despondent cry lighting up the baby monitor. It's the third time Peyton, the toddler I nanny for, has woken tonight. She's teething and she has a cold, the combination of the two making her restless and uncomfortable.

I lie there for a few seconds, waiting to see if the cry is isolated or she's actually awake and needs comfort. A few seconds later another cry filters through the baby monitor, and then again, more insistent this time. I toss my covers off and my feet hit the cold floor. I grab my housecoat and shrug into it as I rush down the hall, wanting to get to her before the cries reach their highest pitch and wake her father as well.

Gavin's been burning the candle at both ends, work taking up more of his time than he'd like, and with Peyton not sleeping particularly well this week, he's been tired. If I can save him another broken night's sleep, I can also save myself from having to drive something to his office because he's forgotten it on the kitchen table.

He steps into the hallway just as I reach Peyton's room. He's wearing nothing but boxer shorts and a thin white T-shirt, his lean, toned body throwing shadows on the wall and floor.

He blinks blearily at me and runs a hand through his sleep-messed hair. "I can handle this." His voice is gruff and thick with exhaustion.

"You have to be up in two hours. She's teething and cranky. I can take care of it."

He glances at the door and then at me, teeth tugging at the skin of his bottom lip before he blows out a breath. "She's been up three times already."

I pat him on the arm. "I know. And you have to function tomorrow. I can take a nap when she does. I've got this. Go back to bed."

"Thanks, Harley." He gives me a weary smile and turns around, disappearing into his bedroom.

As I rush into Peyton's bedroom, she's standing in her crib with her arms outstretched, stiff and shaking. When she sees me, her wailing hits the high notes and she stomps her little feet.

"I'm right here, sweetie. You must be so uncomfortable." I pick her up out of her crib and she snuggles into my neck, sniffling and crying. Her cheeks are red and her fingers go straight into her mouth. At eighteen months, we're in the thick of another round of teething, and this time it's her canines, which are proving to be particularly uncomfortable. And I thought the molar stage was rough.

I carry her over to the rocking chair and cuddle her, singing lullabies until she finally falls asleep again. I don't know how long she'll be down before she wakes up again, so once I have her settled in her crib, I make a trip to the kitchen to grab a teething ring from the freezer.

I stop when I reach the threshold. Gavin is sitting at the

island with a glass in front of him. It's mostly dark, the only illu-mination comes from the light above the stove. His broad back expands and contracts on a sigh, and he drops his head, fingers pushing through his thick, dark hair. He laces them behind his neck and makes a despondent sound.

I don't know whether I should leave him and let him have a moment of peace or offer him comfort.

This week has been difficult for him. Peyton just turned a year and a half, and with each milestone, it's another reminder of how long it has been since his wife died. Add in the sleepless nights, the long work hours, his parents still both working full-time and unable to offer much in the way of babysitting support, and his in-laws in Boulder, it's no wonder he's struggling.

I overheard him on the phone with his mother-in-law before he took it off speaker phone. She doesn't feel it's appropriate that I'm the woman practically raising her granddaughter. I'm too young to be taking care of Peyton. I spend too much time with them as a family. It didn't sit right with her that I was solely respon-sible for Peyton while Gavin was at work. I might be twenty, but I have always loved working with children. I took the babysitting course as soon as I turned eleven and started sitting for family and friends right away. While other teenagers went out with friends on weekends, I spent them taking care of little kids while their par-ents went on dates or out with friends. And with over half a child development degree under my belt, I'm more than qualified to be a nanny. Besides, I've been through more than a lot of people my age, lost more and survived.

My feet make the decision before my head can weigh in, and my heart is already in agreement with my actions as I cross the kitchen and head for Gavin.

I purposely step on the board that creaks, and Gavin's head shoots up. My heart clenches at his expression. Shock, dismay, and embarrassment pass through his eyes, but the pain I see reflected back at me is what stops me from changing course. I bridge the gap between us and settle a hand on his shoulder. "What can I do to help?"

He scrubs a hand over his tired face. "You're already doing too much." His chocolate eyes lift to meet mine. "I'm putting too much on you."

I shake my head. "You're not."

"I am. You're only taking Sundays off. You should be going out on weekends with your friends, going to house parties, doing what college kids do."

I don't understand where this is coming from, or why all of a sudden Gavin is worried about my social life. "I'm more into Disney movies, arts and crafts, baking cupcakes, and making popcorn than I am going to house parties."

"I just mean you deserve to have a life. I need to cut back my hours. I need to be here more." His voice is low and gravelly. "I should be here for Peyton. It's not fair for me to keep piling it all on you. You're too young to be handling all of this."

"I would tell you if it was too much. And you are here for Peyton. You're always home for dinner, and you make sure you're here for bedtime. Sure, you work extra hours once she's in bed, but that's not unusual. Especially since you're helping run a family business. You're doing the best you can, and that's all anyone can ask for."

"But is it enough?" He shakes his head. "I feel like I'm in purgatory, Harley. I feel like I'm stuck in the past, and all I want to do is move forward, but I can't. I don't know how to do this on my own."

"But you don't have to do it on your own, Gavin. You have your family and you have me."

"I don't know how to let go of this guilt." His face crumples and he scrubs a hand over it.

"The guilt over what? What do you feel guilty about?" We don't usually talk like this. Mostly he asks about Peyton, how her day was, and the milestones she's reaching. At dinner he'll sometimes ask about my courses, but he doesn't open up about Marcie. I know it's been a struggle for him to move past the loss of his wife. While she's never a topic of conversation, she's memorialized everywhere in this house.

He shakes his head. "I can't . . . I just want it to stop hurting all the time."

I settle my hand on top of his and squeeze. "I'm here. You can talk to me. I understand what it means to lose someone you love. I know the hurt doesn't go away. We manage, we adapt, we develop armor, but we don't stop missing them and we don't stop loving them."

"Is there no peace?" His expression breaks my heart.

I don't know how to help him with anything other than the offer of comfort. So I do something I normally never would when it comes to one of my charges and their parents. I wrap my arms around his shoulders and hug him.

He stiffens for a moment, and I'm about to release him and apologize for overstepping, but he folds his arms around me and pulls me tightly against him. The sound he makes holds so much torment.

"It's okay, Gavin. I'm here. I know it's hard." We've always kept it professional between us. Sure, I may be living under the same roof, but my job is to care for the sweet little angel that is sleeping down the hall. But tonight is different.

In this moment, I feel like I'm more than the nanny. Right now, it's as though I've become part of this family.

I understand what he's going through. Maybe I don't know what it's like to lose your partner before you've even had a chance to really and truly start your life together. But I know what it's like to lose both of my parents. They died when I was twelve, leaving me and my older sisters, Avery and London, orphaned. Our grandmother stepped in to raise us, but those Mom-and-Dad-shaped holes in my heart can never be filled. There will always be two empty spaces in my chest where they used to be.

Slowly he loosens his hold on me. "I need to get a grip," he mutters, voice thick with emotion.

Goose bumps rise along my skin when his fingertips skim my arm as he drops his hand.

"We all have difficult days. I'm always here. Whenever you need me." My heart is beating so hard, it feels like it could crack my rib cage. I can't seem to find it in me to step back, to break this connection. The longing to feel needed like this clouds my judgment. The intimacy of the moment makes it difficult to separate my desire to comfort from other, new feelings I don't know what to do with.

I lean in until I can feel his sharp exhale against my lips. My stomach flips and my muscles clench in anticipation.

But whatever spell I'm under breaks before I connect.

Gavin's hands wrap around my shoulders and he pushes me back, not forcefully but firmly. "Harley, no."

Peyton's shrill cry is a bucket of ice water over my head and a welcome distraction from my complete horror and mortification. I rush down the hall to Peyton's room and scoop her up like a shield. Panic takes over, and fear and guilt swirl in my gut and make it tough to swallow. What did I do? How could I be so stupid?

"I've got it, Harley. You can go back to bed." Gavin holds out his arms, his expression flat and remote.

I can't say no. He's my boss. He's her father. I'm just the nanny.

And I almost kissed him. I would have, if he hadn't stopped me. He'd been in need of comfort, and I'd taken advantage of that weak moment. Shame and disbelief make me want to disappear, to sink into the ground, to hide from my own mistake.

Uncomfortable, awkward silence follows as I pass Peyton over to Gavin, but her cries grow louder, maybe because she senses the disquiet between us.

"Go to bed, Harley." Gavin's voice is tight and clipped.

I move around him, unable to meet his gaze. I feel numb, as if my emotions have been dipped in liquid nitrogen. Frozen. And one flick will shatter me.

As I step into the hall, Peyton screams, arms stretched out to me. "Momma! Mummy!"

I pause, a sick feeling rolling through my stomach and creeping up my throat, and turn to see Gavin's reaction. She's said it before, at the park I sometimes take her to with a few other nannies in the area, but it's never happened in front of Gavin before. I usually just shake my head and say, "No, not Momma, it's Harley" to her because she doesn't know the difference. To her, it's just words she hears the other kids say.

But his eyes flash with ire, and he gives me a hard, cold look that makes me want to disappear all over again.

"That's Harley, not your mommy. Daddy's got you." He shuts the door with a quiet click, and I stand there, my heart in my throat.

I go back to my room, tears of embarrassment and guilt falling. I don't know what to do. How to fix this. I spend the rest of the night pacing the floor, trying to figure out how I'm going to apologize. That I didn't mean to overstep. That I have no idea what came over me. That it will never happen again.

A few days later, just when I'm ready to express how sorry I am, Gavin tells me they're moving to Boulder to be closer to his in-laws.

And when they do, I don't hear from Gavin or Peyton ever again.

One

THIS MEMORY LANE IS CLOSED

HARLEY
AGE TWENTY-SEVEN

"I need you to work your magic!" London rushes me the second I walk into the Spark House office and thrusts baby Ella at me. "I have a call in five minutes, and I can't take it with Ella losing her mind."

Ella's mouth is open in a wide O, and her face is beet red. She lets out a hearty wail and flails her arms and legs like a tiny human pinwheel.

Without a word, I drop my purse on the floor and hold out my arms, accepting my screaming niece. "What's going on Ella-bella? Why so sad, little cutie patootie?"

She stops for half a second and cranes to look over her shoulder at London, then realizes she's not in her mother's arms anymore and starts up again.

London cringes. "I'm sorry. I'll try to make it quick."

"Don't worry about it. I've got it handled. I'm happy to listen to Ella's woes while you take the call." I kiss her chubby, warm cheek and give her a raspberry. She startles, then giggles, then starts to frown until I do it again.

London shakes her head. "How do you do it? Every single time you get her to stop."

"I distract her. And I'm calm, and you're . . . a little high-strung and stressing about this call."

She opens her mouth as if she's about to argue, then clamps it shut again. "Maybe I need to take up recreational weed smoking or something."

"I'm going to go ahead and say that if you do, please don't make any videos. Remember the turtle-rant incident compliments of Avery?"

She makes a face. "Right. Good point. I'll keep that in mind."

Years ago, Avery's friends accidentally fed her half a dozen pot brownies, and she ended up ranting about the lack of plastic straws and how turtles were smelly and not the only important species on the face of the earth. The rant ended up on social media and did not go over well, especially since we'd been trying to secure a sponsorship. We've moved past that, and more than recovered from that accidental blow to our business, which means we bring it up on occasion, mostly to annoy Avery.

"CBD oil is a good alternative," I suggest and then shoo her off. "Go make your call. Ella and I will be out back setting up for the birthday party."

"What if it goes long? The call, I mean?"

"This is a party for kids. I'm holding an adorable baby. Everyone loves babies, especially when they're as cute as you, right?" I tickle Ella's tummy and she giggles again. "Now go, you've wasted three out of your five minutes to prep standing here fretting with me and Ella."

London rushes back to her desk and drops down in her chair. I take Ella outside, into the yard where the party will be held. I pass the potting shed, which is actually more like a small garage, on the way to the party area. I keep forgetting to suggest we figure out a use for it since it just sits there these days.

My sisters and I have been running Spark House for the past six years. It started as a boutique hotel that functioned mostly as a bed-and-breakfast and a venue for small weddings or celebrations. But over time, and with our older sister Avery's creative brain, we've turned it into an event hotel. We host everything from weddings and bachelor parties, to charity events and hobbyhorse competitions. Yes. That's a real thing, and probably one of my favorite events ever that we host on a yearly basis.

The hotel has been in our family for years, but we officially took it over when our grandmother decided to retire. Avery is the backbone of Spark House and manages the event-planning side; her husband, Declan, deals with finances; and London manages the decorative and creative parts of the events. I run the social media. Or I used to, until Spark House was taken under the wing of London's almost-billionaire husband. Now we have a team of people who manage our social media outreach and I just supplement it.

Since the additions to our team means I have more time to spare, I took on hosting birthday parties, specifically ones for children, which I really love. Today's party is an elaborate setup with a princess theme. The birthday girl is a big fan of all things princess, and this party is right up my ball-gown-loving alley. Today I'm dressed like a magical fairy, complete with sparkly, poofy tutu and star wand. I'm not the only one who will be dressed up, though. There are all kinds of fun costumes for the kids, along with a special princess outfit for the birthday girl.

I set up a crafts station where the kids can make edible

cookie wands. They're shaped like stars and baked with a stick, so they're perfect for icing and sprinkle decorations and making magic.

I keep Ella distracted with things that sparkle as I double-check everything one final time before the guests begin to arrive. I'm making sure all the costumes are labeled with the guests' names—we asked the partygoers who their favorite princess was, and their size, so we could have all the costumes ready ahead of time.

When I read the name PEYTON on a fairy costume, my heart clenches, taking me back in time to when I nannied for a little girl with the same name. She'd have to be close to the same age as the birthday girl by now. I shove those memories down, because the feelings that come with them are never easy. Mortification and guilt are forever associated with that time in my life. Mortification about the lines I crossed. Guilt that those actions are what sent Peyton and her father to Boulder to be closer to his in-laws. Or at least that's how it seemed.

"This place looks like a princess convention." Avery appears in the doorway to the dress-up tent. Like everything else, it's been decorated with balloons, streamers, and all things glittery and sparkly.

"It pretty much is," I agree.

Ella coos, and when Avery tickles her under her chin, she giggles, toots, and ducks her head.

"How are you doing?" Avery asks, her smile questioning and slightly chagrined.

I lift a shoulder and let it fall, working to keep my smile in place and my tone light. "At least my birthday parties are going out with a bang."

"I'm really sorry we can't keep hosting them."

"It's okay. I get it. They aren't a moneymaker, and we need to keep Spark House available for bigger events."

"I know how much you love them." Avery tried to go to bat for me, and so did London when Declan told us the birthday parties were costing us money instead of making it. A two-hour birthday party on a Saturday afternoon isn't as financially lucrative as a wedding where every room in Spark House is booked for two nights.

When I first suggested the birthday parties a couple of years ago, it was a way for me to feel like I was making a more significant contribution. But Declan is right. It isn't financially responsible. They have to be cut. So I'm making the last one as awesome as possible.

"I'll be able to throw kick-butt parties for my nieces and nephews, starting with this little princess." I give Ella a kiss on the cheek.

She takes my face in both of her hands and plants a wet one to the left of my nose.

"You know Ella was crying for half an hour before London palmed her off on you."

"London's stressed. Babies feel that." And I'm sure London thought it would be fine to bring Ella to Spark House since the birthday party isn't going to take the whole day. "Where's Jackson, anyway?" Jackson is London's husband and owns Holt Media, a massive company that started up an initiative called Teamology. It pairs companies with sponsors to help put small businesses on the map. Since Teamology took Spark House under its wing a couple of years ago, we've grown by leaps and bounds.

"He had a meeting this morning. And Declan is out with

the guys." She glances around the tent. "Do you need help with anything?"

"I don't think so. Catering has set up everything in the food tent. Crafts and games are all organized, the adult tent has appetizers and beverages ready to be served, and guests should be arriving shortly. I think we're good."

As sad as I am about my birthday parties ending, I know changes are coming. Recently we've been in talks with the owners of Mills Hotels, who run some of the most luxurious and prestigious hotels in the world. They've expressed interest in helping us expand even further by creating a Spark House franchise. It's a huge opportunity, and if it happens, it could take Spark House to an entirely new level. The kind of level where afternoon children's birthday parties are definitely off the table.

I can see the value in it, especially for my sisters, who are both starting families and need the security and the time. I know that in the grand scheme of things, it will give us incredible exposure. And financially it will help us move forward. But at the same time, the things that I love most about Spark House, and my role here, keep shifting. I feel as though I'm always rushing to try to catch up with the changes. And like we're leaving behind the hands-on approach, which is something I've always enjoyed.

"Okay, well, if you're good here, I'll just leave you to it. Do you want me to take Ella back to London?"

"You can leave her with me for now. I'll let you know if I need backup."

Avery heads in the direction of the main house, and I deflate a little. Just because I know the birthday parties aren't good for our bottom line doesn't mean I'm not disappointed about losing them. They've been my baby for almost two years and I really love planning them. Plus, it's given me an opportunity to work with kids on a semiregular basis, which is something I've missed. It reminds me of the days when I used to be a nanny. It's not a road I'll likely ever go down again. Not after what almost happened the last time.

I swallow the familiar unease that comes with just thinking about that time in my life. Ella's chubby, damp hand settles against my cheek. Her expression is serious when I give her my attention again, as though she can sense the change in my mood.

My phone buzzes from the pocket in my poofy skirt. I have to push layers of tulle out of the way, but I finally manage to find the opening and pull it free. I hold it up to my face to unlock it, and Ella tries to grab it with her spit-covered fingers.

I raspberry her cheek while I open the message from my boyfriend.

Chad: Meet up later for drinks with A&A at the Firkin? Sevenish? I can pick you up.

The sound of tires rolling over pavement alerts me to the arrival of our first guests. "It's showtime!" I say to Ella, who mimics my wide eyes.

I respond to the text with a thumbs-up and slip my phone back into my pocket with just as much trouble as I had retrieving it, then leave the dress-up tent so I can greet the partygoers.

Twenty minutes later the backyard is buzzing with energy. Twelve eight- to eleven-year-olds bounce around excitedly, all dressed up as their favorite princess.

The parents are standing in small groups in the adult tent set up a short distance away from the party. Close enough that they can observe what's happening, but far enough that they're not directly in their kids' line of sight. They have a dedicated bartender who is serving a lovely array of cocktails and a table of appetizers. I've found the adult tent is much needed at these events.

There's also a late lunch scheduled to be brought out at three. It's buffet style, but a heck of a lot more exciting than the pizza, salad, and subs the kids are having. Although I'm never one to turn down a good slice of cheesy pizza.

As far as children's parties go, we set the bar pretty high.

"We're waiting on one more guest," Lynn, the mother of the birthday girl tells me, then takes a small sip of her champagne cocktail. "This is delicious, by the way. Everything is perfect. And all the parents appreciate having their own place to mingle. You've really thought of everything."

"I understand that some parents are more comfortable sticking around. We wanted to make it fun for them too." I wink knowingly. "Would you like me to hold off on starting the craft until the final guest arrives?" I don't want to leave anyone out, but the kids need an activity to break things up. They're currently posing for pictures in the castle-themed backdrop. I'd say we have about five more minutes before they get restless and bored. I'd like to prevent that from happening if possible.

"Oh! There they are! I'll be right back!" Lynn smiles and touches my shoulder, then heads toward a man and little girl making their way across the field.

I squint as they get closer. The little girl has long dark hair, pulled up into a ponytail. She stays close to her dad's side. He's tall, with the same dark hair. Even from a distance, I can tell he's the kind of attractive that turns heads. And the closer he gets, the more familiar he becomes.

And not in the *I've seen him around town* or *he works with my boyfriend and I've run into him at a Christmas party* kind of way. It's more *I wish a UFO would appear out of the sky and beam me up.* Being probed would be preferable to what's about to happen.

A hot feeling creeps up the back of my neck, along with a tickle that's reminiscent of ants crawling on skin. I'm fair-haired, and I don't tan particularly well. So the heat that seems to be spreading over my body like wildfire is also causing it to go pink. Bright pink, in fact. Almost the same color as my tutu.

Oh my God. This honestly couldn't get any worse. I'm wearing a freaking tutu, and I'm dressed like a fairy, and the man who moved across the state because I almost kissed him is heading toward me. Today can suck a giant rotten hot dog soaked in pickle juice.

The little girl is rushed by some of the princess partygoers who drag her toward the dress-up tent, laughing and smiling. I want to run in that direction too. But I can't. Because I can't make my arms and legs move. As it is, I'm barely registering the weight of Ella, or the fact that her hands are now in my hair and she's yanking on it.

My heart is beating so fast, it feels like it's on the verge of busting through my rib cage. I imagine it landing on the ground with a splat and almost let loose a slightly hysterical laugh. Instead, I make a sound similar to a duck being stepped on and plaster what I hope isn't an entirely fake-looking smile on my face.

I shift Ella, more to see if I still have feeling in my fingers. I'm starting to sweat. I can feel it dripping down my back, and it trickles

awkwardly down the inside of my thigh. I'm glad that I have something to do with my hands so I don't touch my hair or adjust my
dress, which incidentally is bunched up on one side because Ella's
foot is caught in the pocket.

She grabs my hair with her drooly hand again as Lynn and
the man approach. They're a handful of feet away now, and Lynn
is pointing out the dress-up tent and the adult tent, which is behind me. There's no option but to pass right by me to get there.

And of course, Lynn being the ever-gracious woman she
seems to be, stops to introduce us to each other.

"Gavin, you have to meet Harley."

It would be awesome if I were a real fairy godmother, and I
could magic myself out of here.

Two

BLAST FROM THE PAST

HARLEY

Unfortunately, no amount of fairy dust is going to get me out of this situation. I'm particularly conspicuous in my pink tutu and my sparkly shirt, but I'd hoped I could blend in with the kids because I'm not a whole lot taller than some of them and they're dressed very much like me.

Thanks to Lynn, that's not going to happen. Gavin's gaze swings my way and his eyes widen, probably because of my outfit and the fact that he's registered that I am not, indeed, one of the children.

Despite my high level of mortification and my desire to be beamed up by aliens, I can fully appreciate how good the past seven years have been to him. He'd only been in his late twenties when he became a dad. Back then, I'd thought he was attractive, but now, he's moved to a whole new level of hot. It's clear that he's spent a lot of time at the gym, or something. He's all broad shoulders and biceps, with thick forearms, and I'd have to guess he's sporting some sweet abs under that navy polo.

He's paired it with gray shorts and casual sandals. His dark hair is a little longer than I remember and definitely the kind of wavy and thick that makes you want to run your fingers through it.

Awesome, not only am I ogling him, I'm also thinking about

doing inappropriate things like touching him. It's as if I've gone back in time seven years, and I'm still the misguided woman who made the embarrassing mistake of almost kissing my charge's grieving father. I'd like to say I've gotten over that, but clearly I haven't.

His smile falters and he tips his head to the side, brows pulling together as he scans my face, then lifting in surprise as recognition dawns. "Harley? Harley Spark? How didn't I put it together until now?" He touches his chest. "Gavin Rhodes. I don't know if you remember me."

I don't know how I could ever forget him. Not when I lived in his house and took care of his daughter for nearly a year and a half. But right now would be a great time for him to develop selective amnesia and not remember me. I raise my hand in an awkward wave as my stomach flip-flops. "Hey. Hi."

"That was Peyton who just ran by." He motions to the dress tent.

I state the painfully obvious, my mouth desert dry, my heart hammering around in my chest like a raver on Molly. "She's growing up fast."

"Yeah. She is." He runs his hand through his hair and grabs the back of his neck, eyes moving over me. "You've done some growing up of your own."

Lynn's eyes go wide, and Gavin makes a face. I choke on a cough and feel a smidge better about my own mortification. Not enough that I stop sweating or wishing that a UFO would pass by, but I'm slightly less interested in being probed.

He rushes on, possibly trying to ease the mounting tension. "I just mean, it's been a long time." His gaze shifts to Ella, as if he's suddenly realized she's not actually part of my body. "Is this your daughter? Did you get married?"

"Oh, uh, no. I'm not married; this is my niece, Ella. My sister

London's daughter. My other sister Avery is having a baby too. Babies all around. But not mine. And I'm closer to thirty than I am twenty these days." Why is my mouth still moving?

I turn to Lynn, who's still standing off to the side, witnessing this very awkward reintroduction. "I used to be Peyton's nanny, before they moved to Boulder. That's where you went, isn't it?" I phrase it as a question, even though I already know the answer is yes.

"Yeah, that's right." Gavin nods.

"Oh! Well, isn't it a small world!" Lynn looks between us, smiling, but I can see the questions in her eyes.

And frankly I have questions of my own. None of which would be appropriate to ask right now.

"It is. Apparently, very small," I agree.

"I think we must have met before. I thought you looked familiar," Lynn says.

And now that I have a frame of reference, I do remember her. I knew she'd seemed familiar when I met her in the planning stages, but we were focused on her daughter's party. And back when I was Peyton's nanny, any previous meetings had been in passing. Sometimes her husband, Ian, would pick Gavin up for dinner events, and Lynn would be there, but the memories are vague at best. "Oh yes, I'm sure we did, but it's been a while. It feels like a lifetime ago, really." At least it felt that way until five minutes ago. Now it feels as fresh as a papercut and almost as painful.

I shift my attention back to Gavin, wondering how much more small talk is required before I can do a runner and hide among the safety of the children. "Are you visiting, then?"

"No, actually, we moved back to the area a few weeks ago. Lynn and Ian are old friends, and Ian works for Greenscapes, my dad's landscape architecture company."

"Oh, well that's . . . good?" The question comes out all high-pitched. It's one thing for Gavin to make an appearance at Spark House, but another to find out that he's moved back to Colorado Springs. It's a big enough city, but it doesn't mean I won't run into him again. As if I need my past coming back to haunt me in the form of mortifying memories on a regular basis. And now my arm is starting to itch in a distracting way. I glance down and notice a couple of raised bumps. We spray for mosquitos, but it looks like we didn't get them all.

"It's been a good move so far." He smiles and tucks a thumb into his shorts pocket.

Thankfully, I'm freed of the responsibility to keep up with the small talk when Lynn's daughter, Claire, drags Lynn off to the photo booth and Peyton bounces our way, dressed in her fairy outfit.

"Dad! Look! They have a costume just for me! And we get to take pictures! It's like being in a play, but I don't have any lines to remember!"

"You look fantastic!" Gavin says, with nothing but genuine excitement on his face.

A happy nine-year-old who doesn't remember me is a lot easier to handle than the father I almost kissed. Peyton turns her excited smile on me. "Are you our fairy godmother?"

I return her grin with a genuine one of my own. "I am! You can't have a princess party without fairies and godmothers."

"Peyton, this is Harley. She used to be your nanny when you were a baby," Gavin says, drawing her attention to me.

Peyton blinks a few times and cocks her head, eyes narrowing as she takes me and Ella in. She pulls one corner of her lip between her teeth, and after a few seconds her eyes light up and she turns to her dad. "Oh! Is she the lady in my baby photo albums?"

He smiles and nods. "That's right."

Peyton turns back to me. "Daddy said you were the angel who was sent to help us when Mommy had to go to heaven."

My heart seizes in my chest and the lump in my throat feels impossible to swallow past. "Well, that's a very nice thing for your dad to say." And not entirely accurate considering how things ended.

"Is this the new baby you're taking care of? Did her mom go to heaven too?"

I open my mouth to answer, although I'm not sure it's going to come out as more than a croak, when a very telling, very rumbly sound comes from the baby in my arms. Ella's eyes are round with surprise, as if the noise that came out of her back end surprised her as much as the rest of us.

Peyton giggles and Gavin chuckles. Ella grins and claps her hands and then the smell hits us both. Her nose wrinkles at the same time as mine.

London, the super mom that she is, comes rushing across the field. The timing couldn't be more perfect.

"I'm so sorry! I didn't mean for that to take as long as it did, but you know what happens, I get chatty and the next thing I know it's been an hour." Her face morphs into something like surprised disgust and she suppresses a gag. "Oh Ella, what has your dad been feeding you?" She glances from me to Gavin and Peyton, who have backed up several steps, likely to escape the green fog that is currently making it very difficult to breathe. "My apologies. I'm just here to collect my stink bomb." She blinks a few times, her brow furrowed as she takes in Gavin. She met him in passing a number of times, but I don't expect her to be able to place him after all these years.

Her gaze darts from me to Gavin and back again as she reaches for Ella. Which is the exact moment I realize that Ella's diaper was unable to manage its job and I'm now wearing its contents.

"If you can let Lynn know I'll be right back to get the party started, I just need to change out of this," I say to Gavin as I keep Ella on my hip to conceal the problem.

"I can take care of it." London tries to take her from me again.

"It's not contained," I mutter.

"Of course I can do that," Gavin replies.

"There are refreshments and food in the adult tent. I'll be back in a few minutes."

"Sure. Okay."

I rush toward the hotel, a now-fussy Ella bumping on my hip.

"Do you want me to stay behind and deal with the party or with Ella?" London calls after me.

"You can come with me!" I shout over my shoulder.

She catches up to me. "Are you sure I shouldn't stay behind?"

"They'll be fine for a couple of minutes. I might need to change. What the hell did you feed Ella this morning?"

"I think Jackson gave her broccoli last night."

"She smells like rotten eggs."

It isn't until we're in the office that I can assess the damage to my fairy outfit. There's no salvaging it. It needs to be washed, probably several times before it's wearable again. I have to change, and my only option is one of the princess dresses that's from the eighties, with huge poofy sleeves that are nearly as big as my head. I wrangle my way into it as London finishes up changing Ella's diaper.

"Who was that man you were talking to? He looked familiar."

"That's because he is. That's Gavin Rhodes. I used to nanny for his daughter, Peyton."

Recognition dawns, and her expression shifts from shock to disquiet. She moves behind me to tie the giant bow at the back of my dress. "Wait. What? Why is he here?"

"For the party." I scratch my left arm, then my right. "I gotta get back out there."

She grabs both of my hands and stretches them out. "Are you having a reaction? These look like hives."

I glance down at my arms and notice that what I originally thought were bugs bites are indeed forming into welts that now cover my forearms and are working their way up my biceps.

"Sugar beets! I need an antihistamine."

For a handful of months after Gavin left, I would spontaneously break out into hives. Often when I thought about what almost transpired in his kitchen.

London puts Ella in her playpen and rushes to the bathroom. I give Ella a kiss and promise I'll be back soon as London returns with the bottle of antihistamines. She shakes one into my palm, and I toss it in my mouth, swallowing it without water. Which is a terrible idea, because it gets stuck in my dry throat. She hands me a glass of water, and I chug it on the way back through the hotel foyer.

"Are you going to be okay out there?" London asks, voice laced with concern.

"Yeah." I nod a bunch of times and tip my head back so I can get the last few drips of water from the glass.

"Are you sure? I mean, you haven't broken out in hives in years."

"It's a two-hour party. I'll survive it."

"Message if you need me, okay?"

I nod and rush back out to the party. I find Gavin in the middle of the kids, wearing an ill-fitting tutu around his waist, pretending to grant wishes. It shouldn't be a surprise. When I used to be Peyton's nanny, he would often wear her cute tutu skirts on his head to make her laugh.

"Thanks for holding down the fort. I can take it from here, if you want," I say as I make my way through the throng of excited kids toward him.

"I feel like you're the more appealing fairy godmother." He passes me his wand and gives me a somewhat-chagrined smile. Then he joins the other adults in the adult tent, minus the tutu.

I spend the next two hours immersed in the excitement of eight- to eleven-year-olds. Their enthusiasm helps take the edge off my anxiety. I try to split my time among the kids evenly, helping where I'm needed, and focusing on Claire, the birthday girl. But it's hard not to steal glances at Peyton every so often.

We decorate edible wands and paint individual photo frames, play games in the field, and finally sit down for pizza, subs, salad, cake, and presents. At the end of the party, each child gets their own gift bag, complete with their edible wand, and a picture of the party tucked into their frame. They're happy, tired kids and it's been a great afternoon, although bittersweet knowing it's the last time I get to do this.

Gavin hangs back with Peyton while the rest of the parents gather their children and head out. "You sure haven't lost your knack with kids. That was amazing."

Peyton holds onto her dad's arm, a wide smile on her face. "That was the best birthday party ever! Can we have my next birthday here? And costumes like this one?"

"We have half a year before your birthday, and you're already looking to plan your party?" Gavin asks with an amused smile.

Peyton props her fist on her hip. "It's already July, next is Halloween, then Thanksgiving, and then Christmas, and then I'll be ten!"

"Wow! I can't believe you're already nine years old! The last time I saw you, I could still carry you on my hip, just like my niece, Ella!" I fight a cringe and the urge to scratch my arm. The last thing I need to do is bring up the past. "Anyway, if you're serious about the party, I'm sure we could plan something fun." I probably shouldn't be promising things like this when this is supposed to be my last birthday party, but I can beg for forgiveness later.

"Can we, please, Dad?" She clings to Gavin's arm and bounces up and down.

"I'm sure we can work something out."

Peyton's bright smile turns down at the corners. "I don't have a lot of friends here yet, though."

"You'll make lots of new friends as soon as the school year starts, kiddo," Gavin reassures her.

Peyton nods and looks to me. "Dad says I make friends wherever I go. I met three new friends today, and they're all going to the same school as me and Claire. Hopefully by the time my birthday comes, I'll have even more friends to invite."

"You sound like my older sister Avery. She's forever making new friends too."

"I miss my old friends, but sometimes we have to embrace change and go on new adventures. Right, Dad?" It sounds like something her dad has repeated in order to help make the transition to her new home easier.

"That's right, kiddo." He ruffles her hair as she brings her hand to her mouth, yawning widely. "I should probably get you home, huh?"

"I might fall asleep in the car," she warns.

"That's okay. It's been a busy day." He gives her shoulder a squeeze.

He turns her in the direction of the parking lot, and she slips out from under his arm and grabs my hand. I guess I'm walking them out. She tugs me along as she regales me with all of her birthday party ideas.

When we reach his SUV, Peyton looks up at her dad. "Can we come back to Spark House again soon?" She turns back to me. "Maybe you can come over and see my new house. My bedroom is decorated with fairies and princesses. We could make magic cookie wands again!"

"Oh, uh, well, maybe we should get the rest of the house unpacked before we go inviting guests over." Gavin gives me an apologetic, chagrined smile.

Peyton frowns. "But you said it's going to take forever to unpack, and I don't want to wait forever before I see Harley again." Leave it to kids to be painfully unaware of the tension in the room.

"If we're hosting your birthday party here, I'll definitely get to see you before forever happens," I tell Peyton, trying to let Gavin off the hook without feeling like I'm being personally snubbed.

Her lips twist and pull to the side. "I guess that's true."

Peyton climbs into the back seat and Gavin closes the door. He gives me another wry, uncertain smile. "I'm sorry about putting you on the spot like that."

I wave off the comment. "No apology necessary. It's great to see Peyton again."

He nods and then pauses for a beat before he says, "Uh . . . I don't know what your schedule is like, but maybe if you have some free time, Peyton and I could take you out for lunch? We could catch up?"

I'm not sure if he's being genuine or he feels compelled to ask because of Peyton, but her comment about not seeing me for forever prevents me from turning him down. "Uh, sure. That would be nice." And embarrassing. I'll definitely need to take an antihistamine if it actually happens.

"Great." He smiles and his shoulders drop, as though he was worried I would say no. "We can exchange numbers? I'll call you later and we can figure out a day that works?"

"Absolutely." I pull out my phone and discover that I still have Gavin's contact, although there are no messages attached to it, which makes sense since I've upgraded my phone a few times since he moved to Boulder. I still remember the last message he sent more than seven years ago, thanking me for all I'd done and letting me know that he'd direct deposited my last paycheck into my account. I'd responded with *keep in touch*. And a week later I'd messaged, asking how the move had gone, but I'd never gotten a reply. I hadn't wanted to push, so I'd stepped back and moved on with my life. I'd tried to bury the guilt along with the memories, but clearly the grave I dug wasn't deep enough, since the day he announced they were moving away lives rent-free in my head.

I swallow down my fears as I send him a message and his phone pings. Part of me would love the opportunity to finally apologize the way I wanted to back then, but the other part of me worries that dredging up the past like this is only going to cause those old wounds to reopen.

He checks the screen without opening the message. "Looks like I still have your contact. I'll be in touch soon." Gavin opens the driver's side door, but pauses before he gets inside. "It's great to see you again, Harley."

"You too, Gavin. Both of you."

He smiles and drops into the driver's seat. I wait until he's pulling down the driveway toward the road before I return to Spark House.

I'm barely in the door before my sisters are on me. "I need to know everything. Tell me what's going on. London said a hot dad you used to nanny for was here. Sorry I didn't come out to help, but I was getting things organized for the upcoming proposal with the Mills brothers." Avery is pretty much on top of me as she follows me down the hall to the office.

"Do you remember Gavin and Peyton?" I ask.

Avery drops into her chair and pats her belly—she's pregnant and finally starting to show. She's also eating like it's her second job. There's a platter on top of her desk that's been picked over. "Not really, no."

"He lost his wife during childbirth," London supplies. "Harley nannied for Peyton for a year and a half."

"Oh!" Avery's eyes light up. "I remember them. They moved, didn't they? Isn't that why you stopped working for them?"

"Yeah, that's right." And Peyton was the last infant I took care of. In fact, I only had one charge after that, and he was older, already school-age, so it was only before- and after-school care, and I didn't live in the house with the family. They ended up moving because the father was in the navy and was being stationed overseas. After that, I started working for Spark House.

"Is he still hot?" Avery asks.

"Yup," London chimes in, letting the *P* pop with affirmation.

"So? What's the deal? Was he just here for the party?"

"I guess they moved back to town. He asked me if I wanted to go for lunch with him and Peyton."

London frowns. "What did you say to that?"

"I said sure. He was probably only being nice, so I doubt he'll call." And honestly, I'm on the fence as to whether I want him to. I had a lot of great memories with Peyton and Gavin, but the last ones overshadow everything else. And they inspired a lot of personal changes. I put college on hold, stopped working with kids and their families, and joined Spark House with my sisters. I didn't trust myself not to let something like that derail my life again.

Two hours later I walk through the door to my apartment and find my boyfriend, Chad, sitting on the living room couch, a controller in one hand and his phone in the other. We've been dating for a few months, and I met him through a mutual friend. "Awesome. You're home. Everyone's already at the Firkin, you ready to go?"

"I should probably change first."

He hits the pause button on his controller and drags his gaze away from the TV. His eyes widen. "Why are you dressed for Halloween?"

"I'm a fairy godmother. I had a birthday party for a ten-year-old today, and it was princess-themed." I drop my purse on the counter and kick off my shoes. They're flats, but it's still nice to set my toes free. I prefer sandals to any other footwear. Unfortunately, Colorado winters are not conducive to open-toed shoes.

"Ah. That makes sense. Too bad there isn't a theme park around here. I feel like you would have loved being one of those princesses." His nose wrinkles as I cross the room. "Are you . . . sparkling?"

I glance down at my arms. The hives are pretty much gone at this point, thank God. "Probably. We had glitter crafts today."

He holds out a hand before I can get close enough to bend down and kiss him hello. "You need to shower, babe. That glitter business gets all over everything. The last time you had a birthday party, I couldn't get it out of my hair for weeks and the guys at work gave me shit for it."

I suppress an eye roll. "You won't have to worry about glitter after today."

"Oh? Well, that's good news. Right?" He unpauses his game.

"I guess."

"Glitter isn't really something you want to wear unless you're a unicorn." He glances up and then back down at the TV. "Why no more glitter after today?"

"Because this is the last birthday party I'll be hosting for kids. I told you that last week, remember?"

"Right. Yeah. I forgot. Those things kind of seem like glorified babysitting, anyway." His phone pings with a message and he glances briefly at the screen. "That's Allen asking when we're gonna be there."

"Give me fifteen and I'll be ready to go." I leave him in the living room and stop in my bedroom to grab a change of clothes before I hit the bathroom so I can wash away the birthday party, and hopefully some of the sadness that goes with it.

Three

LUNCH DATE FOR THREE

HARLEY

Two days later I get a message from Gavin saying that Peyton has been hounding him about seeing me again and asks if I would be up for lunch with the two of them. I wait half an hour before texting back, to see if I break out in hives again. When I don't, I agree. I meet them at Chuck E. Cheese on a Monday afternoon, which is always slower at Spark House since most of the biggest events take place on weekends. I'm dressed in Chuck E. Cheese-appropriate wear—a T-shirt, jeans, and flats.

Gavin and Peyton are already there when I arrive. I stand outside for a moment, take a few deep breaths, and tamp down the familiar embarrassment. It happens every single time I think about Gavin and Peyton, so it makes sense that seeing them magnifies it. I'm hoping that with repeated exposure, it will lessen, not worsen like an anaphylactic allergy. I took a non-drowsy antihistamine in preparation for this event. Just in case the hives decided to come back.

"You can handle this. You can have lunch with a nine-year-old and your former boss," I mutter as I push through the doors.

As soon as Peyton sees me, she slides out of the booth and rushes over. She grabs my hand and pulls me over to the table where Gavin is sitting with a glass of soda cupped between his palms. "Can we play games now that Harley is here?" Peyton is bouncing like she's been mainlining sugar.

"I think we should let Harley have a seat first and order a drink, don't you?" Gavin arches a brow and gives me a wry smile.

"Oh." Peyton's face falls for a second, before she smiles up at me. "I'm really excited. I've never been to Chuck E. Cheese 'cause Granny says there's too many germs and the food isn't healthy." She lets go of my hand and climbs into the booth across from her dad, then pats the seat beside her. "Let's decide what we're going to eat! Then we can play some games!"

"Okay. I like the sound of that." I take the spot beside Peyton, which means she and I are seated across from Gavin, who takes up most of the booth with his broad shoulders. Which I need to stop admiring.

"What do you like to drink? You can have soda, or juice, or even chocolate milk. Dad lets me have chocolate milk when we go to restaurants, or Sprite, but not anything with lots of caffeine because Dad says I already have enough energy and I don't need the kind they keep in colas."

I grin and glance at Gavin who seems amused by this explanation.

"It is sort of a special treat, isn't it?" I agree.

"It's like that movie *Monster Truck*, where they give the monster gas from the gas station instead of the stuff straight from the ground. It has all kinds of other stuff in it, and it gives the monster too much energy," Gavin explains. "And then what happens?"

"The monster has a sugar crash. Have you ever seen that movie?"

"I sure have! It's one of my favorites."

Peyton's eyes light up. "Mine too! I love princess movies, but that movie is so fun, and the monster is so cute. I used to watch it sometimes when I went to Granny's after school."

"Did you spend a lot of time with your granny?" I ask as we scan the lunch options. Peyton has a child's menu on a place mat that she can color.

"Every school day," Peyton tells me. "Except for Friday. Dad would always take me for pizza and chocolate milk on Fridays. I like that it's Monday and I get my favorite foods and I get to see you and we get to play all these games!" She motions excitedly to the open floor where the carnival-style games fill the room.

"Peyton used to go to my mother-in-law's after school and I'd pick her up after work," Gavin explains.

"That must have been nice for you to get to spend so much time with your granny," I say to Peyton and turn to Gavin. "And it must have given you peace of mind to know Peyton was in such good hands." In some ways, this feels a lot like the closure I needed all those years ago. Giving Peyton's grandparents an opportunity to be directly involved in raising her was a good reason to move.

"It was definitely helpful, and Karen loved taking care of Peyton, so it worked out well for all of us, right, kiddo?"

"Yup. And now I'll get to spend time with Nana after school some days, and she makes the best chocolate chip cookies in the world, and she said she'd teach me how to make them too."

"That sounds like a lot of fun!" I reply.

I settle on Sprite to drink, and we decide on a large pizza, half cheese and half with all the toppings.

Peyton wrinkles her nose. "Dad likes mushrooms on his pizza, but they feel like sponges in my mouth."

I chuckle and wrinkle my nose. "They do feel weird in your mouth, don't they?"

She mirrors my scrunched nose, then asks, "Do you like mushrooms on your pizza?"

"Sometimes. It depends on the pizza. You might like them one day. But you know what?"

"What?"

I love the way kids hang on every word, like you're telling them the secret to all of life's mysteries. And I guess in a way, we are, because we've had all the experiences and they're learning little bits about the world with every new adventure. "My favorite kind of pizza is plain cheese too."

"Really?" Peyton's eyes go wide.

"Yup. Sometimes cheese pizza is just the way to go. I've made it my mission to try the cheese pizza at pretty much every place in town."

"You have?"

"Yup. I'm basically a connoisseur of pizza."

"What's a conno-saur?"

"An expert," Gavin says, rubbing his bottom lip while grinning.

"A pizza expert? Is that a job? Can I become a pizza expert?" Peyton asks.

"You have to try *a lot* of pizza to become an expert, but I bet you could be one. Maybe not for a job, but it's a great hobby." I throw a wink Gavin's way. He's sitting back in his seat, his heavily muscled arm stretched across the back of the booth. He grins, obviously enjoying this conversation as much as Peyton and me. See? I can do this. I can have lunch with my former charge and her father without it being super awkward or breaking out in hives. I just need to stay focused on the reason I'm here—Peyton wanted to see me.

"Hmm." Peyton taps her chin thoughtfully. "Eating pizza seems like a fun hobby. But would we have to try a new place every time? Or could we go back to the same place a few times if I really like it?"

"You can go back as many times as you like. The great thing about being a connoisseur is that it takes quite a few years to become one, so you don't have to rush it."

"Okay. That sounds good. Because sometimes when you find a place you like, you want to go there a lot. I think I'll want to come here a lot, but not just because of the pizza. Do you have a favorite pizza place?"

"I sure do. It's called Joe's Great Pizza, and they have the best cheese pizza in all of Colorado Springs. It even says so on their website."

"Then it must be true," Gavin says wryly.

"Maybe we could go there one time? Dad can take us on another lunch date! They're my favorite! But we'd have to do it before school starts because I can't miss school for lunch dates."

"You definitely don't want to miss school." I don't address the rest of the proposed second lunch date since I have no idea what, if anything, is going to come of this. I came into it hoping for closure on that chapter in my life, and so far it's been a positive experience. With no hives. I don't want to push my luck though. "Should we play some games now?"

"Yes! Yay!" Peyton claps her hands and bounces in her seat. "Can we get the tokens now, Dad?"

"Sure, kiddo. Why don't you use the bathroom and I'll buy some?"

"I can take her," I offer, and we all slide out of the booth.

Peyton chatters with excitement as I take her to the bathroom and stand outside the stall. "The day after the birthday party, Dad found my baby photo album and we looked through it together and you were there! You look almost the same, and so does Dad, but his hair is longer, and I obviously look a lot different because I was a baby."

"You have definitely changed the most out of the three of us," I agree.

When she's done washing her hands—we sing "Twinkle" twice through—we head back to the dining area. Gavin is waiting with tokens, and almost as soon as he hands them over to Peyton, he gets a phone call.

"Shoot, this is important, do you mind if I take it?"

"Not at all, Peyton and I can hang out."

"Thanks." He brings his phone to his ear and heads for the front door.

"Dad's been really busy with work since we moved." She glances over her shoulder, out the window to where he's standing on the sidewalk before she drops her voice and whispers, "Sometimes he falls asleep on the couch when we're watching TV at night, and I get to stay up a little later because he sleeps through my bedtime."

I laugh. "Not too much past your bedtime, I hope."

She shakes her head. "Not really, but it's summer break, so I don't have to be in bed as early as I do during school." She looks around at all the games. "Where should we start?"

"Hmm." I tap my lips. "What about the ball toss? Are you any good at that?"

She shrugs. "I don't really play team sports."

"Me either, but my older sister did. Sometimes she'd make me be the goalie when she had to practice for soccer games. Should we see if we're any good?"

"Okay." Peyton bounces over to the ball toss, and we take turns throwing the ball, laughing when we miss—which is often—and high-fiving each other when we manage to get one in the slots.

"How do you like being back in Colorado Springs?" I ask.

"It's pretty good. I like my new room. Me and Dad painted it the first day we got the house, and then we went shopping for decorations and that was fun." Peyton looks over her shoulder, maybe checking to see if anyone else is close enough to listen in. "But it can be kind of lonely. Dad has to work a lot right now, and I only have a couple of friends. I like Claire, but she plays sports all the time and watching her games is kind of boring."

"Do you go to her games often?" I ask.

"A couple of times a week. Sometimes I go over to my nana's house and she always has fun activities planned, but she's busy during the day a lot, so I can't always go there."

"What else do you do with Claire?"

"Sometimes we draw, or color, or play outside. She likes to be moving all the time, and sometimes I just want to make crafts and things like that."

"She sounds a lot like my sister, and you sound a lot like me. I bet when you're in school, you'll find other friends who like the same things you do."

"That's what Dad says. And I'm going to a school with art programs, so hopefully there are lots of people who are like me." She tosses another ball, and this time she gets thirty points.

"Nice work!" I high-five her. "I'm sure you'll make lots and lots of friends."

She nods and bites the corner of her lip. "I miss my friends from Boulder."

"I bet you do." I give her a side hug. "When I was just a little bit older than you, I had to move too."

"You did?"

I toss a ball and miss. "Yup. And we had to move away from our friends too. But I made new ones at my new school. It was hard at first, but the really great part was that I had new friends in my new school and old friends from my other school."

"So you had twice as many friends?"

"I did. And even though I didn't see those older friends all the time, we had a lot of fun when we got to hang out. It made our time together even more special."

Peyton nods thoughtfully. "You have sisters, though, don't you?"

"Yup, two. I'm the youngest."

"Sometimes I wish I had a sister, but I'm almost ten already, so I don't know if that will ever happen." She tosses another ball, and this time it gets fifty points.

We whoop and high-five again, then move on to the dance game. I learn that Peyton loves dancing and she's very, very good at the *Just Dance* video game.

Half an hour later, the pizza arrives, so we take a break from our dancing competition—which Gavin found highly entertaining to watch from the comfort of the booth—and dig into the pizza, rating it on a scale of ten, based on cheesiness, sauciness, and the crunchiness of the crust. Peyton eats two slices before she pushes her plate away and starts coloring her place mat.

"There aren't any brown crayons for the horse." She sifts through the little cup, searching for the right color.

"Why don't you color the horse pink or blue or purple?" I suggest.

Peyton frowns. "But horses aren't blue or pink. They're brown or black or gray, and sometimes they have spots."

"In real life, but in our imagination, they can be any color we want them to. If there was a land full of princesses and castles and magic horses, I bet they'd be fun colors with rainbow tails," I say.

"Kind of like My Little Pony?" She makes her scrunchy face again.

"Kind of, but a bit more grown-up, with some added flair maybe? Like My Little Pony with *The Princess Bride* vibes. Have you seen that movie?"

"I have! I watched it with Dad last year on Mommy's birthday. It was her favorite movie. I'm going to make him a pink horse with a rainbow tail!"

"I think that's a great idea." I help her color in the horse while we wait for dessert.

After Peyton finishes coloring her horse and eating ice cream, she decides she wants to use the slide on the indoor play structure, which leaves Gavin and me on our own, watching from the sidelines. We head back to the booth, and I take a seat beside him, so we can both see her, and I don't have to make direct eye contact the entire time.

It's one thing to have Peyton as the focus and the buffer, but totally another to make small talk with Gavin. Despite having spent a year and a half living in his house, he feels like a relative stranger now. I've changed, he's changed. And obviously both of our lives have done the same.

"Thanks a lot for meeting up with us today. Peyton couldn't

stop talking about you after the party and wanted to know when I was going to message you so she could see you again," Gavin says as his gaze shifts from me to the structure, where Peyton is heading for one of the slides.

"It's honestly my pleasure. It's really great to see her. She's turned into a lovely little girl, which isn't a surprise since she was a great baby." That hot feeling creeps up my spine again.

"She was," he agrees and says softly, "although I think you had a lot to do with that."

"She has an easy personality. She was only ever fussy when she was uncomfortable." My mind goes back to that night all those years ago. She'd had such a hard time sleeping, and Gavin had been so under-rested. And emotional. For months, I replayed that one night over in my head, experienced the mortification time and time again, felt buried in the embarrassment and guilt of it all. If I hadn't gone into the kitchen, would everything have been different? Would they have stayed? Was it better that they left?

"The sleepless nights when she was teething were always the hardest."

"Thankfully that stage doesn't last too long." My voice is pitchy again. While I might want closure, I don't want to relive that night more than I already have. I've done that enough on my own.

He's quiet for a few seconds before he murmurs, "That's true. While you're in it, it seems as though it's never going to end."

"And now here she is, almost ten. She's just so grown-up. Before you know it, you're going to have a teenager." I give him a playful elbow in the side, hoping to lighten the mood and adjust course.

His eyes widen in mock horror. "Do not use the dreaded t-word. She's already asking about a cell phone. She's not even ten. Why don't they come with a manual?"

"Eh, the manual would be useless anyway, since none of them are the same model or make."

"So true." He nods, then gives me a sidelong glance. "You look the same but different."

"I didn't get any taller. I still barely make the height requirements at most amusement parks. Not that it matters, since I'm forever a Tea Cups over roller coaster girl."

He chuckles. "You were always so easy to be around. That hasn't changed."

"Thanks." I refocus on the play structure. "How are you both adjusting to the move? Are you happy to be back?"

"I think we're doing okay, so far. Lynn and Ian are close by, which is good for both of us. It's nice to be in the same city with them again, and Peyton will be going to the same school as Claire, so she has a friend, which is good. They're very different kids, though. Claire is sporty and Peyton is artsy."

"She mentioned that, about her and Claire being different."

"She did?" He's suddenly alert.

"More as an observation than anything else. It's good that she's so self-aware. And school will make a big difference."

"Mmm." He nods his agreement. "It made sense to move in the summer, but it's a challenge to keep her occupied until school starts."

"Do you mind me asking why you moved back?"

He rubs the back of his neck. "A bunch of reasons, but my dad wants to retire, and Ian has been running the Colorado Springs branch of Greenscapes since I moved. It's a bigger outfit now than when I relocated to help open the branch in Boulder. Dad needs me to come back and take over the architectural side of things, so Ian can manage the crews full-time."

"Is that good for you? Were you happy in Boulder?" This is good, I can make polite conversation without things getting overly awkward.

"Workwise, sure. I love the job, and I could have stayed there, but I love working with my dad too."

I give him a quizzical look. "Am I reading into things if I say it sounds like there's a big old *but* in there?"

He smiles somewhat sheepishly. "Not really a *but*, more that I needed a change and a bit of space. I'm grateful for everything my in-laws have done for me and Peyton, but with Peyton getting older and my dad retiring, it made sense to move back. My mom is retiring as well, so they can both help after school when it's needed, and her new school has great extracurricular programs. Peyton is excited about joining their theater group, and those often run several days a week, so I won't have to put all the after-school care on my parents. And because I'm still working with my family, I'll maintain flexible hours."

"That's great." Gavin was always very dedicated to his job and helping grow the family business, and clearly nothing has changed in that department. "That must mean Greenscapes is doing well."

"It's grown a lot in the years since I moved to Boulder." He folds his hands on the table. "Speaking of family businesses, tell me about Spark House. I did a little internet creeping, and it looks like it's doing amazing. Are you working there full-time now? Are birthday parties your gig? When did you start doing that?" He holds up a hand. "Sorry. That was a lot of rapid-fire questions."

I chuckle and relax in my seat. I'd forgotten how easy Gavin is to talk to, although it's been years since we spoke. Some nights after Peyton went to sleep, we'd hang out in the kitchen, make a snack, and talk about life. Spark House was always a frequent topic since both of my sisters had already started working there. "It's okay. Lot of changes, right? So, yes, I am working at Spark House full-time, and I started about six months after you moved. My gran wanted to retire, and I was in between jobs, so I joined my sisters, and I've been there ever since. And the birthday parties are part of my gig. Well, *were*, we had to cut them, but there's always room for exceptions."

"That's too bad about having to cut them. You're so great with kids, and it's such a natural fit for you. Or it seems to be."

"They're a lot of fun, and it still stings a bit, but we need to focus on the bigger events now."

"I saw that on your social. You do a lot of weddings, charity events, and corporate team building, right? You're kind of a big deal now."

I laugh and duck my head, my cheeks flushing, but this time, not because I'm mortified. "I'm not a big deal. Spark House is doing great, but I'm not the reason it is. I'm just along for the ride."

"Now you're being modest. You seem pretty involved for someone who's along for the ride." When his phone buzzes on the table, he flips it over and ignores the message. "Did you finish your child development degree?"

I glance at the play structure, where Peyton is jumping into the foam pit. "I put it on hold when my gran decided to retire, but I started taking courses again last fall. I'm working on it slowly, so it'll be a while before I graduate, but I wanted to finish what I started." It took six years for me to finally make the decision to do that. I'd only been a year and a half from graduation, but what happened with Gavin all those years ago made me reassess my goals. Gavin and Peyton's abrupt move was devastating in a way I didn't know how to handle. I realized that being a nanny was a way for me to heal from the loss of my parents. And that maybe I wasn't ready to fully commit to that career path, so I shifted gears. It helped that I had an excuse to put the degree on hold in the form of being needed full-time at Spark House.

"I'm glad you decided to finish. You're a real natural with kids. And you have the patience of a saint."

I laugh at that. "I don't know about the last part. But I'm not afraid to get covered in glitter, and kids speak to my creative side, which goes a long way in winning them over."

Peyton comes tromping over, panting and sweaty. "Dad, I need a drink of water." She falls against him dramatically, and he wraps his arms around her slight frame.

"Looks like someone's worn herself out."

She nods against his arm. "My fun bucket is empty."

"Sounds like something a nap in the car will take care of." I wink at Peyton and throw a knowing smile at Gavin. When she was a baby, Peyton could fall asleep in seconds if she was comfortable.

I try to give Gavin money for my share of the meal, but he won't accept it. Once Peyton and I have said our goodbyes and she's secure in the car, Gavin turns to me. "It was great to catch up with you."

"You too, the both of you." I smile and fiddle with a loose string on my shirt, not really knowing what to do with my hands, the awkwardness suddenly back.

"I know you probably don't have a lot of free time, but maybe we can do this again sometime?" He flips his keys between his fingers. "Peyton really loves you, and you're a familiar face for her, and I think she could use some of those in her life, especially with all the change."

"Of course. That'd be great. I'd love to see Peyton again."

"Okay. Good." He smiles. "I'll message and we can set something up."

I wave at Peyton as he gets into his car and then return to mine. It's nice to feel . . . needed, even if it's by a nine-year-old girl who's just looking for someone familiar to hold on to.

Four

THE SEED OF DISCONTENT

HARLEY

I'm sitting in my living room, my laptop propped on my thighs so I can finish my assignment for my Mental Health Intervention Planning for Children course before Chad shows up. It's an online class, but more work than in-person. However, it's also more convenient than trying to work around my Spark House schedule. And I'm fascinated by the different ways to create an inclusive environment for children coming from a variety of backgrounds and family structures.

Tonight Chad and I have dinner plans with some of his work friends. I would cook for everyone, but Allen and Andrea are vegan and I'm not a master of vegan cooking, so we usually go to their favorite restaurant when we hang out in our neck of the woods. It's a safe bet, and I don't want them to suffer through me testing out new recipes.

I'm on the last question when Chad lets himself into my condo with the key I gave him a few weeks ago. "Honey, I'm home!" he calls out and adds, "What smells so freaking good?"

I glance around the living room, unsure what he's referencing until I realize it's the candle I lit when I sat down to work on my assignment. It has a mint base and is supposed to be great for stimulating the brain. Which I need right now, because I spent all day at Spark House in meetings to prepare for our upcoming conference call with Mills Hotels to discuss the franchise opportunity. I've needed all the help I can get since my heart isn't fully into this, but with our majority rules motto, and both Avery and London being all in on this, I need to try my best to do what is asked of me. "It's a candle."

He appears in the living room, still wearing his shoes, and also a frown. "Why do candles have to smell like delicious food? I thought you'd made those mint chocolate chip brownies I love so much."

"I'm sorry to disappoint you, but on the upside, this candle apparently lasts for days and the brownies are usually gone inside of twenty-four hours."

"But I can't eat a candle." He drops his messenger bag on the couch. "Do I have a spare suit here? I forgot to bring one with me for tomorrow, and I don't remember if we just talked about me leaving clothes here or if I've actually done it."

"I know you have dress pants and a couple of shirts, but I'm not sure about an entire suit. You do have boxers, though." I know because sometimes I use them as sleep shorts after I wash them.

"Cool, that should cut it." He riffles around in his bag and pulls out his Nintendo Switch, setting it on the coffee table.

Chad is a huge gaming nerd. He works in IT and is part of a thousand different online gaming communities. He basically carries his Switch with him like it's an appendage. "Why are you setting that up? Aren't we going out for dinner?"

"Yeah, but you always pass out early, so I figured I'd get in some gaming after you're lights-out."

"I go to bed at ten. It's not *that* early."

"Babe, some preschoolers stay up later than you."

"That's untrue." And it also makes me sound lame.

"Okay, maybe not preschoolers, but for sure middle-schoolers."

"I have to be up at six, and I need solid sleep."

"I'm just busting your balls, babe. I think it's cute that you can't stay up past midnight to save your life." He leans down and kisses my temple. "It'll make you the perfect roommate when I move in here."

I sit up straighter. "Move in?" It would be great if my voice came out an octave or two lower.

He grins. "Yeah, you know. Eventually. I've still got a few more months on my lease with Marv, but I think him and his girlfriend are getting pretty serious. Don't worry, I'll give you some notice before I rearrange your furniture to make room for my gaming stuff."

Chad lives with one of his coworkers. They're not particularly tidy or good about washing dishes, which is the reason he comes here most of the time. Also, Marv's girlfriend is over a lot, and she is the opposite of quiet behind the bedroom door. While I'm glad she and Marv have a very active sex life, I don't want to know every time she has an orgasm.

"This isn't a frat house, Chad. You can't take over my living room with your gaming stuff."

"Is that a formal invitation to move in?"

I bite the inside of my cheek. We've only been dating for a few months, and moving in seems like a pretty huge step in the commitment arena. "Uh, I'd need to see real, consistent proof that you can pick up after yourself."

"I always pick up after myself."

I point across the room to the end table where he left an empty box of cookies from one of his post-dinner binge-and-gaming sessions from last week. I left them there on purpose to make this exact point.

"That's one empty box and the exception, not the rule."

I raise a finger. "Ah, but that's where you are wrong. There are also three pairs of your socks stuffed under the couch and two hats under the side table."

"Really?" He crosses the room and checks under the couch. "Score! I've been looking for these! Mind if I toss them in with your next load?" They're covered in dust bunnies, and I haven't bothered to move the couch when I've vacuumed the past couple of weeks.

"You can put them in with my gym clothes, but dust them off first." I tack on, "In the garbage can, not right here."

I didn't realize when I gave him the spare key a few weeks ago that he would keep it. He was getting off work earlier than me, and we were going out for dinner with friends. It made sense for him to come to my place to get ready instead of back to his place and then here. And up until now, I felt we were a little too new to be considered serious, but maybe he's on a different page than me, or the kind of guy who's all in right from the start.

He disappears into the kitchen, his footfalls fading as he continues down the hall. Maybe he's going to put a load in the washing machine. Or at the very least, toss his socks in the hamper. Chad is fun to hang out with, but he's still in bachelor mode, and I'm firmly entrenched in adulthood and taking care of my personal space. Unlike Chad's apartment, mine has matching furniture that doesn't include a gaming chair.

He returns a minute later, minus the dirty socks. "You still working on that assignment you needed to finish tonight? We have half an hour before we need to leave for the pub, and I can entertain myself if you need me to." He motions to his Switch.

"I'm almost done, just finishing up the last question."

"No problem, I'll get changed. You need anything while I'm up?"

"I'm good. Thanks, though." I tip my chin up as he bends to press his lips to my cheek on his way to the bedroom.

He returns a few minutes later wearing jeans and a T-shirt. He plops down on the couch and starts setting up his gaming station while I finish my assignment. I'll need to read it over one more time before I turn it in, but at least it's done. I close my laptop and set it aside.

"What are the chances you can get away this weekend?" Chad asks, eyes on the TV and the game he's currently playing.

"We have a wedding on Saturday, so it's all hands on deck. I have the weekend at the end of the month off, though, why?"

"Allen was talking about going camping, and I thought it would be a fun trip, but I don't want to be the seventh wheel with a bunch of couples." He glances at me for a second before returning his attention to the game. "They're leaving Thursday night, though. Maybe you could come up for one night."

"Who all's going?"

"The usual suspects: Allen and Andrea, Belinda and Ted, and another couple from work."

"Would that other couple happen to be Marv and the Howler?" That's my nickname for his girlfriend.

He grins. "No, they can't come this weekend. Try not to look so disappointed about that."

"You can't tell me it's not awkward when people start freaking out thinking we have a wild animal on our campsite." It's happened before. I don't know if it's a good thing that those two are oblivious about the racket they make or not. I check my calendar, even though I already know I can't go. Which is disappointing. Andrea is a mutual friend, and the reason I met Chad in the first place. I enjoy spending time with her and our other friends. "The rehearsal dinner is on Thursday."

"What time will that go until?"

"Probably pretty late, I'm thinking around nine or ten." I bite the inside of my lip, not loving the furrow in his brow or the way he purses his lips. This isn't the first time I haven't been able to make a last-minute weekend getaway.

I feel bad, but there isn't much I can do about the way my work schedule is laid out. "Why don't we plan something for the end of the month? We can organize a camping trip, and if there aren't any sites available, I can always see if we can set up in the back of Spark House. The last weekend of this month is a sporting event, and Avery is always front and center for those."

"That could work. I thought you said you'd be getting more weekends off soon. I get working one weekend a month, but three?" His player dies and he tosses the controller on the table. "Seems like you don't get to have much of a life when all you do is work on the weekend."

This has become a real sore spot for Chad recently. I get it. Summers are short, and we have a limited supply of warm weather weekends here in Colorado before it turns cold again. He's big on camping and hanging out with friends and weekend getaways. But summer is our busiest season, especially on the weekends, which means I have less free time, not more. Add the course I'm taking, and it's been hard to make myself available, particularly for spur-of-the-moment stuff.

"We're working on freeing up more time, but it's an event hotel, Chad," I remind him. "Weekends are when events happen and that's not going to change. We have that meeting with Mills Hotels coming up too. It has the potential to change a lot. We just need to be patient."

He blows out a breath, but nods. "Yeah, I get it. But this is supposed to be the time in our lives where we're making memories, traveling, hanging with friends. We're not supposed to be responsible for at least another five years. Before you know it, you'll be thirty and you'll have missed all the good stuff."

I don't know if I agree with that assessment. I've been responsible all my life. Losing my parents at twelve does that to a person.

Like when London got married, I bought her out of the apartment so I didn't have to move or downsize. Although, "bought her out" is probably the wrong phrase. I paid her a hundred dollars because she's married to a seriously rich man, and there was no way she would take money from me when she could literally fill a pool with hundred-dollar bills and swim in it. I also paid a dollar for our car and the cost of transferring ownership into my name.

"It won't be like this forever. And I'm not missing out on *all* of the good stuff."

"Just three-quarters of it with all your working weekends," Chad counters.

I know he's not trying to lay a guilt trip on me, but I already feel bad about not being able to make most of the last-minute stuff, and this doesn't help. Thankfully his phone pings with a message, distracting him from what had the potential to be an argument. "Allen is on his way to the restaurant. We can meet them there in about twenty. Do you want to walk over or catch an Uber?"

"I'm good to walk if you are." I push up out of my chair.

"Sounds good. I'm gonna use the bathroom, then we can go." He disappears down the hall.

I breathe a sigh of relief, happy to avoid dissension. This isn't the first time my work schedule has thrown a wrench into weekend plans. Or the first time he's made an offhand comment about moving in with me. I thought he was joking, but now I'm not so sure.

Sometimes I wonder if part of the reason moving in here appeals to him is because it's a nicer apartment in a better location. The neighborhood has access to more pubs, and all his favorite restaurants are out this way. Plus, Andrea and Allen live a few blocks away, and we spend a lot of time together.

I've also never lived with anyone other than my family and my sisters. And we really haven't been dating that long, so jumping into that kind of change doesn't seem like the best idea.

My phone rings. I assume it's Andrea, either telling me they're running behind or that they've arrived early. So I'm surprised when Gavin's name flashes across the screen instead. "Hello?"

"Hi, Harley, I hope I haven't caught you at a bad time."

"Oh, Gavin, hey, not at all. What's up? How's unpacking going? How's my favorite fairy-princess-in-training?"

He chuckles. "Unpacking is slower than I expected, and your favorite fairy princess keeps asking when we can see you again because she had so much fun at Chuck E. Cheese."

"Are you sure it's me that's the common denominator, or is it the chocolate milk, pizza, endless games, and amazing prizes?"

"I have proof that you're the common denominator because I asked if she wanted to go back there this week, and she asked if you were coming along. When I said no, she told me she'd rather not."

"Is that so?" I grab my purse and check for my wallet and slip my feet into a pair of sandals.

"Apparently it's not as much fun without you."

"There's a panda exhibit at the zoo. I could take her on Wednesday afternoon if that works for you? Unless it's too short notice."

"It's not too short. I can definitely move a few things around to make that work. She really needs something to look forward to."

"Is everything okay?"

"Yeah, for the most part. But Peyton misses the girls who lived on our street. She's used to running down the street and knocking on a door, but Claire is a car ride away. It's an adjustment period is all."

"I'm sorry. That can't be easy for either of you."

"It'll be fine. School starts soon. But the zoo will be a great carrot to dangle in front of her. I really appreciate you giving up your afternoon for us."

"Honestly, it's my pleasure, Gavin. You know how much I love Peyton. And I love the zoo and was planning to go on my own, so now I'll have company." I'm a bit surprised that he's willing to move his work around for a trip to the zoo, but I guess it would make sense that he wants time with Peyton before school starts.

"Okay. Great. Thanks again. I'll touch base on Wednesday morning."

"Perfect, talk to you then. And if you need anything, just call."

"I will. You're a godsend. Have a good night, Harley."

"You too." I end the call and glance up to see Chad standing in the kitchen, checking his reflection in the mirror by the door.

"Who was that?"

"Just one of the dads I used to nanny for. They moved back into the area and they're just getting settled in."

"How old is the kid now?" He runs his fingers through his hair and checks out his profile.

"Peyton is nine."

"So that was a while ago? How old was she when you nannied for this guy?"

"I took care of her when she was an infant until she was a year and a half."

"Must be nice to be able to afford to have someone else raise your kids for you," he scoffs.

I purse my lips. "His wife died in childbirth."

He stops messing with his shirt and his eyebrows lift. "Shit. That's harsh. I didn't realize that was something that still happens."

"Unfortunately, it can happen. Anyway, I was close with the family, and I'm a familiar face, which Peyton could use a little of with such a big move."

"Yeah. Sure. They do realize that you're not a nanny anymore, right?"

"Yeah."

"Good. Don't want anyone edging in on my time with my girlfriend." He winks. "You ready to go? I'm starving." He leans in and snaps his teeth together close to my jaw in a way that makes me flinch. "Sorry. I didn't mean to startle you." He kisses my cheek softly before lacing his fingers through mine. "Come on, our friends are waiting on us."

Five

CALLING IN A FAVOR

HARLEY

"I have some really great news for you," my brother-in-law says as I drop into the chair across from him.

It's Tuesday afternoon, and the four of us usually spend the morning reviewing the schedule for the week, then we break to tackle calls and anything that needs to be handled for the event later in the week. We follow that with a working lunch to plan for the coming month. Since our events often happen over the weekend, Mondays are sometimes a work-from-home day, depending on the scope of the upcoming event.

"What kind of good news?" I take a sip from my travel mug and set a Tupperware container of scones in the middle of the table. Last night I ended up getting sucked into a foodie show focused on scones, which inspired me to bake some of my own.

"We scheduled a birthday party just for you."

"I thought they were money-suckers, not moneymakers."

"Normally this is accurate; however, it's a sweet-sixteen party, and the family is loaded, so it's going to be huge, like 150 guests and lots of out-of-towners," Declan says.

"And we'll need your party-throwing skills and London's creative brain to pull this one off," Avery adds as she plops down into her chair. She reaches for a scone and takes a huge bite, groaning through a mouthful about how good they are.

Declan reaches over and rubs her pregnant belly as crumbs fall and makes a joke about feeding the beast. Their love is the kind that warms the room. And he calms her in a way no one else can. Having him on board the last few years has been amazing, especially since he's been a regular fixture in our lives since Avery was in college. They're best friends, work partners, and now they're going to be parents.

Chad and I have fun, but I don't think we'd be the kind of partners who would work together. We're more opposites attract. He's an IT and gaming nerd, and I'm a kid-loving, Disney fanatic who enjoys glitter crafts, bakes when the mood suits me, and still prefers family movies to any other kind. I don't think we need to be in each other's pockets for us to date.

"We're going to have so much fun planning this one!" London tosses one of her stars in the jar she carries with her everywhere. Probably even to the bathroom. Those stars are the entire basis for Starry-Eyed Treasures, her Etsy store. She used to make them when she was nervous, and now she makes them so she can keep up with her online store. It's pretty cool.

She's cut back on her hours at Spark House over the past few years, in part because she travels with Jackson and Ella. But since she also loves working with me and Avery, and putting an innovative spin on everything, she spearheads the artistic planning and design for every event, even if it is virtually. I usually fill in for her when she's away, following her plan, because I enjoy the creative stuff too.

"And you know what the best part is?" London taps her fingers together excitedly, and she and Avery exchange a look.

I take the bait. Obviously whatever it is makes them both giddy. "What's that?"

"The birthday girl is a huge fan of that movie with the guy who says *inconceivable* all the time. What's it called again?" London is practically vibrating with her excitement.

"*The Princess Bride?*"

"That's it!" London nods vigorously.

I glance between them. "Seriously?"

"Super seriously." Avery nods.

"I love that movie. I can totally get on board with planning a party around that theme." Obviously there won't be an arts-and-crafts component, but it will definitely be fun to plan with London, who I haven't had enough time with. Understandably so, since she's a new mom and married. But any opportunity to work on an event with her is a good one, so I'll take it.

We chat a bit more about the party and toss some ideas around before we move on to the bigger picture items.

"Next week we're having a conference call with Bancroft and Griffin Mills to discuss their franchise proposal. Obviously nothing is definite, and at this point we're just hearing what they have to say, but we've all done all our research and made our plans, so I think we're ready. This could be an amazing opportunity," Avery says.

"What exactly would that mean for us? From what I understand, other locations would carry the Spark House name, right? Does that mean we'd be split up? Would we have to move to one of the new Spark House hotels to help run it?" The thought alone makes my throat tight. I've been hesitant about this whole thing right from the start, but Avery and London are all in. I know I should probably say something, but my sisters are so excited about this, and I don't feel that anything I say is going to change our trajectory. Making waves and creating conflict isn't something I wanted to do, but maybe I should've.

It's hard enough as it is to find time to spend with my sisters outside of work. If we're all split up, what will that look like? And with Grandma Spark in Italy, all the people I'm closest to could be scattered across the country.

London puts her hand over mine, maybe sensing my unease. "We won't be split up. We'd continue to run Spark House here, just like we always have. But Mills Hotels would like to invest in us. They want to use the Spark House name and our model and open boutique-style event hotels in other locations, and they'll pay us a cut to do that."

"So they won't own Spark House?"

"No." Declan shakes his head. "They'll be able to open new hotels in other states, but since they would be using our name, we would need to give approval before they can move forward with proposed sites. It's like a joint venture."

"Okay. That makes sense. Just as long as we stay together." Lately it's started to feel like I barely know what my role is here. I want to be able to go with the flow, but the things I'm good at keep being taken over. I can't imagine what it would be like if I had to go somewhere else. I'd feel like a fraud. Both Avery and London have very defined roles, and me . . . well, I'm kind of a floater. A jack of all trades, master of none. Or at least that's how I've felt ever since the Teamology initiative streamlined our social media accounts, leaving me to manage "supplemental content."

"We're not going anywhere," Avery assures me. "All it means is that there will be more Spark Houses in the world."

"They'd like to start small to build on exclusivity and make sure the boutique hotels are meeting the same standard of care and attention as the original Spark House," Declan explains. "They have five prospective sites: two in California, one in upstate New York, and two in Vermont. They want to start with Cali and New York, then move on to Vermont. After that, they have three additional proposed sites in the Pacific Northwest."

That seems like a lot of expansion, going from one to six, and then adding three more after that. "What does the timeline look like on that? How quickly is all this going to happen? How are we going to run this place and manage these franchises?" I can feel the panic rising, and I'm surprised London is so calm in the face of all this change. Usually she's the wired one of the three of us. Apparently this is one of my new Spark House roles—resident panicker.

"That's where the Mills brothers come in. They're setting up a core team who will train and oversee the franchise candidates."

"But how are they going to do that if we're here?" I ask, still not understanding. I really should've asked more questions before, but it's all just hitting me now.

"The core team will come out and shadow us during events over the next few months," Declan explains.

"So we'll be teaching them how to run the hotel while *we* run the hotel?" London asks. The lilt in her voice tells me I'm not the only one with anxiety now.

"Yes and no," Declan says. "We're going to teach their core team, and they in turn will train the employees at each new site. All of that will be overseen by the project manager hired by Mills Hotels. And that's *if* we like their proposal and they agree to our terms."

"What are our terms?" We've all been spending weeks pulling data and financials, reviewing proposals, creating systems, but I'm still unsure of the nitty-gritty details. It's like all of these big decisions are being made around me, and I'm running to catch up. My focus until now had been on wrapping up the final birthday party and keeping up with coursework, on top of adding event-specific content to our social media. Maybe I spent a little too much time trying to figure out a way to keep the birthday parties. And it seems to have been for nothing, since they've been cut regardless.

The reality of the franchise proposal is setting in, and it's definitely too late to say or do anything to stop it. Not when we've already done the preliminary work and have all these meetings set up.

"Declan is working with our lawyer to draft everything. Essentially, we're asking that any hotel that bears the Spark House name follows the same ecofriendly model and has green partnerships and sources locally. Jackson has an entire team working on this," London assures me.

"I know it's a lot all at once, but I promise, the long-term gains are worth the short-term stress. It's going to take some work and some juggling, but I'm already looking at additional hires so we have a more robust staff to work with while this is happening. Once everything is in place, we'll have less on our plate and we'll be able to delegate more." Declan glances at Avery. "Which we're all aware isn't your strong suit, babe."

She gives him an unimpressed look. "I'm getting better at it."

"Slowly but surely," London mutters.

"And you're going to have to keep getting better at it with this little nugget on the way." Declan pats her slightly rounded belly.

"I know. I'm a delegating work in progress." Avery struggles with relinquishing control when it comes to Spark House, but she's definitely getting better at it.

"Okay. But will we reasonably be able to carve out more time for ourselves when we're hiring more staff and training people to run franchise locations? We've already done the whole struggling-to-keep-up thing as we're growing quickly, and this seems like it could be another one of those times." Around the time when London and Jackson started dating, we were expanding too fast for us to keep up. Things finally came to a head when London missed an important meeting that Avery dumped on her because she had her own wedding-related emergency. That was when London and I finally put our foot down and told her that we couldn't continue on this path without more support.

That led to us hiring Declan to help with the company-liaising side of things. He was already managing our financial portfolio at the time, so bringing him on full-time made the most sense. Since then, we've hired more than a dozen people to help manage Spark House, which has kept growing every year. And now this franchise opportunity. I worry that we're going to end up more bogged down with work, instead of less. And that we're going to lose what makes Spark House special, which is the fact that it's family-run and owned.

"I promise it won't ever be like how it was before we brought Declan on board full-time." Avery's tone is full of apology.

"We know we need more hands on deck," Declan assures me.

I'm aware Declan means to bring me solace, but for whatever reason, it makes me anxious instead. It sounds like we won't have too much extra work once the franchises happen, since there will be a team for that. Which is great, but it still doesn't help me figure out how and where I'm going to be most effective moving forward, or what that will even look like. I guess this is a figure-it-out-as-we-go kind of situation.

We continue our discussion about the upcoming meeting with the Mills brothers, and I create an extensive list of questions to ask and add new subsections to the staff training manual London and I started working on recently. It's nearing dinner by the time we finish.

As I'm packing up my things, my phone buzzes in my pocket. I check to see who it's from and find a message from Gavin, which isn't unusual. We've been chatting regularly these days, particularly with the zoo trip coming up. But this time the message reads as urgent.

> **Gavin:** mini emergency. Do you have time for a quick call? *cringe face emoji*

I don't bother responding by text and hit the call button instead.

"Hey. Hi. That was fast," he says.

"We're just wrapping up a meeting. What's up? Is everything okay?" I ask as I put the lid on the empty Tupperware container. Avery ate three scones and is now moaning about how full she is and how she needs to go for a walk.

There's a brief pause. "Uh, I hate to do this, but I have an emergency meeting with a client and my parents are out tonight. I know it's really last minute, and you probably already have plans . . ."

The edge of panic I was feeling disappears. "Do you need me to watch Peyton?"

"It would only be for a couple of hours. Lynn and Ian are busy tonight, otherwise I would have asked them to watch her. I don't want to drag Peyton along to this if I don't have to, but I completely understand if you're busy. I need to find a steady sitter here."

"I can make it work. I can't imagine it would be fun for either of you if you have to take her to something like that. Especially at this time of the day. What time is the meeting?"

"At six thirty."

I check the time. It's closing in on five. "Should I come to your place? What time does Peyton go to bed?"

"Usually eight thirty, but I let her stay up until nine in the summer. If she came with me, I'd have to let her entertain herself with the iPad, which makes it hard to get her in bed on time."

"I totally get it. Why don't you text me your address? I'll finish up here and head over."

"Thanks, Harley. I owe you one."

We end the call and a moment later my phone pings with his address. I give him a thumbs-up and slip my phone back in my pocket.

I glance up to find London folding one of her stars, her lips pressed together.

"What's that face about?" I arch a brow.

"You're babysitting for Gavin?"

"He has an emergency meeting and no one else to go to."

"You've been seeing a lot of him lately." She drops her star in the jar and screws the lid on, side-eyeing me.

"I've seen him and Peyton once for lunch."

"Aren't you taking her to the zoo tomorrow?"

"Yeah, but I was already planning to go anyway; at least this way I'll have company." I asked Chad if he wanted to go when they first opened the panda exhibit, but he's not a fan of the smell of animal doody, which he seems to think is the predominant odor associated with the zoo. Ironically they often smell better than his dirty socks. "They're settling in and I'm a familiar face," I add.

"It just seems awfully convenient that you're the first person he goes to when he needs a sitter. Doesn't he have a niece or some teenager he can call on to watch her?" London flips the jar of stars between her fingers before she slips it into her purse.

"Usually he'd ask his parents, but they're out tonight. Why are you so against me helping him?" I feel like I'm getting a chance to right my wrongs, to fix the thing I felt I'd broken all those years ago. But London doesn't know about the almost-kiss, and telling her seven years later doesn't seem like the best idea in the world. I don't want to relive that again.

"It's not that I'm against it. I just . . . don't want you to get taken advantage of in this situation. I remember what it was like when he and Peyton moved. You were pretty broken up about it." I start to interrupt her, but she holds up a hand. "And I know it's been a lot of years, but I saw the way he was looking at you at that birthday party."

"The way he was looking at me? What's that supposed to mean?"

"Oh come on, Harley, you can't tell me you didn't notice."

"Notice what?"

"You're gorgeous. He's got two working eyeballs."

"I'm in a relationship."

"Does he know that?"

I open my mouth and then clamp it shut. I can't remember if I've mentioned Chad to him. "It's not even relevant. He knows I'm good with Peyton. That's why he called to ask for help."

"Okay, if that's what you want to go with, but be careful, okay? I don't want him taking advantage of your kindness."

Six

THE COMFORT OF FAMILIARITY

GAVIN

Thankfully the client meeting doesn't go past the two-hour mark. I'm grateful that Harley was able to watch Peyton. While I could have brought her along, it would have been tough to keep my daughter entertained and it's been a rough go getting her used to sleeping in her own bed in the new house.

When I arrive home, it's closing in on eight thirty. I am not surprised to find Peyton already in her pajamas with one of her frilly tutus around her waist, sitting beside Harley, who is also wearing a tutu—hers is rainbow-colored and the zipper in the back is open, likely because it's not made to fit an adult woman. They're focused on the task in front of them, working together to make a healthy bedtime snack of ants on a log: celery sticks with peanut butter and raisins. It's Peyton's favorite.

Sitting on the counter are a tray of oatmeal cookies and stuck to the fridge is a freshly painted picture of a blue horse running up the side of a glitter rainbow. Both Harley and Peyton have rainbow stickers stuck to their cheeks.

It takes me back to when Harley used to be Peyton's nanny. She was always making creative foods, and, even when Peyton was barely walking, they were doing things like finger painting.

Harley never cared if Peyton was a mess and needed a bath after every meal or a wipe down after playtime. If Peyton was having fun and trying new things, Harley always thought it was worth it.

I stand at the edge of the kitchen, watching the two of them together. There's an ease in their interactions that's been missing from Peyton's life.

It's almost as though no time has passed at all; despite the new kitchen and the different home, Harley is exactly the same. Well, almost the same. The softness of youth has given way to the angles of womanhood. She no longer looks like a college student. She carries herself with poise and sureness. The cute, bubbly teen is now a bright, attractive woman with the same maternal warmth that calmed Peyton. And me. It doesn't seem like that has changed either.

I wouldn't have survived that first year of Peyton's life without Harley. The grief alone would have been too much, let alone navigating being a father without my wife.

"Hey, you're back earlier than expected. Did the meeting go okay?" Harley asks.

"Better than expected, actually." I'm slowly transitioning to take over for my dad at Greenscapes so he can finally retire. It means catching up on how things work and attending a lot of meetings. We're set to break ground on a huge park outside the city, and there were a couple of small issues with the design that needed to be ironed out. Once we have approval on those tweaks, we'll be able to move forward.

"Dad!" Peyton abandons her snack and hops off the stool, running over and throwing her arms around me. "Come see what we made! We had bunny pizzas for dinner and Harley showed me how to make oatmeal chocolate chip cookies and we painted with watercolors!" The words blend together with her excitement.

I let Peyton show me all the things they made in the two hours I was gone, and she informs me that the leftover bunny pizza is for her lunch tomorrow.

Once Peyton is finished with her snack, I send her off to brush her teeth and get ready for bed, leaving me alone with Harley. Over text, conversation between us flows easily. But in person, sometimes I feel she's more comfortable with Peyton than she is with me. I guess it makes sense since I used to be her boss, but I'd like to find a way to change that. "Thanks again for doing this for me. I hope I didn't interfere with your plans."

Harley waves the comment away and then shimmies the tutu over her head and hangs it on one of the chairs. "It wasn't a problem, and I love spending time with Peyton. As you can see, she was determined to make one of her fairy costumes fit me."

"Thank you for indulging her."

She shrugs. "I don't mind. It's entertaining and she has such a great imagination. It's probably one of my favorite parts about working with kids. They're not afraid to get silly and just have fun."

"Oh, I'm very familiar with her amazing imagination. There's rarely a week that goes by that I don't dress up as a fairy and have an afternoon tea party. Mostly I think it's an excuse to eat cookies."

Harley laughs. "Dress-up and tea parties go together like peanut butter and jelly." She points to the fridge, where Peyton's child scrawl fills up a sheet of pink paper. "Aside from all the food making, we also made a list of all the things she needs for school next week. She's excited to start."

"Thanks, my mother-in-law has been taking care of that since she started school, so that list will definitely help."

"I always used to love back-to-school shopping. It helped with the excitement." Harley brings Peyton's empty snack plate to the sink.

"You don't need to clean up. I've got this." I grab a cookie off the plate and shove the whole thing into my mouth. It's been years since I've had Harley's baking.

Karen, my mother-in-law, didn't agree with sweets in the house. And while I understand not wanting kids to overindulge in sugar, I also don't think it hurts to eat a cookie every now and again. Especially when they're homemade and delicious.

"I don't mind. Have you eaten yet?" She arches a brow as I reach for another cookie.

"I'll make myself a sandwich once Peyton is in bed."

"Why don't you have a seat, and I'll whip you up one of my gourmet grilled cheeses, like I used to back in the day." She arches a brow while walking backward toward the stove.

"You still living on grilled cheese and fries? From what I remember, it was your go-to meal of choice. That and the movie *The Princess Bride*."

"My dinner palate has changed, but I still love a good grilled cheese when the mood strikes me. My movie tastes on the other hand . . ." She gives me a wry grin. "You're in for some comfort food, then?"

"I already hijacked your night. You don't need to make me dinner too." But I remember what those grilled cheese sandwiches were like and my mouth is already watering.

"You didn't hijack my night. I basically did all the things I planned to, but with a miniature helper."

"You planned to make bunny pizzas for dinner?" I give her a skeptical look. It's odd how easy it is to slip right back into old ways with Harley. Having her in my house and my kitchen should feel strange, but it doesn't. She fits. Maybe it's the comfort of familiarity.

"I planned to order takeout, so this was much better." She turns on a burner, grabs the frying pan, and waves a hand in my direction. "Sit down. Take a load off. I'm sure you've been going since the sun came up."

"And you haven't?" I do what she says, though. She's right. I'm hungry, and slapping some ham and mustard on bread isn't nearly as appealing as fresh grilled cheese.

"I just spent the past two hours having fun with an adorable nine-year-old. That's hardly a chore." She opens the fridge and pulls out several items, setting mayo and a variety of cheeses on the counter.

Less than ten minutes later she sets a plate with two golden sandwiches in front of me, oozing cheese and smelling delicious. I take a bite and groan as the flavors hit my tongue. "Why are these always so amazing?"

"It's the mayo instead of butter."

"I forgot that trick. I could never make them taste as good as you did," I mutter through a mouthful.

"You were running on very little sleep back in the day. And all you had to do is shoot me a text, asking for my secret. I would have given it to you."

Our gazes lock from across the island for a moment, but she looks away quickly. Not before I catch the hurt lurking behind her eyes, among other emotions. Her cheeks burst with color, and she busies herself with putting away the cheese and mayo.

Thankfully, Peyton comes back into the kitchen, her stuffed bunny tucked under her arm, and saves me from responding.

"You still have Hoppy?" A small smile pulls at the corner of her mouth.

"He's my favorite stuffie. I have to be careful with him now, though, because he's starting to wear out." Peyton holds him out for Harley to see. "Some of his stuffing is starting to poke out of his bum."

"Hmm." Harley plants one hand on her hip and leans in close, tapping her lip in contemplation. "I bet we could give him a little surgery and he'll be good as new."

"Really?" Peyton hugs him gently to her chest.

"Maybe next time I see you, we can work on making sure he's all sewed up. Sound good?"

Peyton nods and rubs his ear against her cheek. "Can you read me a story tonight?"

"Harley probably wants to head home, honey," I tell Peyton.

"It's okay. I don't mind. You eat your sandwiches and I'll read a story."

"You're sure?" I ask.

"Positively positive." Harley winks.

Peyton hugs and kisses me good night before she takes Harley's hand, and they disappear down the hallway.

It's been a long time since anyone but me has put Peyton to bed. It feels . . . odd, but also nice. Especially since I know she's in good hands, and that means I can eat my grilled cheeses while they're still hot. Fifteen minutes later Harley appears. I push my chair back, expecting Peyton will want to say good night again.

Harley holds up a hand. "She's already out."

"She's asleep?"

"Down for the count."

"Can you come over and take care of bedtime every night?" I blurt without thinking.

Harley barks a laugh and crosses the kitchen. "She was worn out. I kept her busy this evening." Her expression sobers. "Is she usually harder to get down?"

"She's pretty good, but it's a new house, new room, new sounds at night. Half the time I wake up in the morning and she's in bed with me," I admit.

"Ah, the old *sneak into bed while Daddy's sleeping* trick. Are you worried about that, or do you think it'll sort itself out over time?"

"I'm hoping for the latter, but I don't know. It's a big change, moving back here. She really loves having you around, and she loves that her nana, my mom, is a lot less . . . of a stickler for the rules."

Harley moves to stand on the other side of the island. "That can be good and bad, can't it?"

"Mm. Yeah. It can." I'm starting to see just how stifling it was with my mother-in-law. The help was great, but it came with a price, which was someone other than me setting a lot of the ground rules that I didn't always agree with. But at the same time, it was coming from a good place and she had Peyton's best interests at heart. And Peyton is the only tie they have to their daughter.

"Is that something you need to address with your parents? Do you think they'll be too lenient with Peyton?" Harley leans against the counter, expression pensive.

"Not too lenient. It's not like they feed her a pound of sugar and let her watch TV all day. It's more that they'll let her have a cookie or a glass of chocolate milk, or watch two episodes of her favorite show instead of one. The rules aren't as . . . rigid. What I'm worried about is how Peyton is going to handle being back with her granny when we do go to visit."

"Ah. I see, because the rules were stricter?" Harley asks.

"Exactly. Things were pretty cut and dry with her granny, but here, there are a lot more gray areas. And my parents haven't had the past seven years with her."

"Does that make them less likely to say no to Peyton?"

I consider that for a moment. "Maybe a bit. But it's more that they're polar opposites to her granny, so it's getting used to a new set of rules. It's not just Peyton making an adjustment, it's all of us."

Harley nods, her smile sympathetic. "I get what you mean. It was tough to get used to my grandmother's rules and how they changed when she went from being a grandparent to a stand-in mom. There were growing pains there, and you're experiencing the same thing. The good thing is that Peyton is old enough to understand there are different rules in place depending on who she's with. Most kids realize their grandparents are willing to sneak them treats that their parents won't allow."

"In this case, it was me always sneaking Peyton the treats when her granny wasn't looking." And getting lectured on my parenting when I didn't do things the same way Karen did.

"Mm." She nods knowingly. "That must have been a tough line to toe, what with how involved they've been."

I nod. "It could be stifling at times. All I was doing in Boulder was working and being a father. I didn't have time for a social life, and most of my friends were still here. In some ways I feel bad for taking Peyton away from everything familiar again, but Colorado Springs has always felt more like home. It's still a lot of change for both of us."

"Change is always supposed to be uncomfortable. It's how you know you're making the right choice," Harley says thoughtfully.

"You're too wise for someone your age," I say.

She laughs. "I'm not twenty anymore, Gavin. And I had to grow up fast. So did you." She blows out a breath. "Anyway, I'm always here to help if you need it."

"Thanks. I appreciate that. I appreciate you." I shake my head at how awkward I'm making things. "I mean, I appreciate you making yourself available for Peyton, especially with how busy you already are."

"I wouldn't have said yes if I didn't have the time." She props her chin on her fist. "How was your emergency meeting? You said it went better than expected?"

"Oh yeah, it was just about getting approval on a couple of tweaks on a design."

"Oh? What are you designing?"

"A park, but it's a much larger scale than the ones I'm used to working on, which has been an amazing challenge."

"Do you have drawings?"

"I do. They're on my computer. Do you want to see them?" I can't quite tell if she's just being polite or if she's genuinely interested.

The way her eyes light up gives me the answer. "Absolutely! But only if you don't mind."

"I don't mind. They're in my office, though." I give her an out if she wants one.

"Lead the way."

She falls into step beside me, and we stop when we pass Peyton's room so I can check on her. It's a habit I doubt I'll be able to break anytime soon. She's curled up on her side with Hoppy tucked under her chin. I pull the door closed and we continue past my bedroom to the end of the hall.

I push through the door to my office, which looks out over the backyard. A trail of lights leads to a pergola where I often work on weekend mornings with coffee.

"Your backyard is amazing. The view of the mountains in the distance is picture-worthy. Peyton and I sat out there and ate dinner tonight."

"You'll have to come back another time and have dinner out there with me," I say as I drop into my chair, then rush to add, "I mean with me and Peyton." I cringe internally. The way that came out made it sound like I'm asking her on a freaking date. Not that I would be completely opposed to that, but Peyton is already attached to Harley, and complicating this with things like dates probably isn't the best plan. Especially when I'm still getting my feet under me after this move, and Harley and I are just getting reacquainted.

"We can make bunny pizzas again since they were such a winner this time around." Harley stands behind me, hand resting on the back of the chair as I pull up the designs and show her the three-dimensional rendering of the park. It's huge, over a square mile of land with trails, a skate park, and a children's play structure, along with several open green spaces lined with trees.

"This is amazing, Gavin. You've really got an incredible eye for this. I've visited some of the parks you designed around here before you moved, but this is really above and beyond." Her fingers brush my shoulder as she leans in to get a better look, and she quickly drops her hand, moving around to stand beside my chair. I inhale the scent of her perfume or whatever she uses that makes her smell the way she does. Like vanilla maybe. Something sweet.

I clear my throat. "Thanks. I've been working my way toward this for a long time. And my dad dangled it like a carrot as a way to entice me to come home."

Harley chuckles. "Obviously it worked."

"Like a charm," I agree. "I was a little daunted by the scope of the project at first, but when you're given this much space to work with and a huge budget, it really lends itself to creativity."

"I can see that. Can you zoom in on the play structure?" She points to the center of the screen. "I want to take a closer look at that."

"Sure. Of course." It's been a long time since someone other than the people I work with have shared my excitement about a project. My dad obviously loves landscape design. He's spent more than thirty years in the field, built his own business from the ground up, and expanded. My in-laws couldn't understand how I managed to get lost for hours in a project and wouldn't even realize I'd miss lunch until my alarm went off signaling it was time for me to pick up Peyton.

"This is really cool." Harley points to the castle-like structure. "What are the chances you could put a rock-climbing wall up the side? Just the first six feet or so, to avoid it being too high and reduce the chances of someone getting hurt, and here"—she points to the wooden bridge connecting the two towers—"you could do a rope bridge, which would be great for balance."

"Those are great ideas." I jot them down.

"Oh my God. I can't believe I did that. Like I know anything about architecture." She tries to take the pencil from my hand, but I grip it tighter.

"But you know a lot of things about kids and what they like. I'm not jotting them down because I need something to do with my hands, I'm jotting them down because I can see how they could work." I stand and roll my chair closer to her. "Here, sit. I'm picking your brain."

"The last thing you probably want to do right now is more work."

"Paperwork no, but design work I would do in my sleep if I could. Sit." I nod to the chair. "Let me scavenge your head for ideas."

She takes a seat in my executive chair, and I grab my stool from my drafting table, rolling back over to her. "Okay. Climbing wall and a rope bridge. What else do you think might work well?"

We go back and forth for the next thirty minutes, discussing potential tweaks and additions. When we're finished, Harley has given me some really great feedback to fix some of the problems I had with the design.

"How much work is this going to make for you?" Harley asks as I start shutting down my computer.

"It'll take maybe a day for me to input all the changes and modifications, but we won't be moving on this structure until the spring. Our first step is creating the trails and setting up the garden and picnic areas, so I can keep making tweaks to this until the winter if you come up with more ideas."

"As if you need me inserting myself into your projects." She covers her mouth with her palm and stifles a yawn. "Oh, wow. That was rude." She glances at the clock on the wall. "It's after ten already! No wonder I'm turning into a yawn factory." Harley rolls her chair back and stands up. "I better get home before I turn into a pumpkin."

I walk her to the front door and out to her car. "Thanks again for watching Peyton."

"It was way more fun than what I had planned anyway." She unlocks her car door. "Are we still on for the zoo tomorrow afternoon?"

"We could postpone it if you have other things you need to do."

"Not at all. And I can totally take Peyton on my own if you're busy. I'm going no matter what, and having Peyton come along will make it way more fun."

"Okay. As long as it's not an inconvenience." I shove my hand in my pocket. "Can I, uh, can I pay you for tonight?"

Harley blinks a few times and her expression shifts to something like irritation. "No. I don't want money for spending a couple of hours with Peyton."

I rush to explain. "I feel bad not giving you anything."

"You can foot the bill for the zoo, how about that?" she says.

"Yeah. Absolutely." I'm grateful for the save. "I'll even splurge on overpriced popcorn and ice cream."

That puts a smile back on her face. "Ice cream is a must at the zoo. And funnel cakes." She opens the driver's side door and gets in her car.

I wait on the front steps until she backs out and pulls away before I go back inside.

The smell of fresh baked cookies lingers in the hallway.

I've missed this. The hominess that comes with having someone around who bakes not because they feel obligated to, or because Peyton had to beg them, but because they honestly and truly derive joy from doing it.

I move through the house, shutting off lights as I go, and

stop in the kitchen, stealing one last cookie as I survey the room, my eyes catching on the picture Harley and Peyton painted this evening, which is stuck to the fridge with magnets.

This is what Peyton has been missing. Someone in her life who loves the same things she does, who will have fun with her, be silly with her. And maybe I've been missing that too. I feel like I robbed us both of that when we moved to Boulder and away from Lynn and Ian and their daughter Claire, and the other friends we had here. But Karen had been right in a lot of ways. I had family who was willing to help care for Peyton; it didn't make sense to keep paying someone to care for my daughter when she had other people who wanted that time with her. And I felt like I owed them that after losing my wife, Marcie.

But I have to admit, being back in Colorado Springs feels right. And it's good to have Harley back in our lives.

Seven

A TASTE OF HAPPINESS

GAVIN

The following afternoon Peyton and I meet Harley and her niece, Ella, at the entrance to the zoo. I tried to invite Ian to come along, but he has a late meeting and Claire has one of her many lessons, so it's me, Harley, and the kids.

It's a warm afternoon, the sun is shining, and there's a slight breeze. Harley is dressed for the weather in a tank top, shorts, running shoes, and a baseball cap to shield her face, pushing a stroller with the adorable fair-haired toddler who pooped all over Harley's tutu at the birthday party.

"Harley brought Ella, Dad! This is going to be so much fun." When I don't move fast enough for Peyton, she lets go of my hand and skips the last few steps over to Harley.

She gives her a big hug, then bends down to say hello to Ella.

"I hope you don't mind me bringing Ella along. I figured it was a good opportunity for my sister and her husband to get in some alone time, or a nap. Or both. Ella's teething, and the broken sleep is killing London."

"I remember those days only too well."

"Those could be some long nights." She busies herself with adjusting the stroller to make sure the sun isn't on Ella's face.

She's wearing a T-shirt that says ME AND MY AUNTIE GOT IN TROU-BLE TODAY.

"Can we visit the meerkats first? They're so funny," Peyton asks, breaking the sudden tension.

"For sure. Let's get our tickets." Harley pushes the stroller while Peyton tells her all about the day camp she's been attending this week. It's arts- and drama-focused and right up Peyton's alley.

"One adult and three kids?" the girl at the ticket booth asks. Her name tag reads Stashia.

Harley's head is tipped down, her face covered by the brim of her WE'RE ALL PRINCESSES ball cap. She's trying to open her backpack, which also happens to be princess-themed and probably belongs to Ella. Harley's head snaps up and Stashia's eyes go wide. "Oh! I'm so sorry. Family of four."

My lips press together, and I try not to react, but I give Harley a sidelong glance. Her eyes are wide and darting between me and Stashia.

"Harley used to be my nanny," Peyton, my ever-observant daughter, pipes up.

The girl in the booth, who looks to be in her late teens, glances back and forth between me, Peyton, Harley, and baby Ella, a whole range of emotions including scandalized crossing her face before her mouth turns up in a very awkward, very fake smile. "That's so nice," she says in a pitchy, strained voice.

I have to give it to her, she's really trying to keep it together.

And of course because Peyton loves to talk and tell random strangers things they definitely don't need to know, she tacks on, "My mommy went to heaven before I had a chance to meet her, so the angels sent Harley to take care of me when I was a brand-new baby. We're going to see the pandas today and the meerkats because they're fun to watch."

Harley raises her palm to her mouth and covers a laugh with a cough. "I'm so sorry. Allergies." She motions to the flower beds nearby and fakes a sneeze that sounds like someone stepped on a dog toy.

Stashia hands over the tickets, and Harley thanks her while barely maintaining her composure as we make our way through the gates. It isn't until we're out of hearing range that she bursts into laughter. "Oh my gosh." She grabs my arm. "Did you see the look on her face? She was trying so hard not to react."

"*She* was trying not to react?"

"She thought I was your daughter at first!" She sucks in a gasping breath and wipes tears of laughter from the corners of her eyes.

"I don't get why that's funny," Peyton says.

"She thought we were the same age, or close to it." Harley motions between her and Peyton.

"Because your head was down, and you're wearing a princess hat." I flick the brim. "And you were rummaging around in a princess backpack. And in a few years Peyton is going to be taller than you."

Harley plants a fist on her hip and tips her chin up, all adorable annoyance. "Are you height-shaming me?"

"No, I'm just stating facts."

She meets my gaze with a narrowed one of her own. "Sounds a lot like height-shaming to me."

"I don't need a step stool to reach the top shelf in my kitchen cupboards, but you do." A flash of memory hits me. One day, at the very beginning, when Harley had just moved in after Marcie died,

I'd come into the kitchen and found her hoisting herself onto the counter so she could reach a bowl on one of the top shelves. I'd scared the crap out of her when I asked what she was doing, and she'd almost fallen off the counter. After that, I went out and got a step stool so she didn't have to parkour around the kitchen.

She points a finger at me. "Height-shamer."

"You have a vertical deficit."

She scowls and I grin. After a few seconds she rolls her eyes and covers her mouth with her hand, obviously trying to hide her smile. I like this easy friendship we seem to be forming. It's been a long time since I've spent time with a woman, even just on a friend level, and Harley is fun to be around.

Ella makes a disgruntled sound from her stroller, and Harley turns her attention back to her niece, giving her back her teething ring.

We head for the meerkat exhibit, which is on the way to the pandas. Pretty much all the exhibits are. It's clearly been designed to entice people to visit the entire zoo in order to get to and from the pandas.

Peyton skips ahead of us as we reach the meerkats. They're full of personality and mischief, which we witness firsthand when one of the meerkats drops a number two right in front of the window and then picks it up and lobs it at another meerkat. Like poorly behaved children in a cafeteria, other meerkats start picking up scraps of food and other, less appealing things and tossing them around.

Peyton's expression turns from joy to disgust. "Are they throwing poop at each other?"

"Yup, they definitely are." I give her a solemn nod and glance at Harley, who looks gleeful.

Ella is giggling away in her stroller, clearly enjoying the antics.

"Ew. But that's so gross," Peyton exclaims.

"It definitely is, but it's also hilarious," Harley agrees.

"Maybe we should come back later when they're acting less gross." Peyton takes my hand, and we continue on toward the monkey enclosure, which is another exhibit that Peyton usually loves.

We make a stop at the giraffes, and Peyton leans her head against my arm. "It's kind of sad that all the animals here can't be free to run around like they do in the wild."

"You're right, it is." Harley nods her agreement. "But we're so close to the city, and it definitely wouldn't be good for the animals to be wandering around the streets, would it?"

Peyton shakes her head. "The animals could get hurt in the city. We've been talking about wildlife sanctuaries in social studies, and some places help wild animals that have been hurt get better and then they release them back into the wild, but sometimes they have to stay at the sanctuary because they can't make it on their own."

"Maybe we could visit a sanctuary," I suggest.

"That would be fun. Come on, let's go see the monkeys." Peyton tugs my hand.

Harley is a few steps ahead of us, and she slows considerably as we approach the baboons. "Um, I don't know—" She stretches her arm out and grabs my wrist.

Peyton lets go of my hand and skips past her. Harley releases my wrist and tries to grab Peyton's hand, and at first I'm not entirely sure why. Until I notice what she notices. "Oh my God," I mutter. "What the hell is wrong with them?"

"They're in heat." Harley's gaze stays fixed on the sea of very enflamed-looking baboon butts.

I come to a stop next to her, unsure if I'm fascinated, disturbed, disgusted, or a combination of all of the above. "They look like they've contracted an STI. And how in the world do you know they're in heat?"

"Because I visited the zoo with my sisters when I was about Peyton's age and witnessed the same thing." Her cheeks are close to the same color as the baboon butts.

Peyton glances over her shoulder and then points at a pair of baboons. The female—she's easy to identify—is being followed around by one of the males, who is practically sniffing her butt. "Why is he doing that? And what's wrong with that baboon's butt? Is it sick? It looks sore."

Harley and I share a panicked glance, and she raises both hands in the air. "Not it."

I give her a look. "You're gonna throw me under the bus like that?"

"I'm not throwing you under the bus. I'm just here to see the pandas, not give a nine-year-old a sex-ed lesson thanks to some randy baboons. That's your job." She backs up a couple of steps, heading in the opposite direction of the monkeys.

"Can't she stay nine forever?" I grumble, not wanting to go any farther, but Peyton is almost at the fence, apparently enthralled by the weirdness we're witnessing today.

"Wouldn't that be lovely." She calls out, "Peyton, let's get ice cream before we head to see the pandas."

She spins around, her eyes lit up with excitement, and she skips back over, the baboons completely forgotten. "Can we get a funnel cake?"

"Absolutely." I'm not above bribing her with all kinds of food to avoid a conversation about baboon romance.

"Saved by the funnel cake," Harley says with a grin. "For now."

We stop for funnel cake, which proves to be just as entertaining as the exhibits. Little Ella can't get enough of the ice cream, and her excitement is hilarious and infectious.

Ella manages to get the spoon out of Harley's hand, and ice cream goes flying. At first I think she's missed everyone, until Harley turns around, face scrunched up, vanilla ice cream and strawberry sauce dripping down her cheek.

"Hold still. I'll get it." I grab a napkin and tuck a finger under her chin, tipping it up so I can wipe the ice cream off.

"I got it." Her tongue peeks out, catching a drip as it reaches the corner of her mouth. She cracks a lid. "Did I get it?"

"Your tongue needs to be about three inches longer for you to handle this on your own, and then you'd be part lizard. If you hold still, I can get it for you." I stick my tongue out, like I'm going to lick it off her face, and her expression shifts from amused to horrified.

"I have wipes!" Peyton stands on the chair and waves them around.

Harley steps on my toe and pushes away, grabbing the wipe from Peyton at the same time. She cleans the ice cream off her face with one hand and holds the other one out, fending me off.

I burst into laughter. "I wasn't actually going to lick your face."

"You looked way too serious."

"Um, Harley? Daddy? I don't know if the wipes are going to be enough to clean up Ella." Peyton looks like she's not sure if she should laugh or not.

We both turn at the same time to find Ella with one hand in the ice cream and the other one in her mouth, her whole face and shirt covered in sticky ice cream and strawberry sauce.

"Oh Ella!" Harley claps a hand over her mouth and points to me. "You're helping me clean her up."

We spend the next fifteen minutes in the family bathroom, cleaning ice cream off Ella, who needs an entire change of clothes. And even though I basically need a full shower when I get home, and so does Peyton, I can't stop smiling.

Harley is a ray of sunshine peeking through the clouds. Warm and bright and full of life. And I'm glad the initial awkwardness is giving way to friendship. It makes me feel a little less alone and like this kind of happiness isn't out of reach anymore.

Eight

THE SMALL THINGS

HARLEY

"We're still on for tonight, right?" Chad asks.

"Absolutely. One hundred percent." I have him on hands-free because I'm driving to Spark House. I'm only half paying attention to our conversation because I'm nervous. We have a video conference scheduled with the Mills brothers to discuss the Spark House franchise, and every time we talk about it, I get all sweaty. I don't know if it's psychosomatic or what, but I keep having to wipe my hands on my pants because they're damp.

And apparently Selene Angelis is going to patch in because she's part of the Mills Hotel social media team. We've been working with her ever since Holt Media created Teamology, the program that partners small family-run businesses like Spark House with green sponsors.

I get starstruck and tongue-tied every time I see Selene, even if it's through a screen. She's a powerhouse when it comes to social media influencing, and at times I feel woefully inadequate next to her. She has a sixth sense for exactly what works and when to post for maximum reach. Social media has its own science, and Selene knows what makes people tick and how to inspire them. She was a big part of what made the Teamology partnership so successful and helped take Spark House to the next level.

"I probably won't be there until closer to seven thirty, but can we go for a late dinner, maybe? And I have to be online for a bit because the fantasy hockey draft is tonight, but after that I'm all yours." Chad's obsession with fantasy sports leagues isn't something I understand, but then my love of all things crafty and glitter can be equally consuming.

"That's okay. I have an assignment to finish, so I'll do that while you're handling the draft." Staying on top of the online coursework is a part-time job of its own.

"Perfect. Okay, babe, I gotta run, but I'll see you later."

"Sounds good."

We end the call as I pull down the Spark House driveway.

Jackson's Tesla and Declan's SUV are already parked out front.

I'm barely in the door before Avery grabs my arm. "Apparently there's already a ton of interest in the Spark House franchise locations, and the Mills brothers want to iron out the financials sooner rather than later so they can get started. This is so freaking exciting, isn't it?" She squeezes my arm.

"So exciting." I wish I felt her enthusiasm the same way, but with every new change, I feel like I get further away from the things I love about Spark House. It's like we're moving full steam ahead, and the brakes are shot on this adventure. My degree felt like something I should do for me. But I'm starting to look at it as a legitimate fallback plan. And secretly I've been worried about what it's going to be like when both of my sisters are trying to juggle kids and working here full-time.

I enter the conference room where we've been holding more

and more meetings lately. Around the table is London, Jackson, his personal assistant, Mitchell, and Trent, who is Jackson's best friend and Selene's husband, all of whom are affiliated with Holt Media and Teamology. And projected from one of the screens is Selene. I wave to everyone, including Selene's two-dimensional face, and take a seat at the table.

We all felt the connection with Teamology was something that should be part of the franchise, which makes sense, since they're a huge part of the reason the opportunity presented itself in the first place. We'd been doing well on our own, but with the help of Holt Media, Teamology, and Selene's social media skills, we've grown our base substantially.

"Excellent, everyone is here! We can get things rolling." Selene directs her warm smile my way. "Harley, it's so great to see you again. I loved last week's posts and the focus on the symbiotic relationships you have with so many local companies. You're doing amazing with the supplemental promotion."

"Thanks, I'm glad I can help," I manage to squeak out, feeling both good and bad. The praise is nice, but "supplemental" is a glaring reminder that my role as the social media manager has shifted, and now I'm only responsible for additional content. But I love taking photos and capturing candid moments around Spark House, so it's never really felt like actual work. I used to spend a good part of my day setting up shoots and planning out photo sets, but now I'm lucky if I can devote an hour or two a day to it.

"You're doing a great job and making mine that much easier." She shifts her gaze to Jackson. "Let's have the Mills team join us so they can fill us in."

"Sound good to me." Jackson brings up the Zoom meeting and connects us.

A few seconds later Bancroft, Lexington, and Griffin Mills appear on the screen. They're all huge, formidable-looking men, dressed in suits and sitting at a conference table side by side. Griffin is slightly shorter and leaner than Bancroft, and despite being older, his face is softer. Lexington looks like a model and is nearly as broad as Bancroft, who used to play professional rugby. He has a few facial scars and a small bump on his nose from it being broken more than once, which somehow makes him even more attractive.

After some pleasantries, we get right down to business, and I find myself overwhelmed by the conversation. Despite all the time we put in to prepare, I wasn't aware of exactly how much work goes into creating a franchise or how detailed the business plan would be. We discuss everything from the styles of the rooms, to the estates that are being purchased and renovated to fit the unique Spark House model, to the sponsor liaisons who will be assigned to each new hotel.

I take notes and listen while Avery and London do most of the talking. Half an hour into the meeting, I glance over at London, whose hands are laced together, her chin resting on her pointer finger. She unclasps them and tucks her hair behind her ear which is when I notice an issue that will be impossible to hide soon. I'm also aware that in a few minutes she's going to talk about the creative side of this venture, and the tutorials we've been creating to help the new teams with things like centerpieces and events.

She's sitting across the table from me, so I slide down in my seat and try to kick her under the table without alerting everyone. Unfortunately my legs aren't long enough. I resort to texting her instead, but she ignores the message.

So I switch to texting Jackson who's seated beside her. Unlike London, he's forever multitasking. His brows pull together when he notices the message. His gaze darts to me and then back to his screen. I flare my eyes, hoping he takes the bait and I don't have to do anything else that's going to draw more attention to myself or my sister.

Thankfully, he checks the message. His brows lift, then he glances quickly at London, recognizing the issue is indeed dire and she needs to make a swift exit before anyone else notices what I have. He extends an arm across the back of her seat and leans in, whispering in her ear. She glances down at the front of her blouse and claps a hand over her mouth. There are two very obvious wet spots on her chest. London is breastfeeding and trying to wean Ella, but it's been a slow transition, and every once in a while her body is a jerk. Like right now.

I slide a folder across the table, and she uses it as a shield while she excuses herself from the meeting and rushes out the door. Jackson mouths *thank you* to me.

"Is everything okay?" Avery asks.

"Everything's fine. London will be back in a few minutes."

"Should we wait? I know London wanted to talk about the creative aspect of Spark House," Selene asks.

"Maybe you can step in, Harley?" Avery suggests.

"Oh, uh, sure." My face heats with the unexpected attention, but I clear my throat. "London and I have been creating a video tutorial series for her centerpieces. She's been doing it for years for the staff here, but we thought putting together something more official would be a good way to streamline it." But as I consider the scope of this venture, I'm not so sure it's all that important anymore. "It's a small part of what we do. And with everything else that goes into setting up a franchise, maybe it's not something we should focus on right now. It was just an idea." And one London could have explained way better than me.

"I actually think this is a great idea," Selene interjects.

"I know the centerpieces are a small part of the events, so I don't know if it's really a valuable use of resources. And we already have lots of mini-tutorials. I could always clean those up," I offer, not wanting to make more work for London or the rest of the team.

"I definitely think it's worth having a look at those old videos. At the very least, it would be good to take a few professional ones to showcase just how much care goes into every aspect of running Spark House," Selene replies.

"Okay. In the past we've made step-by-step videos for different centerpiece prototypes. We know they're usually unique to the event, but we thought it would be helpful in giving the franchise staff a jumping-off point." I feel a bit better having Selene on my side for this. It makes me feel more confident in my role again. Plus, this is the kind of thing I enjoy, and it would give me a side project to be excited about.

"That is exactly what we need, especially when it comes to the small details. Do you think London would agree to a crew coming in to film her for these?" Selene taps a pen against her lips. "It would be some great additional content for social, which we're going to streamline further so we make it consistent across all franchise locations."

"What do you mean by streamlining it further?" I ask, and catch Jackson and Declan exchanging a look.

"Selene has agreed to head the social media for the entire Spark House franchise. We thought it made more sense to have her team managing that, so we could free you up to focus in-house," Jackson explains.

"Right. Yeah. I guess that makes sense." I sink back into my chair as Jackson, Selene, and Avery volley ideas. I'd been planning to take videos for London, and we started getting things organized for it, but it looks like that job isn't going to be mine. And it also looks like the job that *was* mine isn't going to be anymore either. Which puts me back at square one. It's hard not to feel defeated.

London returns a few minutes later, wearing a different blouse in the same color, so no one notices the change but me and Jackson, and they fill her in. She glances at me, but I just smile and say I think it's a great plan, so she rolls with it.

Once the meeting wraps up and everyone leaves but Declan, Jackson, and my sisters, we convene in our office. "Thanks for the heads-up. That would have been super embarrassing if any-one else had seen what was going on," London says to me.

"Seen what?" Declan asks. "Why'd you disappear all of a sudden?"

"She had a wardrobe malfunction," I offer and turn back to London. "And no problem. I tried to text you, but you ignored me, and I knew Jackson wouldn't."

"What kind of wardrobe malfunction? Did you pop a button or something?" Declan drops into his chair and shoves half of his chicken wrap into his mouth at once.

"Not exactly." London's cheeks flush.

"What happened? I feel like I missed out on something here." Avery plunks down beside Declan and starts loading up her plate like she's eating for four, not two.

"I sprung a leak. Can we drop it now? It's not really lunch-time conversation."

"A leak?" Declan asks through his mouthful of food.

Jackson doesn't say a thing, just sits back and lets Declan try to figure it out.

"Oh man! But don't you have those pad things?" Avery asks.

"Pad things?" Declan echoes.

"Yeah. I soaked right through them. This whole weaning business is not a lot of fun."

"Oh. Oh!" Declan finally puts two and two together. "Well, that's . . . more information than I expected." He gives Jackson, who's busy hiding a smile, an unimpressed look. "Why didn't you help a guy out?"

"Because it was entertaining to watch you flounder. And you'll be familiar with it soon enough."

"As if it wasn't embarrassing enough when it happened in real time," London mutters.

"Anyway, I think that meeting went well, don't you?" Avery changes the subject.

There's a murmur of agreement, and London turns her attention to me, likely happy not to have to talk about leaky boobs anymore. "Are you okay with Selene hiring a professional team to film the centerpiece tutorials?"

I glance from her to Jackson, who suddenly looks concerned, and back to London. I don't see the point in turning this into a point of conflict. "Oh yeah, of course. It makes more sense to have professionals film you, especially since it's for more than just a thirty-second post on social or a ten-minute tutorial for staff." I often spend an hour or two editing those videos. With a professional team coming in, I'm not sure there's a point.

She regards me seriously for a moment. "It does, but it was something we'd planned to do together. I want to make sure you're not feeling like every idea you've come up with is being taken away from you."

"We can discuss this further with Selene if it's something you want to handle, Harley," Jackson adds.

I set half of a veggie and cheese wrap on my plate, my appetite disappearing. "Am I still taking pictures and videos to post on our social?"

"Of course. Selene still wants you to supplement. I think they'll want individual social media accounts at every location, so it's personalized to the unique hotel. But for the franchise, it makes more sense to have everything uniform, and that's way too big for you to tackle. Am I right, Jackson? That's the plan?"

"Yes, and we can make sure it's all cleared with Selene so your toes aren't being stepped on."

"I wouldn't even know where to begin with the franchise stuff anyway, so it's better that Selene handles all of that," I say, only half meaning it but wanting to erase the look of concern on London's face.

My phone pings with a couple of messages, one from Gavin with a picture he took last week of Peyton, Ella, and me in front of the panda exhibit—they seemed to be the only animals not acting up. There's also a new one from Chad asking what we should do for dinner—cook or go out.

Chad's cooking is limited to spaghetti and sauce or boxed mac and cheese, so when we cook, it's usually me giving him small, manageable tasks, like setting the table or spinning lettuce. He does the dishes, though.

I suggest we go out and see if Allen and Andrea want to join us if they don't have plans. He gives me a thumbs-up.

"How are things with you and Chad?" London asks.

"Fine. I'm seeing him tonight. Why?" I set my phone down and focus on my lunch, which I'm no longer hungry for.

"I don't know. You've been spending a lot of time with Gavin and Peyton. Is he okay with that?" She tosses a puffy star in her jar and starts another.

"We're just friends, and I had Ella with me when we went to the zoo last week," I remind London. I laughed off the whole family-of-four thing with the girl working the ticket booth at the time, but I hadn't really considered how it might look from the outside. Not that it matters.

"Someone want to fill me in on this Gavin guy?" Declan asks, glancing between me and London.

The tension is clear, mostly because this isn't the first time London has mentioned this.

"Harley used to nanny for him when his daughter, Peyton, was a baby. He lost his wife during childbirth and was on his own and needed help," Avery explains then glances at me. "You were with the family for what, a year and a half?"

"About that. Then they moved upstate to Boulder." I swirl a carrot stick in ranch dip. "They moved back to the area not long before we hosted the last birthday party. Peyton really needed some stability and a familiar face, so we went for lunch and to the zoo."

"And you watched her for him when he had that meeting," London says. Obviously she's keeping a running tally of how often I see them.

"That was an emergency situation, though." And now I sound defensive.

"Is he remarried or does he have a girlfriend?" Declan pops an olive into his mouth.

"He's not remarried." He wouldn't be asking for my help if he was.

"But he has a girlfriend?" Declan prompts. It's a leading question and I don't bite.

"I don't know. I've never asked." I cross my arms. This feels a lot like I'm getting the third degree.

Declan raises a brow. "How old is this guy? Is he in his forties or fifties or something?"

"He has a nine-year-old," I point out.

"Lots of people have kids later in life. A fifty-year-old with a nine-year-old isn't unheard of. I'll be in my mid-forties by the time Ella is ten, which means we should probably get on giving her a brother or a sister." Jackson winks at London.

London rolls her eyes. "Can I just get her weaned before you go trying to knock me up again, please?"

"You know patience isn't my strong suit." Jackson turns back to me. "So? How old is this guy?"

I blow out a breath, aware I'm not getting out of this conversation easily. "He's in his mid-thirties."

He glances at Declan, and they both share a raised eyebrow and a chuckle, before he turns back to me. "And you really think the only reason he's making plans with you is for the benefit of his daughter? How often have you seen this guy since you stopped being his nanny?"

"The first time I saw him and Peyton since they moved away was last month at the birthday party."

"And why'd they move again?"

"You mean back to Colorado Springs?"

"Yeah. What was the motivation to come back?" Jackson asks.

"His dad wants to retire, and their landscape company has grown so much that he's taking over the design and project management side of things."

"Okay. Have you stayed in touch over the years?" He flips a pen between his fingers.

"No. The first time I spoke to him since he moved away to Boulder was at the birthday party."

"Hmm." He sets the pen down. "That's interesting."

"Why is that interesting?"

"Because it raises even more questions, and Jackson finds all interpersonal relationships interesting," Declan jumps in. "And, if I was Chad, I don't know how excited I'd be about this established guy moving in on my girlfriend, but maybe that's just me."

"We're just friends," I argue.

"If you say so."

I want to toss glitter in Declan's face to make his smile disappear.

"Men and women can be friends. Look at you and Avery. You were friends and roommates for years." As soon as I say it, I know it's a weak argument. Declan's smile grows wider.

"Exactly. And look how well that turned out," he says as he rubs Avery's belly.

Darn it.

"Yeah, well, Avery hangs out with Mark and Jerome, and neither of them have made a move on her or led her to believe they had feelings for her."

Declan rolls his eyes. "That's because they already knew I was in love with Avery. But if you say you're just friends and that he wants to spend time with you because of his daughter, that's cool. Just don't be surprised if Chad gets jealous is all."

The conversation with Declan stays with me for the rest of the day. Gavin hasn't done or said anything that would make me think he was interested in more than friendship with me and stability for Peyton. That was always his primary concern and a big part of the reason he ended up moving. Besides, he probably still sees me as twenty-year-old Harley.

I arrive home at five and tidy up before Chad comes over, even though he isn't due for a couple of hours. Allen and Andrea aren't available tonight. Andrea is a teacher, and she's too swamped with lesson planning. She sent me a bunch of sad face emojis and promised we'd have a girls' night soon with Belinda. Since it'll just be the two of us, we're probably better off ordering in. I should be able to finish my assignment before he gets here, but if he has the draft thing, going out doesn't seem like the best plan. Besides, the pub isn't nearly as fun without friends. Usually Chad will get sucked into whatever game is televised at the bar, and I'll end up scheduling posts for Spark House social media.

I'm in the middle of vacuuming the living room when my phone goes off. But it's not a message, it's a call. I glance at the screen and turn off the vacuum cleaner when I see it's Gavin.

I answer the call and put it on speaker phone. "Hey, how's it going?"

"Good. I'm good. How are you, Harley?" It sounds like he's driving.

"Great. Just doing a little cleaning. What are you up to?"

"I just picked up Peyton from painting class, and she wanted to tell you how much she loves it. I hope that's okay."

"Of course it's okay. I'm so glad to hear that."

"Today we worked with watercolors! It was so much fun, Harley, and next week we get to paint clay figurines!" Peyton calls out.

"That's awesome. I can't wait to see it. Maybe the next time we hang out, you can show me how to paint with watercolors too." I put the vacuum back in the closet and close the door.

"Maybe I can show you tonight? Dad, can you drop me off at Harley's instead of taking me to that meeting? Then we can paint with watercolors!"

"Honey, I can't do that. Harley probably has plans, and it's not nice to put her on the spot like that. I'm sorry, Harley. I promise when we called it was to tell you how much Peyton is loving her art class, not for any other reason."

"That's okay." I pick up the dishcloth and give it a cursory sniff test to make sure it isn't funky before I start wiping down the counters. "What kind of meeting do you have? Do you need me to watch Peyton for a bit?"

"No, no. It'll only be a couple of hours. And we have her iPad already loaded with movies. Peyton will manage."

"But Harley is way more fun than watching a movie alone on an iPad," Peyton argues. "Please, Harley? Can I come over?"

"Oh my God," Gavin grumbles, and suddenly the sound of traffic is gone.

"Please tell me you're not driving and holding your phone at the same time."

"I popped in an earbud. I'm so sorry, Harley. This wasn't my intention at all. I should have known Peyton had other plans."

"Honestly, it's okay." I glance at the clock. It's just after five. If his meeting is a couple of hours he'll be done by eight thirty.

It won't interfere with my plans. "You can drop her off here. I'm just hanging out. And she's right, movies aren't a whole lot of fun alone."

"I can't. I'll feel awful."

"I wouldn't offer if I didn't mean it. Drop her off. Go to your meeting. She and I will have loads of fun."

"Are you sure? I feel like I'm taking advantage of your kindness."

"You can't take advantage when I'm the one who's offering. I'll send you my address and you can head this way. Sound good?"

"You're sure, you're sure?"

"Positively positive."

He sighs. "Okay. We'll be there in less than an hour."

"Great. Tell Peyton I'm excited to see her."

"I will. And Harley?"

"Yeah."

"Thank you. Again. You really are an angel, and I really, really owe you for this."

He ends the call and I smile to myself, whistling on my way down the hall to the bathroom. I need to shower and freshen up before Peyton gets here.

Nine

WHAT'S THIS BOYFRIEND BUSINESS

HARLEY

Forty minutes later the buzzer goes off, and I let Gavin and Peyton in. It doesn't take long before they're knocking on my door. Normally I see Gavin in his casual clothes, but tonight he's still dressed in a suit, carrying a purple metallic backpack with a llama face on it.

Peyton is standing at his side, a wide grin on her face. She throws herself at me as soon as I open the door. "Yay! I get to see you again! Want to see my watercolor painting?" She holds it up in front of me.

"Oh, that's amazing!" I tell her.

"Dad said I can take lessons on Wednesday after school sometimes. Maybe you would want to come too. I told him that I want you to be my nanny again, but he said you have a different job now and I'm too old for a nanny. But Claire has a nanny, and she's a year older than me."

"Lynn and Ian have four kids, and three of them are under the age of seven, honey. That's why they have a nanny." His expression is apologetic.

Peyton twists her lips to the side. "Their nanny's name is Tessa. She's nice but she's not as much fun as you."

I bring my finger to my lips and wink. "Let's not tell Tessa that, though."

Her eyes go wide. "Oh, I would never. That could hurt her feelings, and I don't want to do that."

"I wouldn't want to do that either. Besides, one person's idea of fun might be different from yours and mine." I turn my attention to Gavin. "Do you want to come in?"

"I would, but I need to head straight to the meeting. It should be done by eight thirty, but Peyton has pretty much everything she needs apart from jammies in here. Oh, and she's been fed and watered, so you don't have to worry about that."

"I had chicken nuggets and fries," Peyton offers.

"Dinner of champions, huh?" I arch a brow.

"Better than the donuts she asked for, but probably not by much." His smile is chagrined. "Thank you again. I really owe you one." He gives Peyton a hug and a kiss, and then he's off.

Fifteen minutes later we're sitting in the living room with a pile of rainbow construction paper, my glue gun, several pots of glitter in an assortment of colors, and watercolor paints. I have a plastic lid, and we're tracing circles and cutting them out. Then we're decorating them with glitter before we make flowers out of them. After that we'll paste them onto white sheets of paper that have watercolor skies painted on them. Is it messy? Yes. Will we both be covered in glitter by the end of the evening? Absolutely. Will I find glitter on my clothes and everywhere else for the next month? Probably, but it's so worth the smile on Peyton's face.

"Granny never let me use glitter or paints. She says it makes too much of a mess."

"What about your Nana? Does she let you use glitter?"

"Sometimes, but we have to put down a plastic sheet, and

it takes a lot of work to set up, so we don't do it much." Peyton's tongue peeks out of the corner of her mouth as she carefully tries to follow the line she traced.

"You must really be loving the art camp you're at this week."

"Oh yes! It's been so much fun. And Claire's sister is there too, so I had a friend already when I got there. I get a tummy ache when I have to go somewhere and I don't know anyone, but I haven't had one this week."

"Does meeting new people make you nervous?"

Peyton scrunches up her nose. "I don't know. My stomach gets all these butterflies, and I feel like I've just been on the tea-cups at the carnival. And then my hands get sweaty and I have to wipe them a lot on my shorts, but once I'm there, I'm okay."

"That makes sense, and I think a lot of people feel the same way you do. I know sometimes I get nervous when I'm going to meet new people. How are you feeling about starting school next week?"

She lifts a shoulder and lets it fall. "I wanted to be in the same class as Claire, but I'm not. And now I don't know anyone in my class and everyone else has known each other for a long time."

"I bet you won't be the only new person in the school, though. And think of it this way—you still have someone to talk to at re-cess, and you'll get to make a whole new group of friends. What about the kids who were at the birthday party at Spark House? Don't some of them go to your new school?"

She bites the inside of her lip. "Oh! Yes! A few of them do."

"So maybe you will know someone in your class. Even if you know them just a little." I hold two fingers half an inch apart.

"Maybe." Her eyes light up.

"You could ask Claire if she knows anyone who will be in your class. Do you call each other?"

Peyton nods. "Oh yes. We have FaceTimes almost every day on Dad's iPad."

"Will you talk to her tomorrow?"

"Yup, after dinner."

"You could ask her then," I suggest as I shake some pink glitter onto my yellow petal.

At the sound of the door opening and closing I check the clock. It's already twenty to eight.

"Hey, babe! I picked up pizza! I hope you're cool with that!" Chad calls out.

Peyton frowns. "Who's that? Do you have a roommate?"

"It's Chad. I know you had something before you came here, but he picked up pizza for us." His *us* didn't include Peyton, but she doesn't need to know that. "I'll be right back, and then I'll introduce you." I hop up and rush to the kitchen.

"Hey! Thanks so much for picking up dinner."

"I figured we could have a romantic night in." He sets the pizza on the counter and grabs me around the waist, nuzzling into my neck.

"You might want to put a pin in that. We're not alone."

"Oh. Did you invite Belinda and Ted to hang out?" He backs off, his expression hard to read.

"Uh, no. You remember that family I used to nanny for?"

"Uh, yeah?" Based on the questioning lilt and his confusion, he doesn't remember.

"Gavin had a meeting, and Peyton asked if she could see me. I figured we were just hanging out anyway, so it wasn't a big deal for him to drop her off here." I lower my voice. "It's only for a couple of hours."

"Oh, okay. That's cool. How old is she again?" He sounds slightly disappointed, but otherwise, he seems like he's okay with it.

"Nine. I'm really sorry if I messed up your plans for us." I do feel bad, and maybe I should have told Gavin I couldn't do it because I had legitimate plans. "She shouldn't be here much past eight thirty, and I figure since you had the hockey draft thing it wouldn't be a big deal. I should have warned you, though." I bite my lip, fighting a grimace.

"Do nine-year-olds like hot peppers on their pizza?" He flips open the lid, showing off the mouthwateringly delicious-looking pizza, covered in hot peppers.

"She's had dinner, but if she wants a slice we can pick them off. Or I can make her something else if I need to. Why don't we grab plates and you can come meet her?" I'm relieved he's not upset.

"Sure. Sounds good."

I give him a smile and a big hug. I gather all the things we'll need for dinner and bring them to the living room, Chad following behind with the boxes of pizza and wings. Peyton is sitting at the coffee table, still cutting out circles of paper. She glances up when we come back into the living room, her gaze flitting to Chad and back to me.

"Peyton, I want you to meet my boyfriend, Chad." I motion between them. "Chad, this is Peyton."

"Boyfriend?" Peyton tips her head to the side.

"Yup." I don't know how to read her expression, but I suddenly feel a whole lot awkward about having Peyton here while Chad is too. Which doesn't make sense.

"Oh. I didn't know you had a boyfriend." She chews on her bottom lip for a moment and then gives her attention to Chad. She looks at him the same way a kid would regard a toy they aren't too sure about. "Hi, Chad. I'm Peyton. My dad and I have known Harley my whole life. When I was a baby, Harley used to take care of me because the angels took Mommy to heaven, so Dad said they sent Harley down to help us. And I missed her and now she's back." She twists her fingers around each other, smiling at the end and dropping her hands to her lap.

"Well, that's . . . really great that you got Harley back. She's cool, isn't she?" Chad rubs the back of his neck and glances from me to her as if he's looking for direction.

"She's the coolest. She lets me use glitter, and my granny never does," she announces. "And Harley lets me have chocolate milk with dinner too."

"But not all the time, right?" I prompt.

"On special occasions and weekends because too much sugar isn't good for us." Peyton sighs, as if this information frustrates her.

I put a blanket on the floor, and Peyton and I pick all the hot pepper and mushrooms off her pizza slices. There are also bread sticks, which she's a fan of, so she polishes off a bunch of those while Chad hoovers down half the pizza and an entire pound of wings.

I've never seen Chad interact with kids before. I don't think he's ever been around when London has had Ella with her either. It becomes clear that he doesn't have much experience with kids and that he has no idea what to say or do when it comes to Peyton. He's the youngest in his family and doesn't have nieces or nephews yet, so that makes sense.

"Do you want to make glitter rainbow flowers with us?" Peyton asks, obviously trying to be nice.

Chad makes a face. "Did you say *glitter* rainbow flowers?"

Peyton nods enthusiastically. "They're so fun, and when we're done, we can hang them on the wall, and it will look like a sparkling flower bed!"

"Uh, I'm gonna pass on that, but thanks." He picks up his phone.

Peyton shrugs, and we continue making glitter flowers while Chad manages his hockey draft.

At eight fifteen, I start winding things down, making Peyton a snack and cuddling with her in a chair so I can read her stories.

At five to nine Gavin shows up. Peyton is tucked into the over-size reading chair, sleeping soundly. I slide out carefully so I can get the door and hopefully not disturb Peyton. "I'll be right back." I leave Chad on the couch, still engrossed in the draft, and let Gavin in.

"Hey, sorry I'm later than I meant to be." He's lost the suit jacket and the tie, the top two buttons of his dress shirt are open, and the cuffs have been unbuttoned and rolled up to expose his forearms. He has nice forearms. And biceps. Which is not something I should be appreciating.

"It's not a problem. She fell asleep about twenty minutes ago. She's passed out on my reading chair, looking adorable. Wanna see?" I thumb over my shoulder, toward the living room.

He gives me a lopsided grin. "I never pass up a chance to see my daughter looking adorable."

I motion for him to follow me to the living room, and I point to Peyton, tucked under a blanket, her bunny cuddled against her cheek. We gave him some light surgery before story time so the stuffing stays inside instead of peeking out of his bum.

Chad's easy smile drops as his gaze lands on Gavin and then

shifts to me, before returning to Gavin. I glance between the two of them, wearing matching displeased expressions.

Chad's cheeks puff out, and he drops his phone on the couch and pushes to a stand. He, too, is wearing a dress shirt and dress pants, although his are a lot more wrinkled at this point in the day, and the dress shirt has a pizza stain on the left side of his chest. He stands, his shoulders rolling back. "Hey, you must be Peyton's dad. I'm Chad. Harley's boyfriend." He crosses the room and holds out his hand.

Gavin looks at it, and for a moment I'm unsure what's going to happen. As it is, there's tension in the room that makes me uncomfortable.

"Gavin." He takes Chad's hand and gives it a firm shake. "Harley and I go way back."

"Yeah. I heard. Harley was Peyton's nanny when she was a baby. It's really good of her to help you out with babysitting until you find someone else."

I fight a cringe at how awful that sounds coming from Chad, despite it being true.

"Peyton adores Harley," Gavin says.

"She and I have that in common, then." Chad smiles stiffly.

Gavin clears his throat. "Yeah. Of course."

They shake hands for what seems like several seconds too long before Gavin drops Chad's hand and turns to me. "Can I talk to you for a second?"

I glance from Chad, who looks highly unimpressed, to Gavin, who ironically is wearing a similar expression. "Uh, sure?" It comes out sounding like a question.

"Probably in the kitchen so we don't wake Peyton." He looks from Chad to Peyton to me, as if he's not 100 percent sure about leaving his daughter alone with Chad. Which makes me bristle. Chad might not have experience with kids, but he'd never do anything to hurt anyone, let alone a child.

"We'll be right back," I tell Chad as Gavin follows me to the kitchen.

I don't have a chance to address the awkwardness before he does. He props a hand on his hip and glances over his shoulder, then turns back to me and drops his voice to a whisper. "Why are you bringing strange men around my daughter?"

"Excuse me?" I feel like I'm actually the babysitter getting scolded for inviting a boy over. Which is insulting and ridiculous since this is my house and I'm a grown-ass woman.

"I don't know that guy." He points in the direction of the living room. "I had no idea he was going to be here."

I hold up a hand to stop him. "Back the bus up, Gavin. I'm watching Peyton as a favor. Chad isn't a strange man. He's my boyfriend."

"Does he live here? With you?"

"No. Not yet, anyway." I don't get what this has to do with anything, or why he's suddenly grilling me like he has a right.

"Yet?" Gavin's brows lift.

"What is this about? I'm sorry I didn't tell you that my boyfriend was going to be here, but since I'm the one doing *you* a favor, I don't really think you have much of a right to get upset about that. Next time maybe you should ask more questions." The only time I've seen this side of Gavin was back when Peyton was a baby and I'd invited one of the nannies from the park over for lunch without clearing it with him first. I realized my error after the fact. It was his house; he didn't know them. But this isn't remotely the same.

This time Gavin holds up his hands, both of them, in submission. "I'm sorry. It just . . . took me by surprise. That's all. You're right, I should have asked more questions. I didn't expect there to be anyone else here."

I cross my arms. "Don't you trust my judgment? Chad's harmless."

"I'm sure he is. I don't typically leave my daughter with people I don't know and haven't met before."

"You left her with me, and unless I'm wrong, you trust me with her. Shouldn't my judgment of character count for something?" I'm frustrated about this. What do they say about no good deed?

He pinches the bridge of his nose. "I know you're a good judge of character. You should have said something if I was interfering with your date night."

"I wasn't going to let Peyton down like that, and I wanted to see her." And I hadn't thought it would interfere much with date night. But I don't say that out loud.

"Which I appreciate. But you clearly have a life of your own, and I don't want to get in the middle of that." He exhales heavily and rubs the back of his neck. "I should get Peyton home. She has an early morning."

"Let me help you get her down to the car." I gather up her things, and he carefully picks her up from the chair, murmuring to Chad that it was nice to meet him. I help him get her down to the car, impressed that she's still mostly asleep by the time we get her buckled in.

"Thanks again. I really appreciate you letting us interrupt your night, Harley. I owe you, and I'm sorry about how I reacted up there. I know you would never put Peyton in a dangerous position."

"No, I wouldn't."

"Tell Chet I'm sorry for crashing your date night."

"His name is Chad, and it wasn't a big deal. We were just hanging out."

We say good night, and he gets in the car and drives off. I stand there for a few seconds, watching his taillights disappear down the street before I turn around and head back inside. I don't know how to feel about how he reacted to Chad. I don't know what would be worse, Declan and Jackson being right that he's interested in more than my babysitting skills, or that he could be taking advantage of my kindness like London said.

When I get back up to the apartment, Chad is sitting on the couch with his arms crossed. "Want to tell me what that was all about?"

"What exactly are you referring to?" I don't know why I'm playing dumb, other than I'd like to avoid an argument. I don't think I've done anything wrong, but for some reason I feel guilty.

"What am I referring to? Are you kidding?" He gives me a disbelieving look.

"You're going to have to give me a little more to go on here." Guess I'm committed to pretending I don't know what he's talking about.

He huffs and shakes his head. "How old is that guy? He's gotta have a decade on you."

"Gavin? Mid-thirties maybe? What does that have to do with anything?" I don't like the hot feeling creeping up my spine.

"What does that—" He clamps his mouth shut. "How old were you when you were his nanny? Nineteen?"

"I was close to twenty when I started taking care of Peyton. I don't understand what my age when I took care of her has to do with anything."

"Babe, I know you're a Disney-loving woman, and most of the time I think it's pretty cute, but you can't be this naive."

I throw my hands in the air. "Naive about what?"

"That guy has the hots for you. You didn't see the look on his face when he walked into the room and saw me sitting here." He pokes himself in the chest. "I did. He was not happy. He looked at me like he was sizing up his competition."

"He didn't know you were here, and he's never met you before. He's the father of a little girl. He was wary about having a guy he didn't know around his daughter." But the pit in my stomach opens up, and I have to wonder if I'm the last one to see what's been happening here and whether I even want to deal with whatever that is.

He holds his arms out. "Have you never mentioned me? He looked pretty shocked about my presence in general."

"Of course I've mentioned you!" I say, but there's a squeak in my voice, and I don't know if that's actually true at this point, because Chad is right, Gavin was definitely surprised.

"Are you sure about that? What kind of history do you two have? Why exactly did he move away again?" His eyes narrow, expression full of suspicion.

Chad has never been like this before. He's always so laid back and chill. I cross my arms, my posture just as defensive as his, but now for very different reasons. "I don't appreciate what you're insinuating." I swallow down the guilt, not because I've done something wrong now, in the present, but because I did back then. And now I'm afraid that the same thing might be happening again. Have I let myself get too close to Gavin and Peyton for a second time?

"Why not? Because there's validity in it? He was what? In his late twenties when he had that kid? And you were nineteen fucking years old taking care of his baby for him. Were you taking care of anything else?"

I grind my teeth, angry, frustrated, and feeling very attacked. "His wife had just died. It wasn't like that." Except I almost made it like that. And that's not something I want to admit to Chad, not when I've only ever admitted it to one person, and that was Gran.

"What was it like, then, Harley? Tell me." He's just as riled up as me. It's disconcerting because the only time I've ever seen him this heated before is when he's lost one of his fantasy leagues.

"It was complicated," I say, but it doesn't come out with anything but uncertainty.

He pokes at his cheek with his tongue. "Were you a live-in nanny?"

"Why would that matter?" I hate that I'm just starting to see the way this puzzle pieces together, and Chad has figured it out before me in a matter of minutes. I scratch my wrist, then clasp my hands together. I better not be breaking out in freaking hives.

His expression turns remote. "So that's a yes."

"It was more than seven years ago."

"You slept across the hall from him in your fucking Disney tanks and shorts?" He nods knowingly. "Yeah. I'm sure it was super complicated."

I raise a hand. "You need to stop before you say something so regrettable, you can't recover from it. I have never had an affair with one of my charge's parents. And nothing inappropriate ever happened with Gavin." But it almost did.

"Then why do you look so damn guilty, Harley?" Chad brushes past me and heads for the door. I don't stop him.

Because even though I didn't do anything wrong now, if Gavin hadn't stopped me then, it would have been a very different story.

Ten

BECAUSE YOU'RE JEALOUS, DUDE

GAVIN

"Want to tell me why you've got a bug up your ass?" Ian leans against the doorjamb, coffee raised to his mouth. The mug reads: BEFORE COFFEE, EVERY DAY FEELS LIKE MONDAY.

I toss my pencil on my drafting table and lace my hands behind my head. "I don't have anything up my butt."

"Your tone implies something different." Ian pushes away from the doorjamb and takes a seat in one of the rolling chairs. He crosses one leg over the other, obviously planning to stick around for more than a minute. Ian and I have been friends since college. We were each other's best man in our weddings; his wife, Lynn, was in our wedding party; and my wife, Marcie, was in hers. It rocked us all when we lost Marcie.

Even when I moved away, he and I have stayed close. And he's been an integral part of my family's landscaping company, and part of the reason I needed to return to Colorado Springs. The family business has grown with his forward-thinking and smart financial mind. It's great to be back in the same city again, working together.

"The in-laws are talking about coming for a visit sometime in the next few weeks."

"Ahh." He takes a sip of his coffee. "And you have concerns?"

Since I've moved back to Colorado Springs, I haven't had much of an opportunity to visit Marcie's parents. Peyton and I made the trip up to see them a couple of weekends ago, but we only stayed for one night. Karen griped about the fact that she wasn't getting enough time with her granddaughter. It didn't help that all Peyton could talk about was Harley and the fun things they did together.

And that was only made worse when Karen realized that Harley was Peyton's former nanny. Back before we moved to Boulder, she'd been displeased that I had a twenty-year-old basically raising my daughter. It didn't seem to matter that Harley turned out to be one of the most maternal women I'd ever met—and continues to be that way. Her age was a problem for Karen.

The friction it caused wasn't something I wanted to contend with while I was still grieving the loss of Marcie, trying to single-parent a toddler, and balance a career. So I conceded and moved to Boulder to help get the new branch of Greenscapes off the ground and give my in-laws a chance to get to know their granddaughter.

"I don't think Karen's very happy that Peyton and Harley have reconnected," I tell him.

Ian's brow furrows. "You mean your old nanny?"

"Yeah, my former nanny." Harley isn't old by any stretch of the imagination.

"Okay, so first of all, it's not just Peyton who's spending time with Harley, you are too."

"It's been helpful for Peyton to have someone who provides stability in her life with all of this change." I feel like I'm on repeat, I say this so often, but no one seems to believe me.

Ian arches a brow. "Is that so?"

"Well, yeah. It was a big step to move back here. Having a network of people to rely on is important." In Boulder my social circle was limited to my in-laws and the people I worked with. That transition was rough—mostly for me—and I'm grateful coming back here means being close to Ian and Lynn again. But for Peyton it's been more of a challenge because all her school friends are back in Boulder.

"Refresh my memory. Harley is the woman who hosted the birthday party for Claire, who was dressed like a fairy godmother, right?" He sips his coffee noisily.

"That's her, yes."

"And the only reason you've been seeing her pretty much once a week since you've moved back is because you want Peyton to have stability and someone familiar in her life?" He does that annoying thing where he repeats what I've said back to me.

"Yeah, exactly, and Karen has her back up about it."

"To be fair, Karen gets her back up when she's down to the last seven rolls of toilet paper." He picks up my box of paper clips and fishes out a small handful.

I chuckle. "This is true. I don't want to feel like I'm walking on eggshells the entire time they're here. And I'm not going to stop letting Peyton see Harley just because Karen doesn't approve for whatever reason."

"Maybe she doesn't approve because you've got the hots for Harley and she's picked up on that," Ian suggests.

I scoff. "I don't have the hots for Harley."

"Are you sure about that?" He starts connecting the paper clips. I'd be annoyed, but he always pulls them apart after he's done.

"She's almost a decade younger than me."

"So? There's twelve years between your parents, and they've been together for what? Nearly forty years?"

"Harley has a boyfriend."

"Oh?" He sets the paperclips down and gives me his full attention.

"I met him when I had that late meeting and Peyton wanted to hang out with Harley instead of come with me," I explain.

"And?"

"And what?"

"What was he like?"

"Young. Immature." Not her type. Definitely not happy to meet me.

"Had she mentioned him before you met him?" Ian asks.

I shake my head. He'd been a surprise, and based on his reaction to me, he hadn't expected me to be . . . me.

"That's interesting." He steeples his hands.

"You're reading into things." I roll my eyes at him.

"Am I, though? I remember Harley from when Peyton was a baby. She was a cute kid back then, but she's an adult now. And it seems a little suspect that she hasn't so much as mentioned the fact that she has a boyfriend. Maybe it's casual and they're not serious, which is why she's been so willing to spend time with you and Peyton. And while I get that maybe at the beginning it was for Peyton's benefit, I'd also like to point out that she wasn't even two years old when you moved, so the only memories she has of Harley are from photo albums."

We go through Peyton's baby albums on a fairly regular basis, so Harley's face has become familiar to her. But I hadn't considered that maybe I didn't want just Peyton to have stability, but myself, as well. "She made my life and Peyton's better."

Ian gives me a patient, knowing smile. "I get that, but I'm going to go out on a limb here and say that you're spending time with Harley not only because Peyton likes her, but because you do too."

"Well, of course I do. She's fun to be around." What I don't like is how defensive I sound.

"She's also attractive."

I think about how often I cave and reach out to Harley when Peyton asks if we can see her again, even when I tell myself I'm not going to do it. And how much I look forward to the times when it's the three of us together. "Shit." I run a hand through my hair. "Maybe you're right."

"I know I'm right. Your face lights up like a pinball game every time you talk about her."

"It does not."

"It does. And you've been grumpy as hell this week, which coincides with you meeting this boyfriend of hers."

"So what the hell do I do? It's not like I can pursue her when she's already dating someone." Even if she wasn't, I don't know if it's a good idea, anyway.

"Are they exclusive?"

"I don't know. But she referred to him as her boyfriend." And when I asked if he lived with her, she said not *yet*.

"So they're at the make-it-or-break-it phase of their relationship. Have you talked to her since you met the boyfriend?"

"We've messaged back and forth." But it's been awkward; mostly on my side, though, if I'm honest. Because I realized that I'd acted like an ass and that I had no right to question who she allows in her personal space. But now that Ian has forced me into the light, I can see that part of my reaction was because I had no idea a boyfriend even existed and I wasn't sure what to do with that information at the time.

"Do you have plans to see her again?"

"She wants to take Peyton to the park after school one day this week, but we've kept it open-ended because school just started."

"Maybe you need to find out exactly where she's at with this boyfriend."

"Maybe." I tap my lip. "I don't want to mess with her relationship with Peyton though. Not right now." Despite how I may or may not feel, I have to put Peyton first.

"I'm not saying you need to make a move right now. In fact, it's probably better that you're getting to know each other, but it doesn't hurt to find out how serious this relationship is. I know Peyton is always going to be your number one, Gav, but remember that she's not the only one who needs stability and people she can count on. You need the same thing. You've been without a partner for a long time. And maybe this isn't the right time for a relationship, and maybe it's not the right relationship, period. But you won't know if you don't at least try to put yourself out there again."

"I know. You're right." And he is. But it doesn't make it any easier for me to take the leap.

Not when I already know what it's like to lose the love of your life.

And not when it could take someone important away from my baby girl.

The risk seems too high.

I do see Harley later that week when she drops Peyton off after going to the park, but I don't have the balls to talk to her about the boyfriend situation. Not that I would have had a chance anyway since Peyton talks her ear off about school and how much she loves her teacher and that she's already made four new friends.

On Friday I pick Peyton up from my parents' place after work. She's all hopped up, and at first I think it's because my parents fed her a pound of sugar. Until she pulls a letter out of the front pocket of her backpack. It's rumpled and looks like it's been sitting at the bottom of her bag. "I forgot to give this to you! You have to come though because our class is going to perform a song in front of the whole school and all the parents!"

My mom gives me an apologetic look. "I must have missed it earlier this week."

Peyton wrinkles her nose and twists her hands together. "I forgot all about it, and then Mrs. Horton reminded us. It isn't until next Friday, though. Mrs. Horton said she emailed all the parents, but maybe you didn't get it?"

I scan the letter. There's a parents' welcome assembly next Friday evening, and some of the older grades are going to perform in front of the school, which seems lofty for only the second week of the school year, but this is a private school, with a special focus on the arts, and much different from the school Peyton attended in Boulder.

"That's okay, honey. Do I need to confirm your attendance?"

"I already did that this afternoon as soon as I found the letter," my mom says. "It looks like they had the wrong email address on file, so I had the secretary change it. I said all three of us would be there."

"Okay. Thanks. I didn't realize there was an issue."

"It was probably just a clerical error. They had Marcie's parents as their top contact."

"I thought I changed all of that." Although there was a lot of paperwork, so it's possible I missed it.

"I'm sure you did and it just didn't go through. It's all ironed out now."

"Do you think Granny and Grampa would be able to come too?" Peyton asks.

"I'm sure they would love to. Let me ask your teacher if we can invite them. I'm sure they'd love to see your new school and meet Mrs. Horton." And it should definitely make Karen happy; one of her biggest fears was not being able to see Peyton enough.

"If there isn't room, your dad and I can always go to the next one," my mom offers.

"I'm sure it'll be fine. They've had plenty of opportunities to attend Peyton's school events; you guys haven't."

"I know that, but missing one isn't a big deal when we get to see our favorite little girl all the time." Mom kisses me on the cheek and gives Peyton a hug.

It turns out that it's not a big deal to add two more family members, so we extend the invitation to Karen and Kyle, who apparently already knew about the event because they've been getting the school emails. They already RSVP'd and it looks like that plan to come for a visit is happening sooner than anticipated. They're overjoyed that they're going to be able to see Peyton's new school.

Peyton is extra-excited all through the weekend and into the next week, rehearsing the song her class is performing at the assembly when she's in the bathroom, getting ready for bed, and basically every waking moment. By the time the assembly rolls around, I'm going to know the song by heart too.

On the day of the assembly, I head home early to make sure I can get Peyton there on time. My in-laws arrived just after lunch, so Peyton was able to take the bus directly home instead of going to my parents' place like she often does after school.

As soon as I walk in the door, Peyton comes rushing down the hall. "Daddy! Yay! You're home! When are we leaving? I have to be there at five thirty so we can make sure the whole class is ready. We had a dress rehearsal today, and Tony Burton threw up in a wastebasket because he gets nervous performing in front of people. Mrs. Horton said he didn't have to participate tonight, but I think he has FOMO because he said he still wanted to even though it makes him sick to his stomach. I'm really glad I don't get sick to my stomach when I get up on stage. Harley says I'm a natural and that instead of getting nervous, I get excited and that's how you know you're an extrovert and not an into-vert."

Karen appears at the end of the hallway. She's wearing an apron, wiping her hands on a dish towel. "Peyton, honey, you need to finish your snack before we go."

"Okay. Can we leave as soon as I'm finished?"

"Of course, dear. Just give your dad a minute to get in the door." She pats Peyton on the shoulder and turns her in the direction of the kitchen.

"It's okay. I know she's excited," I say as Peyton skips down the hall. I accept the hug and kiss on the cheek from Karen. "How was the drive down?"

"It wasn't bad, a little busy when we got close to the city, but otherwise fine." She picks at a loose thread on her apron. "I worry about how much of a challenge the trip will be in the winter, though. It feels like we hardly see Peyton at all now that you've moved, and with winter coming, that drive is going to be that much more of a challenge."

I don't love that this is the first thing she brings up when I walk through the door. I don't want this visit to become another guilt trip. "You could always catch a flight in, and we could pick you up from the airport."

"Oh, I'm not sure flying is a safer option. Especially with the storms we get."

"We'll figure out something that works for everyone."

She hums and tucks her hands in the apron pocket. I notice that the one she's wearing was a gift from her to Marcie when we first got married. I think it was at a bridal shower. Marcie had always been a fan of cooking, and she and her mom had spent a lot of time together in the kitchen. I didn't even realize I still had that apron or where I even kept it.

"Are you sure that you're going to want to stay in Colorado Springs indefinitely? Maybe all it will take is a year to get Greenscapes where it needs to be. Then you could think about moving back our way. Peyton was saying how much she misses seeing us all the time," Karen says. Her tone holds a hint of accusation, and I hate how easy it is for her to play on my guilty conscience.

I force a patient smile. "You could always move out this way now that Kyle is retired. Then you'd be able to see us all the time, and no one would have to worry about winter driving."

"Oh, I don't know about that. We've lived in that house for the past thirty years. Marcie grew up there. I can't imagine leaving all of those memories behind."

I bite my tongue, not wanting this to be the focus of their visit. Part of the problem for my in-laws is that they're stuck in the past, and it's made it very difficult for me to move on with my life.

Even now, Marcie's room is still decorated the same way it was when she left for college. She used to joke about how by the time we had kids, that room would be retro. The sad reality is, that's exactly what it's become. And Peyton is only allowed in there with supervision. It's like an exhibit in a museum. "I'm going to get changed and then we can leave."

"Okay. I'll tell Kyle he'll have to watch the game highlights."

"We can record it for him."

"Oh, that would be great. It's his team playing, and you know how much he hates to miss a game. I'll make sure Peyton's done with her snack." She heads for the kitchen, and I go in the other direction, dropping my briefcase in my office before I go to my bedroom.

I change out of my suit into a collared shirt and a pair of dark dress pants, wash my face, and comb my hair before I return to the kitchen. Karen is loading plates in the dishwasher, and my father-in-law is sitting at the kitchen island, eating a sandwich and sliced carrots.

"This is quite a nice place you have here, son," he says after he swallows his bite and washes it down with milk.

"Thanks, we like it."

"Peyton seems to be settling in okay, isn't she? Loves her new room and can't stop talking about that Harley woman who used to take care of her when she was a baby. I didn't realize the two of you had kept in touch." He smiles, but it seems tense.

"We hadn't actually. Lynn and Ian had a birthday party for

their daughter at Spark House, the event hotel Harley and her sisters own, and we reconnected there."

"I already told you that, Kyle," Karen reminds him.

"Hmm. I must've forgotten. Well, it's nice to see Peyton getting comfortable here, even if we do miss her a lot." He finishes his sandwich and wipes his hands on a napkin.

"You're always welcome to visit, and now that we're settled in, I'm sure we'll be able to schedule regular trips out your way too," I placate, wanting to make sure they know that just because we moved doesn't mean we won't make the effort to see them.

"That'd be nice. I think Karen is missing all the time with her granddaughter."

I feel the guilt like a weight on my chest, getting heavier with each jab. I'm sure I'm reading into things and turning their comments into something they're not.

Peyton comes skipping into the kitchen. She's changed into a new dress that Harley picked up for her and refused to take any money for, saying it was a back-to-school present, even though the three of us went back-to-school shopping and she bought Peyton stuff then too.

"What in the world are you wearing, Peyton?" Karen purses her lips in disapproval.

"It's my new dress. Harley bought it for me!" She does a twirl and the sparkly, poofy skirt fluffs out.

"What's wrong with the dress I laid out for you?"

"I want to wear this one."

"I think it's perfect." I put an end to that unnecessary conversation. "And we should really think about heading out since it's already quarter after five."

We pile into my car, Karen sitting in the back with Peyton, and Kyle up front with me. We chat about my work and the projects he's started around the house, and how he's been trying to fit in as much golf as he can before the courses close for the season.

When we get to the school, Peyton bounces excitedly, pulling me along, telling me all about her classmates and how much she loves it here already. She points to a piece of artwork on the wall outside her classroom.

"Why is the horse pink, Peyton?" Karen asks.

"Because when we use our imagination, they can be any color we want, and I wanted my horse to be the color of cotton candy," she announces.

"Oh, well that's . . . interesting," Karen mutters.

We peek inside Peyton's classroom, which is bustling with students, most of whom are dressed up for tonight's performance. Peyton waves to another girl who, like Peyton, is dressed in a frilly, poofy skirted outfit, except hers is purple and Peyton's is green.

I do a double take when I notice the petite blonde standing next to the classroom teacher. At first I think I'm seeing things until Peyton claps her hands and shrieks, "Yay! Harley is here! Come on, let's go say hi to her!" She takes her granny's hand and pulls her into the classroom, calling out Harley's name.

Back when Harley was Peyton's nanny, I would give her weekends off when Peyton's grandparents came to visit, in part to avoid any conflict with Karen, but also because she couldn't work seven days a week.

Harley's smile widens when her eyes land on me.

We're introduced to Peyton's teacher, Mrs. Horton, but the classroom is filling up quickly, so Karen and Kyle say they'll meet us in the hallway, while I hang back.

"I had no idea you were going to be here," I say, more than a little surprised.

"Emily, Peyton's teacher, got married at Spark House last year. When I picked up Peyton the other day, we got to talking, and I offered to help with the class since it's a lot to handle on her own. I hope that's okay." She picks a piece of lint off my shirt, then absently smooths out my lapels before dropping her hands.

"Why wouldn't it be okay?" I glance toward the hallway, where Karen and Kyle are waiting for me. Karen's expression is pinched, and I can only guess what she must be unhappy about this time. Probably that she's not the one talking to Peyton's teacher.

Harley follows my gaze, but Karen and Kyle move out of my line of view. "My intention wasn't to overstep. I honestly didn't think anything of it, but I probably should have let you know when I volunteered."

I refocus my attention on Harley. "I don't mind at all, and you're not overstepping. Peyton and I love spending time with you. And you being here is obviously a good thing for her." It also means she's not hanging out with the boyfriend, which irrationally makes me feel better.

"I'm glad you feel that way. I have a little something for Peyton after the assembly, so I'll meet you in the foyer when it's over?"

"That sounds great."

Mrs. Horton calls out to Harley for some help, so I head back to the hall where I find my parents and my in-laws waiting outside the auditorium. Unlike her previous school, where all the assemblies were held in the gym and we sat on plastic chairs, this school has a real theater with plush seating.

"This is better than movie theater seating," Kyle says as he relaxes back into his chair.

"There seems to be a strong focus on the arts in this school. Will you be encouraging Peyton to try out for any of the sports teams? How are the academics here?" Karen asks.

"If Peyton wants to try out for a team, I'll support that, but she seems to have her mom's artistic flair, so she's been very excited about the drama club, and there's a yearbook club here. She's still young, and with the move being new, I want her to feel settled before I fill her schedule up too much." I don't know if it's just me projecting, but I feel like I'm under Karen's parenting microscope.

"I didn't realize that Harley was volunteering in her class," Karen says.

I was waiting for this. "She knows Peyton's teacher personally, and she's great with kids. I think it's pretty selfless that she's giving up an evening to help out a friend and be a familiar face for Peyton."

The lights go down, ending that conversation. For now.

An hour and a half and some pretty cute performances later—I'm ridiculously impressed they were able to put all of this together in under two weeks—we meet up outside the school. My parents have to leave because they have a brunch with friends in the morning, but we're supposed to see them tomorrow evening for dinner.

Harley appears a few minutes later, one hand tucked behind her back as she approaches us, her smile widening as her gaze moves from me to Peyton. "You were amazing up there! Even better than during rehearsals!"

Peyton grins shyly. "We practiced really hard this week."

"I heard! And I have something special for you." She pulls out a bouquet from behind her back. But it's no regular bouquet. It's made of cookies.

Peyton's eyes go wide. "Oh wow! This is better than flowers!"

"You should probably save those for tomorrow. Too much sugar before bed will keep you up late and that's not good for your teeth," Karen says, raining on both Peyton and Harley's parade.

"I don't think one cookie would hurt. And it's Friday night. Peyton is allowed to stay up a little later," I say with a wink at my daughter, hoping to keep Karen from saying anything that will offend Harley or upset Peyton. I know she's particular about parenting, but I feel like I've been under attack since I walked in the door after work.

"She hasn't even had dinner yet," Karen reminds me.

"Oh!" Peyton tugs on my sleeve. "Can Harley come with us?"

"Honey, we haven't seen you in almost a month. This should really be just about family." Karen gives me an imploring look.

Peyton's face falls, and Harley, bless her kind, thoughtful soul, smiles brightly. "We have an event tomorrow, and I need to stop by Spark House to give my sisters a hand, but we can do dinner later next week. Sound good, kiddo?"

Peyton's lips twist in disappointment, but she tries to cover it with a smile. "Oh, okay. Thank you for the cookie bouquet."

"You're so welcome and it's so well-deserved."

Harley hugs Peyton and says goodbye to everyone, getting yet another frosty response from Karen.

I don't want to say anything in front of Peyton about how rude Karen was to Harley, so I wait until she's asleep in bed. But by then, Karen's already in bed too, leaving me with Kyle, who's watching the highlights from tonight's game.

Obviously it's a conversation that's going to have to wait.

Eleven

WHAT THE HECK AM I DOING?

HARLEY

"Well, that was a level of awkward I'd rather not experience again," I mutter to myself as I get in my car. I try not to read into the way Karen reacted to me, but it's difficult with how frosty her reception was, even after all these years.

While we do have an event tomorrow night, we've already finished setting up. So I don't need to be at Spark House until later tomorrow morning. And that's a good thing, because I could use a couple of drinks right about now, not just one.

I haven't seen Gavin's in-laws in years, and I can't say much has changed. Kyle seems blissfully oblivious to everything, and Karen is about as warm as the Antarctic in the middle of a cold snap.

I leave my car at the apartment and head over to the pub on foot, so I don't have to drive home at the end of the night. It's already ten by the time I arrive, and Chad and our friends are seated at a table in the back corner. Andrea and Belinda see me first and wave me over.

I slide into the free chair next to Chad, which puts me kitty-corner from Belinda and across from Andrea.

Chad slings his arm around my shoulder and gives me a peck

on the cheek. "Hey, babe, how was the work thing tonight? Did you have another birthday party?" He isn't looking at me, though; his attention is on the hockey game on the screen above the bar. Seattle is playing, and it's one of the teams he favors for his fantasy league, or at least that's what I gather from the way he gets all heated when someone doesn't play as well as he needs them to.

I told him I was going to help at an event tonight, but I didn't specify what kind of event. "It was good."

"Good. Good. Glad to hear it." He whoops in my ear when Seattle's goalie deflects a shot on net.

I shift my chair a couple inches away so he's not yelling in my ear and let Chad chat about the game with Allen and Ted. Since Belinda is a nurse and Andrea is a kindergarten teacher, we always have great, lively conversations.

"How have the first couple of weeks of the school year been for you?" I ask Andrea.

"Full of accidents," Andrea sighs.

"Oh no! I hope not serious ones."

She waves a hand around. "Oh, not like, broken bones or anything. Half the class seems like they missed their potty-training lessons."

I make a face. "That can't be fun for you."

"Not really. Some years it's worse than others, but this one is particularly bad. Usually it's worked out by the end of September, but one of the moms is still sending her kid in Pull-Ups and he's totally capable of using the potty. And they have to be able to go on their own. Sending a kid who doesn't understand how to aim has been . . . special."

"Can you use the Cheerio method? Can you suggest it to the parents?" I ask.

"Oh yeah. I've had to send a bunch of YouTube tutorials home and set up a reward system in class. It's wild."

"So ironic that you and I both deal with potty issues, except I'm usually dealing with the other end of the spectrum," Belinda says. She works in a hospice.

I can't imagine how hard it is to watch people as they struggle through the last days of their life. It takes a special person to do that job. "That must be so tough."

"More for them than for me. It's about trying to preserve their dignity. I just try to make them laugh and keep their spirits up. Anyway . . ." She waves the comment away. "Enough about that, what event were you at tonight?"

"I was helping out a former client who happens to be a teacher at the Art Academy. They had a performance tonight, and she needed an extra set of hands to get the kids ready," I explain.

"I would literally sell a kidney to work there. They have such great programs and forward-thinking staff." Andrea's tone is full of respect and awe.

"Can you apply for a position?" I ask.

"Postings rarely come up, but I have an alert for when they do." She taps her phone.

We continue chatting while the guys remain immersed in the game. Eventually Andrea and Allen and Belinda and Ted have to leave since they all came together and Belinda has a shift tomorrow morning. Like me, she doesn't always have weekends off. When it's just me and Chad, I suggest that we get our bill.

"Yeah, I just want to see the highlights on the basketball game 'cause I missed it earlier," Chad says.

I pull out my phone while I wait and notice that I have a message.

Gavin: Thank you for helping out with the performance tonight and the cookie bouquet. It was a thoughtful gift and Peyton is really excited about trying every single kind of cookie in the bouquet. She also couldn't stop talking about how nice it was to have you there. I plan to let Peyton eat one for breakfast tomorrow, but keep that on the down-low. ;) I'm sorry about my MIL, she's having a hard time with us living so far away. Looking forward to seeing you soon ~G

"Are you dealing with work stuff? You need to take a break, babe." Chad puts his arm around my shoulder and glances at the phone screen, brows inching toward each other.

"Don't worry, it's not work-related." Before I can close the message, Chad grabs my phone out of my hand.

"What are you doing?" I don't have anything to hide, but it's certainly disrespectful for him to go through my messages. He reads the text, then starts scrolling through my messages.

"Do you talk to this guy every day?"

I grab my phone out of Chad's hand and stuff it back in my purse. "Not every day." At least I don't think it's every day. We often iron out plans for me to see Peyton, confirming what works for both of us. And then there have been the times when he's needed my help in a pinch.

The server comes over with our bill, and Chad tosses some cash on the table. He shoves his chair back, and it scrapes loudly across the floor. "Let's go."

"What about the highlights?" I point to the screen where they're still playing.

"I'll catch them later." I don't like the set of his jaw, or the way I suddenly feel the weight of guilt pulling me down. I was helping a friend tonight. It just happened to be at Peyton's school.

As I follow him out of the bar, my stomach does an uncomfortable flip. I'm worried Chad is about to go off, and for the first time since I started talking to Gavin again, I'm uncertain as to whether or not he has a right to be upset with me.

Technically I haven't done anything wrong.

But I have been spending a lot of time with Peyton and Gavin, even though this time wasn't on purpose. And I realize now that I haven't been very forthcoming about it.

"Are you okay to drive?" I ask Chad as we approach his car.

"I had two beers." His tone is frosty.

"Okay, but you also seem agitated, which isn't a great combination with any amount of alcohol," I point out.

"I seem agitated? I wonder why that is!" He crosses his arms, eyes narrowed, expression fierce. "Are you cheating on me with that Garrett guy?" Normally I'm grateful to see some level of emotion from him, but lately it's been only about Gavin.

I don't bother to correct him. I don't know what it is with men and being incapable of remembering someone's name. I mirror his pose. "Of course not."

"You talk to him all the time! You message him more than you message me, and that's based on the week's worth of texts I scrolled through," he snaps. "How often are you helping out with his kid?"

"I don't know. Once a week, maybe? I already told you, I took care of Peyton when she was a baby. I'm familiar and comfortable for her." But as I say it, I realize there's a hole in the story I've been telling everyone, including myself. Because Peyton doesn't remember me taking care of her. She has stories and pictures, but not actual memories.

"So you're babysitting her? Is that it? Or are you spending time with him too?"

"Sometimes I take her to the park."

"And other times?" he presses.

"I took Ella to the zoo, and Gavin and Peyton met me there. I asked you to come with me, but you weren't interested," I point out.

"Oh, so now you're going to put this on me? The zoo is for kids."

"And I took Ella."

"And then met up with this guy and his daughter. You can't tell me you don't see how bad this looks from the outside, Harley. I can barely get you to commit to a weekend away, and here you are spending all your free time with a guy and his nine-year-old daughter."

As I stand here, in the middle of the parking lot, Chad the angriest I've ever seen him, I recognize that he's right. There's a big difference in the time I spend with Chad and the time I spend with Gavin and Peyton. Chad and I are rarely ever alone together. We always go out with friends, and half the time it's me, Andrea, and Belinda who organize things so we can get in girl time. And my weekend plans with Chad are never about the two of us; they always revolve around group activities—with Andrea and Allen and Belinda and Ted. And occasionally Marv and the Howler. Whenever Chad comes over, he spends a good chunk of time playing video games. And the sex . . . is okay. Not bad, but not mind-blowing.

"The look on your face says everything, Harley."

I run a hand down my face. "I didn't mean for this to happen."

"For what to happen? Please don't tell me you slept with that guy."

I recoil at the insinuation. "Of course not. I would never do something like that." And it makes feel sick to think that he could believe that I would.

"So what didn't you mean to happen if you're not sleeping with him? What's going on between you? Is this an emotional affair or something?"

I rub the space between my eyes, trying to figure out how to explain. "No. It's not like that. I just didn't mean to start spending so much time with Peyton and Gavin. I honestly thought I would go to lunch with them that one time, but—"

"He kept messaging and texting and you kept saying yes." He cracks his jaw.

I nod.

"But you can't find time to spend with me."

As I absorb his words and his anger, our situation becomes clearer. "You're right. But do you really want to spend time with me?"

"Of course I do. Why would you even ask that?"

"How often do we see each other and it's just the two of us?" I ask.

"You're always working, or you have assignments, or you're hanging out with that dad and his kid, so not that often," he snaps.

I sigh, aware he has a right to be upset. Because he's not wrong. But he's also not entirely right. "We're always with friends. We make group plans, and when you come to my house, you're always playing video games. We don't make plans as a couple." I motion between us. "We never have."

Chad's expression shifts, the anger still there, but another new emotion covers that. "But it's more fun to go out with a group. You're always inviting other people to come along."

"And you never say no, or that you just want time with me. But you don't really like hanging out with my sisters and their husbands." I hold up a hand. "I'm not trying to play the blame game here, Chad, or deflect. You're right about a lot of things. I always invite our friends and you're always game for more people. I just think . . ." Am I really going to say this out loud? Admit what I know is probably true? I guess I am. "Maybe you and I aren't meant for each other."

"Seriously? That's how you're going to play this? So what now? You're gonna hook up with this guy instead?" He rolls his head on his shoulders.

"No. That's not . . . we're not involved like that." Although Gavin has helped me see what was missing in my current relationship, which is a true connection. We met through Andrea and Allen, and that's who we spend most of our time with. Without them, there's not much of a relationship. It's not a foundation at all. We're comfortable with each other, and we have friends in common, but that's where it ends. The spark isn't there. It's probably why the thought of him moving in makes me cagey. This is Psychology 101, and I completely missed the signs. "We're at very different places in our lives. What I want and what you want isn't the same thing."

"So you want to be someone's stand-in mom? You know this guy is only interested in you because you're a built-in babysitter, right?"

I don't like the way that comment cuts me. Or that I don't even know if what Chad is saying holds merit or not. "This isn't about Gavin."

"Like hell it isn't. I saw the way he looked at you. And you were with him tonight."

"Not technically. I was helping at a school event." My motivation for helping doesn't matter; it's that I didn't factor in how Chad might perceive it. I'm beginning to see that I'm the problem.

"For his fucking kid!" He shakes his head. "You know what, have fun playing mommy. If you want to lose all your good years taking care of some forty-year-old dude's kid, go for it." He turns around and yanks open his car door.

"You have a right to be angry with me, Chad, but this is the most passionate I've ever seen you get about anything other than your fantasy leagues and sports. That has to tell you something, especially about our relationship."

His lips press together in a line. "Just because you're letting yourself off the hook doesn't mean I have to."

He gets inside and slams the door, turns the engine over, and leaves me standing in the parking lot, questioning everything. Especially myself.

It's late and walking home at this hour on my own doesn't seem like a good idea, so I call an Uber. I message Chad to make sure he made it home safely.

> **Chad:** Don't worry. I didn't drive off a bridge. The only thing you have to feel guilty about is lying to yourself about what's going on with that dude. Have a nice life.

I stare at the words for a long time, wondering if he's right. If I've been more invested this entire time without realizing it.

But I'm not wrong about Chad and me. We aren't meant for each other. Andrea, who I befriended a few years ago at a pottery class, invited me out for drinks with her and Allen and a few of their friends, one of whom was Chad. We sat beside each other, the two single people amidst a pair of couples, and seemed to hit it off. We exchanged numbers, and the next week I met up with him at the same pub, with the same group of friends. He was fun, easygoing. We were instantly comfortable with each other, maybe too comfortable. I knew we had our differences, but I thought we'd grow into them in an opposites-attract way.

I wanted it to work. I liked having a group of friends and a boyfriend to hang out with that wasn't attached to my sisters. Chad is fun to be with, but he and I weren't an ideal couple. We were just passing time, and maybe dating each other was a way not to be a fifth wheel in a group of couples.

It took Gavin and Peyton coming back into my life to make me see that.

And where does that leave me: back at square one?

Twelve

COURSE CORRECT

HARLEY

I know I made the right decision in breaking it off with Chad. As awful as I feel, it's not heartache that's the problem, it's guilt over realizing I was in a relationship with him for all the wrong reasons. And now that I'm no longer dating him, I can see all of those clearly, in a way I couldn't or wouldn't allow myself to before.

We were never each other's endgame. As angry as he was last night, and I think he had a good reason to feel that way, I truly believe once he has some time to really think about it, he'll see that I'm right.

Hindsight is always twenty-twenty.

I get ready for work on autopilot, feeling a lot like Eeyore with a black rain cloud hanging over my head. I should be in a good mood because we're preparing for the huge sweet sixteen party, but my excitement over that is completely overshadowed by the breakup. I hate that it happened the way it did and that I hurt Chad.

On the way to work I stop at my favorite bakery, pick up pecan cinnamon rolls and order myself a coffee milkshake—because all breakups require sugar in copious quantities—and head to Spark House.

"Uh-oh." London's gaze goes directly to the shake in my hand. "It's only nine and you're drinking ice cream. What happened?"

"I broke up with Chad." I slurp on my shake. It's salted caramel.

"I'm sorry." Her expression shifts to understanding, and she pulls me in for a long hug. When she finally releases me, she steps back and tucks my hair behind my ear. London has always been half-sister and half-mom to me, which is ironic since Avery is the oldest. "How did he take it?"

"He was . . . hurt and upset." I feel like a bag of crap about the whole thing.

She tips her head to the side. "Do you want to talk about it?"

I nod and finally the tears well. I wish I'd seen the truth of our relationship sooner, so I could have avoided hurting Chad like I did.

"He thought I was cheating on him with Gavin," I tell her.

She takes my hand and pulls me over to the chairs in the center of our office where we often have our brainstorming sessions. "Because you've been spending so much time with him?"

I nod and drop down into the chair beside her. "I would never sleep with someone else while I was in a relationship. But I realized last night that I *have* been spending a lot of time with Gavin and Peyton. More time than I've been spending with Chad. And the worst part is realizing I prefer spending time with them over him."

London gives me a sad, patient smile. She's familiar with being in relationships that don't work out. She had a few of them before she finally met Jackson. And even then, she was pretty oblivious to how into her he was, until he laid his cards on the table. She'd never allowed herself to love someone deeply until him, maybe because we know what it feels like to lose the people we love the most. Love is scary because it has the power to make you feel whole and tear you apart.

"Sometimes an emotional affair feels just as damaging as a physical one."

I bite the inside of my cheek. "Do you think that's what I've been doing?"

"No. Not consciously, anyway. I think Gavin and Peyton fill a hole for you, but I'm a little worried about what that looks like in the future. I remember how hard it was on you when they moved away all those years ago. You really struggled with that loss. I wasn't sure if there was more to it than just missing Peyton. I guess the question you need to answer for yourself, honestly, is if this is about spending time with Peyton, or are you are as invested in Gavin as you are her?"

I run my hands down my face. "I don't know. I think I've been trying to convince myself that Peyton is the reason we're spending so much time together, but now I feel like I've been burying my head in the sand and it's taken this breakup with Chad for me to see that. I like spending time with them. Both of them."

London turns a strip of paper into a star and sets it on the arm of her chair. "What if you take Peyton out of the equation?"

"I can't do that."

"Would you still have feelings for Gavin if she wasn't a factor? Do you want to spend time with him without Peyton?" she asks.

"I . . . I think so? But I just broke up with Chad. It's probably not a good idea for me to get involved with anyone at all. And this is a complicated situation. Peyton is comfortable with me."

London hesitates before she finally says, "Please don't take offense, but are you sure Gavin isn't pulling you back into his and Peyton's life because of exactly that reason?"

I think about all the time we've spent together. How we have fun together, but it always revolves around Peyton. Now that I look back on his introduction to Chad and my never mentioning the fact that I had a boyfriend, I have to wonder if subconsciously I'd done that on purpose. Even then I'd known why Chad was upset, but I'd brushed it off as nothing.

And then there's the giant elephant that's still stomping around between us in the form of what almost happened before he decided to move.

"I almost kissed him once," I blurt.

London's eyes go wide. "Recently?"

I shake my head. "When Peyton was a baby, just before he moved away."

London nods slowly. "I wondered if there was more going on back then. You were so broken up about it when they moved. At first I thought it was because you'd lived with the family for more than a year, which you hadn't done before. But you seemed so unsure of your path after that."

"I was unsure. I couldn't believe I had crossed that line." I wanted to find a way to heal from the loss of losing our parents, but instead, I was creating even bigger holes. So I switched gears and surrounded myself with the people I loved and relied on the most: my sisters.

"Do you want to tell me what happened to inspire the almost-kiss?" London asks.

So I explain what transpired that night. How Peyton had been teething, that Gavin was overworked and not coping well, and

I'd found him in the kitchen and consoled him. How I leaned in to kiss him, and he stopped me before I did.

"Have you ever talked about it since then?"

I shake my head. "I had just gotten up the nerve to apologize when he told me he was moving to Boulder to be closer to his in-laws."

"What about since he's moved back?" Her expression is full of concern.

"No. I haven't had the guts to ask him. And we're always with Peyton, so . . ." But that's not entirely true, because we have been alone since then, not for long periods of time, but long enough that I could ask.

"Are you afraid of the answer?" she asks softly.

I sigh. "He told me he wanted to be closer to his in-laws."

"But you didn't believe him."

"I always felt like I was the reason he made the move. Or at least the thing that pushed him over the edge. And after they moved, it made me question everything. I felt . . . betrayed, maybe? Lost? I'd spent all that time with Peyton, taken care of her, made things as easy as I could for her and Gavin, and they disappeared from my life. It hurt, maybe more than I wanted to admit or even re-alized at the time. But I couldn't do that again, get attached like that. I understand that he was still grieving over losing Marcie, but that didn't make their moving any less difficult."

"Is he still grieving her now?" London asks.

"I don't know." Do you ever stop grieving a loved one?

London reaches out and squeezes my hand. "Give yourself some time to get over Chad before you jump into something new. Just because you weren't in love with him doesn't mean you don't need some time to get your head around the breakup. And whatever is going on with you and Gavin, if and when you decide to pursue it, please take it slow. It's not just you and Gavin that you need to think about."

"I know. Peyton is a big part of the equation."

"Whatever you choose, make sure that you're doing this for the right reasons, and not as a way to keep Peyton in your life again," she says gently.

I want to be reassured, but I'm nervous.

And she's right. Regardless of whether breaking up with Chad was the right thing to do, I need to give myself time to let go of that relationship fully before I pursue another one.

Not to mention I still have no idea whether Gavin is interested in me like that.

I throw myself into work over the weekend, not wanting to focus too much on what's going on in my life or how it feels a lot like I'm floating through it, never really able to find my footing.

On Sunday afternoon Grandma Spark calls me on video chat. We try to make it a weekly thing, but sometimes her internet reception isn't all that great.

Today, though, she's sitting outside, drinking a glass of red wine, wearing a wide-brim hat, looking relaxed and happy. Her hair is longer these days, pulled back in a ponytail, flyaway wisps fluttering around her face. It's been white for as long as I remember. Like me, she was a blond when she was younger, but it went white when she was in her mid-forties. The corners of her eyes crinkle when she smiles, and there are laugh lines around her mouth. She always talks about how she's earned every one of her wrinkles and that they're an homage to everything she's been through.

"How's my favorite Harley?" she asks.

"I'm good. How are you?" I prop my chin on my fist and smile.

Her eyes narrow and she purses her lips. "I don't believe you for a second. What's wrong? Did you have a fight with your sisters? Is it Spark House–related?"

I shake my head. "No. Nothing like that. Spark House is doing great."

"Hmm." She sips her wine. "Spark House is becoming its own force, which is wonderful and awful. It can be hard to keep your head above water when the current is too strong."

I chuckle. "You see everything, don't you?"

"I've been keeping my eye on social media. I know when it's your posts or when it's the ones that the Wizard of Social Media Oz is posting. There's a difference in voice. Let's come back to Spark House though, since it's not going anywhere. What's happening that's making you look like a lost soul?"

"It's annoying that you can read me this easily," I mutter.

"I raised you, it's my job to be able to read you," she reminds me. As much as I wish my parents hadn't died in that car accident, I loved being raised by Grandma Spark. Because I was the youngest, I spent the most time with her, especially when Avery and London were in college. When I put my degree on hold, she was understanding, being the only person who knew what I was truly going through. But every once in a while she'd throw out a passing comment about whether I wanted to finish it at some point. She was beyond elated when I told her I was going to take that step.

"I know." I blow out a breath and tell her everything. She already knew about Gavin and Peyton coming back to Colorado Springs and us reconnecting, but I fill her in on the breakup with Chad.

"Oh, sweetheart, I'm so sorry. Breakups are never easy, but I will say, from the beginning I knew he wasn't the right one for you." She adjusts the brim of her hat.

"Why didn't you say something if you knew?"

"Because sometimes we have to find the wrong man before we find the right one. I met your grandfather two days before I turned down a proposal from my high school sweetheart."

"I didn't know that."

"That's because I was saving the story for the right time." She winks. "Your grandfather delivered a bouquet of flowers sent from my boyfriend. At the time, flower delivery wasn't common like it is now, and he'd been running errands and said he was happy to drop them off. Now, I'd seen your grandfather around town, but only in passing. He took the opportunity and jumped on it, knowing that my boyfriend was sending them as an apology."

"What did he do that would warrant flowers?"

"He missed a date or something. I can't remember now." She waves the question away. "The important part is that your grandfather brought me the flowers and said if my current boyfriend was truly sorry, he would have delivered the flowers himself. And he was right. Sometimes it takes seeing it through someone else's eyes before we realize the path we're on isn't the right one."

"I think I just wanted someone for myself, if that makes sense."

She nods knowingly. "It does. You and your sisters are very close, but they both have partners, and I'm sure that makes it more of a challenge for you."

I nod. "I needed someone other than my sisters in my life. I think I was so caught up in the idea of having someone that I didn't really put enough focus on whether we were a good match."

"He was a good-for-now, not a good-forever boyfriend and

that's okay, Harley. You'll find your person. And maybe you already have."

Later that afternoon I get a message from Gavin asking if I'm around. I tell him I'm at Spark House managing cleanup for last night's event, and he asks how long I think I'll be there. I tell him probably a couple more hours.

I don't hear anything back from him after that, so I continue with cleanup and then sit down at my desk to schedule social media posts for the beginning of the week, highlighting the businesses we partnered with for the event over the weekend and the ones we're working with for this coming week. This is one part of my job that hasn't changed, and I'm grateful for that. I enjoy setting up mini-photoshoots and coming up with new, creative ways to showcase the businesses who help make our events so special.

I'm in the middle of programming Tuesday's posts when there's a knock on my office door. "Come in!" I call out.

I'm not expecting anyone, but sometimes people driving by will pop in and ask for a tour. So I'm surprised when Gavin steps into the office.

I glance past him, expecting Peyton to be his shadow, but he's alone. "Hey, sorry for the surprise visit, but, I uh . . . wanted to talk."

"Talk?" Suddenly my heart is in my throat. And for a moment I wonder if this is how Chad felt on Friday night when I broke up with him.

I feel awful all over again, because the sudden roll in my stomach is a lot to handle.

He glances around the office. "Are we alone?"

I nod, and resist the urge to scratch my wrist. I do not need a hive attack to go with the rest of the unsettled feelings.

He takes a few steps forward, then tucks his hands in his pockets. For some reason he looks nervous. "I need to apologize."

"Apologize?" I can't think of a reason he'd need to be sorry for something.

"For the way my mother-in-law acted on Friday. At the assembly."

"Oh." Friday feels like it was a million years ago. The whole breakup with Chad overshadowed Karen and her frostiness.

"Karen is having trouble with the move. She misses Peyton, and she doesn't like how easily she seems to be settling in." He rubs the back of his neck. "That sounds bad. What I mean is that she's used to being the center of Peyton's world, and with us living here, that's not how it is anymore. It's been tough for her to manage, and I need to make more of an effort to plan visits with them, but my focus has been on getting Peyton settled." He blows out a breath. "Not that this is your issue, or your fault, but she lashed out at you and that wasn't fair. She's worried about her role in Peyton's life."

"That's understandable. It has to be a big change for all of you." Although I have to wonder how much those feelings are being directed my way because of my previous role in Peyton's life. It makes me question exactly how much she knows, but I don't have the guts to ask. Not right now, when everything feels so unsteady.

"It doesn't make it acceptable, though. I didn't want you to think I was okay with the way she acted."

"I appreciate that. And I appreciate your apology, even though it's unnecessary."

"It felt necessary to me." He tucks a thumb in his pocket and rocks back on his heels. "So, uh, there's a theater in the park event coming up next weekend. I know you probably have plans with your boyfriend, but I'm taking Peyton, and I wanted to extend the invitation. My treat. As a thank-you."

"Oh, uh, Chad and I aren't together anymore, so my social calendar is wide open, unless I'm working a Spark House event." I wish that had come out way less pitchy.

Gavin's eyebrows shoot up. "What? When did that happen?"

"We broke up this weekend." I amend that statement. "I broke up with him."

"Oh. I'm . . . sorry?" It's phrased more like a question than a statement.

I shrug, and once again the blanket of guilt weighs heavy on my shoulders for not seeing what I should have weeks ago. "He and I weren't on the same page, and we weren't right for each other. I wasn't as invested in our relationship as I should have been."

Gavin takes a seat on the chair across from me, his expression shifting to disquiet. "Is this my fault? Is it because of how I reacted when I came to pick up Peyton?"

I look away, struggling to meet his concerned gaze. Now that I've officially ended the relationship with Chad, I can see there's an attraction to Gavin that I've been working to keep buried along with the memories and the guilt. I just had a reason before now not to acknowledge them.

"Harley?" His voice is soft, and he leans forward, his elbows resting on his thighs. "Is this because of me?"

"Sorry." I shake my head. "No. It's not because of you, Gavin." I don't need him feeling bad about this. I can carry that on my own. He has enough of his own baggage without taking on mine too. "I realized he and I are in different places in our lives, and what I want and what he wants isn't the same thing."

"Are you okay? Is there anything I can do?" Gavin laces his fingers together, and his foot taps restlessly on the floor.

"No, I just need a bit of time to process. Let me check my schedule and see about the outdoor theater event. That would be fun if I can swing it."

"Are you sure? I don't want you to feel obligated."

"I'm sure. It'll be a good distraction."

A week after Chad and I break up, I drop off a box of the things he left at my place at his apartment. It wasn't much, just a single outfit, a couple of ties and button-downs, a pair of pajama pants, and a toothbrush. We hadn't spoken since the breakup, apart from me texting to ask if I can drop off his stuff. London asked if I wanted her to come with me. But I told her I needed to do it on my own.

My stomach flips as I knock on his door. My palms are sweaty. I don't know what to expect, but I'm hoping it doesn't end with me feeling worse than I already do about this whole thing.

Chad opens the door. He's dressed in jeans and a T-shirt with a game logo on it. He looks good and not like he's been sad or moping for the past week. And that's a relief.

I swallow down my anxiety. "Hey."

His gaze roves over my face and drops to the box in my hands. "Hey. Thanks for bringing my stuff back."

"Don't thank me." I purse my lips and close my eyes, giving my head a quick shake. "I'm really sorry, Chad."

"For what?" He takes the box from me and hands over the key to my apartment, which means I have something to flip between my fingers.

"For not seeing what you could before I did."

"You mean about that Gavin dude? He ask you out on a date yet?"

"Yes, and no." I blow out a breath and shove my thumbs in the back pocket of my jeans. "I mean, he hasn't asked me out."

"He knows we broke up, though?" He tucks the box under one arm and leans against the doorjamb.

"Yeah. He knows."

"I figured." Chad nods once and gives me a wry smile. "And he'll ask soon, if he's smart, anyway." He blows out a breath and nudges the toe of my shoe with his. "Look, I know you're kind of used to holding on to blame like it's yours to own, but I've done a lot of thinking this week, and you weren't wrong, about us, I mean. I really like you and you're an awesome person, but we were missing something. So don't beat yourself up over this, okay?"

"You don't have to let me off the hook, Chad. I know I was in the wrong," I tell him.

"I'm not letting you off the hook. I'm telling you to let yourself off the hook." He gives me a wry smile. "We both deserve to be happy, even if it's not with each other."

Over the next month I continue to see Peyton and Gavin about twice a week. Whether it's dinner or a trip to the park, they've become a regular fixture in my life. I can't decide if things have started to shift or if it's all in my head. But with some closure for Chad and me, I feel like I can move forward, whatever that's going to look like.

It's a Wednesday afternoon, and Peyton is staying after school for drama rehearsal. She loves her new school and has become very involved in the theater group. I'm supposed to pop by to watch her for a bit, and the three of us are planning to go for dinner. We're trying another new pizza place. Peyton is very committed to trying every single pizza joint in the city.

I have a new message.

Gavin: Finished my meeting early, want 2 grab a coffee before we pick up Peyton?

I've just finished programming posts and am about to pack up, so the timing is perfect.

Harley: Sure, see you in twenty?

I pull into the school parking lot less than twenty minutes later, but I don't see Gavin's SUV, so I message him about an ETA.

Gavin: At the coffee shop across the street. Your dose of sugar is waiting for you.

He sends along a pic of a steaming cup of hot chocolate topped with whipped cream and chocolate shavings sitting in front of an empty chair.

When he said grab a coffee, I thought he meant to-go coffees, not sit down and drink them at the coffee shop. Nothing and everything has changed since I told him Chad and I broke up. Gavin and I text on a nearly daily basis. But he's been flirtier with me, and he often asks how I'm handling the breakup, maybe gauging where I am on an emotional level.

My heart does a silly flip-flop in my chest when I spot him

sitting in the back corner of the coffee shop in a pair of cozy chairs. He waves me over. "I figured we had lots of time and could afford to hang out for a few minutes, if that's okay with you."

"That's totally okay with me." I drop down in the chair across from him.

"It's salted-caramel hot chocolate." He points to the steaming cup. Next to it is chocolate caramel biscotti. "That's what you usually get, isn't it?"

"It is. Thanks. What do I owe you for this?" I start to dig my wallet out of my purse, but Gavin leans over and covers my hand with his. It sends a jolt up my arm. "My treat."

I lift my head and meet his warm gaze. "Thank you."

"No thanks necessary." He removes his hand and sits back in his chair, crossing one leg over the other. "Tell me about your day."

We chat about work. Things are progressing with the Spark House franchise slowly. One of the prospective locations turned out to have too many restrictions on the property, but the other four have been fully vetted and approved. The Mills brothers have already found an alternate location for the fifth one, and it's a matter of time before that one is signed off on too. The delay hasn't been the worst thing in the world, at least not for me, because it's given me time to get used to the idea and get more comfortable with the changes.

I move away from talking about Spark House and ask Gavin about his work instead. He tells me about all the developments with the park he's working on and how he and Ian have already been by the site to survey the bike and walking trails, and they've brought in landscapers to prepare the gardens for the spring.

We move on to what the rest of our week looks like and the

upcoming events at Spark House, including a very out-of-the box wedding.

"Oh, before I forget, what does next week look like for you? I thought maybe I could take Peyton to this really cool graffiti class." I sip my hot chocolate. It's deliciously sweet with a hint of salt at the end of every sip.

"Graffiti class?" Gavin's eyebrows pop.

"Yeah! It's so cool! We have a client who's getting married in the fall, and they have these amazing graffiti murals they're bringing in. Let me show you!" I pull up the artist's Instagram page where some of his pieces are featured and lean over so I can show it to Gavin.

"Oh wow. Is that the side of a building?" Gavin's fingers graze mine as he shifts the phone so the light above us doesn't obstruct his view.

"It is. They commission him to create these pieces. So amazing, right? So he's going to bring in pieces for the wedding. He teaches classes for all levels, and they have a family class. It might be fun to take Peyton, give her exposure to another form of art since she's so hungry to express her creative side." I tip my chin up.

Our faces are inches apart. And his gaze drops to my mouth for a second, the air suddenly thick with new tension. Or maybe it's been there all along and I wasn't ready to acknowledge it until now.

"I think we'd love that." He clears his throat and drops his hand, leaning back in his chair. "Unless you just want to take Peyton."

"We could go together. The three of us? Maybe go out for dinner after? The class is from five to six. If she really likes it, they have courses. But I'm getting ahead of myself." I wave a hand in the air. "I thought it would be a neat new thing to try. And the best part is that the classes are in a park, so lots of great entertainment and outdoor time."

"Your out-of-the-box thinking is one of my favorite things about you."

His smile sends a kaleidoscope of butterflies loose in my stomach. "Wednesday at five, then?"

"Wednesday at five." He programs it into his phone. "We should probably head over to the school so we can catch the tail end of rehearsals." He stands and extends a hand, helping me to my feet.

On the way out of the coffee shop, his fingertips rest against the small of my back as he opens the door and ushers me outside. Little gestures, smiles and sidelong glances individually don't mean much, but added up, it's starting to feel like this friendship we've formed is shifting, and I'm not sure what to do with that, if anything.

I don't want to ruin this good thing we have.

I wish the butterflies in my stomach understood that.

Thirteen

IT'S NOT REALLY A DATE, YET

GAVIN

"Dad, when are we going? Aren't we supposed to meet Harley soon?" Peyton comes bounding into my room and launches herself onto my bed, bouncing on her butt.

"Yup. I just need one more minute." The five o'clock start time for this class doesn't leave me with a lot in the way of time. I basically picked Peyton up from my parents' house and forced her to eat a snack—which ended up being cookies because I still need to get changed out of my suit. I'm wearing a pair of jeans and a T-shirt, with a zip-up hoodie in case it gets cool later. It's only late September, but the days are shorter, and when the sun goes down, there's a chill.

I splash a little aftershave on my hands and slap at my neck.

"Do you want to smell good for Harley?" Peyton asks.

I pause and glance up at her knowing smile. "I don't want to smell *bad* for Harley, or anyone."

"Those are your going-out jeans," she says haughtily.

"How do you know they're my going-out jeans? I have more than one pair of jeans you know."

"Yeah, but you have your work-on-the-house jeans, the mow-the-lawn jeans that have grass stains on them, and then you have two pairs of going-out jeans." She holds up two fingers. "These are your going-out ones."

"Well, I'm going out, so I guess it makes sense that I'm wearing my going-out jeans, doesn't it?"

She chews on her bottom lip for a second before she nods. Her lips twist to the side. "Is Harley's friend going to be there again?"

"Which friend is that?"

"Um." She taps her chin. "Chad?"

"Oh. Uh no. Harley and Chad aren't seeing each other anymore." I'm a little unsure how to navigate this conversation with my nine-year-old. We mostly watch princess movies and cartoons, and while I've dated a few women over the years, I only introduced one of them to my daughter. Not because I didn't think she could handle it, but because I didn't think it was a good idea to bring women into her life who might not stick around. And my mother-in-law made that very difficult.

Maybe more difficult than I realized, based on her reaction to Harley at the assembly a few weeks ago, and we're not even dating.

Not yet. But maybe soon. I don't exactly know how long I should wait on that, though. Probably not too long. I don't want to give anyone else a chance to swoop in and ask her out before I get a chance.

I hope she'll say yes when I do. To a date that doesn't involve a nine-year-old. Not that I don't love having my daughter around, but I'd like to spend more time with just Harley. And I can't explore the chemistry we seem to share when she's reading bedtime stories and making glitter crafts.

"What does that mean?" Peyton asks. "Not seeing each other anymore?"

"Well, you know in *Frozen*, when Princess Anna starts to fall for the bad guy?"

"Hans." Peyton makes a face. "He's not nice. He's selfish and mean."

"He is. And Anna sees him for who he really is, and instead, she falls for Kristoff, even though he smells kinda funny because his best friend is a reindeer and he's a little weird."

Peyton scrunches up her nose. "So was Harley's boyfriend a Hans?"

"Well, no . . . I mean, maybe. You know what, this is a bad comparison. Harley decided that she didn't want to be Chad's girlfriend anymore. Sometimes that happens. People grow apart instead of together." Man, I really suck at this conversation.

She twists her hands together. "Do they sometimes grow back together after they've been apart?"

"Um. Sometimes? Why?"

She bites her bottom lip. "Is that what happened when I was a baby? With Harley? Did you grow apart and now you're going to grow together again?"

I feel like I'm digging myself a huge hole with this conversation. The kind that can easily get too deep to climb out of. "No, honey, we moved to be closer to Nana and Grandpa, not because of Harley." But that's not entirely true either. I'd been on the fence about moving, not wanting to start over again. In fact, Ian had been ready to put an offer in on a house in Boulder and take on the task of getting the Greenscapes out there up and running. A few days before he and Lynn were going to go out there and look at a house, I decided Peyton and I should be the ones to make the move. We went to the house showing and I put in an offer right away.

"But now that we live here, we see Harley again," she points out.

"That's true. But Harley was your nanny when you were a baby. She helped me take care of you."

"The angels sent her to help because they took Mommy to heaven." It sounds almost rote, like a line from a story she's been told often.

"That's right."

"So did the angels send her again because we needed her?" Peyton asks, head tipped to the side.

"Maybe," I answer honestly.

Because as much as I'd like to believe we reconnected by chance, it's hard not to wonder if the universe is trying to tell me something I wasn't ready to hear all those years ago.

Half an hour later we meet Harley at the entrance to the park. She's dressed in a pair of jeans that hugs all her slight curves and a long-sleeved shirt that reads I BELIEVE IN FAIRY TALES. Peyton skips over to her and Harley crouches down, catching her around the waist. "How's my favorite nine-year-old?"

"I'm so excited! I can't wait to do graffiti!"

Harley smiles. "I can't wait either!"

"Every time Granny sees it on a wall, she says it's the riffraff who do it, and if they get caught, they get in trouble," Peyton announces.

"If we painted graffiti in places it wasn't supposed to be, that would be bad, but today we get to learn how to do it in a place where it's okay."

"Okay. That's good. I don't want to get in trouble for having fun." Peyton takes one of Harley's hands and takes mine in the other, and we walk toward the other side of the park, where I can see, very clearly, the wall of graffiti art.

Today, there are half a dozen kids, a couple as young as Peyton and a few who look to be a little older. There's a boy who appears to be on the verge of becoming a teenager, wearing what I would consider skater clothes and a ball cap with the name of the artist instructing the class on it.

We spend the next hour learning all about the art of graffiti and creating our own designs that we get to photograph, but the paint is water-soluble, so it will stay up for the night and then get washed away.

Afterwards we grab a bite to eat from one of the food trucks and take Peyton to the park, so she can run around for a bit before we take her home. "Just stay where we can see you, okay, kiddo?" I ruffle her hair.

"Okay!" She leaves her popcorn with Harley and bounds off to the play structure. Harley and I sit on a bench so we can keep an eye on her.

"Just stay off the climber, please!" I call out, then mutter, "I wish they wouldn't make them so enticing for kids her size. She's too small to go up that high."

"I'm guessing you've taken that into account with the park you're working on."

"I have. I have new sketches for the play structure. I'd love for you to have a look when you have some time."

"Absolutely. Whenever works for you works for me."

"Maybe sometime next week, then? You could come over for dinner?" I suggest, but know I'm taking an easy out by inviting her to the house instead of out on a proper date.

"That would be great." She crosses one leg over the other

and her foot bumps my shin. "Oh sorry." She leans over to brush away the smudge of dust off my jeans and tugs at the material. "I like these."

"You like my jeans?"

"They look good on you." She glances at me out of the corner of her eye and smiles, then pops a piece of popcorn into her mouth. "Usually you're in a suit."

This is true. Most of the time Harley sees me when I'm coming home from work. And even when I dress down, I still tend to wear khakis and collared shirts. "You always look good, no matter what you're wearing," I tell her.

Her smile widens. "Even when I'm dressed up as a fairy godmother?"

"Especially when you're dressed up as a fairy godmother."

She laughs and shifts so she's turned toward me and props her elbow on the back of the bench, resting her cheek on her fist. "So aside from the big park project, how are things? Are you happy to be working with your family again? And Ian too?"

"Honestly? It's been great. It's nice to be back in the place I consider home and working alongside Ian again. I don't think I realized how much I missed working with my dad until I was again."

"Is that hard then, since he's retiring?"

"Well, I don't know if he'll ever fully retire, but he's going down to part-time and planning to take a lot more holidays than he used to. He and my mom want to plan a monthlong trip to Europe. Isn't your grandmother out there?"

"She is, yeah." Harley smiles fondly. "She went to Europe for a vacation, but ended up staying a lot longer. I think she's been there for nearly three years. She comes home every few months to visit, but she has a boyfriend out there."

"That must be tough for you, though. She basically raised you, didn't she?" I remember vaguely that she used to take Peyton to the park and meet up with her gran fairly often.

"She did. I miss her, but she deserves happiness, and if that's in Italy, then that's where she should be. We talk pretty regularly, and I have my sisters around, so it all balances out in the end."

"How are things with your sisters? How's Spark House and the franchise?"

Harley tucks a piece of hair behind her ear. "Spark House is good. The franchise will be good for our bottom line, but the whole thing is a little overwhelming. There are so many big-picture things to account for now. Every time I think I have a handle on my new role, it changes again. I feel like I'm constantly trying to figure out where I fit in at Spark House, and it's been a challenge to get a foothold."

"Do your sisters know that?" I ask.

She lifts a hand, waving at Peyton who has climbed to the top of the structure and is waiting her turn to go down the slide. "They're trying their best, but we have a team of people working with us on developing a franchise model. It's a lot of moving parts. My sisters' roles have shifted too, but they were always more set than mine. We'll figure it out."

"I'm sorry it's a challenging transition."

"All transitions are a challenge in one way or another."

I decide now is as good a time as any to segue. "It can't be easy, though, especially when you throw a breakup in there. How's Chet handling it?"

Harley gives me a sidelong glance and suppresses a half smile. "Do you purposely get his name wrong?"

"No, I just don't think I spent much time wanting to get to

know it or him, if I'm going to be quite honest." I shrug and give her my best chagrined smile.

"Well, I dropped all of *Chad's*, not *Chet's*, stuff off at his place a couple of weeks ago. By that point he'd had some time to think things through, and he agreed that we weren't right for each other. On paper, we ticked all the boxes, but we don't have enough in common, and we were better off as friends. It was nice not to be the single friend in the group, but the spark wasn't there the way it should be. And he's still into spending all weekend in a pub, drinking beer and watching sports. I'm past that. In fact, I think I skipped over that phase entirely. My sisters and I will go for drinks once in a while, but when we do, it's to hang out, not because we have seven different fantasy sports leagues to keep track of."

"That's a lot of fantasy sports," I remark.

"I'm exaggerating, but probably not by much. Anyway, last I heard, he'd gone on a date with one of the bartenders at his favorite sports bar."

I cringe. "Ouch."

Harley lifts one shoulder and lets it fall. "I'm actually happy he's putting himself out there. I think if I'd had deep feelings for him, it would hurt, but it doesn't."

"That makes sense. Does that mean you're ready to move on?"

"Yeah." She nods and her bottom lip slides between her teeth. "I'm past the *feeling bad* stage, if that's what you mean."

I weigh my options and decide to go for it. I shift and mirror her pose, my forearm resting on the back of the bench and my fingers brushing her arm. "Is it too soon to ask you out for dinner, then?"

"Dinner? You mean with you and Peyton?"

"I'm always happy to take you both out." I motion between us. "But I was thinking just you and me."

Fourteen

UNCHARTED TERRITORY

HARLEY

"Without Peyton?" I don't know why I ask; clearly this is what he means.

"I'm a fan of pizza, but I was thinking more along the lines of a place without paper menus. Where they have an actual wine list consisting of more than house white and red." He chuckles somewhat nervously.

"Do you mean like on a date?" Apparently all my current questions fit in the stupid category.

"Unless I'm reading this wrong," Gavin backtracks.

"You want to go on a date with me?" Now would be an excellent time for that rogue UFO to appear and beam me up, and maybe spit back out a less awkward version of me.

"Um, yes?" Now he sounds uncertain.

"Why?"

"Why do I want to go on a date with you?" Gavin arches a brow.

I open my mouth to respond, but it's cut off by a loud shriek. Our heads whip over to the play structure, and we push up off the bench at the same time, scanning the area for Peyton. We find her on the ground by the climber.

We rush over to her, and Gavin scoops her up in his arms. "What happened, honey? Are you okay?"

"I f-fell off the climber! My knees and my h-hands hurt!" Peyton stammers through a sob.

I put my hand on Gavin's arm. "Let's take her to the bench so we can have a look."

He carries her to the bench and sits, setting her in his lap. Gavin wipes her tears away and kisses her forehead, then gently takes her hands in his so he can have a look at the damage. Her palms are scraped, beads of blood welling, but nothing serious. Her knees are in worse shape, but it's all surface wounds.

He kisses the back of her hand. "Oh sweetie, I bet that hurts, doesn't it? This is why I want you to stay off the climber."

"It just looks so fun." She sucks in a tremulous breath.

"I know, but that one is a little higher than normal, and it's probably slippery from the rain we had earlier," he explains.

I pass a tissue to Gavin. "Give me a second. I have an emergency first aid kit in here somewhere." I set my purse on the ground next to me—it's huge and can basically carry my entire life in it without much trouble—and rummage around until I find the first aid kit.

I pull out the iodine wipes, so I can clean the dirt out of her wounds, starting on her hands and then moving to her knees. "It's going to sting a little, but we want to get the dirt out of the cuts, okay, sweetie? You hug your daddy and it'll be over in a minute," I tell her.

"Okay." She sniffles and wraps her arms around Gavin's neck.

He kisses her cheek and turns his head toward me, murmuring, "Thank you."

I smile reassuringly. "No problem."

"I shouldn't be surprised that you have a first aid kit in your purse, should I?" He gives me an impish grin.

I shrug. "You can never be too prepared." It was a habit I got into when I was a nanny, and I never stopped.

I wipe down her right knee first, blowing on the wound to help with the sting before I cover it with a bandage, then do the same with the left one.

"All done," I announce.

Peyton releases her iron grip from around her father's neck and looks down at her knees, decorated in Tinker Bell Band-Aids. She bites her lip and sniffs. "Tinker Bell is my favorite."

"Mine too." I wink.

"Should we head home?" Gavin asks.

Peyton nods, and he picks her up, carrying her across the parking lot and back to the car. He buckles her in and walks me over to my vehicle, which is a few rows over.

He tucks a hand in his pocket. "Sorry about the abrupt end to the evening."

I chuckle. "These things happen."

"I'm very glad you were prepared with the Band-Aids, so thank you for that."

"Kids and scrapes go hand in hand."

"That they do. And the boo-boos get bigger the older they are."

"This is definitely true." I adjust my purse. "No, is the answer to the question you asked earlier." Gavin's expression starts to fall until I rush on. "It isn't too soon to ask me on a date."

A grin spreads across his full lips. "Not too soon?"

I shake my head.

"So I can take you out for dinner? Just you and me?" His tongue peeks out to drag across his bottom lip.

"I'd like that."

"Me too. Do you have a weekend free soon?"

"I actually have this weekend off." I don't know what to do with my hands, so I grip the strap of my purse.

"I'll check with my parents and see if they can take Peyton for an overnight. Would Saturday work for you?"

"Saturday would be perfect." I bite my lip and blurt, "I still want to know why."

He grins and tips his head to the side. "Why I want to take you on a date?"

"I thought maybe you . . . I don't know what I thought." Great, and now I've made this super awkward.

"Well, Harley." He slips his finger under the strap of my purse, freeing the hair that was trapped underneath. "I have a lot of fun with you, and as much as I love having my daughter around, and how much she enjoys you too, I feel like we have a connection and I'd like to explore in a setting that doesn't include screaming children."

I laugh and duck my head.

"I actually realized more than a month ago that I wanted to ask you out. But then there was Chad, and he created some challenges. Which I think have proven to work in my benefit, since it's given me time to get to know you even better. But patience is key, as I've learned." He gives me a lopsided smile. "Does that answer your question?"

I'm almost afraid to answer, for fear the butterflies in my stomach decide to come out of my mouth instead of words. I swallow down my nerves. "Yes, that definitely answers my question."

"Great. I'm really looking forward to taking you out, Harley."

He steps forward and leans down, lips brushing my cheek and lingering there.

"Me too." It's mostly a whisper.

"Until Saturday, then." He steps back, chest rising and falling on a deep exhale.

"Until Saturday."

He waits until I'm inside my car before he returns to his.

And I wait until I'm driving down the street before I shriek with excitement.

I have a date with Gavin.

On Saturday afternoon I bring half of my wardrobe to Spark House. This weekend's event is a sports dinner, so the bridal room is open, which means I can use it to prepare for my date. Could I have gotten dressed at my house on my own? Yes. But it's been a long time since I've gone out on a proper date.

Chad and I never really did the date-night thing, not unless you count going out with friends or nights spent on the couch with his Switch an actual date. Which I do not.

Since the breakup, Andrea and I have messaged back and forth, and we've made plans to go for coffee just the two of us, but Allen is Chad's friend and coworker, and so is Ted, so I understand that our breakup makes it a challenge. I have my sisters, and most of the time, they're more than enough.

"This is the dress," London says as I step out of the changing room.

It's mint-green chiffon: light, flowy, and elegant.

"Are you sure the black dress wouldn't be better? Isn't it sexier?" It sure does hug all my curves.

"The black dress is sexy, but this dress is *you*." London taps her lip. "And I say you accent with gold. Here." She passes me a pair of heels. "See how these look."

I try on the heels, and London outfits me with jewelry and a clutch before I get to work on my makeup. While I'm applying mascara, she checks on Avery to make sure everything is running smoothly with the event. She slips back into the bridal room ten minutes later.

"How's everything going out there?" I ask.

"Running like clockwork. It's so much easier now that we have the staff to support the events instead of it being the three of us running everything all the time. Here, let me help you with your liner." She takes the brown pencil from my hand and forces me into a chair. "Close your eyes."

I do as I'm told and tip my chin up. "It's hard to believe we tried to run every single event with just us and a skeleton staff for years, isn't it?"

London mm-hmms. "It honestly blows my mind sometimes when I think back to how we used to run things around here. And with the franchises, it's really going to be about us overseeing the events and letting the staff take the reins more and more. It's why we hired all of these competent people."

"Do you think we'll be able to free up two weekends a month soon?" It had been in the works before the franchise opportunity, which delayed us because our staffing needs have grown even more. I'd say something about how I'm worried about what the future is going to look like for us, but this isn't a great time, not when I'm about to go on a date.

"Honestly? I'm pretty sure we could make a case for it now. As it is, Avery's handling things fine out there on her own."

As if she can hear us talking about her, Avery knocks on the door and then slips into the room. She lets out a low whistle. "Wow. Nice dress pick, London."

"How do you know it wasn't me who chose this dress?"

"Because London is the fashion guru."

"Fair. How's everything going out there?" I ask, even though London and I were just talking about it.

"Great, apart from my freaking swollen feet." She drops down into a chair and toes her shoes off. She grunts and leans forward, rolling off a sock. "Good lord, how much water can one person retain?"

London and I both look down at her feet. The print of her sock is embedded in her skin and there's a dent where the top of her shoe ends. "You have to take it easy on the salt."

"I have been! All my food today has been boring and bland."

"On the upside, at least it's fall, and you don't have to wear sandals until well after the baby is born," London points out.

"I don't know if I'll be able to fit my feet into shoes by the time I'm ready to pop this baby out."

"I had to give up heels about four months in," London replies. Out of the three of us, she's the only who willingly wears heels most days of the week. I tend to stick to flats unless it's an event night, and Avery avoids them altogether. She wore flip-flops on her wedding day and running shoes during the obstacle course wedding party introduction at the reception.

"You would have worn heels to the delivery room if you'd been allowed," Avery scoffs and rubs her belly.

"That's untrue."

"Only because you were like Griselda, trying to jam your swollen feet into shoes that were way too small." Avery arches a brow. "Anyway, enough about swollen feet, do you know where Gavin is taking you for dinner?"

"Nope, he just said wear something nice," I reply.

"Did you pick up some sexy lingerie to wear under your dress?"

"I guess it depends on whose version of sexy we're talking about."

Avery's version of sexy lingerie is upgrading from a sports bra to one with padding and black bikini briefs. London, on the other hand, loves all things lace and satin and delicate. I'm somewhere between the two.

London stops messing with my eyebrows and gives me a stern look. "Please tell me you bought new underwear for this date."

"Who says he's going to see my underwear at the end of the night?" I challenge.

"Oh please." London props a fist on her hip. "Isn't Peyton sleeping over at her grandparents' place?"

"As far as I know, yes."

"So he'll be able to come back to your place and stay the night if he wants," London says.

"Do you think I should invite him back to my place?" I glance between my sisters.

"Why wouldn't you?" Avery rubs her belly.

"It's our first date."

Now it's Avery's turn to give me a look. "You've been seeing him on a weekly basis since July. It's October."

"Because of Peyton."

"Uh, we all know that's bullshit." Avery makes a circle motion and points at me.

"I was in a relationship for most of the time I was spending with them," I argue.

Avery rolls her eyes. "Chad was a nice guy, but he was a fun-for-now boyfriend, not a get-serious boyfriend. And he was way too into fantasy sports. No one should be in that many fantasy leagues. It's not normal, and that's coming from a self-professed sports junkie."

"Still, don't you think I should wait a while before jumping into bed with Gavin?" I bring my fingers to my lips then drop them to my lap so I don't ruin my gloss or my nails.

"Do whatever feels right." London seems to be changing her mind about this. "And you want to make sure that you're actually into Gavin on his own, rather than the Gavin-and-Peyton package."

"How is she going to figure that out unless she gets naked with him?" Avery argues.

"Sex complicates things. You know that better than anyone," London says pointedly. She's referencing the way Avery and Declan nearly imploded back when they crossed the line from best friends to best friends with *a lot* of benefits.

"My situation with Declan is not even remotely the same as what's going on with Harley and Gavin. Declan had major commitment issues, and I made a stupid mistake. Now we're super happy and totally in love and having a baby." Avery turns back to me. "I think you need to do whatever is right for you. It's up to you whether you let him see your underpants."

London sighs and shakes her head, then her eyes go wide, and she takes me by the shoulders. "Please tell me your underwear is not cotton."

"There's nothing wrong with cotton underwear. It breathes," Avery says defensively.

"There's nothing wrong with them in the general sense, but for a date and potentially the first underpants sighting, cotton is a no-no."

"They're not cotton," I assure her.

She arches a brow and I sigh.

"They're satin with a lace waistband and a floral print."

"Okay. As long as they don't have a cartoon pattern on them, we're good," London says with relief.

My phone buzzes on the vanity, and Gavin's name flashes across the screen. I nab the device and check the message. He's just pulled into Spark House. "He's here. I'm so nervous. Why am I so nervous?"

"Because you want to get naked with him," Avery says.

"Because you like him, and you're changing the dynamic of your relationship," London says.

"And you want to find out if he's got the moves between the sheets." Avery grins. She gives me a fist bump. "Just remember, you don't need to wait five dates before you get in the sack with this one."

"But don't feel like you need to rush into anything either." London turns me around once to make sure my dress isn't wonky in the back, and then they're ushering me into the hall.

I reach the front entrance as Gavin walks through the door. And I nearly melt into a puddle on the floor. He's dressed in a navy suit, hair styled, dark eyes roving over me on a heated sweep.

"You look stunning." He crosses the room and takes my hand in his, bringing it to his lips. "And you smell divine. What is that perfume?"

"I think it's called Boardwalk Taffy body lotion."

He chuckles. "Well, you certainly smell and look absolutely edible."

I bite my lip and fight the blush working its way into my cheeks. "Thank you, so you do."

"Are you ready to go?"

I nod, and my sisters wave me off, Avery looking ridiculously excited and London smiling softly, but I can see the hint of worry in her eyes.

Gavin opens the passenger door for me and helps me in before he rounds the hood and takes his place behind the wheel. He slides his key into the ignition and turns the engine over, then grips the wheel for a moment before he turns to look at me, giving his head a little shake.

"What?" I ask, suddenly feeling nervous and uncertain.

"This feels a little surreal, that's all."

"The date part?"

"Mmm. That you're back in my life. That I asked you on a date and you said yes. You're sure about this? You didn't say yes to be nice?"

I grin. "I didn't say yes to be nice. Did you ask just to be nice?"

He gives me a wry smile. "I wasn't trying to be even a little nice." He shifts the car into gear. "If I'm going to be completely honest, when I picked up Peyton from your place and Chad was there, I wanted to punch him in the junk. Or the face. Or both."

This time I laugh. "I think it was the same on both sides. He was not . . . not happy to say the least."

"Really? Why?"

"I, uh, I think he was under the impression that you were older."

He arches a brow. "I am older. I have nearly a decade on you."

"Less than a decade, but yeah, I think in his mind you were like, closer to fifty with a bald spot, not this." I motion to his general hotness.

"He expected me to have a dad bod?"

"I think so, yes."

"What else did he say?"

"That you had the hots for me."

He nods once. "Well, he wasn't wrong about that. But it wasn't until after that night that I realized there was more to me wanting to spend time with you beyond how well you and Peyton get along."

"We were two peas in a pod, then. I had my head buried in the sand too. When he freaked out about you and all the time I was spending with Peyton, I started questioning what I was doing with him." I don't tell him what Chad said about Gavin just looking for a mom for his daughter, or about London worrying that I was interested in dating him in part because of Peyton. This date will give us an opportunity to figure out if the chemistry between us is as real as I think it is.

"As bad as I feel about being part of the reason you broke it off with him, I'm glad we get the chance to explore us," Gavin tells me.

"Me too." I hold my clutch with both hands so I'm not tempted to touch my hair or bite my nails. "Is Peyton excited about having a sleepover at her grandparents?"

"She is. My mom is great at keeping her entertained, and she always has fun with them."

"That's good. Does she sleep okay when she's away from you?" I ask.

"Probably not as good as when she's in her own bed, but my parents have a special room for her in their house, and she really loves it there. My mom will let her stay up a little later than usual, and the next day she can be a bit of a grumpy bear, but you're absolutely worth it."

"I'm glad you think so."

He reaches across the console and squeezes my arm. "I didn't tell her I was out with you tonight. I don't want to confuse her or put that kind of pressure on you or us." He pulls into the parking lot of one of the nicest restaurants in the city. I've never been here before, but I've heard great things about the food. He pulls into an empty spot and shifts the car into park. "I don't want to get ahead of myself, though, so let's enjoy the evening and figure things out as we go."

"Okay. That sounds reasonable." I know eventually, if one date turns into more, we're going to have to talk about what this will look like. I don't think it's a good idea to jump right into a new relationship with both feet, not when there's a child involved. And I have no idea what relationships have looked like in the past for him. I'm aware we want to be very careful about how we address it with Peyton.

Gavin gets out of the car and rushes around to the passenger side, offering me a hand as I climb out. He closes the door, and instead of slipping my arm into his and guiding me toward the entrance, he raises my hand and presses his lips to my knuckle. "Can I make a suggestion?"

"Sure," I say breathily.

"You look utterly delectable to the point of distraction." His lips move against the back of my hand.

"Oh. Is that going to be a problem for you?" I'm not sure where he's going with this, but his eyes are hooded, and they keep roving over me in a way that makes me feel naked.

"Nothing I can't handle, but I was thinking . . ."

"About?"

"The order of things." He keeps rubbing his bottom lip and looking at my mouth.

"Would you like to elaborate on that?"

"Well, usually the kiss comes at the end of a date. I pick you up, take you somewhere nice—" He motions to the restaurant. "We eat and talk and laugh, and at the end—"

"You'll ask for permission to kiss me."

He nods. "Exactly."

"Hmm." I tap my lip. "Are you thinking that maybe we should be a little . . . deviant and turn this date on its head? Start with a kiss and work backwards?"

"I love how you think outside the box, Harley."

I slide my hand along his chest and up over his shoulder, taking a step closer until our bodies are flush. It's the closest I've been to him in years. But so much has changed, and now instead of seeking comfort, we're looking for something else. The anticipation feels electric. My skin pebbles, and the hairs on the back of my neck stand on end. I tip my chin up, gaze meeting his.

His eyes search mine. "You are so beautiful." He cups my cheek in his palm, thumb brushing back and forth, his lips hover over mine for a suspended moment. And for the briefest, uncomfortable second, I remember what it was like all those years ago. When I'd been this close to kissing him and everything changed. My whole world turned upside down.

But before the memory truly takes hold, he drops his head. And for the first time our lips meet. The kiss is gentle at first. Chaste.

For a moment I think that's going to be it. That he's going to drop a PG kiss on me and leave it at that. So I dig my nails into the back of his neck and suck his bottom lip between mine.

He makes a deep, throaty sound and winds his arm around my waist, pulling me tighter against him. We tip our heads, lips parting as our tongues meet. It's sweet at first, soft and tender. But I bite his tongue, and his hand slides down my back, gripping my ass as his hips press forward and I feel him, hard and demanding against my stomach. The sound of deep bass thumping from a passing car reminds me that we're standing outside, in the middle of the parking lot.

I tear my mouth from his, and his lips immediately latch onto my neck. I cup his chin in my hand and push him back just enough that he can't reach my mouth again. His gaze is all fire and his lip curls up in a salacious smile. "You're a minx under all that soft and sweet, aren't you?"

"You'll find that out later."

His brow arches. "Is that so?"

"Take me for dinner, Gavin."

His smile widens and his fiery gaze roves over my face again. He drops his head, his mouth at my ear. "One day, hopefully not long from now, I will most definitely eat you like you're my last meal."

I throw my head back and laugh, swatting at his chest. "Now that's a line."

"That's a promise, and one I intend to make and keep more than once." He winks, does a little surreptitious rearranging in his pants, then threads his fingers through mine and tugs me toward the restaurant.

Fifteen

SWEET WITH BITE

HARLEY

I'm excited to get more of this version of Gavin, flirty and play-ful. When it's just the two of us, it's as though he gives himself permission to let some of the walls down. And I understand why they've been in place while we're with Peyton. I'm not sure it will be particularly easy to stay in check all the time if that kiss is anything to go by.

The host takes us to a private table at the back of the restaurant and hands Gavin a wine list. "Do you prefer red or white?" he asks, flipping through the book.

"Um, I prefer margaritas to wine. Or sex on the beach." I bite my lip when his gaze lifts and one brow arches.

"I'm sure I can accommodate the second request at some point in the future, maybe next summer. Unless a tropical get-away is in the cards this winter."

"We're on our first date, Gavin. You might want to hold off on planning vacations until at least date six or seven," I tease.

My stomach flutters at the thought that he's already folding me into his life. And another part of me worries that this is all too fast. As if being able to ask me out on a date suddenly opened a door he's been waiting to walk through, and now he can't help but build a fictional future that somehow includes me every step of the way. It's as elating as it is terrifying.

And maybe that makes sense, since he knows exactly how I am with kids, and that I'll put my heart and soul into his daughter. It makes me wonder what his previous relationships have looked like. I don't want to dampen the light mood with that kind of conversation, though.

He sets the wine menu aside. "Sorry. That kiss has scrambled my head."

"Mine too," I admit.

"I thought you in this dress was going to be a distraction, but now I know how tempting your lips are." He taps his own with his index finger.

"I can hold my hand in front of my mouth if it helps. I could even draw fake lips on my fingers so it looks more authentic." I start to lift my hand.

Gavin grabs it and laces his fingers with mine. "I want to see every part of your gorgeous face, especially that beautiful mouth."

"Who are you and what have you done with Peyton's dad?"

"Am I too much for you?"

"Not at all. This is just a very different side of you. I like it."

"Good. I'm glad to hear that." He smooths his thumb back and forth over my knuckles. Even that small, innocent touch sends warmth through my veins.

I settle on a Bellini—it's part sparkling wine, part juice—and Gavin orders a glass of red wine.

The server glances between us, looking a little nervous before his gaze finally settles on me. "May I see some identification, miss?"

I'm used to being carded. I don't look my age at all, and the fact that I'm short doesn't help. I slide my identification out of my wallet and pass it over to the server. His eyes widen in surprise. "Oh. I'm so sorry for the inconvenience, ma'am. Thank you."

"It's not a problem."

The server rushes off, red-faced.

"How often do you get carded?"

"Basically every time I order alcohol." I slide my ID back into my clutch. "I'm used to it."

The server returns with our drinks, and we decide to share the gnocchi as an appetizer.

While we wait for our appetizer, we talk about the event at Spark House tonight, and the other events we're hosting in the coming months, including a small cosplay convention, which Gavin is entirely too fascinated by.

"Isn't it just adults dressing up like it's Halloween?"

"In a general sense, but these are like super fans. They really get into role-play and they're passionate about the characters, and we're not talking just people who are into the movies. These people read all the graphic novels. They collect them and keep them in sealed packages and temperature-controlled rooms to make sure they stay in perfect condition."

"I might want to stop by Spark House that weekend."

"They have makeup artists who come in and do the coolest things. I'm going to be dressed as Poison Ivy."

"I shouldn't be the least bit surprised that you're going to get dressed up for that event."

"I was probably born to cosplay. I feel like it was a missed calling."

The server returns with our shared appetizer. We leave it in the center of the table and pick at it while we chat.

Our meals arrive. I ordered the salmon and Gavin ordered the steak, and we talk all through dinner, not even caring that our food is tepid by the time we're finished.

We order the chocolate lava cake for dessert, to share, of course.

I decide I can't let this night end without addressing the one thing that's been eating at me all these years. "Can I ask you something?"

"Of course."

I set my fork down and take a sip of water, steeling my resolve.

"Harley? Is everything okay?"

"Do you remember that night when Peyton was teething and kept waking up?"

Gavin sets down his own fork and leans back in his chair. "She had a few of those nights."

"You were in the kitchen. I was going to get a glass of water and I found you there."

"Ah." His gaze drops to the table. "Yes, I remember that night."

I swallow down the nerves with a sip of my Bellini. "Is what almost happened that night the reason you moved to Boulder?"

His head snaps up, brows pulled together in confusion. "What?"

"Because I almost kissed you then." My heart feels like it's going to beat its way out of my chest and my mouth is desert dry, but I need the answer to this question, so I can finally move past it, instead of hanging on to it. "Is that why you moved?"

Gavin rubs his bottom lip and sighs. "No. That isn't why we moved, but it did force me to see that I was heading down a path that was dangerous for both of us. And Peyton calling you Momma . . . that was . . . I had to look critically at what I was doing. You were young and so full of life, and I was . . . broken and grieving. It would have been a mistake to do anything back then. I wasn't in the right frame of mind."

I nod and cover my mouth with my hand, the emotional weight of it all still pulling me down. "So it wasn't my fault that you moved to Boulder?"

"What? No, Harley." He takes my free hand in his. "Hey, listen to me, it wasn't about you. You didn't do anything wrong. People get caught up in the moment, but everything about the timing was wrong. You were so young, figuring yourself out. I was in a bad place, and you were a lifeline. You kept me from sinking, and I relied on you a lot, which I'm sure made things confusing. I realized that after that night, and I knew I needed a reset. And I needed more help with Peyton than I was willing to admit. Did you honestly believe you were the reason we moved away?"

"I never heard from you again."

"My headspace wasn't good at the time. Those were lines I couldn't cross, not then. I felt like I had the potential to really upend your life in a way I didn't want to. I cared about you, for you, but I couldn't entertain a relationship. I didn't and couldn't look at you that way then." He squeezes my hand. "It wasn't fair to you, but I needed a clean break and I'm sorry for that."

I exhale a long, slow breath, and with it lifts the weight of guilt. "You weren't the only one in a bad headspace. I realized I was trying to fill up the holes in my heart by taking care of other people's kids. And living with you and Peyton, it made me feel like I was part of a family. I can see now how hard that all must have been for you too. I just thought I was the reason and held onto that belief because I didn't know what the other side looked like for you."

"There were a lot of reasons, Harley. What almost happened in the kitchen that night isn't on you." He raises my hand to his lips and kisses my knuckle. "I should have realized the lines were blurring, but I'd been so caught up in my grief and trying to keep my head above water. When you messaged after we moved, I wasn't in a good place. The adjustment was hard. And by the time I was ready to reach out, it had been so long, and I felt like it was probably better for me to leave it and you alone. Let you move on with your life. I'm sorry it's taken this long for me to tell you that. I can't imagine how hard it all was for you."

"It's in the past. We can leave it there now." There's relief in getting that off my chest. I spent so much time feeling like I had been to blame, unable to see his side of things, and now the weight of that shame has finally lifted.

"We can start from here instead. Sound good?"

I smile. "It does."

"Good. Do you want to get out of here?" He raises his free hand and asks the server for the bill.

Gavin laces our fingers together as we cross the parking lot to his car. We chat about his weekend plans with Peyton as we drive toward my place. "We could go to the park by my house tomorrow if you want," I offer.

"You haven't had enough of me yet?" Gavin asks.

"Not nearly." I grin.

"Peyton would love that, and so would I."

"It's a date, then." As we approach my building, I clutch my purse in my lap and point to the underground parking sign. "Do you want to come up for a drink?"

"I was hoping you would ask." He pulls into the underground lot and parks in the visitor's spot. We take the elevator to my apartment, and I unlock the door, ushering him inside before replacing the safety latch.

The last time he was here, I was still dating Chad. But that relationship feels like a lifetime ago. And this one . . . well, it feels like it's already been a lifetime of waiting to get here.

Gavin stands in the front foyer, one hand shoved in his pocket, gaze flitting from me to the hallway.

"What are you thinking?" I ask on a whisper.

"About how irrationally annoyed I was when I realized that Chad kid was your boyfriend."

"He's twenty-nine. He's not a kid."

"He lives on a steady diet of video games—in my head he's a kid."

I arch a brow. "I'm twenty-eight."

"And you successfully run an event hotel, and you can get a nine-year-old to follow rules and go to bed on time, which makes you very much a woman."

"I also love glitter crafts and dressing up like a fairy godmother."

"Which makes you a special breed of woman and a bit of a badass. Glitter can be a nightmare."

"Yes. Yes it can." I take a step closer and pick up his tie, winding it around my hand. "You know what I've been thinking about all night?"

He makes a low sound in the back of his throat. "What's that?"

"Our conversation in the parking lot, pre-dinner."

"And what were you thinking about that conversation?"

"That I'd like to pick up where we left off."

"What about that drink you invited me up for?"

"We can have one later." Say eight or so hours from now, in the form of coffee.

I tip my chin up and tug on his tie, pulling his mouth down. His lips touch mine, soft and gentle, just like last time. But unlike our first kiss, this one isn't tentative. We tip our heads and part our lips. His velvet tongue meets mine, and I sink into him and the kiss, looping my arms around the back of his neck, melding my curves to his hard edges.

One of his arms wraps around my waist, keeping me close, and the other one cups my cheek. This kiss holds the promise of more. Of patience and decadence.

Seven years ago, I was young and inexperienced. He was grieving and full of guilt.

But now . . . we're in much different places in our lives. Older, wiser, and hopefully better prepared to deal with the feelings that existed before and have been dormant all this time.

Unearthing them ignites raw desire. I moan into his mouth and press my hips into his, taking his bottom lip between my teeth and tugging before I suck the soft, plump flesh and release it. Then stroke inside his mouth again, searching for his tongue. He makes a matching, low, feral sound, and his hand on my hip travels up my side, along my arm, causing goose bumps to rise in its wake.

He takes my face in both his palms and pulls back, his fiery gaze locking on mine. "Should we be slowing this down?"

I answer his question with a question. "Do you want to slow this down?"

"Not particularly, no."

"Then no, we shouldn't slow this down." I try to meld our lips back together, but his hold on me tightens, two inches separating us.

His warm breath fans my face. "I'm trying to keep my head with you, Harley."

"Why? I want to lose mine with you." It's blatantly, painfully honest. All the years between that almost-kiss and now seem to disappear. As if they never happened. As if time were suspended, waiting for our paths to converge again.

He huffs a laugh, and an emotion I can't quite catch passes over his gorgeous features, before his gaze lowers to my mouth and then his lips are on mine again. This time, it isn't gentle and patient. It's full of pent-up emotion. Desire and need wash over me. I find the knot in his tie and tug, loosening it until I can get to the buttons underneath.

We don't make it past the kitchen before I tug his shirt from his dress pants and work the buttons free, pushing the fabric over his shoulders and down his arms. It ends up on the floor, along with his tie and my dress.

"Fuck me," Gavin groans when I step out of the puddle of green fabric at my feet.

His eyes sweep over me, teeth trapping his bottom lip as he takes me in. "You are an utterly delectable walking contradiction, Harley." He picks me up by the waist like I weigh nothing and sets me on the island.

I part my knees and hook a foot around the back of his thigh, pulling him into the empty, waiting space between mine. "How do you mean?"

"You look so sweet, but you've got bite." He drags a fingertip along the lace trim of my bra. "This." He drops his head, lips finding my collarbone. "So pretty and sweet." His lips travel up the side of my neck. "So gorgeous."

I wrap my leg around his waist and pull him closer, one hand finding his belt buckle, the other sifting through his thick, wavy hair, gripping the strands so I can guide his mouth, bringing it back to mine.

"So assertive." He grins against my cheek.

I turn my head and catch his bottom lip between my teeth, before I tip my head and our mouths connect again.

"There's the bite I was talking about." He chuckles, and then groans as I slip my hand down the front of his pants and cup him through his boxers.

He's gloriously hard and thick.

We kiss and grope, fingers exploring, touching, coaxing moans and gasps and dirty words out of each other until we're both naked and panting. His wallet sits beside me on the countertop. He flips it open, fumbling for a few seconds—distracted by my hand stroking his erection and my mouth nibbling a path along the edge of his jaw—until he finds the condom.

"Shit. Let me check the expiration date," he mutters.

I have condoms in my bedroom. And I've been on the pill since I was eighteen. But safety is important, and we haven't talked about previous partners.

He squints at the date stamped into the foil wrapper. "Good for another six months."

"Perfect." I nab it and tear it open, rolling it down his length.

And then he's pushing inside, stretching me, filling me, connecting us in the most intimate way. He grips my hip, pulling me closer to the edge of the counter, and I wrap one leg around his waist, letting the other dangle, my toes brushing along the side of his thigh.

Instead of wrapping my arms around his shoulders, I lean back on my palms, taking in the sight of him, sweaty and naked, standing between my thighs. He's such a delicious treat.

I roll my hips, encouraging him to move. His thrusts are slow at first, long and languorous. I drop a hand between my thighs and rub tight circles, sensation gathering and building until I'm at the edge of an orgasm. I balance there for a few seconds, then tip over into bliss, fingers moving furiously as Gavin continues to pump his hips.

As soon as I drop my hand back to the counter, he slides both of his under my butt and lifts me, forcing me to wrap myself around him. He lifts and lowers me, faster and harder, my sensitive skin rubbing up against him, sending another wave of pleasure rushing through me.

We end up in a heap on the kitchen floor. Still wrapped around each other. I blink at him, running my fingers through his sweaty, messy hair. "Hey."

"Hey yourself." His voice is more rasp than words.

"Wanna sleep over so we can do that again in the morning?" I ask.

He grins, his eye twinkling with mischief. "I was thinking more like the middle of the night, but yes, I definitely want to sleep over."

Sixteen

LITTLE BITS OF TRUTH
TO MAKE THE WHOLE

HARLEY

Over the weeks that follow, Gavin and I try to find time to spend together, just the two of us. It isn't always easy because my schedule still doesn't allow for frequent weekends off. But some nights, after we're sure Peyton is asleep, we'll sneak into his office, lock the door, and have frantic, quiet sex.

We decide not to tell Peyton that we're dating. Gavin and I try to keep it platonic when it's the three of us, so as not to confuse her. We want to be careful, not only for her sake, but also for ours, as we navigate this new version of us.

One night in the middle of the week, about a month or so after we start seeing each other, I slip out of her bedroom after reading her three stories and find Gavin sitting in the living room with the TV on, clearly not watching it since the volume is too low to hear. We haven't had a night alone in a couple of weeks, and mostly it's been stolen moments.

He tosses the *Architectural Digest* magazine on the table. "Is she asleep?"

"Out like a light."

He pushes up off the couch. "My office?"

I nod and turn around, hightailing it down the hall. He follows close behind and pulls the door shut behind him, turning the lock before we're on each other, groping, grinding, and trying to rid each other of our clothes as quickly and quietly as we can.

"We need another sleepover. These quickies aren't cutting it." He drags my pants and underwear down my legs and drops to his knees, gripping my hips and nuzzling my center. His mouth finds my sensitive skin for a too-brief moment before he stands up and pulls me over to the couch.

He drops to his knees again and pushes my legs apart. In the weeks that we've been sleeping together, I've discovered that Gavin is very gifted in bed. I've never been with someone who can make me come every time we have sex, or who makes sure that I'm satisfied completely before he finds his own release. Even if it doesn't happen quickly—which sometimes is the case if I'm listening for the sound of feet in the hallway—he's always patient and attentive, coaxing delicious orgasms out of me.

He runs his palms heavily up the inside of my thighs and licks his lips, gaze dropping between my thighs. "I can't wait to get my mouth on you," he groans.

"Daddy! Harley! Where are you? Daddy! Daddy!" The sound of Peyton's feet coming down the hall has us both shooting up off the couch. I rush to grab my pants and shirt and slip into the bathroom that adjoins his office and the spare bedroom to dress while Gavin tugs his pants up his legs and yanks his T-shirt over his head.

I struggle into my own clothes, my face on fire, eyes wild, and the rest of me ridiculously sweaty, likely from the embarrassment. I feel like a teenager who's sneaking around, except it's not a parent I'm worried about catching me, it's a nine-year-old. I can hear Gavin consoling Peyton from the other side of the door.

I make sure my hair isn't a mess and that my clothes are smoothed before I open it. "Is everything okay?" I ask, forcing a smile and hoping I don't look as guilty as I feel.

"I didn't know where you were. You weren't in the living room and usually that's where Daddy is after he puts me to bed." Her fingers go to her mouth. "I had a dream that the angels had come to take Harley back, and this time they took you with them."

"Oh, sweetie, that's not going to happen." Gavin wraps his arms around her.

"Why are you in your office? It's late for working," she mumbles into his stomach.

"I was showing Harley some drawings for one of my projects."

"Is it a secret project? Is that why the door was locked?"

Gavin's gaze darts to me. I didn't manage to get my bra back on because I couldn't find it. I cross my arms over my chest to hide my peaked nipples and scan the floor. I spot the floral printed cup at the edge of the couch, about five feet away from where Gavin is hugging Peyton. I take a few steps closer, moving in so I can shove it under the couch with my toe.

"Do you want your dad to take you back to bed?"

"Can you both come? Can you sing me a song, Harley?"

I glance at Gavin, taking my cues from him. "That sounds like a good idea."

Gavin picks her up and carries her back to her room, me following close behind. He climbs into her princess bed with her, and I sit in the beanbag chair and sing her favorite lullabies until she falls asleep.

I help him roll out of her bed, and we steal out of her room and head back to the living room. "That was close." I drop down on the couch next to him.

"Very close." He rubs at his lips with his fingertips.

"Tell me what you're thinking?"

"That I'm glad I locked my office door," he mutters.

I nod my agreement. "It would have been very hard to explain what was going on if she'd burst in on us like that."

He runs a hand through his hair. "I think we need my parents to take her for an overnight again."

I've been patient with Gavin while we've been navigating this new us, but at some point me always going home and us only being able to spend the night together once a month has to change. We've been seeing each other for a while now, and although his parents know we're dating, I'm not sure what he's told his mother-in-law, if anything at all. At this point, it's only my sisters who know I'm even spending time with him as anything other than a friend. I understand that we need to be cautious, but I'm starting to feel like a dirty little secret.

"We can definitely do that. Plan another date night where you get to stay at my place," I say, then decide now is as good a time as any to address one of the other issues. "I know that we want to approach this carefully for Peyton's sake, but I think we probably need to talk about how long we're planning to keep this from her. Or at least at what point you're going to feel comfortable telling her we're dating, if that's what we're doing."

His brows pull together. "What do you mean? If that's what we're doing?"

I struggle to find the words, not wanting to create unnecessary tension, but needing to know what we are to each other. "I'm just not sure what it is exactly we're doing. We've only been on one date and that was a month ago. Most of the time we have Peyton with us, and our alone time is relegated to sneaking off to your office. Are we friends with benefits? Are we secretly dating?"

His eyes flare with shock. "Shit. Is that how I'm making you feel? I don't want you to be a secret indefinitely. And I don't see this as a friends-with-benefits situation. Not for me anyway. Is that how you see us?"

"No, but we've never really defined what we're doing." The lump in my throat softens. "I'm glad we're on the same page, but how do we move forward?"

Gavin taps on the arm of the sofa and pokes at his cheek with his tongue. "I've always been very careful to keep my personal life separate from Peyton, and I realize this is a lot different because you two are already close." He blows out a breath. "Karen didn't exactly make it easy for me to date in the past. I don't think I realized how hard she made it until now."

This is what I've been waiting for, a peek into Gavin's dating history. How he's managed relationships prior to me. "Why? What would happen when you dated before?"

He shifts so he's looking at me, instead of across the room. "She had an opinion on who I should be with, and sometimes she would make it hard for me to go on dates."

This is new information, and I want more of it so I know what to expect. "How do you mean?"

"She would offer to take Peyton for the night, and then halfway through a date I'd get a call saying Peyton was having a hard time, and she needed me to pick her up. It made it difficult to establish new relationships. And if I hired a babysitter that she didn't know about, she'd give me a hard time about having someone who wasn't family watching Peyton."

I nod slowly, wanting to be careful about how I approach this with him. I know there's tension between him and his mother-in-law, and based on what he's told me, it might explain why she's been so frosty with me in the past. "Did you ever introduce anyone to your in-laws? Or Peyton?"

"Only once," he says.

"Once?" I can't hide my surprise. While I understand not wanting to introduce a slew of girlfriends to Peyton, because that would be confusing and challenging should the relationships not work out, one girlfriend in seven years is . . . not what I expected. "How long did you date for?"

"Before or after the introduction?" He looks away, his jaw tensing.

"Both?"

"We dated for six months before I introduced her to Peyton and my in-laws. We broke up a month later." He runs his hands down his thighs, like this conversation makes him uncomfortable.

"What happened?" I ask.

"I don't know that it was any one thing, but Karen didn't think she was good with Peyton, and she was the first woman I'd been serious about since Marcie passed. I think it was too much for all of us."

"How old was Peyton?" I ask.

"She was five. She only met her a few times, so she didn't have time to get attached to her, but she had a daughter too, and she and Peyton got along, so it was still tough. I didn't want to do that to her or myself again, so I kept my relationships separate after that."

"Were there many?" This is information I need, not because

I'm jealous or prying, but I want a clear idea of the challenges that lie ahead, not just for Gavin, but for Peyton and for me.

He shakes his head. "Only a couple, and they didn't last very long."

"Thank you for sharing this with me." I take his hand in mine, feeling a lot like, despite our age gap, I'm the one with more relationship experience. I haven't had a lot of boyfriends, or even cohabited with anyone other than my sister, but Gavin has a lot of baggage. He and Marcie were together for nearly a decade, from the start of college until Peyton was born. Since then, he's only had one girlfriend he deemed worthy of meeting his in-laws and Peyton. That tells me a lot about where he's at when it comes to relationships.

And it means I'm going to have to be extremely patient with him as we move forward.

"This whole situation is uncharted territory for me, Harley. I know I've been holding back when it comes to telling Peyton, but I think we can make a plan to tell her soon."

"You let me know when you're ready."

"Okay." He slips his hand into my hair and kisses me softly.

I can't tell if it's full of apology or need, or both.

I'm not going to push Gavin to say anything to Peyton until he's ready. But it grows increasingly difficult when he does things like link our fingers when we're out in public with her. Or he'll put his arm across the back of the bench when we're sitting at the park and she's playing on the slide or the swings. He'll absently rub his thumb back and forth on my shoulder, and I'll have to remind him that we're not alone.

Individually, those small affections don't mean much and can be brushed off, but the more they happen, the more Peyton starts to notice, until finally, one day she catches us in the act. Well, not *the* act, thankfully.

Most Mondays I pick Peyton up from school and take her to the park—it's our off day at Spark House, or as off as we can reasonably have with everything that's going on—and it means that Gavin's parents aren't on the hook every day of the week. It's not that they don't want the time with Peyton, but five days a week of after-school care is a lot to ask of a couple on the verge of retirement, and it gives me and Peyton some bonding time.

On this particular Monday, Gavin gets home from work around five thirty. Peyton is feeling fairy-ish, so the moment we walked through the door, we donned our tutus and our wings and spent half an hour dancing around her bedroom. As soon as Gavin arrived home, he was instructed to change by fairy Peyton.

Currently he's wearing a pair of running pants that don't hide much, and a blue tank top that looks like it was made for a teenager, and a very sparkly deep-blue tutu. I don't know if it's normal that I find him incredibly sexy dressed up like this. He's just such a great dad.

The three of us gather in the kitchen, Gavin and I moving around each other as I cut up strawberries for Peyton to nibble on while we make dinner. Gavin puts his hands on my hips and moves me over enough so he can get into the drawer with the spatula. We're having breakfast for dinner, one of Peyton's favorite meals.

It means we're having pancakes, bacon, and fresh chopped fruit.

When I turn to smile up at him, he drops a kiss on my cheek. For a second I don't think anything of it, until I refocus my attention on the bowl of hulled strawberries and push it toward Peyton, whose eyes are wide as saucers. "Dad kissed you!"

I can only imagine what my expression must be. I glance at Gavin, and he wears the same panic I'm feeling.

I don't know how to address this, or what exactly to say.

"Harley and I like each other," Gavin says.

"Like each other how? You only kiss Nana and me on the cheek. Is Harley like part of our family now? Did you kiss her on the cheek when she was my nanny too?" Peyton lobs questions at her dad.

"I didn't kiss her on the cheek when you were a baby." Gavin taps on the counter. "But that was a long time ago, and things are different now."

"Different how?" Her eyes light up. "Is Harley your girlfriend? My friend Josie has an older sister and she's in high school and she has a boyfriend named Davis who's always over. She says she saw them kissing, but it wasn't like a kiss on the cheek. She said it looked he was trying to eat her face. Bobby Cooper wants me to be his girlfriend, and he wants to hold my hand sometimes, but one of the other boys said he doesn't wash his hands after he goes to the bathroom, which is gross. And I don't think I want him to kiss me." She wrinkles her nose then turns her attention to me. "Do you want my dad to kiss you?"

I chuckle, because her nine-year-old brain is hilarious, and look to Gavin to see how he wants to handle this. I'm relieved when he doesn't lie to her. "How would you feel if Harley was my girlfriend?"

She tips her head to the side. "Would it change anything?"

"What do you mean?" Gavin asks.

Her lips twist to the side, and it's clear she's thinking. "Will Harley still come over and spend time with us?"

"Of course," I say.

"So you won't just want to spend time with Dad? You'll still spend time with me too?"

"I'll always want to spend time with you," I assure her.

"It doesn't change anything, honey. It just means that sometimes we might hold hands, and that you might see Harley more, instead of less."

She ponders that for a minute before she nods. "Okay. Then I think I would feel good about Harley being your girlfriend. If she wants to. Do you want to be Dad's girlfriend?" she asks me, her expression serious.

"I would like that," I tell her honestly.

A wide grin breaks across her face and she claps once. "Yay! And Dad always washes his hands after he goes to the bathroom, so you don't have to worry about not being able to hold his hand."

"That's very good news." I smile up at Gavin, and he gives my hand a squeeze in return, but I worry that this was too easy and the hard stuff is yet to come.

A couple of weeks after we tell Peyton that we're officially dating, I pick her up from school. I've been added as an emergency contact since I'm often Gavin's fallback plan should a meeting run late or his parents aren't able to grab her.

"Harley! I hoped you would be picking up Peyton today! Do you have a minute?" Her teacher, Mrs. Horton, gives me a bright smile when she sees me.

"Of course." I hug Peyton and give her a kiss on top of the head.

Mrs. Horton asks Peyton if she would mind putting away the art supplies, and Peyton, being the helpful kid she is, rushes off. As soon as she's out of earshot Mrs. Horton turns back to me. "I've sent out an email already, but I wanted to tell you that Peyton's getting an award for being such a great help with her peers at the assembly next week. It's on a Friday afternoon, and the assembly starts at one. I was wondering if you think her dad will be able to attend?"

"I'm sure we'll be able to figure something out. He wouldn't want to miss this. Let me check his schedule." I pull up my calendar and scroll through his meetings and mine. "I'll just block it off for him, so he doesn't add anything to the calendar. Do you need my help organizing?"

"Really? Are you sure you have time?"

"Absolutely. You know I'm more than happy to help. Do you need me to come in for setup or anything?"

"Usually we set up on Thursday after school, but even if you're here around noon on Friday to help get the kids organized, that would be great."

"I can do both. Just send me a message or an email if you need me to pick stuff up. I know how busy these things can be."

She tells me she'll email me the details of the assembly, and I take Peyton to the park before we meet Gavin at home. Almost the second we're through the door, his in-laws call and Peyton gets on the phone to tell her granny about the assembly and that she's supposed to get a special award, but she doesn't know what it's for exactly, so it's sort of a surprise, sort of not.

And of course, that means all of a sudden they're coming for a weekend visit. Based on Gavin's expression, he's not particularly excited about that. And it makes me wonder what he's said to his in-laws about me and how they're going to respond to my being there.

On Friday I arrive at the school about an hour before the assembly to help set up. Yesterday afternoon I brought balloons, and the kids blew them up and stuck them to the walls and the podium, so today it's just about getting the students organized based on the award they're receiving.

Not only are Gavin's in-laws here, but so are his parents. As much as I'm not super excited to see Karen again, considering the frosty reception I received last time, I can appreciate the lengths they'll go to be present for Peyton and to support Gavin.

The assembly is an amazing celebration of community and good deeds, and Peyton receives an award for being empathetic and helpful. I love that this school celebrates not only academic achievement, but also kindness and compassion.

Once the assembly is over, I meet up with Gavin in the foyer, where they have refreshments and baked goods which were donated by one of the local businesses that Spark House also works with. I might have pulled a few strings to make that happen.

I find Gavin in the crowd, standing with his parents, his in-laws, and Lynn and Ian. Claire received an award for being an excellent team player.

My stomach flips as I head in their direction. Gavin said he's told Karen we're dating and that Peyton knows, but I'm unsure what her reaction to that information was.

Lynn is the first person to notice me. She waves and steps away from the group to pull me in for a hug. "It's so great to see you again! We really need to get together for dinner one of these nights."

"I would love that."

"I keep mentioning it to Ian, but organizing dinner dates aren't his strong suit. Let's exchange numbers and see if we can't make something work. Claire just started hockey and the early-morning weekend practice schedule is killing me, but she loves it, so it's worth the five thirty A.M. ice time."

"Ouch, that's early."

"I don't even get up that early on weekdays." We promise to arrange something soon, and when Lynn gets a call, she excuses herself and steps outside for a moment.

I move to join the rest of the group. Judith, Gavin's mother, gives me a warm smile and lifts her hand in greeting. I steel myself as Karen turns to see who she's waving at and her smile falters.

"Harley, how nice of you to offer your time to help out with the assembly. One of these times I should do that too." Judith pulls me in for a warm hug, just like Lynn did.

"That would be great! I usually come in to help with assembly prep when I don't have a Spark House event. You're always welcome to join me." I turn to Karen, wanting to make sure she feels included. "And if you're ever visiting, you're obviously more than welcome to join anytime."

"That's kind of you, but I think my time is better spent with my granddaughter since I get so little of it these days." Talk about passive-aggressive guilt tripping.

I try to make small talk with Gavin's parents and his in-laws, but Karen seems determined to ignore me as much as possible. Thankfully, Peyton's teacher stops by to say hi. Of course, Karen hijacks that conversation, asking about the academics and what level of math they're teaching. Judith and Gareth, Gavin's father, excuse themselves to use the bathroom while I stand off to the side, feeling awkward since Kyle is talking Gavin's and Ian's ears off about golf and I'm left on the sidelines.

Peyton and one of her classmates, Krissy, along with Claire, come bouncing over, their awards in their hands.

Gavin has enough time to congratulate them and hug Peyton before a woman who looks to be in her mid-thirties and is clearly a huge fan of athletic wear pushes her way into the group. She's wearing fuchsia Lycra pants, hot pink running shoes, and a matching zip-up jacket. Her hair is pulled up in a ponytail with a matching hot pink scrunchie, and her skin is glowing. Not because she's radiant, but because she's wearing foundation with a sheen to it. Her eyelashes are longer than my fingers and her eyebrows are so perfect, I can't tell if they're stenciled on or maybe she had them tattooed. Regardless, she's a lot of visual input.

She makes a beeline for Gavin and thrusts her hand out. "You must be Peyton's dad. I'm Larissa, Krissy's mom. It's so great to finally meet you."

"Gavin. It's a pleasure." He glances down at Larissa, and then at his arm, which Larissa is holding onto with her very perfect, very manicured nails.

She throws her head back and laughs, despite Gavin not making a joke. "Really, the pleasure is all mine. Krissy tells me you're a single dad. That must be so tough. You know, I'd love to have Peyton over for a playdate. Anytime. I'm divorced, and I work from home, so really, she's always welcome. Why don't we exchange numbers and we can set something up?"

I'm rendered speechless as this woman hits on my boyfriend right in front of me and his in-laws. I take a step forward to make my presence known.

Larissa's gaze drops from Gavin's stunned face to me. She gives me a once-over that turns from assessing to dismissive. "Oh, it's so great that you include your nanny in these kinds of events and supersmart for mingling with the other parents," she simpers and drags her gaze back to me. "Why don't you be a doll and take the girls outside to play on the swings."

Gavin's expression is somewhere between disbelief and horror, while mine, I'm sure, reflects my desire to shove thumbtacks under this woman's nails and then cover her in honey and throw her into a forest with hungry bears.

Gavin puts an arm awkwardly around my shoulder. "Harley is my girlfriend, not the nanny."

"Oh." Larissa's extremely perfect eyebrows arch even more, and her cheeks hollow out as she looks me over again. "Wow. You barely look like you're out of college. You need to tell me your secrets."

I give her a saccharine smile. "I go to bed early and I don't let stress get to me." I sincerely hope Peyton won't be going over to her house for a playdate.

Karen coughs and leans in close to Gavin so she can whisper, but not quietly enough for me not to overhear. "I'm not the only one who sees the issue with this."

If this were a cartoon, steam would be shooting out of my ears and the top of my head would lift off. Peyton, who followed Krissy to the snack table, comes skipping back over. "Harley, can I show you the art project I'm working on? Mrs. Horton says I have a few minutes before she locks up the classroom."

"Absolutely." I turn to the group and plaster on what I hope is a successful smile, even though my face feels a lot like it's made of stiff plastic. "We'll be right back. It was nice to meet you, Lisa." I purposely get her name wrong. Now I understand why Chad and Gavin did that.

Gavin looks like he wants to stop me, and also laugh at my clear snub, but I give his arm a squeeze and take Peyton's hand, letting her lead me down the hall, away from all the catty bitches.

Seventeen

WALKING THE TIGHTROPE

GAVIN

Larissa collects her daughter and excuses herself, flitting to another family like a drunk bee. I turn to my mother-in-law and give her a stern look. "That was not okay."

She rolls her shoulders back. "I didn't say anything others weren't already thinking."

"Harley is my girlfriend. She volunteers at the school, she spends time with Peyton because she cares about her, and I care about both of them. Belittling Harley in public is not a good way to win points with me, and you're certainly not going to win points with Harley either."

She purses her lips and laces her fingers together, dropping her head slightly. It makes her look repentant, but I'm not sure I buy it. "I'm concerned about the influence she's having on Peyton. What happens if this relationship doesn't work out? What kind of damage will that do to Peyton?"

"The influence she's having?" I say, my voice laced with incredulity. "She's fostering Peyton's creative side, and she's always giving her opportunities to play and have fun and be a kid. What's wrong with that?"

"What about structure and rules and consistency? What will

happen to all of that if you and Harley don't work out? She's young."

"She's twenty-eight. Last I checked that's considered a full-blown adult."

"She's almost a decade younger than you."

I cross my arms. "My parents are a decade apart, and they worked out just fine."

"You know boys mature slower than the girls. I'm still trying to catch up to you, Kay-kay," Kyle says with a smile.

"You're not helping," she snaps at her husband then turns back to me. "Those were different times, and she is at a very different place in her life than you are."

"How do you know? You haven't even talked to her to be able to make that assessment."

Before Karen can respond, my parents return from the bathroom.

My mother looks between me and Karen, probably picking up on the hostility. "Is everything okay?"

"Everything's fine." Karen smiles, but it's just as stiff as my posture.

"We should get Peyton and all go out for lunch. I'm starved." My dad pops a brownie into his mouth. The man has an endless sweet tooth that's rarely satisfied.

"You'll ruin your appetite if you eat any more of those," my mother says, her tone disapproving, but she smiles and rolls her eyes.

"They're one-bite brownies. They're not going to ruin anything, dear." He gives her a cheeky smile before he turns back to me. "You can fill me in on how things are going with the park project over lunch."

"For sure. There are a few things I'd like to pick your brain on."

"I peeked at the most recent blueprints, and it looks great, but I'm always happy to give you feedback."

Peyton and Harley return, and my dad, who is completely oblivious to the tension between Harley and Karen, invites her out for lunch with us. Which makes sense, she's often invited for meals. Sometimes, when I'm working late on a project, she'll pick up Peyton and my parents will invite her to stay for dinner. They adore her. Which makes Karen's animosity toward her that much more obvious and glaring.

Of course, I want Harley to join us, but I'm also aware of how uncomfortable this has to be for her. And navigating Karen isn't easy.

"You have to come with us!" Peyton holds onto Harley's arm while she jumps up and down. "Daddy, can we go to Chuck E. Cheese again?"

"Chuck E. Cheese? Is that the horrible place with all the games inside the restaurant? That's a breeding ground for sickness and germs. Why would you even entertain taking Peyton there?" Karen's lip curls with disdain.

"Because it's fun. And because Peyton is a kid, and she has the immune system of a superhero since she's surrounded by germs all day, every day." Harley motions to the school.

I don't know whether to high-five her or put my hand over her mouth so she can't say anything else that's offensive to my easily offended mother-in-law. Instead, I divert the conversation. "Maybe we should save Chuck E. Cheese for another day. It's pretty busy in there, and we want to have time with Granny and Grandpa, since they don't get to see you as much as they used to."

We finally agree on a place to eat after Karen shoots down

three more options, and I call ahead to make a reservation for the seven of us. We head out to the parking lot, and of course, because Peyton is a kid and because Harley is fun and she loves her, she asks if she can ride with Harley.

"I need company in the back seat, honey. We'll see Harley at the restaurant." Karen puts her arm around Peyton's shoulder and guides her toward my SUV. Peyton glances over her shoulder to Harley, who, thankfully gives her a wave and a wink.

When they're out of earshot, she turns to me, adjusting the strap of her purse. "Should I even come?"

I tuck a hand in my pocket. "Of course, you should. I'll talk to Karen."

"In front of Peyton?"

"I'll remind her to be on her best behavior." I know I need to deal with this, but putting my mother-in-law in her place in front of my parents and her granddaughter isn't ideal. "Please, Harley, Peyton will be disappointed if you don't come and so will I."

"Are you seriously giving me puppy-dog eyes right now?" She arches a brow at me.

"Is it working?" I take her hand in mine and pull her closer, bringing her knuckles to my lips.

She laughs and shakes her head. "Fine. I'll come. But I'm only taking one for the team because of Peyton."

"Not me?"

"You're a big boy, you can handle a family lunch without a sidekick. I won't disappoint Peyton." She pushes up on her toes and drops a kiss on the edge of my jaw. "I'll meet you at the restaurant."

When I get into the SUV, I find that my mom and Karen are in the back seat with Peyton. "Where are the grandpas?"

"They went together. You know how Kyle and Gareth are. They love to talk shop."

"Ah, that makes sense. Maybe my dad can talk Kyle into semi-retirement." My dad is an architectural engineer and my father-in-law is an environmental engineer. They're different, but have enough in common that the two of them can talk for hours and not even realize they're the only two people left in the room.

"I feel like semi-retirement is the best I can ask for. I really can't see Kyle stopping completely," Karen replies with a sigh.

"I think I'll be lucky if Gareth goes down to a couple of days a week," Mom says sympathetically.

My mother and Karen aren't quite as compatible, but my mother is kind and soft, and she can carry on a conversation with anyone, so it makes bringing both families together easy. The added dynamic of Harley, not as my nanny but as my girlfriend, is turning out to be a lot harder to navigate. Especially with how much my mom loves her and how much shade Karen has been throwing her way.

I don't have an opportunity to pull Karen aside before we reach the restaurant. But I do get told no less than six times to slow down and to watch my speed. I was driving two miles over the speed limit. By the time we get there, everyone else is waiting inside for us. The hostess ushers us to the table.

"Can I sit between you and Harley?" Peyton asks as chairs scrape across the floor.

Karen holds onto her hand and pats the chair next to her. "Why don't you sit next to me? You can tell me all about school and your new friends. I haven't had nearly enough time with you yet, and Harley and your dad see you all the time."

Peyton's lips pull to the side, and she glances from me to Harley. "Oh, okay." It's clear she's disappointed, but she takes the seat anyway.

Karen fusses over her for a few minutes, peppering her with questions about school and friends while we wait for our drinks to arrive. I stretch my arm across the back of Harley's chair. "I didn't realize you were going in early to help out with the assembly."

"Oh, it's no big deal. Emily and I were talking last week, and I didn't have anything this morning and it's my weekend off."

"How often do you help with Peyton's class?" Karen asks, a forced smile stretched across her lips.

Harley drags her gaze away from mine. "Maybe once a week. It really depends on what's going on in the school. More hands make light work."

"That's very true, and convenient that you have that kind of availability." Even that simple statement seems like it's steeped in suspicion and judgment.

"It is. And it's been nice to work with kids again, even if it's indirectly and just on an occasional basis." I can tell Harley is trying to keep things light and remain polite and cordial. It's something she's good at, likely because of her job at Spark House and all the people they deal with on a regular basis.

"Does that mean you're not taking care of children anymore?" Karen absently strokes Peyton's hair.

Harley's smile falters, and she shifts around in her chair, as if the direction of this conversation makes her uneasy. "Peyton was actually my last infant charge. After Gavin and Peyton moved to Boulder, I worked with a family who had a three- and a five-year-old for about six months."

"What happened that you stopped working for them?" Karen folds her hands under her chin.

"Their dad was in the navy, and when he was stationed overseas, the rest of the family moved with them. At the time, my
grandmother wanted to retire, and my sisters needed my help
running Spark House, so I changed course."

"And you enjoy that? Working with your sisters?"

"They're my only family, aside from my grandmother. I like
that I get to be close to them." Harley takes a sip of her water,
making the ice cubes clink together.

I notice that she doesn't quite answer the question, and I'm
also aware that the changes recently at Spark House have been
challenging for her. Sometimes I wonder if being there is more
about being close to her sisters than it is the actual job. "Harley's
been taking classes part-time to complete her degree."

"Oh?" Karen props her chin on her index finger. "Well, edu-
cation is always good to have, even if it's later in life. What kind
of degree?"

"Childhood development. I was two years in when I put it on
pause to work with my sisters," Harley explains.

It seems like a lot of things have been put on hold for her
and that she's spent a lot of time putting other people ahead of
herself. Something I'm not unfamiliar with.

The server returns with our drinks and takes our orders.
When she gets to Peyton, Karen speaks up. "She'll have the
grilled chicken and steamed vegetables."

"But I want the chicken fingers and fries," Peyton says, her
gaze darting from her grandmother to me and back again.

"Those are deep-fried, honey." Karen gives her a gentle smile.

"But Daddy said I could have whatever I wanted for lunch."

Karen looks to me, with slight disapproval on her face. "Well,
I suppose if your dad said, but you should get the carrots and cel-

ery instead of the fries. You need to have a vegetable with every meal."

Peyton concedes to the carrots and celery. I want to argue, but she's already ordered her meal and going back to change it seems passive-aggressive. And I don't want to embarrass Karen in front of my parents and Harley, which seems likely given how sensitive she can be. If Peyton really wants some fries, she can pick off someone else's plate. While I'm not sure that's any less passive-aggressive, at least it saves me from having to call Karen out.

When the server reaches Harley, she orders the adult chicken fingers and fries and adds a side salad. I pinch her thigh under the table, and she blinks up innocently at me. I order a burger, which incidentally comes with fries—not in a bid to irk my mother-in-law, but because it's one of the best things on the menu here.

The server sets a cup of crayons in front of Peyton, who immediately flips her menu over and plucks the pink one from the cup and begins coloring the rabbit in the center of the menu.

"Bunnies aren't pink, honey." Karen pulls the gray and brown crayons from the cup and sets them beside her.

"Not in real life, but they can be in my imagination," Peyton tells her.

Karen harrumphs and purses her lips, turning her attention to my mother, who is seated on her other side. They start chatting, leaving Peyton to color her bunny whatever the fuck color she likes.

I'm uncomfortable with the way this lunch is going, and I don't feel like I can say anything without creating more rather than less conflict. With one look at my mother, I can tell she too is biting her tongue. Karen is very used to being in charge, and it's only now that I'm no longer living in Boulder, depending on her for support, that I can see exactly how much control she had over the way I parented Peyton.

Things go from bad to worse when Peyton reaches for her kid's cup of milk and it's not what she asked for.

"This isn't chocolate milk, it's white milk."

"You're already having chicken fingers, which aren't healthy. White milk is good for you, and chocolate milk is full of sugar, especially at restaurants," Karen chides.

"But Daddy said I could—"

"That's enough whining, Peyton," Karen snaps. "And you're supposed to save your drink for dinner instead of filling up on sugary junk before you've even had your meal."

"It's just one meal, Karen. And she won an award," my mom says.

"One meal quickly turns into every meal," she gripes.

Harley's nails dig into my thigh, and I can basically feel her biting her tongue. As it is, I'm struggling to figure out how the hell I'm supposed to deal with this situation without it exploding in my face. When we lived in Boulder, Peyton spent a lot of time with Karen and Kyle, and it seemed like allowing Karen to mother Peyton gave her back what she'd lost when Marcie died. But now she's blatantly undermining me, and I can't figure out what the point of it is, especially when all it's accomplishing is causing friction between everyone.

Before I can figure out what to say and how to say it, Peyton bursts into tears and Karen huffs a sigh.

"What are these dramatics?" She gives me a withering look. "Obviously your parenting is getting lax if this is the kind of behavior you get at a restaurant."

Eighteen

PULL THE PIN

HARLEY

I think my head is going to explode. It's everything I can do to keep my mouth shut and not tell Karen where she can shove her white milk. Peyton only drinks white milk when she's forced to. Like right now.

What is the point of her getting an award and being celebrated when someone is policing her entire meal? And why the hell is Gavin allowing it and not putting her in her place? I don't know how to deal with this kind of . . . passive parenting. Not when he's usually so great about balance with Peyton.

I push my chair back, needing to take a breather and collect myself before I lose my shit on Gavin's mother-in-law. "Peyton, why don't you come to the bathroom with me and wash your hands before lunch comes out."

Her chair scrapes against the floor, and she practically flings herself out of the chair, tripping over her feet to get to me. She buries her face against my stomach, leaving wet marks on the fabric, probably a combination of tears and snot. I take her hand and guide her away from the table. My neck is hot and I'm practically shaking, I'm so angry.

This whole meal feels like a lot of posturing. Unnecessary

posturing. The kind that makes me want to smack this woman upside the head. I'm not the enemy. I'm just a woman trying to navigate a relationship with a man who has a very complicated past, and a control freak, overbearing mother-in-law.

We cross the restaurant, Peyton sniffling and using the back of her hand to wipe her nose. As soon as we're inside the restroom, I dig around in my purse and find a tissue and crouch down in front of her. "Here, sweetie, blow your nose."

"I wanted to sit next to you."

I push her hair back from her face and tamp down my anger. This isn't Peyton's fault, and I want to make sure she understands that. "Your granny doesn't get to see you often, and I get to see you all the time, though."

"But she won't even let me get what I want. And Dad already said I could have whatever I wanted."

Half of me wants to tell her we'll have a do-over, but I don't want to do the same thing Karen is by undermining Gavin, and I'm not Peyton's parent. I'm the girlfriend, and Peyton's former nanny, which puts me in a difficult position. My instinct is to protect and try to gently discipline. If I were still the nanny, I would sit Karen and Gavin down and have a discussion about reasonable expectations, consistency, and supporting each other. But I can't, because I'm now directly involved in so many ways.

And despite the friction between me and Karen, I want her to like me. Because no matter what, she's always going to be connected to Peyton, and whether I like it or not, she's been a huge part of her life.

And I feel like she sees me as a threat.

"I know that, but maybe Granny didn't. She just wants to make sure you eat good things to go with the not-so-nutritious stuff. Remember when you wanted the extra scoop of ice cream because you couldn't decide, and your dad said you had to pick one and then you couldn't even finish that?"

"But this is different. It's just chocolate milk and french fries." Her mouth screws up in a scowl.

Agreeing with her isn't going to help the situation. "I know, honey, but this is Granny's way of telling you she loves you."

"I wish she would tell me with words and hugs."

I wrap my arms around her and she melts right into me. I have her use the bathroom and wash her hands before we return to the table. The server brings out our meals, setting Peyton's chicken fingers and carrots and celery in front of her. She reaches across the table for the ketchup and squirts a generous amount on her plate.

"You need to start with the vegetables, Peyton," Karen tells her.

I move my plate of chicken fingers aside—in hindsight I shouldn't have ordered the fries—and dig into my salad. Peyton follows my lead and dunks her carrots into the ranch dip.

When she's finally able to move on to her chicken fingers, Karen stops her from putting more ketchup on her plate when she runs out after the first chicken finger. "Ketchup is all sugar. You don't need any more."

"But I need something to dip my chicken fingers in," Peyton says, eyes darting to her dad and me and then back to her plate.

Because I've been stewing this entire time, I don't even give Gavin the chance to jump in before I give my own two cents. "She's nine; ketchup might as well be its own food group. I know it was one for me when I was her age, and Gavin still uses half a bottle every time we have grilled cheese sandwiches. It doesn't mean he's a bad parent, and if my parents were still alive, I'm pretty sure one of their regrets in life would not be letting me use ketchup liberally when I was Peyton's age. Loving ketchup is not a crime." I realize I'm on a rant, and that my behavior is only going to cause more tension, not less, but I'm annoyed.

The table falls into an uncomfortable silence for a few long seconds, at least until Gavin clears his throat. "I'm pretty sure Peyton got her love of ketchup from me, and I got mine from my dad." He points to his plate and then nods over at his dad's plate: both have a puddle of ketchup that takes up nearly a quarter of the plate.

Peyton smiles and Gavin's mother chuckles. But the atmosphere is still tense, and it's my fault for making it this way. At the end of the meal Gavin's parents suggest they take Peyton for a few hours and invite Karen and Kyle to join them, giving Gavin and me some time on our own. Which we obviously need after that shit show of a lunch. Judith hugs me and tells me everything will be fine. I'm unsurprised when Karen barely acknowledges my existence before they depart with Gavin's parents, taking Gavin's SUV, and leaving the two of us alone.

Once we're in my car, I go off. "How in the world did you deal with that woman on a daily basis? She's damn well infuriating. Does she always undermine everything you do? How am I ever going to get along with her when all she does is make me feel two inches tall?" I continue ranting, pissed and frustrated that this woman has such a hold on Gavin's life, and she doesn't even live in the same city. "Why do you let her talk to you like that? All she does is criticize your parenting. I've never felt so judged in my life. I don't understand why you'd take that kind of shit from her. You sure as hell wouldn't take that from me."

He's quiet for a while, staring out the window. I wonder if he's even listening to me when he finally speaks. "I didn't want to embarrass Karen in front of you and my parents. She's usually not that . . . overbearing. Opinionated yes, but not like that. I didn't think calling her out in the middle of a public restaurant would make the situation better."

"Do you have any idea how hard it was for me to keep my mouth shut?" I grip the steering wheel tightly, feeling it squeak under my hands.

"Well, to be fair, you didn't keep your mouth shut." His voice is low and tight, and it almost sounds like an accusation. Or maybe that's just how I'm receiving it.

"She criticizes everything I do! I think I managed to keep it together for a decent amount of time. No one should be talked to the way she talks to me. And maybe I'm a little easier going when it comes to rules, but you told Peyton she could have what she wanted, and Karen came in and criticized your parenting in front of your own parents." I pull into the underground lot and park my car.

"I know, and I need to talk to her, but as I said, I didn't feel a restaurant was the best location for that conversation to take place. Besides, Peyton had fries because I shared mine with her. So she got what she wanted anyway."

Gavin is quiet in the elevator as we head up to my condo, giving me a little time to cool off, although I'm still pretty fired up. Once we're in my apartment, I head for the fridge and grab myself one of the coolers Andrea brought the last time I had her and Belinda over. It's been a while. Neatly coinciding with the amount of time I've been with Gavin. My sisters and I like to have girls' nights in, but with London still breastfeeding and Avery preggers, that's not going to be in the cards anytime soon.

"Can I get you something to drink?" I'm snappy, which isn't normal for me.

"It's only four." He glances pointedly at the clock.

"It's Friday and it's been a day," I reply and take a hefty gulp of the too-sweet liquid.

Gavin leans against the counter and sighs. "I know the way Karen has been behaving is a problem."

I'm relieved to hear him say that; unfortunately, it feels like there's a *but* at the end of that statement. "So how do we manage this? What am I supposed to do, Gavin? Walk around on eggshells? Bite my tongue? Let her undermine both of us? I don't know what I'm allowed to say and not say. What's my role here? It's like she still treats me as though I'm the nanny, not your girlfriend. And if you know she's a problem, how are we going to fix it?"

He sighs heavily and rubs his temple, like this conversation is giving him a headache. Like it's me that's the issue, not the woman who constantly makes me feel like shit. And honestly, Gavin's unwillingness to stand up to her is . . . not the most attractive quality at the moment. "I realize I let Karen get away with a lot more than I should."

This conversation feels like pulling teeth. Like he's holding back. "If you realize it, why do you let it keep happening?"

He drags his tongue along his bottom lip, eyes on the floor. He shakes his head a couple of times and finally, quietly, says, "Because, Harley, I'm the reason their daughter is dead."

I suck in a shocked breath. "I thought she died during childbirth."

His jaw tics. "She did." His eyes flick up to mine. There's anger, hurt, and frustration lurking behind them. And guilt. So much guilt. "But if I'd taken their daughter to the hospital two hours earlier, when she said we should probably go, instead of needing to finish mowing the fucking lawn, then maybe she would still be here."

He swallows thickly, lip curling in disgust, and I see that under all the anger is self-loathing. "If I'd put my wife ahead of a fucking household chore, they would still have their daughter. I took her away from them." He points to his chest, voice as hard as his eyes. "It's my fault she's gone. Because I didn't take care of her when I should have. Peyton is the only link they have left to their daughter, and letting Karen mother Peyton was the only way I could see to give her back some of what I took from them when Marcie died. I get that I need boundaries, but calling her out in a public place is cruel."

"I'm so sorry." I didn't realize until now that Gavin has been holding onto the blame for that for all these years. Not like this. And it reframes so much of what's happening. When he moved to Boulder, Karen stepped in as the mother Peyton didn't have, and when he moved back here, he took that away from her. It explains so much about the way they deal with each other, and how Karen deals with me.

I take a step forward, wanting to find a way to console him. To tell him I understand what it's like holding on to guilt, because I did it with him for years, but he puts his hand up to stop me.

"Don't, please. I can't handle this. I don't deserve pity, or understanding, or any of the things that you want to give me right now, Harley. I know that Karen is making this difficult"—he motions between us—"but my moving back here has been hard on her. She's struggling too. To her it's another loss. I can't take more away from her than I already have."

"I'm not asking you to take things away from her. I'm asking you to stand up for us and for Peyton. There has to be some kind of balance, Gavin," I say gently.

"I took their daughter from them. I robbed Peyton of a

mother. There isn't any balance. There's just me trying to make up for the biggest fucking mistake of my life," he grinds out.

I realize in that moment, as much as Gavin might want us to work, he still has a lot of work to do. His guilt is a heavy chain that's keeping him shackled to the past. "I don't know how to help you with this," I say honestly.

"You can't. This is mine to deal with." He runs a hand through his hair and blows out a breath. "I'm going to grab an Uber. I want to be here, but I think we both need some time after today. I'm not telling you that you don't have the right to be upset right now, Harley, with me, with Karen, but I don't think any conversation we have today is going to be productive. Karen will be this way with any woman I bring into my life—"

"But it's worse because we already have a history," I finish for him.

"It makes it harder. There are memories attached to you." He looks away. "Not just for Karen, but for me too. I just"—he closes his eyes and shakes his head—"I need some time to think, okay?"

"Are you asking for permission or are you telling me?"

"I don't know. Both?"

I set my cooler on the counter and cross my arms. "If you need time, take it. I don't want to push you into things you're not ready to handle."

He sighs again and crosses the room. He kisses my cheek, lips lingering there for a second, and when I feel him move toward my mouth, I turn my head away. I can't give affection when he won't give emotion. And that's what this feels like—excuses drenched in his guilt.

A reason for him to keep me safely inside a box. His heart tucked away, out of reach and maybe too broken to be mended.

Nineteen

THE PATH TO HERE

HARLEY

Despite it being my weekend off, I dump the rest of the cooler—I drank a quarter of it—and head to Spark House. If I'm not spending the evening with Gavin, I might as well help my sisters and give one of them the night off, if they want it.

I show up at Spark House just before dinner and expect to find my sisters in the kitchen, or at least London, since she's always been a bit of a micromanager, but they're both sitting in the office, snacking on appetizers.

"Hey, what are you doing here?" Avery cocks a brow and pops a tiny puff pastry into her mouth.

"My night opened up." Even though I came from a late lunch only a couple of hours ago, I grab a fig-and-cream-cheese tart and bite into it. I know exactly where this came from, and they have the best appetizer platter known to man. I will avoid dinner altogether and fill a plate with these if I have the opportunity. And tonight I feel like stress eating.

"Peyton not feeling good or something?"

"Or something," I say through a mouthful of tart. "Why aren't you two in the dining room, doing dining room things?"

"Because we hired people to do the dining room things three

months ago and figured we should probably let them do the dining room things without us constantly interfering and hovering,"
London replies. "And I threatened to tie Avery to her chair if she
went to check on them before seven. Now, back to why you're
here and not with Gavin. I thought you two were supposed to
have some alone time tonight."

My sisters always have been and always will be my sounding
boards, so I fill them in on what happened at the restaurant, the
conversation I had with Gavin at my place, and the fact that he
took an Uber home because he needs time to think. "Am I in too
deep here?" I ask, dragging a hand down my face.

"Probably," London says.

Avery shoots her a look. "You hit a bump in the road. And
when you think about it, it makes sense that he's struggling, you
know?"

"Am I being unreasonable, wanting him to stick up for me?"
In the moment my reaction felt justified, but now I'm not so sure.

Avery flips a tiny soccer stress ball between her fingers. "Of
course, it's justifiable that you'd want him to stick up for you, especially when his former mother-in-law is being a super bitch.
But I can see where he's coming from, because if he truly believes
he's the reason his wife died during childbirth, then of course he's
always going to feel like he owes them something. And in this
case, that something is his passive acceptance of their criticism."
She sets the ball on the table and reaches for another appetizer. "It
really does make a lot of sense on all sides. She feels threatened by
your presence in Peyton's life. They've moved back here, and he
immediately reconnects with you."

"It's not like I sought him out," I say defensively.

"No, but it doesn't change the fact that you have history with both Gavin and Peyton. He cares about you and always has. And let's be really real about this, he probably had feelings for you back when you were taking care of Peyton. Maybe not developed ones, because of the age difference and how glaring it would have been since you started taking care of Peyton when you were nineteen, but they existed all the same. And they would have been completely understandable for both of you. You were literally a stand-in mother for Peyton. There are so many layers to that. And a lot of confusing emotions on all sides. You were probably a threat to Karen back then, and this is bringing up all those old feelings. Likely not just for her, but also for Gavin."

"You sound like a therapist," I tell her.

She shrugs. "Declan's had a lot of therapy. And we've had a lot of couples' counseling."

"I didn't realize that. You two seem so solid." Avery and Declan's love is the kind that I want for myself. They're best friends and lovers. They always have each other's back—at least that's how it looks from the outside.

Avery raises a hand. "Calm your tits, sis. Everything is fine with me and Deck. And I want to keep it that way. He's got a lot of baggage when it comes to trust and family issues. He's super nervous about becoming a father, so we've been seeing his therapist together. And honestly, I've got baggage too. Between trust issues because of my relationship with Sam, and us losing our parents, Deck and I could use someone to bounce things off of. It helps us keep the lines of communication open."

"Well, that's . . ."

"Smart?" Avery offers. "Declan is my best friend and my partner for life. I don't want anything to mess that up. Anyway, back to you and Gavin and his monster-in-law, something I can totally relate to, by the way. Give him some time to sort through things. Especially if they're in town. He might need some space to work through this on his own."

"How do you keep your mouth shut with Declan's mom? She's so much drama."

"She's what tabloid gossip columns were made for. And I've learned that getting angry about the way his mother manages things isn't helpful for either of us. Her behavior is a result of her own issues, and I can't control those, or own her crap. I've made it very clear that if she wants to have a relationship with her grandchild, she's going to have to learn how to keep Declan and me out of her family drama." She pats her belly. "This kid isn't going to be used as a pawn in any of their ridiculous games."

"I know there are some similarities in your situations, but there are some key differences too," London says softly.

"What do you mean?" I ask.

"You and Gavin started off as friends, and it shifted into a relationship. Don't they usually suggest waiting until after the six-month mark to introduce a significant other when there are kids involved? And you were already part of Peyton's life. You've taken over a lot of the roles his mother-in-law was playing when he lived in Boulder."

I hate how defensive I feel, and how the past seems to be following me as I try to navigate this new path with Gavin. "What are you saying?"

"Just that it's not quite the same. I know you have feelings for Gavin and that he has feelings for you, but I want you to be careful. Sometimes I worry that you're just as in love with Peyton as you are with him. And I'm not saying that's a bad thing, but you could be looking at a lot of heartache, especially if his mother-in-law doesn't back down and he won't stand up to her."

This isn't what I *want* to hear, but it's something I have to face, because she's right about all of it. I already feel like I'm in too deep and it scares the hell out of me.

"I think we need to give him a chance to stand up to her before we go condemning their relationship," Avery jumps in.

"I'm not trying to condemn their relationship. I just worry, that's all. This is very complicated for a lot of reasons. And now you're telling us that Gavin's clearly still harboring guilt over losing Marcie the way he did. That's a lot of trauma to carry around. And I know it's still early in your relationship, Harley, but you're going to want kids of your own at some point, aren't you?"

"Well yeah, of course, but I have lots of time for that. I'm only twenty-eight."

"It's not your age I'm worried about. Or his. It's how he's going to cope with a pregnancy when he lost his first wife during childbirth. If he can't deal with his mother-in-law or his guilt now, what is that going to look like in the future?"

"Geez, London, way to go down the most depressing rabbit hole in the history of the universe." There's warning in Avery's tone.

London purses her lips and gives me an apologetic smile. "I'm sorry. I'm making things worse."

"But you have a point. A good one." I bite the end of my nail and look across the room to the fireplace where a family photo hangs on the wall. Three generations of Sparks, my grandmother, our parents, and us as kids. It was taken the year before we lost our parents. A snapshot of our history.

I would never have a mother of my own to lean on for support in situations like these, but I have my grandmother, who was very much like a mom, and my sisters, who always stand by my side.

I wanted Karen to like me, to accept me, to deem me worthy of the man who had once loved her daughter, but so far, all I've done is be defensive and combative. I'm not sure if it's all Karen, or if maybe I've expected her to dislike me and that's part of the problem. Finding a middle ground seems impossible if Gavin can't let go of his own guilt and stop living in the past with all the ghosts that haunt him.

And I don't know what our future looks likes anymore. London is right, even if I don't want her to be. Gavin has been through a lot, and so have I. But giving up on the idea of mother-hood isn't something I thought I'd have to consider, and I'm not sure how to handle that possibility.

I spend the rest of the weekend immersed in Spark House, tak-ing photos and creating posts to highlight the sponsors and their contributions and the event itself. I also hang out with London and spend time with her, making centerpieces, being creative, and documenting it all. This is the part of Spark House I enjoy the most, spending time with my sisters. And staying occupied is preferable to sitting at home, wondering how Gavin's weekend with his in-laws is going. And what kind of conversations they've had about me.

On Sunday afternoon Griffin Mills and Lincoln Moorehead stop by with their wives. They were in Colorado on business, and we thought it was a great opportunity to meet in person and discuss how the first franchise locations are shaping up. I really like them and their wives. While we did talk business, it felt like a meeting of friends. And I'm starting to accept the franchise idea, which is good, because it allows me to think about what's next for me.

After lunch I offer to take Ella into the makeshift playroom since she usually has a nap and sometimes it takes her a bit to settle.

"I didn't realize that Spark House has childcare," Cosy, Griffin's wife, says as we stop at the playroom and London passes Ella over.

"Oh, we don't have daycare. We just set this up so I can bring Ella to work when it's not quite so busy," London explains.

"This used to be a storage room, but we converted it after this little bean came into the world." I tickle under her chin, and Ella giggles and tucks her head against my neck, sucking on her fingers.

"Regardless, it's a great space and maybe something to consider down the line. We have a program at all the Mills Hotels for the staff so they have affordable daycare options on site," Cosy replies.

I really hadn't thought about Spark House needing something like that, but with all this growth, I can see the potential. And one of the upcoming projects for my class is the development of a daycare program. I can see the benefit of creating something that would work here.

"That's wonderful, although Mills Hotels have a robust staff," Avery says.

"This is very true. It really depends on staff needs, and we employ a lot of people at each location, so it made sense to set something up in-house."

Just as the wheels start turning in my head, Ella yawns loudly, and I excuse myself into the playroom.

London seems reluctant to leave me out, but I tell her it's fine and they can fill me in later.

Normally I'd put Ella down after a few minutes in the rocking chair, but she looks so sweet with her hands curled into fists, one of her knuckles in her mouth because she's never quite grasped the concept of sucking her thumb.

As I sit in the glider, rocking back and forth, singing a soft lullaby, I realize that London's fears for me and Gavin, while not something I want to consider too closely, are very real. I have no idea if Gavin is going to want more children. And while I can completely understand why he would have reservations—the fact that he has a nine-year-old daughter and has already been through the diapers and sleepless nights stage of parenting and may not be too excited to go through that again being one—the other reasons hang heavy in my heart.

Losing Marcie during childbirth was a huge trauma, and possibly one he might be unable to learn to live with. Would I be willing to give up the opportunity to ever have a baby of my own for him? I think I already know the answer to that question, and that makes things more difficult to handle emotionally.

Avery pops her head in and surveys the room. "Hey, I was coming to see if you needed any help, but it looks your baby-whispering skills are in full effect and you've got it handled."

I smile and realize I'm on the verge of tears.

"Or maybe not. Are you okay?" She closes the door behind her and steps into the room.

I wave a hand around in the air. "I'm fine."

She arches a brow. "Liar, liar pants on fire?" It's phrased as a question. "Did something happen with Gavin?"

I shake my head. We've messaged a couple of times over the

weekend, but I've left him alone for the most part, because I know his in-laws are there.

"No, nothing happened." The lack of conversation post monster-in-law dinner isn't exactly reassuring.

"Is that a good or bad thing?" Avery asks, as if she can read my mind.

"His in-laws leave tonight. I figured he needed some time to process, like you and London said."

"Okay." She sits down in the other glider and settles a hand on her rounded belly. "So what's going on, then?"

"I've been thinking about what London said."

"She's protective of both of us, and she doesn't want you to get hurt. She was the same way when Declan and I got involved."

"That was different." Avery had been in a serious car accident and Declan stepped into the role of caregiver. London struggled with it because it echoed the loss of our parents, something that will continue to affect us for our entire lives.

"It is, but her worrying is the same. Try not to read too much into it, or let it mess with your head."

I bite the inside of my lip. "The thing is . . . she's not wrong."

She stops rocking and tips her head to the side. "About what?"

"About me wanting to have kids in the future. The blended family isn't an issue for me, but I can't imagine *not* having a family of my own. I want to experience pregnancy. I want the swollen ankles and getting up twenty times in the night to pee. Which sounds . . . ludicrous, I know, but it's a part of the process I'd been hoping to have. I have no idea if that's something Gavin would or could entertain in the future after what he's already been through. I get that we're early in our relationship and a lot of things can change, but his guilt is a real thing."

"And you think that's going to make it impossible for him to entertain you having a baby?"

"Maybe. I probably shouldn't even be contemplating it. But this—" I stroke Ella's cheek, and she makes a small noise, snuggling in closer. "This makes me happy. This fulfills me in ways nothing else does."

Avery nods slowly. "Would you consider adoption if having your own baby is a deal breaker for him?"

"Adoption is always an option, but I'd only want to go in that direction if I couldn't conceive. There are so many families out there who can't have their own children. I wouldn't want to take that opportunity from someone else if the only thing standing between me and having a baby is my partner's fear, if that makes sense. And then the other part of me wonders if I'm being selfish for wanting something like this at all. And for even thinking about it. Especially when we haven't been together for very long."

"You're not off base for thinking about it, not with me being pregnant and Ella being adorable and you trying to figure out how to navigate your relationship with a single dad," she says.

"I spent all that time raising a baby that wasn't mine and taking care of other people's children. I want that experience for myself too. I really want to be a mother, and I don't think I realized how much until now."

"And you should be one, however that's going to look, and whoever is lucky enough to have your love. Whether it's Gavin or someone else."

I sigh. "I love being an aunt, and I feel like I could be a good stepmom to Peyton, if Gavin and I are meant for each other, but I don't know if I would be satisfied if that was where it ended for me."

"It's a lot to think about," Avery says softly.

"It is. And I know he and I just started dating, but with our history and my relationship with Peyton, it's hard not to think about what the future is going to look like. It's days like these that I wish Mom were still here. Not that she would be able to tell me what to do, or that I can't pick up the phone and call Grandma Spark in Italy, but it would just be nice to have a mom to go to with things like this."

"I get exactly what you mean." She reaches out and takes my hand. "At least we have each other, right?"

"At least we have each other." I squeeze her hand back.

I love my sisters more than anything, but as much as I'd like them to be a replacement for the mother we lost, they can't be. And maybe that's the hardest part about all of this, knowing what it's like to grow up without a mom, and how different life is when you have two loving parents, instead of none. More than that, it's seeing the possibility of a family with Gavin and Peyton, but being unsure whether it's enough. Especially when his mother-in-law keeps putting up roadblocks, and Gavin doesn't seem capable of knocking them down.

Twenty

THIS WINDING ROAD

GAVIN

For the first time since Harley came back into our lives, I feel unsteady. I know there are a lot of things I need to deal with. Namely my mother-in-law. But there's a minefield surrounding her, full of guilt and a lot of other emotions I'm not sure I'm capable of managing.

What worries me most, though, is my uncertainty over whether I'll be able to get a handle on them eventually, if at all, and what that means for my future.

On Sunday morning I stop in at the office to pick up some things I forgot on Friday. They could probably wait until Monday morning, but I need a few minutes to myself, and having my in-laws in my personal space all weekend is a lot.

I'm surprised when I find Ian in the office too. "What are you doing here on a Sunday morning?"

"I could ask you the same thing." He closes his laptop and unplugs it. "I have a meeting off-site tomorrow morning, and I needed some files. It's on the other side of town, closer to my place, so I figured I'd grab my stuff now so I can go directly to the meeting from there. And I can pick up cinnamon buns from Lynn's favorite place on the way home, so it's a win all around.

You using the excuse that you forgot something at work to escape the in-laws?"

I drop down in the chair opposite him. "Yeah, basically."

"Everything okay?"

I blow out a breath. "I don't know."

"That doesn't sound good. Did something happen?"

I fill him in on the restaurant fiasco and the way Harley went off and also the way I left her place on Friday night instead of staying and dealing with the situation.

"Have you talked to her at all since then?"

"Just a few text messages back and forth. It was supposed to be her weekend off, and I guess she went into work because her sisters needed help."

"So she went to work because you bailed on her, and it was better than being alone and angry at you?" Ian supplies.

"Probably." I rub my bottom lip. "I need to deal with Karen."

"Yeah, you do," Ian agrees. "What's stopping you?"

I run my hands over my face. "I don't know. When I moved here, I thought I'd be able to have an actual fucking life, and it seems like she still has as much control over my social life as she did when I was living in the same city as they were."

"Do you want me to be honest with you, or do you want me to pat you on the shoulder and say things like, it'll all work out in the end?"

"I'd rather you be honest than feed me lines of bullshit."

"Okay." He nods once and grips the armrests of his chair, crossing one leg over the other. "The reason she still has control is because you let her have it."

"She lives two hours away," I point out.

"And yet here you are on a Sunday morning, in the office

because you're trying to get away from her. You know where you should be right now?"

"At home with my daughter."

"No, asshole, you should be balls deep in your girlfriend."

I give him an unimpressed look. "Shouldn't you be balls deep in your wife, then, instead of here?"

"I was before I came here. You're welcome for that information, and if you ever tell my wife I've used the term 'balls deep' in reference to our intimate encounters"—he makes air quotes around the phrase—"I'll disown you as a friend. I get up at stupid o'clock in the morning on Sundays so I can get in some alone time with my wife before the kids are awake. And instead of sneaking off to your girlfriend's house for some surprise morning nookie, you're here, looking like a sad sack, bitching about how hard your life is because of your mother-in-law. I think the real question is, why won't you tell her to back off?"

"Because I feel fucking guilty." I look out the window, unable to meet his gaze.

"For moving back to Colorado Springs?"

"That's one reason."

Ian sighs. "Gavin, man, you can't blame yourself for the rest of your life for what happened to Marcie. It's not your fault."

"If I'd listened when she said we needed to go to the hospital—" I choke on the words, unable to spit the rest of them out. The wound feels especially fresh considering the conversation I had with Harley on Friday.

Ian's eyes grow sad. "She called Lynn that morning, while you were mowing the lawn, and Lynn told her it would be fine. That she didn't need to go right away."

"But I'm her husband."

Ian stares at me, one brow arched.

"Was. I was her husband."

"You gotta let go of the guilt, Gav, or you're never going to be able to move on, and you're going to keep letting Karen dictate your future."

"She thinks Harley is too young for me."

"She'll find a reason for any woman you date not to be suitable. We already talked about Harley's age, and the fact that your parents are more than a decade apart and have been married for nearly forty years, so we know that argument doesn't hold a lot of water, unless you're the one who has a problem with Harley's age."

"Someone thought she was the nanny at the school event on Friday."

"And? Did she get upset about it?"

"No."

"Did you?"

"No, I told the woman she was my girlfriend." And then Karen had to be an asshole about it.

"I feel like we're talking in a circle here, Gav."

I knead the back of my neck. "That's because we probably are."

He nods once and steeples his fingers. "What do *you* want? If you could put everyone else aside and just focus on you, what would you want?"

"I can't put Peyton aside."

"Okay, but you can still put you ahead of everyone else. What do you want?"

I don't even have to think about it, the answer just rolls off my tongue. "To be with Harley."

"Why?"

"Why?" I echo.

"Yeah, why do you want to be with Harley? And don't list any reasons that have to do with Peyton."

That makes me pause, but he has a point. "I like spending time with her, she's fun to be around, she makes me laugh, she's full of adventure, we have a lot in common, and the sex is out of this world."

He smirks. "You can still keep up in bed, then, huh?"

"I'm in my thirties, not filing for my pension checks, a-hole."

"I know. I'm kidding. I just wanted to get a reaction out of you. Do you have any concerns about how she is with Peyton?"

"No. None. She's great with her, and Peyton loves her." I tap on my armrest. "Which is a problem on its own."

His brows pull together. "That seems like it should be a good thing, not a problem?"

"It is and it isn't. Peyton's already attached to her, and that makes me really want this to work out, and not just for myself."

Ian nods. "When you say work out, what exactly do you mean?"

I frown. "I want us to be a couple that lasts."

"You've only been seeing each other officially for a few months, though, so you can't know that for sure." I can hear the concern in his voice. "It's good that you're into her the way you are, and that it seems mutual, but there's a lot more that you both need to deal with."

"I just don't want Peyton to end up getting hurt if Harley and I don't work out. She's already lost enough."

Ian blows out a breath. "That's a lot of pressure to put on yourself and this relationship. You need to take it one step at a time. Don't start building the picket fence before you've even had a chance to look at house plans."

"You're right. I know you're right." But now that I have this, I don't want to lose it, and I'm terrified of fucking it up, if I haven't done that already.

"You haven't had a lot of opportunities to date over the last decade, and most of the women you've been involved with have been short-term and haven't even met Peyton, let alone your mother-in-law, who isn't easy on a good day. I think you need to give credit where credit is due. Harley's got a backbone and Peyton's best interests in mind. It's not like this is easy for her either."

"She doesn't want to step on toes," I agree.

"That's not what I'm talking about. Didn't she lose both of her parents in a car accident when she was twelve? Unless I've got it wrong?"

"You're not wrong." It's what sold me on hiring her in the first place all those years ago. She knew what that loss felt like. She could relate, and because of that, she seemed like a smart, safe choice for me and Peyton, despite how young she was.

"You both understand what it's like to lose someone important, and she knows what it's like to grow up without a mom, just like Peyton. And now she's contending with a mother-in-law who's making it clear she doesn't like her. That's gotta be tough."

I've been so focused on how to keep the peace that I didn't even take that into consideration. "My parents love her."

"Because she's awesome, but to Karen, I have a feeling she's a threat."

I tap my lip, trying to see it through Karen's eyes, but I can't. "Why would she see Harley as a threat? It's not like she's going to replace them as grandparents, and she doesn't even have parents who are going to come into the picture either."

"But if Harley doesn't like your mother-in-law, she could make it difficult for them to see Peyton in the future."

"Harley wouldn't do that, though. That's not her style at all. And shouldn't Karen be nice to her instead of cutting her down?"

"Probably, yes, but all Karen sees is the fact that you moved back to Colorado Springs and within a couple of weeks, you rekindled your relationship with the nanny you left behind. She didn't love that a twenty-year-old was having a hand in raising your kid then, and clearly that hasn't changed. If you want this thing to work between you and Harley, and it's clear that you do, you need to put Karen in her place. If you don't, she's going to keep doing this because she can get away with it. How long do you think Harley will put up with this?"

He's right. And I've known this all along. Harley might be patient, but there's only so much she can be expected to take. I can't ask her to tolerate the way Karen is treating her, or the way I'm letting her treat Harley. It's not fair to anyone. "Probably not long."

"Talk to Karen, tell Harley you're working things out, and ask her if she's interested in coming to our place for dinner. Lynn's mentioned that she sees Harley at the school all the time. If you're serious about her, stop keeping her all to yourself and start folding her into your life."

When I return home, it's close to noon and I bring cinnamon buns with me. I consider leaving them in the car until after my in-laws go home this evening, but decide that's me pandering to Karen and what she thinks is an acceptable brunch. There's nothing wrong with an occasional cinnamon roll at noon on a Sunday.

I pass the living room, where Kyle is napping in my lounger with the football game droning in the background. His Sunday routine has been the same for as long as I can remember: armchair quarterback. He sleeps through 50 percent of the game, but the second anyone changes the channel, his eyes pop open. I leave him where he is for now and continue to the kitchen, where Karen is sitting at the table with Peyton, her math workbook in front of her. Peyton looks about as excited as a dead fish.

"Hey, how's it going?"

"Dad!" Peyton jumps up from the table and rushes across the room, throwing her arms around me like I'm a life preserver. "Yay! You're home! Does that mean we can go to the park now? Can we call Harley and ask her to meet us there? Can we go to that bakery with the sugar cookies?"

Every word out of her mouth makes me cringe and makes Karen's scowl deepen. "We have three more questions to finish before we can do anything, especially go to the park. And I'm only here for a few more hours, honey. I'd love to spend my afternoon with you. We could go to the museum instead of the park. Wouldn't that be fun?"

"But we always go to the park with Harley on Sundays," Peyton explains.

"You only get so much Granny time, and Harley's picking you up tomorrow after school to take you to the park." At least I'm hopeful that's still happening. I should've dealt with this sooner, like when it happened, instead of dancing around it all weekend.

"But we always see Harley on Sunday afternoons," she says

adamantly. "Can we call her and see? Can't she come with us today? She makes everything more fun."

"That's because she doesn't enforce any rules," Karen mutters under her breath, but not quietly enough that I don't catch it.

"Sweetie, can you take your math books to your room for me and wash your hands? I brought home a treat." It's time I had that talk with Karen, and I'd prefer Peyton not be in the room when it happens.

"We're not finished with her homework yet," Karen informs me.

"Peyton and I will finish it later. Wash your hands and wake up your grandpa, so we can all eat together." I pat Peyton on the head and usher her down the hall.

"The math will only take fifteen minutes to finish. I don't think giving Peyton a treat for half-finished work is setting a good example," Karen says primly.

"The muttered comments need to stop, Karen. And you can't talk down about Harley in front of Peyton, and you certainly shouldn't be doing it in front of me. This isn't about Peyton's math homework, which she and I will finish later, *after* you and Kyle head home."

Her fingers go to her throat, and she fidgets with the heart-shaped locket she always wears. Inside is a picture of Marcie. "Well, she doesn't seem to enforce much in the way of rules, and I was just trying to be helpful with the math homework."

"I appreciate that you want to help out, but this is about more than the math homework. I realize that things are different than they were when we lived in Boulder, but the snide remarks and undermining my parenting decisions aren't helpful. Peyton is *my* daughter and what I say goes. I didn't say anything when we were at the restaurant because I didn't want to cause a scene or embarrass you in front of everyone, but I can't and won't ignore it or leave it unaddressed."

Karen scrunches up her face. "I used to be so involved in Peyton's life, and now this Harley woman has reappeared, and all of a sudden I feel like you're making me out to be the bad guy. For seven years, I made all of Peyton's after-school snacks and dinners, she and I did all her homework together so you wouldn't have to when you picked her up from work. And there were plenty of times when you'd have to work late and she'd sleep over, and now I'm only seeing her once a month! I feel like . . . like I've lost Marcie all over again!" She blinks rapidly and turns her head, dabbing at her eyes with a tissue that was tucked into her sleeve.

And I feel like shit all over again. There's no way I can win this. I ease off a little, trying to see this through her eyes. "I'm not trying to take your granddaughter away from you, and I know this transition isn't easy, but the condescension and negative commentary on my lax parenting don't make me feel particularly good. I understand that us moving here has been difficult, but crapping on my parenting isn't a good way to make things better."

"I've had a hand in raising her!"

"And I appreciate everything you've done for us. You've been a great source of support for a lot of years, but you can't come in and railroad all my decisions. It's not good for me or Peyton, and all it does is cause confusion and dissention. And you need to stop belittling Harley. It's not okay. I'm invested in her and so is Peyton. She's a good person, and she doesn't deserve to be treated the way you're treating her."

She folds her hands on the counter, looking somewhat contrite. "I just miss my granddaughter, that's all."

"Then we can make plans for you to see more of her. And now that we're settled, we can come visit more frequently, and you're always welcome here, but you need to let me be the parent. Just be her grandmother. Have fun with her. Let me be the heavy since that's my role."

Peyton comes bouncing down the hall. "Can I have my treat now, Dad?" She clasps her hands behind her back and rolls up on her toes. "Please?"

"You sure can." I lift the brown paper bag from behind the island, and she shrieks her excitement.

I hope I've made an impact with Karen, and that this is the last time I have to have a conversation like this with her. And that the next time she sees Harley, she's warmer with her. Harley doesn't deserve that kind of coldness. Not from anyone.

Later in the evening, after Karen and Kyle have gone home, Peyton and I sit at the kitchen table. She's dressed in her fairy costume, and I'm wearing a pink tutu that used to fit Peyton as a hat. We do this sometimes, play dress-up and have tea parties. Tonight she asked if we could have grilled cheese sandwiches in lieu of the leftover casserole Karen made for dinner last night. It's not that it's bad; it isn't, Karen is a great cook. However, nine-year-olds aren't always a fan of all the parts of their meal in a mash-up. And we both felt like grilled cheese. Plus sandwiches and tea parties go hand in hand. We're drinking chocolate milk out of plastic tea cups to complete the meal. And despite having had cinnamon buns earlier, she and I made those grocery store-bought sugar cookies that I found in the freezer for dessert.

"Are we going to see Harley again now that Granny has gone home?" Peyton dips her grilled cheese in the small lake of ketchup on her plate.

"Want me to make sure she can take you to the park tomorrow after school?"

She nods, and her mouth twists to the side, a sign she's thinking about what she wants to say. "Granny and Grandpa aren't coming down again next weekend, are they?"

"No, sweetie, why?" I take the tutu off my head and set it on the table; in part because it's tight, and also because this seems like a bit of a serious conversation.

She lifts a shoulder and lets it fall. "Why doesn't Granny like Harley?"

I fight not to react to that. "Why would you say that?"

Peyton picks at the crust and focuses on her plate. "The things Granny says sometimes. It seemed like she was upset that Harley was at lunch with us. And she didn't want Harley to come to the park with us today, but it's always more fun when Harley is around. It's not that Granny isn't fun, but Harley is . . . softer. Granny is like a stale marshmallow, and Harley is like a fresh one."

I smile at the comparison. "I don't think Granny doesn't like Harley. I think she just isn't used to me having a girlfriend."

"It's not going to be like when you had that girlfriend before. Trista, I think?"

I blink in surprise. I didn't think she remembered Trista at all. "What do you mean, it's not going to be like Trista?"

"She was nice. I liked her. She reminds me of Harley a little. But she wasn't around for very long, and Granny didn't like her either. I don't want that to happen with Harley. I don't want her to stop coming to pick me up from school, or taking me to the park, or making glitter crafts."

"Trista didn't stop coming around because of Granny," I tell her, but as I say it, I'm not entirely sure that's the truth. "I know it might seem like that, but Trista and I just weren't right for each other."

"Do you think you and Harley are right for each other?" she asks.

I smile softly, struggling for words. "Harley and I have a lot in common, and she understands me in ways that not everyone can."

Peyton tips her head to the side. "I have lots in common with Harley too. We both like fun art stuff, and we're not afraid to make a mess because they can always be cleaned up. And we both don't have a mom because they're up in heaven."

"That's very true." I swallow past the lump in my throat.

"Harley says they're up in heaven watching us. And if we pay attention sometimes, they send us signs."

"Is that so?" Sometimes I wish Marcie would send me a sign. Something to let me know that she approves of my choices. That Harley is the right one for me and Peyton. That she's okay with me moving on.

She nods. "Do you think Mommy would have liked Harley?"

I have to clear my throat to answer. "I think she would have."

"Me too. I wonder if Mommy and Harley's mom are friends in heaven. That would be nice, wouldn't it?" She takes another bite of her grilled cheese.

Her gentle innocence breaks my heart and makes it swell at the same time. "It would."

Twenty-One

AN UNCERTAIN TRUCE

HARLEY

At ten on Sunday night, just as I'm getting ready for bed, my phone rings. I check the screen, and my heart does a little leap and spin in my chest.

I answer the call with, "hey."

"Hey, yourself. I missed you this weekend." Gavin's voice is soft and raspy. He clears his throat. "I'm sorry."

"For what?" I drop down on my couch, put the phone on speaker, and set it on the armrest.

"For the way Karen acted on Friday, and for not putting her in her place. For not sticking up for you the way I should have, and for letting her undermine my parenting," he says softly.

"I'm trying to understand why you allow it and what exactly I've done to make her dislike me so much. Does she know about what happened before you moved? That I tried to kiss you?" Even now, after our discussion and his assurances, I still feel the familiar heat of embarrassment creeping up my spine. Especially at the idea that he might have confided something like that to his mother-in-law.

"God no. I never told anyone about that."

"Not even Ian?"

"No. Not even Ian." He sighs. "It's not about you, Harley. Karen is struggling with the fact that she was basically a mother figure for Peyton, and now she feels as though that's been taken away from her because of the move. And now we have you."

It takes a few seconds for it to sink in. "Oh. *Oh.*" I consider how hard that would be, going from seeing Peyton almost daily to only once a month. It would be similar to a divorced parent losing most of their custodial rights. "And she sees me as a re-placement?"

"I guess in a way. I knew it was going to be hard for her. I don't think I realized exactly how hard. And it's made that much harder for her because Peyton has settled in here so quickly. And she talks about you a lot." Gavin's voice is full of apology.

Some of my frustration with Karen disappears. "This is a delicate balance for you, isn't it?"

"It is, and I can't control Karen's behavior, but we sat down and talked it through, and I think we're in a better place. I assured her that her role in Peyton's life hasn't changed, and that she needs to let me do the parenting, since it's my job. And that she needs to cut out the snide comments because they're not going unnoticed and it's unfair to you."

"How did she take that?"

"She was defensive at first, but I think she understands where the lines are now, and I'm hoping she's going to toe them."

"That seems like progress? Baby steps?"

"Baby steps." He pauses for a moment. "That's all we can ask for, isn't it?"

"I think it's reasonable." I'm going to cross my fingers that the next time I see Karen, there's less hostility from her, and I don't have to protect my feelings with battle armor. "And this is uncharted territory, isn't it? We can't expect it to be seamless."

"No, I guess we can't. How are you so wise?"

I glance at the gallery of photos on my wall, my gaze catching on the last family photo we had taken before my parents died. We were standing in front of Spark House, Grandma Spark standing to the right of my dad, her hand on my shoulder. Even then, she felt more like an additional parent than a grandparent. I imagine it's much the same for Karen. "Loss at a young age does that, I think."

He makes a noise, but doesn't comment otherwise. "Are you still able to pick up Peyton after school tomorrow?"

"Absolutely."

"Great." He sounds relieved. "She really wanted to see you today. We both did. I missed you."

My heart squeezes at the admission. "Me too."

"I'm looking forward to tomorrow and seeing your beautiful face."

I chuckle. "And I'm looking forward to seeing your handsome one and Peyton's cute one."

He laughs along with me, and then clears his throat, his voice suddenly shy. "Maybe you want to pack an overnight bag?"

"You want me to stay the night? Do you think we should talk to Peyton about that first?"

"Maybe?" It sounds like a question. "Am I jumping the gun?"

"I think it's probably a conversation we need to have first, in person, before we go making sleepover plans."

He sighs. "You're right. I just want some time with you, especially after this weekend. And I don't want to have to wait until

Peyton can have a sleepover at her grandparents' place before I can spend a night with you beside me."

My heart stutters. "Then maybe we need to broach the subject with Peyton and see how she feels about me staying overnight at your place. And we can go from there. Baby steps, Gavin."

He chuckles again. "I would come over there right now if I had access to a sitter."

"I don't doubt that for a second, but it's late, and you have work tomorrow, and so do I, and staying up until midnight so we can sneak in some sexy time seems irresponsible."

"Sometimes being responsible is overrated."

"It's after ten. My carriage has already turned back into a pumpkin."

He huffs. "This feels like a punishment."

I bite back a grin, aware that I could go to his place right now, but that dropping everything for him sets a bad precedent. "You'll see me in less than twenty-four hours."

He makes a discontented sound, then asks, "Where are you?"

"What do you mean, where am I? I'm in my apartment."

"I mean, what room are you in?" I hear rustling in the background.

"My living room, why?"

"What are you wearing? Are you ready for bed?"

"Nothing you can say is going to persuade me to leave my house right now."

"I know, you've told me that. I'm improvising. I'm going to end this call and video chat you."

My screen goes blank and lights up again a few seconds later. I answer the call, and Gavin's handsome face appears. He shifts the phone around, setting it on one of the stands he has sitting around his house so he can have hands-free video chats. That's when I realize he's in his bedroom, and he's shirtless.

His gaze moves over me in a hot sweep. "Wanna have a little fun with me?"

I bite my lip. "What kind of fun are you talking about?"

"The naked kind." He arches a brow. "Unless that's outside of your comfort zone."

Have I ever had phone sex before? No. But that doesn't mean I'm not interested in trying new things. "I can get on board with naked fun."

I push up off the couch, grab my own phone stand, and walk down the hall to my bedroom. My stomach clenches with excitement as I set the phone on my nightstand and adjust it, making sure it's set up to give Gavin an excellent view of my bed.

I open the nightstand and toss a few helpers on the mattress.

Gavin curses softly. "Have I told you lately how much I appreciate your willingness to try new things with me?"

"Does that mean you're ready to have some fun?" I climb up onto the bed and arrange myself so I'm facing the screen and lift my top over my head. I'm already in pajamas—just a T-shirt and shorts—so I'm instantly topless.

Gavin groans. "What I wouldn't give to be able to put my hands and mouth on you right now."

"What would you do first, if you were here?" I drag my fingertips along my bottom lip.

"I would start by kissing that sweet, sexy mouth of yours." His biceps flex and release, hand moving over his erection in slow, unhurried passes. "Then I'd trail them down your throat."

"Would you use teeth?" I let my fingers drift down my throat and over my collarbone.

"Maybe a little, just to tease you." He adjusts his own phone so I have a better view of his hand moving over his straining erection, thumb sweeping the crown on each upward stroke. "I wouldn't linger there too long, though."

"What would you do next?" I let my fingers drift down between my breasts. "Would you stop here?" I circle a nipple. "Maybe here is where you'd use teeth?" I pinch the taut peak.

He nods once, tongue sweeping across his bottom lip. "That's exactly what I'd do. But I wouldn't stop there, would I?"

I shake my head. "No. You'd keep going, wouldn't you?" I walk my fingers down my stomach and past my navel, slipping my hand inside my sleep shorts. "You'd tease me some more, kiss the inside of my thigh, bite and suck, and leave whisper-light kisses where I need you the most."

"I think you should lose the shorts, Harley, so I can see what you're doing."

I hook my thumbs in the waistband and drag them down my thighs, tossing them over the side of the bed.

Then we guide each other to orgasm, whispering hot words and needy sighs and groans until we tip over into bliss.

Gavin talks to Peyton about how she would feel if I spent the night at their house. It's a conversation he needs to have with her on his own, without her feeling pressured to say what she thinks we both want to hear.

A few days after he talks to her about it—he told me she seemed receptive and okay with me staying over, but I still wanted to give it a little more time before we dive into it—I pick her up from school with the intention of taking her to the park, trying to make the most of it before we get hit with snow.

I run into Lynn in the parking lot. "Hi, Harley! How are you?" She pulls me in for a quick hug.

"I'm good. You?" We head toward the pick-up area.

"Same, same." Her phone pings with a message, and she checks it before sliding it back into her purse. "I've been meaning to invite you over for dinner for months now. Actually, I've told Ian to ask Gavin probably half a dozen times, but he always forgets." She rolls her eyes, but she's smiling. "What are you all doing tonight? Ian just messaged, apparently he and Gavin have a meeting and it's literally two blocks away from our place. I know it's short notice, but we could do something easy? Order pizza and throw together a salad? But only if you don't already have plans."

"I was just going to take Peyton to the park. We don't have anything else going on that I know of," I tell her.

"Do you want to check with Gavin?" she asks as we push through the front doors.

"Yeah, I can do that." I type out a quick message, and Gavin answers almost immediately with a thumbs-up and that sounds like a great plan.

"Perfect! Claire has hockey practice until four, but we'll be home by four thirty if you want to come over after that? And you don't have to wait for Gavin, just come by whenever."

"Okay. That sounds great. Peyton and I will pick up dessert."

"Fantastic. I'm really looking forward to it. It's been ages since Gavin has been over for dinner."

The bell rings and kids rush out of the building. Peyton and Claire find us, and we tell them that we're having dinner together, which makes them both happy. We wave goodbye for now and head for our respective cars.

"Your birthday is coming up in a couple of months. Do you know what you want?" I ask Peyton as we make the short trip to the park.

"If pink ponies were real, I would want one, but since they're not, I think I want a dog."

"A stuffed dog or a real one?" I pull into the lot and park the car, holding Peyton's door open for her as she climbs out of the back seat.

"A real one. I've wanted one my whole life, but Granny is allergic to dogs, and she thinks they're too much work, so we never got one. But now that we live here, we can have a dog."

"Does your dad know you want a dog?" We head straight for the swings.

"Yup." She hops up onto a swing and I take the one beside her.

"And what does he say?"

"He says, 'we'll see.'" She mocks his deep voice.

I laugh. "And what do you think that means?"

"I don't know. But he said if I want a dog, I have to prove that I'm going to be responsible and take care of it."

"Well, that's true. Dogs can be a lot of work. It's like having a little kid that doesn't grow up. They need you to walk them and feed them and play with them." All things I would love if I didn't work such long hours.

"I think I would like that." She pumps her feet. "There's one thing I want more than a dog, but I can't ask my dad for that."

"Why can't you ask him?"

"Because I asked once before, and it made him . . . sad." She twists her lips to the side. "Or maybe he was mad. Mad or sad. Maybe both."

"What did you ask for?"

She chews on her bottom lip for a few seconds before she finally says, "I wanted a baby brother or a baby sister. That was back when his girlfriend was Trista. I was five. She had a daughter too. Her name was Hilary and she was four. She was fun, and I wanted her to be my sister, but then they stopped seeing each other and I stopped seeing Hilary."

My heart clenches. "That must have been really hard."

She purses her lips. "I was sad, and I cried. And so did Dad. But he doesn't know that I saw him cry. I wanted to give him a hug, but I've tried to hug him when he's been sad before, and he gets more upset and tries to hide how sad he is. So I leave him alone instead."

I reach out and squeeze her hand. "Is it hard to see your dad upset?"

She tips her head to the side. "It depends. Every time I watch the movie *Onward* with my friend Abby, and her mom watches with us, she cries. But that's a different kind of sad. Granny always cries when she takes me to visit Mom at the cemetery. And then she hugs me a lot and tells me I look just like my mom when she was my age." She kicks at the stone in the dirt, her eyes on the ground. "I don't like going to the cemetery, but Granny says it's important to visit Mom. Sometimes I feel bad because I don't ever cry about her. I know I grew inside her, but that was before I had memories, and she died before I could meet her. I like it better when we look at the photo albums at Granny's house."

"Do you do that a lot? Look at photo albums?" I ask. This is the first time Peyton has ever opened up about her mom, and I can't pass up the opportunity to learn a little more and maybe understand Karen better, and how Gavin has dealt with this loss as well.

All I have are my memories of Peyton as a baby, and Gavin sometimes struggling with being a new father and losing his partner. Seeing it through a different set of eyes helps give me perspective.

"Oh yeah, every time I stay at Granny's overnight. Before my bedtime snack and stories, we always pick one album, and Granny will tell me stories about my mom when she was little just like me. I think you would have liked my mom," she tells me.

"I think I would have liked her too." I give her a soft smile. "Do you and your dad ever talk about your mom, or look at photo albums together?"

Peyton shakes her head. "It always makes him too sad, so sometimes I'll look at the albums we have on my own. My favorite is the wedding album. She looked so pretty in her dress, and Dad was all dressed up. In pictures, he looked at my mom the same way he looks at you."

I feel like I can't breathe for a few seconds. As if the air has been stolen and my lungs are frozen. "Oh? And how is that?"

"Like you're one of his favorite things." She pumps her legs again. "We still have Mom's wedding dress, but I'm not supposed to touch it. He keeps it in the closet in the spare bedroom. Once I tried it on, and he got really mad at me. I got grounded and couldn't play with my friends all weekend."

"Oh no. That must have really upset him."

"It did. Sometimes when he's working, I sneak in there and look at the dress. It's in a plastic bag, so I never get to touch it, but I can look and not get into trouble for that."

"I bet it's a beautiful dress."

"It is. One day maybe you can look at it too."

"Maybe one day," I agree.

"Dad said you might sleep over at our place sometimes."

The abrupt change in topic throws me. "Oh? And how would you feel about that?"

She pumps her legs harder, swinging higher. "I think a sleepover would be fun. You used to live with us before, when you were my nanny."

"That's right. I did." I swallow down my nerves, uncertain where she's going with this, and what I should or shouldn't say. I probably should have asked more questions about what all Gavin said to her.

"You had your own bedroom. But Dad said it would be different because now you're his girlfriend and not my nanny."

"Do you understand what makes it different?" I want to get a good sense of how she feels about all of this. If she's confused. Or if she feels okay about it. And especially if she doesn't.

"When you were my nanny, you took care of me when Dad was at work."

"That's right. It was my job to take care of you. And even though I got paid to do it, I loved taking care of you very much."

"Do you get paid to do that now?"

I shake my head. "No. I spend time with you because I care about you and it's fun."

"And because you like my dad."

"Yes, I do. I like him very much."

"He likes you too. He told me that if you sleep over, it wouldn't be in the spare room or my room, but in his room, with him." She glances up at the sky, following a bird making circles above our heads.

"How would you feel about that?"

She lifts a shoulder and lets it fall. "Sometimes I get scared in the middle of the night, and I want to sleep in his room with him. If you're in his room, would that mean I can't sleep in there too?"

"No, it wouldn't mean that you couldn't come in and get a snuggle with your dad. But he might take you back to your room and cuddle with you in your bed."

"Would you cuddle with me?"

"Of course, if you wanted me to."

"Okay. Then I think it would be fun for you to sleep over. Sometimes Claire and I have sleepovers, but now that she has hockey practice, it makes it harder." She drags her toes along the ground, slowing herself down.

"Hockey practice can be early in the morning," I agree. "Speaking of Claire, should we stop at the bakery and pick up something yummy for dessert?"

"Oh yes! We should go to Whimsy's, they have all the best desserts." She hops off the swing and waits for me to hop off mine. Then she slips her hand in mine. "I really like that we all get to go to Claire's tonight. It makes it feel almost like a weekend instead of a weekday."

"It does, doesn't it?" I agree.

"Her mom is really nice. I like her a lot," Peyton says.

"I like her a lot too." I squeeze her hand.

Peyton looks up at me. "You know what would be really great?"

"What's that?"

"If one day you became my mom."

My heart stutters in my chest, then swells. I'm scared to let that hope take root, but the seed is already planted.

Half an hour later, Peyton and I pull into Lynn and Ian's driveway. I'm surprised to find Gavin and Ian already there, with takeout pizza. Gavin gives me a kiss on the cheek and hugs Peyton, who promptly runs off in search of Claire.

The next few minutes are a flurry of activity as we get the girls to help us set the table. We sit down to dinner, and the girls tell us all about their day and the things that happened on the playground at recess. Once they're done, they excuse themselves to go play while we finish up and enjoy adult conversation and a glass of wine.

Gavin stretches his arm across the back of my chair, thumb brushing the nape of my neck, causing a wave of goose bumps to flash along my arms. I lean into him, enjoying the innocent affection.

The conversation is light and easy, and despite the fact that Ian, Lynn, and Gavin have a long history of friendship, I feel like I'm part of things. Like this relationship exists outside of just him and me and Peyton.

And that little seed of hope that Peyton planted at the park starts to sprout. I hope it's not too soon to let it grow in my heart.

Twenty-Two

TEST RUN

HARLEY

The weekend following the conversation about me sleeping over, we give it a test run. I'm a little uncertain as to how it's going to go. Peyton is excited, and so is Gavin, but I'm not entirely convinced it's going to be one of those situations where everything runs smoothly.

We dress up, as seems to be a pretty regular occurrence these days, and Peyton makes ponytail horns in Gavin's hair, but he draws the line at glitter hairspray when they keep popping out. We order pizza for dinner, and at seven we all put on our pajamas—modest ones, obviously—make popcorn, and cue up a movie with Peyton seated between the two of us on the couch. At bedtime we read her stories together and say good night, and I promise chocolate chip pancakes for breakfast.

And then it's just Gavin and I.

I'm not naive enough to believe that Peyton is going to go to bed without a fight tonight. We're changing the routine, doing something different. The holidays will be upon us soon enough, and there will be family events and probably more sleepovers. So we want to see how this is going to work in familiar surroundings.

"These pajamas are killing me," he mutters as we walk quietly down the hall, back to the living room.

I glance down at my outfit. I'm wearing leggings and a long, oversized nightshirt. I even have a sports bra on. "This is the opposite of sexy," I reply as I start to make the right into the living room.

"Whoa, where are you going?" He grabs my wrist and nods in the direction of his bedroom.

I laugh and pat him on the chest. "I appreciate your enthusiasm and your desire to get me out of these super sexy jammies, but this is not the last we've seen of Peyton."

"Bedtime is done. She'll be asleep in ten minutes."

"I still think we should wait it out for a bit." I pull him toward the couch.

He follows grudgingly.

And, as predicted, it doesn't take long for Peyton to come down the hall, stuffed bunny tucked under her arm, telling us she's afraid of the monsters in the closet. Gavin takes her back to her room. While I wait for him to return, I check my phone and find a message from Avery.

Avery: How's the sleepover going?

Harley: Exactly as I predicted.

Avery: So you're sitting by yourself while Gavin puts Peyton to bed.

Harley: For the second time.

Avery: LOLOL. You totally called it!

Harley: It's cute that he thought we'd actually get some alone time.

Avery: Dating a guy with a kid is eye-opening. And she likes you!

Harley: Lucky for me. Now I just need to work on his MIL.

Avery: *eyeroll gif* You do realize you're basically my only babysitting option when I pop this kid, right? Declan's mom is too busy online shopping to remember to feed a toddler.

We message back and forth until I hear the soft click of Peyton's door closing and let her know that date-night sleepover is resuming.

Avery: *crossed fingers emoji* Good luck having slightly frantic, awkward, and quiet sex while simultaneously being worried it's going to get interrupted by a cockblocking nine-year-old.

Gavin appears in the living room as I drop my phone back on the coffee table. "Everything okay?"

"Suddenly she's afraid of the monsters in the closet. She's never been afraid of monsters. Not even after we watched the Harry Potter movie with the Voldemort dude."

I grin. "Funny how kids can develop new fears just like that." I snap my fingers.

He drops down on the couch beside me. "You're so gleeful about this."

"She's a kid, and this is new. Didn't you ever try a sleepover with any of your past relationships?"

He frowns and shakes his head. "No. Not when Peyton was home anyway. We never got to a point where I felt comfortable enough to try it. Or maybe I was too nervous? I don't know."

"So this is new for all of us. She's excited, but she's also nervous. She likes me, but this is very different, so she's going to push some boundaries." I run my fingers through his hair. It's still kind of wonky from the mini horn ponytails. "Relationships with kids involved take time and patience. She needs to know that you're still here for her, and that I'm not going to take you away from her. Did you really think tonight would be about more than sleeping?"

He shrugs and gives me a chagrined smile. "I wasn't banking on it, but a guy can hope."

"We'll get there eventually, but it might not be tonight."

"Karen offered to take Peyton next weekend, sort of as a peace offering. We could drive her to Boulder and rent an Airbnb. Have some us time. The uninterrupted kind."

I bite my lip. "Us time would be amazing."

"I'll call Karen tomorrow morning. As long as you're sure you can get the time off." He laces our fingers together.

"We've hired a bunch of new people to help with events, so I'm pretty sure I can make it work. Let me double-check with my sisters, but next weekend is a corporate event and Avery typically handles those." One of the positive things that have come out of the franchise opportunity is the hiring of additional staff. We've been able to bring in new people and promote some of our other employees. It's freed up more and more of our time recently, and has allowed me to focus more of my energy on the parts of the job I love the most.

"I'll keep my fingers crossed then." Gavin brings my hand to his lips and kisses my knuckle. The creak of a door opening has him closing his eyes and exhaling heavily through his nose. "Crap. I can't stand up right now."

"I haven't even touched you."

He cracks a lid. "I know, but talking about alone time is making things happens. My control is on par with my teenage self from two decades ago."

I laugh and lean in, giving him a quick peck on the lips. "Would you like me to see if I can get her to stay put this time?"

He nods once, and I push to a stand, meeting Peyton at the threshold to the living room. She glances from me to her dad and back to me. "There's a scratching sound outside my window."

"Why don't we check it out?" I offer her my hand.

"Can I hug Daddy one more time?"

"Of course. Go give him a hug, and then we'll see if we can figure out where the scratching is coming from."

She rushes over and gives him a hug and then comes back to me, slipping her hand into mine. I pull her curtain aside, and we discover it's just a branch that's swaying in the wind.

"Can you sing me a song?" Peyton asks as she climbs back into bed.

"One song and then it's bedtime, okay?"

"Okay." She nods and pulls the covers all the way up to her neck.

I brush her hair away from her face. "But before I sing you a song, I want to ask you something."

"Okay."

"Were you really afraid there were monsters in your closet?"

Her mouth twists to the side.

"It's okay if you weren't. And it's okay if you said you were because you wanted your dad to tuck you in again, honey. I know this is different and that maybe you were excited at first, but now you're nervous about me sleeping over here."

Her fingers go to her lips. "I want you to sleep over, but I want to be part of the sleepover."

I nod in understanding. "Because you don't want to feel left out?"

She nods.

"I get that, but the best part of a sleepover is waking up and making breakfast together, and then spending the day having fun. Nighttime is for sleeping, and if we don't get a good sleep, it's hard to have a good next day."

"When I go to bed late, I'm grumpy."

"And we don't want to be grumpy for chocolate chip pancakes, do we?"

She shakes her head.

"So I'll sing you a song, and then you have to try your hardest to stay in your bed and go to sleep, okay?"

"Okay."

I curl up beside her and start singing a lullaby. When I get to the end, Peyton whispers tiredly, "One more?"

"One more."

Before I start singing she takes my hand in hers and laces our fingers together. "I love you, Harley."

"I love you too, Peyton." I kiss her temple and fight to keep my voice steady as I sing the second lullaby. I repeat the final refrain twice, her hand going lax. I give it one more minute before I finally slip out of her bed and steal out of her room.

This definitely isn't a long-term strategy, but she needs reassurance. And hopefully, with time, these sleepovers will become part of her normal.

Gavin is sitting on the couch, staring at the TV, a hockey game playing with no volume.

He glances in my direction and his eyebrow lifts. "Is she actually asleep?"

"I'd give it five minutes, but I think so."

"Fingers crossed." He pats the cushion beside his, and when I sit down beside him, he wraps an arm around me and pulls him into his side, bending to press his lips to my temple.

We watch the game on low for fifteen minutes before we deem it safe and turn off the TV and most of the lights, apart from the hallway. Gavin makes sure the doors are locked before he takes my hand and we pad quietly past Peyton's closed door. I'm very grateful that Gavin's room isn't right across the hall or right next to Peyton's, and that there's a bathroom between them.

Once we're inside his bedroom, he turns the lock on his door and takes my face in his hands, planting a searing kiss on my lips. I moan quietly, gripping his strong arms. I find the hem of his shirt and slip my fingers underneath, skimming the taut ridges and planes of his abs, up his chest, dragging the fabric with it.

His hands leave my face, and he yanks his shirt over his head, then crouches and grabs me by the ass, hoisting me up. I wrap my legs around his waist, and he lowers me until I can feel him, hard and thick between my thighs. He claims my mouth again, his kisses hot and demanding, full of pent-up desire. It's been weeks since we've been able to steal any alone time. More than a week of talking about it, of late-night video chats from across the city where we talk about what we plan to do to each other when we're finally naked and alone.

He carries me across the room to the bed, sets me on the edge, and grinds himself against me. I buck and groan quietly, especially when he tears his mouth from mine and nips his way across my jaw and down my neck. He shoves my nightshirt up and my sports bra along with it and latches onto a nipple, sucking roughly.

I gasp, and one of his hands presses over my mouth to stifle the sound. Which is a good idea, because he follows with teeth. "You think you can be quiet if I go down on you?"

I grab one of the pillows from the top of the bed. "With a little help, maybe?"

He chuckles and stands up, fingers dragging down my stomach and curling around the waistband of my leggings. I'm already throbbing between my legs, and he hasn't even touched me yet.

I'm about to lift my hips when the patter of feet in the hallway puts me on alert. His doorknob turns, but thankfully it doesn't open. "Daddy? I had a bad dream!" Peyton calls out.

"Give me a second!" His eyes flare as he looks down at his pajama pants, which are tented rather impressively. He tucks himself into the waistband, which doesn't look all that comfortable, and pulls a shirt over his head. And then a sweatshirt for good measure. "We really need that weekend away before I die of blue balls," he grumbles as he heads for the bedroom door. I bite back a smile, because I'm sure it's uncomfortable, even if it's kind of funny how perturbed he is.

Gavin ends up falling asleep in Peyton's bed, and I fall asleep in his. He steals back into the bedroom at two in the morning, and despite us both being groggy and only half awake, we have quiet, lazy sex before we pass back out.

I'm unsurprised when Peyton ends up back in his bedroom at six in the morning, worming her way between us and alternating between hugging me and her dad, and then asking when it's time to make pancakes.

I know Gavin might consider this a wash of a sleepover, but it's another baby step in the right direction. And I'll take every single one of those we can get.

Twenty-Three

A LITTLE PRIVATE TIME

HARLEY

On Friday Gavin picks me up at four in the afternoon for our weekend getaway. Peyton is sitting in the back seat, which is full of her things. There are blankets and pillows piled on one side, her backpack perched precariously on top. On the other side are her stuffies, including the gnome family we made earlier this week, lined up beside her, ready for the ride to Boulder.

Gavin meets me at the truck and takes my bag, setting it beside his. When his hands are free, he leans down to steal a kiss. "Just a few more hours and you're all mine."

"And you're mine."

"Damn right." He smirks and winks, then closes the trunk and walks me around to the passenger side, opening the door and giving me his hand so I can climb in.

I twist in my seat so I can look at Peyton. "Are you excited to spend the weekend with your granny and grandpa?"

She nods. "Granny said she's going to take me to a play."

"That sounds like tons of fun!"

"I love plays. But you have to be very, very quiet. Because it's not like a movie where the actors can't hear you, and when people talk, it can be distracting."

"And you have personal experience with that, don't you?" Peyton has a role in every skit the school puts on during assemblies. It means she often stays after school once or twice a week for rehearsals. She loves it, though, and doesn't mind the longer days.

On Mondays I'll often sit in the audience and work on assignments for my class. Most people can't handle all the noise, but I seem to be able to tune it out.

The trip to Boulder takes a little less than two hours. My palms start to sweat when we pull into Karen and Kyle's driveway. Their house is a pretty ranch-style bungalow with a white picket fence, manicured lawn, and gardens that have been put to bed until spring.

We hardly have the vehicle in park before the front door opens, and Karen steps out onto the front porch, an apron tied around her waist. Peyton clambers out of the car and bounces up the steps, throwing her arms around Karen.

Gavin waits for me and places a hand on the small of my back, patting it once, possibly to reassure me that everything is fine. Gavin hugs Karen, and I stand back, uncertain what the protocol is. Eventually Karen turns to me and gives me what I'm guessing is her version of a warm smile. "Harley, it's so nice to see you again." At least it seems like she's trying.

"You as well. Your house is beautiful."

"We've lived here since we got married, almost forty years this year."

"Oh wow. That's amazing. My parents would have been married for nearly forty years too, if they were still here." I cringe internally. Nothing kills a conversation quite like bringing up your dead parents. "It's definitely something to celebrate."

"It is." She nods her agreement. "Why don't we bring in all of Peyton's things. Dinner is almost ready."

Gavin glances at me and then Karen. "Oh, you don't have to feed Harley and me."

"Nonsense. There's plenty for everyone, and the table is set for six."

"I made a dinner reservation for Harley and me for eight tonight," he explains.

"Oh, I didn't realize. That's unfortunate. I wouldn't have gone to all the trouble if I'd known." She drops her gaze and smooths her hands over her apron.

"We can stay for dinner," I assure her.

"I wouldn't want to interfere with your weekend plans." Karen smiles, but it's stiff.

"Not at all. We can cancel the dinner reservations. We have tomorrow night anyway." I don't want to start this weekend on the wrong foot, and it's obvious that Karen has gone to a lot of trouble to make dinner for us. There must have been a communication failure if Gavin didn't explain that we had dinner reservations tonight.

"Are you sure you don't mind canceling?" Karen looks between me and Gavin.

"Stay for dinner! Please, Harley." Peyton grabs hold of my arm and bounces twice excitedly.

"Of course I'm sure. We'll get you settled in, and have dinner before we leave," I tell Peyton.

Gavin mutters an apology that I wave off as we carry several loads of stuff into Karen's house. It's clear that Karen is making an effort, and I want to acknowledge that, even if it means canceling our dinner reservation.

Karen and Kyle's house is exactly what I expect from Karen. Not a thing out of place, pristine, organized, and clutter-free. The house is a little dated—everything looks like it was purchased in the previous decade—but it's all been well-maintained.

I don't have much of an opportunity to check out Peyton's room since all I manage to do is drop an armload of stuff in the space that's been carefully decorated for a little girl who is a big fan of fairies and princesses. But as I walk down the hall, I glance at the framed photos lining the wall. I follow Gavin down the stairs and notice that he keeps his gaze trained ahead of him, as though he purposely avoids looking at the pictures.

It's a family history laid out in photo form. Some are of grandparents and great-grandparents. Yellowed and faded black-and-white photos in pretty, decorative frames show smiling younger men and women in wedding attire. They slowly change to color photos, Karen and Kyle, young and in love at their own wedding. Their entire lives ahead of them. Blissfully unaware of the tragedy that would strike their family when they were gifted their first grandchild.

I soak in as much as I can as we make our way back downstairs, Peyton leading the way. We bring the last of her things inside, and then we're ushered into the dining room for roast beef dinner.

We make small talk, the conversation not easy like it is with Gavin's parents, but it's not nearly as tense as it was the last time Karen and I were in the same room together. After dinner I help clear the plates and bring them into the kitchen. Gavin doesn't leave me alone with Karen for a second, and I'm unsure if that's intentional.

When she offers tea or coffee, Gavin declines, saying we

should probably get going. We give Peyton hugs and kisses and tell her we'll see her on Sunday. It's after seven thirty by the time we pull out of the driveway.

"I'm so sorry about that," Gavin says as soon as we're on the road again.

"You don't need to be sorry. It was probably just a miscommunication."

"I swear I told her we had dinner reservations, but maybe I didn't."

"It's fine. We have dinner tomorrow night." I give his hand a squeeze. "Besides, I doubt I'm going to want to leave our room once we're in it. We can order something later if we need a midnight snack to get us through until morning."

He brings my hand to his lips and plants a kiss on my knuckles. "That sounds perfect."

Twenty minutes later we pull up to an estate that's been converted into a bed-and-breakfast. Gavin's rented us the one-bedroom cottage at the back of the property. It's stunning and private, surrounded with lovely gardens and a covered porch with a swing. It's the perfect setting for a romantic weekend.

There's a fire crackling in the hearth, a bottle of champagne chilling, and a platter of chocolate-covered strawberries on the table by the fireplace. "This is amazing."

"I wanted privacy and this has it. There's a hot tub out back that we can make use of later." He kisses the side of my neck and drops his bag on the floor.

He barely has the door closed and the lock turned before our mouths are connected. I part my lips and stroke my tongue out. A wave of need washes over me, intense and overwhelming. In all the months we've been seeing each other, there have only been a handful of nights where it's just been us. And there's something intoxicating and exhilarating about knowing that for the next day and a half, he's all mine. I have his complete, undivided attention, and he has mine. And I plan to take full advantage of that.

He cups my face in his palm and the fingers of his other hand slide into my hair. Gripping lightly, he angles my head to the side and deepens the kiss, a low feral sound humming across my lips. I go for his belt buckle, flicking the clasp and pulling it free. Popping the button on his dress pants and pulling the zipper down, I cup him through his boxers, already hard and ready for me.

I squeeze once, then dip inside the waistband of his boxers to skim the length. He groans and I sigh as I wrap my hand around him.

He breaks the kiss for a moment, both of us panting hard. "The first time is going to be quick and dirty, but the second I'll take my time."

"Is that a promise or a warning?"

The corner of his mouth turns up in a salacious half grin. "Both?"

"Good. You can romance me later. I just need you in me." I pull my dress over my head, dropping it on the floor and leaving me in a pair of lace panties and a matching bra. Gavin cups my breasts in his hand and drops his head, sucking a lace-covered nipple between his lips.

We're frantic as we undress each other, desperate and needy. My panties end up a casualty, too delicate for Gavin's rough fingers as he drags them down my thighs.

He grimaces and tosses them on the floor. "Sorry about that. I'll replace these." He licks up the length of my sex, nuzzling in for a moment as he passes me the condom.

"We could go without if you want," I suggest breathlessly.

He lifts his head, expression questioning.

"I'm on the pill. I'm very regimented about taking it." I bite my lip, waiting, wishing I'd kept my mouth shut.

"It's better to go with. We don't want any accidents." He presses a kiss at the apex of my thighs, eyes holding gentle warning mixed with apology.

"Of course."

My eyes roll up when he strokes at me with his tongue again. I let my head fall back for a moment, my worry dissolving with need. I tear the condom open, and he plucks it from my fingers, sheathing himself. As he rises, he grips under my thighs and lifts me. I grab onto his shoulders and wrap my legs around his waist. He doesn't carry me across the room to the bed; instead, he pins me to the door. "You okay with this?"

"More than okay." He nudges at my entrance. "Fuck me, please."

"Your wish, my command." He lowers me onto him, filling me completely with one quick thrust.

My head falls back against the door and my eyes roll up. I hiss a quiet *yes*, reveling in the fullness.

"You feel so damn good." His lips move across my jaw, nipping gently.

"I can't get enough of you," I tell him, breathless and heady with desire.

"Good, because I don't think we're going to get much in the way of sleep this weekend." His hips pull back and shift forward again. Fill. Retreat. Fill. Retreat.

The door is hard and cold against my back, but the heat of his chest and his hungry kisses, the way his fingers dig into my thighs, gripping tightly as he moves, warm me from the inside. I can feel the orgasm building. The slow spiral, sensation spreading, moving through my limbs, funneling in, like the eye of a tornado, violent and overwhelming. I'm being dragged down, down, down, and then I burst like an exploding star. And all I can do is feel.

Gavin moves inside of me, groaning my name. Bodies already slick with sweat and suddenly lax and lazy with pleasure. To his credit, he doesn't sink to the floor. I'm boneless, struggling to keep my legs locked around his waist, and he carries me across the room, to the bed, which is close to the fireplace. The room is one big open space, the only door leading to the bathroom. He stretches out on top of me and kisses along my throat. "I have zero plans to leave this bed now that we're in it."

He pulls out slowly and removes the condom, dropping it on the floor. And then he kisses his way down my stomach and settles between my thighs, teasing me with his mouth, taking his time with me, like he promised.

After a ridiculous number of orgasms we take a hydration break, and we stretch out on the bed. I run my fingertips along his arm. "I'm sorry about the condom thing earlier." I probably should let it go and leave the subject alone.

"You don't have to apologize." He folds an arm behind his head. "You just caught me off guard. I don't want to take that kind of risk."

"You don't want to take that risk ever, or now?"

He blinks a couple of times. "Honestly, I see a future with you, and you're amazing with kids, so I want to keep an open mind about what that could look like for us, but for now, I need us to be safe." He blows out a breath. "I want time for us to be a couple, and an unplanned pregnancy would make it difficult for us to have the time we need to figure us out. Does that make sense?"

"Yeah, it makes perfect sense. I just . . . I wasn't sure because of what you've already been through." I don't want to push too much, but I'm honestly surprised that he feels this way.

He traces the edge of my jaw. "I'm not going to lie, the idea is scary as hell, but I think it's a lot easier to deal with if we know it's coming than if it happens by accident. Okay?"

"It's absolutely okay. It's more than okay, actually."

He smiles gently and leans in to kiss me, lips soft but insistent. And I let myself get lost in the kiss, seeds of hope for the future taking root.

I pull back when I feel the nudge against my hip. "How in the world can you still manage to get a hard-on? We've had sex three times in two hours."

Gavin shrugs. "I've always been able to go twice in a row."

"Always?"

"For as long as I remember. The first time is usually fast, but the second time I can go a lot longer. Then I need maybe twenty minutes to recover."

I gape at him. "No offense, but you're on the left side of forty. Shouldn't that particular skill set be reserved for guys in their twenties?"

Gavin narrows his eyes. "That's ageist."

I roll mine. "It's not ageist. It's basic biology. Usually twenty-year-olds can do the whole back-to-back thing without having to take a break, but recovery time gets longer as you get older."

He tucks his arm behind his head. "And you know this how?"

"Conversations with girlfriends."

"So it's not from experience." He seems amusedly pleased by this possibility.

"No. You're actually the first man I've ever been with who's over thirty-five."

"Over thirty-five?"

"Usually I ended up dating guys closer to my own age. In part because people often think I'm younger than I am."

"You're all woman in a slightly smaller-than-average package," Gavin says.

I shrug. "Either way, I think it's probably part of the reason most of the guys I dated before you were under thirty."

"And did any of them possess my particular skill set?"

"Would you really want to know if they did?"

He considers that for a moment. "Not really, to be quite honest." He rolls to his side and props up his cheek on his fist. "Your class finishes soon. Do you have an exam to study for?"

"No, just a paper. I'm mostly done. I might need a couple hours tomorrow morning to work on it, but it's not a big deal if I don't tackle it until I'm home on Sunday night."

"Is that going to give you enough time?"

"Oh yeah. I've tried to stay on top of things, and it's been easier the last little while since we hired new staff to help with the events."

He tucks my hair behind my ear, fingertips following the contour of my jawline. "What would it take to finish your degree if you didn't have to juggle courses and your job?"

"One semester plus one additional course."

"Is that something you would consider?"

"I think before now, probably not, but with the way things are going at Spark House and my job always shifting and changing, maybe?" I trace a vein in his arm with my fingertip.

"What's holding you back, then?"

I put a lot of things on hold after Gavin and Peyton left, and it was easy to use Spark House as an excuse. Now things are different. I'm different. "It would take me away from my sisters, and I love working with them."

Gavin nods. "But you don't love the actual job."

"I don't dislike it."

"In an ideal world, if you could still work with your sisters and do what you love, what would that look like?"

I don't even need to think about it, since the paper I've been working on is based on what my ideal role at Spark House would look like. "First I'd bring back the kids' birthday parties because they bring me joy and they don't feel like work. And I would keep it separate from the rest of Spark House, so it would be its own thing and wouldn't interfere with the big events. It would be its own side venture, and I would be in charge of overseeing it. And—" I tap my lips. "I'd love to set up a daycare program, not necessarily just for big events, but possibly for our staff. Cosy, the wife of one of the Mills brothers, mentioned it, and I've been thinking about how that might be a great way to support the people who work for Spark House. Having an on-site daycare program could be amazing. London and Avery could bring their kids there, and if it made sense, we could make daycare available for some of our bigger events. That way, when families are at Spark House for weddings, we'd have a program for the kids to keep them entertained. It's a big project, but I think it could roll out in stages. First daycare for weddings, so we can learn what we'd need and the logistics, then opening it up for potential on-site daycare."

"You've really put a lot of thought into this, haven't you?"

"It's the focus of my final paper for the course I'm taking, so yeah, I've had lots of time to think it through and develop an implementation plan." I mirror his pose, propping up my chin on my fist. "So much has changed with Spark House over the past couple of years. And at first, the franchise seemed like it was undoing everything we'd worked for. But now I can see so many great opportunities that could come from it. We have all these full-time staff who are there to help manage. It's good in a lot of ways, but half of our job has turned into meetings and planning sessions. I know when the franchises are up and running, that will shift again, and so will our roles. It would be nice to have something that's mine to foster."

"Do you think your sisters would be open to something like this?"

"I don't know. We already have a lot going on with the franchises, so I'm not sure if adding more now is the best plan."

He tucks a lock of hair behind my ear. "It might not hurt to at least mention it. I know in the past you've put your own happiness aside because you want the closeness with your sisters, but maybe you don't have to anymore."

"I've been reluctant to make any suggestions because we're in the middle of the franchise start-up, and it's been a bit overwhelming. But you're right, if I don't say anything, nothing will change."

Gavin's phone chimes from somewhere close by. He frowns. "I should shut my phone off tonight." He reaches over and grabs his pants, pulling the device free. He glances at the screen and the furrow in his brow deepens. "Shit. Karen's called twice."

"I hope everything's okay with Peyton."

He hits a few buttons and brings the phone to his ear. I only hear one side of the conversation, but it sounds like Peyton couldn't find her stuffed bunny and that they've managed to recover it. We both say good night and assure Peyton that she can still call us in the morning, but not too early.

An hour later Gavin gets another phone call from Karen because Peyton is having a hard time sleeping. I sing her a lullaby over the phone and say good night again. Twice more Karen calls, but finally around eleven it stops. We get to enjoy the hot tub, sort of, but we're both on alert and basically waiting for another phone call.

Which comes at eight the next morning. Incidentally, that's when Gavin's phone is set to receive calls; he put it on do not disturb from midnight until eight.

Gavin rolls over, grumbling, and answers the call. He scrubs his hand over his face. "What do you mean she's not feeling well? Does she have a fever?" There's a pause on his end. "Did she throw up? Was it something she ate? . . . No. . . . No. Can I speak with her? . . . We'll be there as soon as we can." He ends the call and tosses the phone on the bed.

"Peyton's not feeling well." I try not to let the disappointment seep into my tone or show on my face.

"According to Karen, she's not." The set of his jaw tells me he's not happy.

"Do you believe her?"

"I don't know, but she seems worried, and I don't want to leave Peyton with her grandparents if she's not feeling well."

"Should we stop in and see how she's doing, or would you rather us pack up and go?"

Gavin rubs his temples. "I'd like to say we can just stop over and check on her, but this isn't going to be much of a weekend if we keep getting phone calls from Karen the entire time with false fucking alarms. I really thought she was coming around."

"Maybe it isn't false alarms? Maybe Peyton really is unwell. Let's pack everything up, and if things are fine, we can come back here, but if they aren't, we can take her home. You're right, leaving her with Karen and Kyle if she's unwell isn't a good idea, and we don't want to set it up so that future weekends are stressful for us or her."

He leans over and kisses me. "Thank you for being so understanding."

"You don't need to thank me. Peyton is always your top priority." I hope for Karen's sake, Peyton truly is unwell.

We pack our things and arrive at Karen's an hour later. We find Peyton in the kitchen with Karen, tracing shapes on paper with cookie cutters, which is something I taught Peyton to do so she could make her own holiday garland to string up between her bedposts.

I don't have to look at Gavin to know he's not pleased. It bleeds through in his tone. "I thought you said Peyton wasn't feeling well."

Peyton looks up from her tracing, eyes wide. "Daddy?" She jumps up from her chair and rushes over. "I thought you weren't coming to get me until tomorrow."

"Granny called to let us know you weren't feeling well. But you look like you're okay now." He strokes her hair and smiles down at her, his expression shifting and his smile stiffening when he glances at Karen, who pushes back her chair and clasps her hands in front of her.

The forced contrition is a lot to handle. I hang back, aware this isn't my fight and I need to let Gavin deal with his mother-in-law.

"I was thirsty this morning and I drank my milk too fast. But I feel good now. Are you staying here tonight? Can we go to the park you built this afternoon?"

"I'm so sorry I interrupted your plans. Why don't I whip up some scrambled eggs and you can stay for brunch? Then I can take you to the park, Peyton."

"We packed up all of our stuff thinking that Peyton was ill and had come down with something," Gavin says.

"I just had a sore tummy. It's okay now," Peyton says.

I glance between Gavin and Karen, aware that Gavin is not happy about this situation, or the fact that Karen called several times last night and we started our morning off with this. It all seems too intentional.

I turn to Peyton. "I didn't really get to see your bedroom yesterday. Do you want to show it to me now?"

"Okay." She nods and takes my hand, leading me down the hallway and up the stairs to the second floor. I want to stop along the way and check out all the pictures on the wall, but I can hear Gavin's less-than-impressed voice filtering down the hall, getting heated.

"Is Dad mad at Granny?" Peyton asks once we're in her room.

"I think there was just a miscommunication." It's a small lie, but she's nine and dragging her into this family stuff isn't necessary. "Did you sleep okay last night?"

"It was okay. Granny kept checking in on me, and it made it hard for me to fall asleep because she kept opening the door and it was creaking a lot." She pushes her door open, revealing the mint-green room decorated in a fairy theme. Based on the room alone, it's very clear that Peyton's grandparents adore her and dote on her when they have the chance. I feel bad that there's so much animosity between her and Gavin. And that I seem to be the catalyst for much of it. "After you sang me the lullaby, she stayed in my room for a little while and rubbed my back and then I went to sleep."

"That's good." I give her a reassuring smile. "Tell me about these pictures." I motion to the wall of photos.

"That's my mom when she was pregnant with me. Granny says I look like her when she was my age, except my hair is darker, like Dad's."

I stand beside Peyton, staring at the same picture she is. I can see Marcie and pieces of her dad in her. She has her father's smile, but her mother's delicate mouth and her dark eyes and the same wavy hair.

"You do look a lot alike, but I can see your dad in you too."

"Granny says we're alike, me and my mom. My mom liked arts and crafts like me. And she loved books and dressing up like a princess." She points to a picture of her mom and Gavin on their wedding day. "Granny says she looked like a real princess on her wedding day, and that she wanted to start a family right away. Granny says she wanted a big family and to give me at least one brother and a sister, but she didn't get the chance."

"That would have been nice, wouldn't it? If you'd had a brother or a sister or both?"

Peyton nods. "Sometimes it's lonely being an only child, but Granny tells me I'm good at keeping myself entertained."

"You are definitely good at that." I point to a picture of Marcie with a group of women. I recognize one of them as Lynn. "Were these your mom's friends?"

"Yup. They were her best friends." She goes on to name the rest of them. "When I come to visit sometimes, Granny sets up playdates with their kids."

"Does your dad still keep in touch with them?"

Peyton shakes her head. "Only Ian and Lynn. He doesn't really ever talk about Mom, and when he does, he gets real sad for a couple of days, so I try not to bring her up, but Granny loves to talk about her, so we do that a lot."

"That's good. I'm glad you and your granny can have those talks. It's important that you learn about your mom, especially since you never got to meet her yourself."

Peyton nods. "I wish I could have met her. Just one time. And Granny says one day when I go to heaven, I'll get to meet her. But I don't want to go to heaven anytime soon, because I'd have to leave Dad, and I don't want him to be alone. And I have a lot of things I still want to do. Like become an architect like my dad, and get the lead role in a play and ride a horse and go to Disney World."

I swallow down the lump in my throat. "Those are all good reasons to be here."

"I think so." She twists her hands. "Sometimes I think Granny gets worried about Dad finding someone new to love because she thinks she won't get to see me as much. And I guess maybe it's true because I used to see her almost every day when I lived here, and now I only see them sometimes because the drive is a lot longer."

My heart clenches, and as I stand here, in a guest room that's been converted into their granddaughter's special bedroom, I can see how difficult this must be for Karen. Especially since it seems a lot like Gavin has put Marcie in a box that he doesn't like to open.

Of course it makes sense that she's worried about me coming in and taking away Gavin and her granddaughter. Replacing a woman who has only been a photograph for the daughter she never got to meet.

It's a tricky situation, and Gavin is clearly struggling with keeping Karen appeased and moving on with his life.

I hear raised voices coming from downstairs, mostly Gavin's. And a minute later, Peyton's door swings open. His gaze moves around the room in a quick sweep, not stopping at the pictures on the walls.

"Is everything okay?"

"We're going to head back to Colorado Springs."

"I'm not staying another night with Granny?" Peyton wrings her hands.

"No, honey, we're going to head back now."

"But we were supposed to go to the park. Granny said we might meet up with Patty and her mom there." Peyton looks like she's about to burst into tears.

"I'm sorry, kiddo. We'll have to do this another time. It looks like there's a storm rolling in, and we don't want to get stuck here. I have meetings on Monday, and I can't afford to miss them. Let's pack your stuff so we can head home."

It sounds like a hollow excuse, even to me. And Gavin won't meet my gaze as he crosses the room and starts helping Peyton gather her things.

The goodbye is stiff and awkward, and the ride back to Colorado Springs is quiet and tense. Something clearly happened with Karen, I just don't know what. And poor Peyton sits in the back seat, sniffling occasionally because she's disappointed they had to leave and she couldn't see any of her friends.

We stop and pick up pizza and junk food, and watch a movie with Peyton when we get home. Peyton is so exhausted from her broken sleep the previous night that she passes out on the couch before nine. We transfer her to her bed and make sure she's settled before he opens a bottle of wine and pours us both a glass.

"I'm sorry our weekend got cut short," he says once we're back in the living room.

"What happened with Karen?"

He sighs. "What she always does. She did this before, when I was dating Trista."

"Did what, exactly?"

"She . . . meddles, is the best way I can explain it. I honestly thought I'd dealt with it last time. I thought this weekend was her way of apologizing, but really her whole plan must have been to make it as difficult as possible. If it isn't one thing, it's another. I'm sorry I rushed us out of there like that, but I needed to leave before I said something I couldn't take back."

"I don't understand why she would offer to take Peyton for the weekend and then sabotage it."

"I can tell you exactly why. Fuck. I can't believe I didn't see this coming. She did the exact same thing the last time I was in a relationship." He huffs and shakes his head. "And it ended because Trista couldn't deal with how much Karen meddled. Half the time our dates ended prematurely because there was always some kind of emergency."

"Do you think she even realizes what she's doing?" I ask.

"She has to know." He runs a hand through his hair. "I owe you a do-over. But next time I'll ask my parents to take Peyton. At least then I can be sure we'll get an entire weekend together."

He sets his wineglass on the table and takes my hands in his.

"I'll make this up to you. We can have a naked weekend. No interruptions." He kisses my knuckles. "This will be the last time Karen interferes."

I want to believe he's right, but I worry that we're just scratching the surface, and that there's more to deal with than just Karen.

Twenty-Four

AT THE EDGE

HARLEY

On Monday morning my sisters and I gather in the office to go over the plans for the week, and I fill them in on my botched weekend with Gavin.

"Karen sounds almost as bad as Declan's mom, minus all the divorces."

"Karen and Kyle probably sleep in twin beds with a nightstand between them. I can see her in *Little House on the Prairie* sleepwear."

"She's that uptight?" London seems disturbed by the prospect.

"Why can't we find guys with normal parents? Why do they always have to cause problems?" Avery rubs her stomach. She's getting to the point where she's always uncomfortable. Her hips are achy and she's constantly rubbing her low back.

"Gavin's parents are great. It's just the in-laws who are a problem. I really hope we can find some kind of balance. At least we have some time before the holidays. I feel like I need to mentally prepare myself for what that's going to look like." I would prefer to have home-field advantage with Karen the next time we see her. "Enough about that." I change the topic, because I need to focus on something positive. "I need to ask you two for a favor."

"What do you need?" Avery asks.

This seems like a good opportunity to broach my idea and see what my sisters have to say. The majority rules stipulation might be the one thing standing in my way on this, but I won't know if I don't at least put it out there.

"I know that we said birthday parties for kids were a no-go, but I was hoping we could host one for Peyton. We could do it on a Sunday afternoon, that way we're not interfering with our own events."

Avery and London exchange a glance.

"Do you have time to organize something like that?" Avery asks.

"Yeah, I already know what Peyton wants, so it would be easy. And I wouldn't expect you guys to help. I would organize it on my own, so it won't interfere with anything else we have going on."

"I think it should work, but it would be good to check the calendar and make sure it's not going to conflict with the events we're already hosting," London says.

"I can run it by Gavin and see what weekends would work, since I know we're basically booked out for the next eighteen months."

"Two years, actually," Avery says.

"Right. Yeah, I'll ask if something during the week would work, just in case. Hopefully we're planning out far enough in advance that it should be okay." I flip a pen between my fingers. "There's something else I wanted to talk to you about."

"Okay, what's going on?" London flips a puffy star between her fingers, probably trying to read my expression.

"I have an idea, and I'm not sure what it would look like in the grand scheme of things, but I wondered if maybe for one of the upcoming weddings, we could offer in-house daycare for parents with young kids."

Avery frowns. "How would that work? We'd need to hire extra staff for that."

"I would be the person in charge of running it, and maybe I could see if there's anyone in my program who would be interested in helping out."

"That seems like a lot of work and planning." London folds one of her paper stars and tosses it on the table.

"I just figured that sometimes parents with younger kids have to leave the reception early, so it might be cool to offer a play space for a couple of hours. Nothing extensive, or permanent, just something we could try out for the events where the little kids wear out early."

London and Avery give each other another sidelong glance.

"This all sounds great in theory, Harley, but if you're running a daycare during the event, who's going to take the photos?" Avery asks.

"I think this is a much bigger undertaking than you realize. We'd have to have a room safetied, and we'd need licensed professionals. You still have at least a year or two before you've finished your degree. This might be something we could consider in the long-term, but we're in the middle of setting up a franchise and that needs to take precedence," London says gently.

"Right. Yeah. Okay. It was just an idea."

"I don't think it's a bad one," Avery says. "But I think there's a lot more planning that we'd need to do, and we have other things happening that take top priority."

"Just forget I said anything." I'm frustrated, and I don't want to lash out or say something I'm going to regret. While majority rules works for the most part, it's times like these I wish it were more than the three of us making decisions. I get what they're saying, that maybe the timing isn't the best, but every time I try to create a place for myself that might make me happier here, it's either shot down or taken away.

"We're not saying no forever, Harley," Avery says. "Only that we need to put a pin in it for now. I think it's a great idea. But we've all got enough on our plates without adding another thing to it. Plus, now you're going to plan a party for Peyton, so that should be good, right?" Obviously she's trying to smooth things over.

"Yeah. It'll be fun," I agree.

"I'm still sorry that we had to take the birthday parties away," Avery says.

"I knew they weren't helping our bottom line at all, though. And they were a lot of work for something that wasn't lucrative and took away from planning time on the other, bigger events, which is where we want our focus." They sound like words with no real emotion behind them.

"Exactly." London seems relieved. "I know all the changes haven't been easy, but this is what we've been working for."

"I know it's for the better of Spark House." And it is. We've turned a family-run business into a burgeoning franchise over the past five years. It's an accomplishment, and Spark House has been Avery's passion for a lot of years, so seeing it flourish is amazing.

I just want to figure out where I fit into all of this. And hope-fully, in time, I can find a place for myself in Spark House that gives me the same kind of joy Avery and London have.

Later that afternoon, I pick up Peyton from school. The fall colors are long gone, trees bare and the grass faded, having lost its summer vibrance. The first flakes of snow start to fall on the way to the park, swirling around us and melting as soon as they touch our clothes or skin.

"I can't wait to make snowmen this winter! Dad and I usually make two for the front yard, one of him and one of me, but this year we can make three, and you can have your own snowman too. We dress them up in our old clothes and change their outfits sometimes." Peyton skips along beside me, chattering away.

"That sounds like a lot of fun."

Peyton slips her mitten-clad hand in mine. "It is. On Christmas Eve we always go to Granny and Grandpa's place, and then on Christmas Day we see Nana and Grampy. Will you spend Christmas with us?"

I glance at her, taking in her hopeful, expectant expression. I don't want to overstep, and this isn't a conversation I've had with Gavin yet. "I usually spend Christmas Day with my sisters, but we'll have to see what works."

She nods and her smile turns wistful. "It must be so fun to have sisters at Christmastime. At Granny and Grandpa's my auntie Louise and uncle Frank come too, and they bring my cousins Jasper and Jennifer. They live all the way in Boston, so it's a long trip for them, and last year Jasper was brand-new and he couldn't do much but stare at things, but this year he's talking and walking, and Granny says he's a going concern. I think that means it's going to be a lot of fun. If you don't see your sisters on Christmas Eve, maybe you could come to Granny and Grandpa's with us and meet my aunt and uncle and cousins."

Gavin doesn't talk about Marcie's siblings, but from what I

know, they're spread across the country and they only really see each other during the holidays. "That sounds like it would be a lot of fun. And your birthday is coming up soon too. You must be excited about that."

"I am. I sort of thought maybe I wanted to go to Chuck E. Cheese for a party, but I also kind of want to have a princess party. And I want one of those before I'm too old to love dressing up like princesses. But I don't know if that will ever happen because I want to be in plays, and then I'll get to dress up and pretend to be princesses, or whatever role I get in the play. This year I get to play Santa's lead elf in the Christmas play, and I'm really excited. I have lots of lines and I have almost all of them memorized."

"Maybe tonight you can rehearse some of them for me."

"Do you think you can come to rehearsal next week? They're so much fun. At least when we're not messing up scenes and forgetting lines. Sometimes that happens. That's why we have to practice a lot."

"I would love to come. We can check my schedule and you can tell me what day will work the best."

"Yay! Dad sometimes stays for them, but he always has work to do, so he can only watch part of it. But he comes to every performance."

It sounds exactly like something Gavin would do. When we get to the park, we head for the swings. It's quiet, only a few kids and their parents around, the cool temperatures and darker days sending people inside earlier. We only have half an hour before the sun starts to set.

When Peyton runs over to the slides, I take a moment to message Gavin, asking if he has any thoughts about dinner, and if he's not quick about responding, there's a good chance Peyton will want mac and cheese, and not the good kind either.

His response is almost immediate.

> **Gavin:** I'm a fan of mac and cheese, but I was thinking I could pick something up. Takeout from the Pasta Bar? Their lobster mac and cheese is second only to your homemade.

I message back with a thumbs-up. As nice as homemade mac and cheese is, takeout sounds so much more appealing tonight.

I glance up, searching the slide for Peyton's bright yellow puffy coat. It's easy to pick her out in a crowd of pink or blue coats, which seems to be fairly common in her age group. For a second my heart jumps into my throat because I don't see her on the slide at all. And then it settles back in my chest when I spot her on the climbers. I'm about to warn her to be careful and to remind her that her dad doesn't love it when she climbs up there, but I don't have a chance, because her foot slips and she falls.

The scream that rips out of her makes my skin break out in a wave of goose bumps. I rush over, climbing through the bars to get to her.

She's sobbing, sucking in big gasping breaths and wailing at the top of her lungs. I cross my fingers that she didn't break anything. I drop to my knees in the gravel beside her and pull a tissue from my pocket, dabbing at her eyes. She's clutching her ankle, and tears are streaming down her face.

"Hey, hey. I'm here." I smooth her hair back from her face, trying to get her to focus on me. "What hurts, honey?"

"My ankle! I want Daddy!" she cries out.

"I know, sweetie. Let me take a look, okay?"

I roll up her pant leg. I can already see a bruise forming at her ankle, but I can't tell if it's broken or just a sprain or what. I finally get her to calm down, but when she tries to put pressure on her ankle to stand, she breaks into tears all over again.

It's getting dark fast, so when I finally get her out of the climber, I fireman carry her across the park. She's not particularly heavy, but she's almost ten and I'm on the short side, so I'm not the best candidate for carrying a near-tween. But I finally get her back to my car and buckled into the back seat. I make sure she's as comfortable as she can be considering the pain she's in. The tears have slowed to a trickle instead of a full-on waterfall. Peyton isn't one for dramatics outside of when she's in a play, so I know she's really hurt herself.

As soon as I'm in the car, I call Gavin to let him know that Peyton had a fall and that we're on our way to the closest urgent care.

I feel sick to my stomach that Peyton got hurt on my watch. Especially how she got hurt. Gavin is forever warning her to be careful on that climber, and he never lets her go on it when it's been raining. I should have been paying closer attention. All I can do is hope that she didn't break anything and that whatever the injury is, it will heal quickly.

Twenty-Five

MORE THAN JUST A FALL

GAVIN

The panic in Harley's voice makes the hairs on the back of my neck stand on end. "What happened? What's going on?"

"Peyton fell at the park and hurt her ankle. I'm on my way to urgent care right now."

"How badly? Is it broken?" I grab my keys and jacket and head for the door, leaving my laptop open and my design plans on my drafting table.

"I don't know. It's bruised and swelling, and she can't put weight on it. We're at the one a few blocks from your place. Can you meet us there?"

"I'm on my way right now." I end the call without saying goodbye and pause in Ian's office door to let him know I'm leaving. "Peyton had a fall at the park and Harley's taking her to urgent care."

He pushes out of his chair. "Is she okay?"

"She hurt her ankle, that's all I know."

"Hopefully it's just a sprain. Give me a call later and let me know how it goes and if there's anything Lynn and I can do to help."

I nod and then I'm off, down the hall and into the elevator.

A strange numb feeling settles over me. I don't particularly love the doctor, or anything that resembles medical treatment or care. The last time I set foot in a hospital was when Peyton was born, and while I love my daughter, that day is also one of the saddest of my life. I gained a daughter and lost my partner. So while I'm aware that Peyton isn't in grave danger, I also thought my wife was going to be fine after the birth of our daughter.

No one expected her heart to fail during labor, or for the doctors to be unable to safely deliver Peyton and keep Marcie alive. I shake my head and blow out a steadying breath, trying to keep my focus on the road and not on the past. Peyton is going to be fine. Kids have accidents all the time. But the memories I've shoved to the back of the closet and closed the door on are pushing to the surface, none of them easy to handle.

The drive to urgent care seems to take forever, even though I get there in less than twenty minutes. By the time I arrive I'm sweaty and clammy. It's hard to focus on the receptionist, but eventually I manage to explain. "My daughter, Peyton Rhodes, was brought here by my girlfriend. She's nine. She hurt her ankle?" I say the last part as a question because I don't have a lot of information about her injury.

"Oh yes, they're in room number three. Let me take you there." The receptionist guides me down the hall, the sharp scent of bleach and the bite of latex gloves brings back more memories. Before we moved, Karen would often take Peyton to doctor's appointments. Those I could handle better, the office a slightly less sterile place.

But this feels different, likely because it's an emergency clinic.

The receptionist knocks on the door and peeks her head in before ushering me inside. Peyton bursts into tears as soon as she sees me and throws her arms around my neck when I get close enough, telling me she's sorry. I don't understand why she would apologize for getting hurt, but I console her as best I can and pat her back, kissing the top of her head and grounding myself in the knowledge that she's safe and okay and nothing truly bad has happened to her.

This is all fixable.

The doctor comes in and checks her ankle, then sends us to the X-ray clinic to make sure there isn't a hairline fracture. It turns out to be a bad sprain, which unfortunately means she's going to need crutches for at least a week, if not longer, depending on how she heals. It's not ideal, considering she has a major role in the holiday performance. Hopefully they can adjust as needed and make it work.

Harley is beside herself, chewing nervously on her bottom lip as I carry Peyton out to my SUV. I get Peyton into the back seat and Harley puts the crutches in the trunk.

"Should I stop and pick up a treat for Peyton? Maybe something from Sweet Sensations?" she asks softly, wide concerned eyes lifting to meet mine.

I look to the side, unable to handle her remorse. I feel like I'm on the edge, and I don't know how I got here. "Yeah, sure. That would be great."

"Okay." She nods once. "I'll meet you back at your place?"

"Yeah. That works." I turn away, but she grabs my wrist.

"I'm sorry, Gavin. I didn't mean for this to happen."

"I know. I'll see you back at my place. I just want to get her home and comfortable."

"Okay." She releases my wrist, and I round the hood of the car, slipping into the driver's seat.

Peyton sniffles from the back seat. "I'm sorry, Daddy. I didn't mean to get hurt."

"You don't have to apologize, sweetie. You didn't do anything wrong. Accidents happen." I offer her a smile in the rearview mirror, then keep my hands at ten and two while I drive us home.

Harley arrives twenty minutes later with takeout from the Pasta Bar and a treat for Peyton from Sweet Sensations. The stress of the afternoon has gotten to Peyton, and the pain medication has set in, making her groggy and her tummy feels off. She has two bites of dinner and then asks to go to bed.

I leave Harley in the kitchen and help Peyton get ready for bed. I don't even make her brush her teeth, and I only get about halfway through her bedtime story before she's out cold.

Even still, I lie there for several minutes, watching her chest rise and fall. Thinking about what could have happened. If she'd fallen and hit her head. If she'd broken something. Because of someone else's carelessness. Because Harley wasn't watching her closely enough. If it had been worse, then what would I have done?

I push down the memories of what happened with Marcie, struggling to keep them locked down. I know it's not the same thing, but it feels a lot like it is, and I don't know how to process it all.

Eventually I slip out of Peyton's bed, kiss her on the forehead, and leave her bedroom, closing the door behind me. Harley is sitting in the living room on the couch, her hands in her lap, her gaze fixed on the blank TV screen. Her head lifts when I cross the threshold. "How is Peyton? Can I go in and give her a kiss good night?"

"She's already asleep."

"Oh. Did she go down okay? You were in there for a long time."

"She was fine." I cross the room and grab the back of the chair. "What the hell happened? Why weren't you watching her?"

Harley's eyes flare. "I was watching her."

"Obviously not closely enough if she fell! What was she playing on? How did that even happen?" I can hear the panic and accusation in my voice, but I feel powerless to moderate it.

"She was on the climber. I was messaging you. I was distracted for all of a minute."

"You *let* her go on the climber?" I motion to the window, where flakes swirl around in the dark night air and create a fine white blanket on the ground. "It was snowing and wet!"

"I didn't *let* her do anything. She was on the slides. I was messaging you about dinner, and when I looked up, I realized she wasn't on the slides anymore and that she'd moved to the climber."

"You know how I feel about the climber, let alone when it's raining. It has accident written all over it. Why would she think it's okay to go on it unless you let her do that all the time?"

"Excuse me? What exactly are you saying, Gavin? That I go behind your back and let her do things you wouldn't?"

"Well, that's what it damn well looks like. What if she'd been hurt worse? What if she had to go to the actual hospital and not just urgent care?" Memories keep surfacing, ones I can't control and don't want, and I lash out, because it's the only thing I can do. "Maybe Karen's right. Maybe you are a bad influence. Maybe I shouldn't be putting this kind of faith in your ability to take care of my daughter."

Harley recoils, like my words are a physical blow. "Why

would you say something like that? Where the hell is this coming from?"

"She could have broken something. Or hit her head!"

Her gaze turns cold, and she pushes up off the couch. "Keep your voice down," she whispers angrily. "Unless you would like your daughter, who has just been through a pretty serious trauma tonight, to hear us arguing."

She moves toward the kitchen, away from the bedrooms, and I follow, my frustration mounting with every passing second. She whirls when she reaches the kitchen and crosses her arms. "I understand that you're upset about Peyton getting hurt today, and I'm very sorry that happened. But what you're insinuating isn't fair. I'm always careful with Peyton, and I pay attention when I take her out. I was seconds away from telling her to be careful and reminding her that you don't like the climber. Accidents happen. Kids fall and get hurt. It's part of growing up, and blaming it on me and saying I'm a bad influence is hurtful and frankly untrue."

"You obviously weren't paying attention this time."

She exhales heavily through her nose. "What is this really about, Gavin?"

"It's about making sure my daughter doesn't end up in a cast or worse!"

She purses her lips. "Sometimes that happens, and not because anyone did anything wrong. I think you're allowing this accident to drive a wedge between us. I just don't understand *why* you're doing this."

"The only thing I'm doing is trying to protect my daughter and myself. She's all I have left. I can't and won't let anything happen to her."

I watch Harley deflate, the anger leaching out of her, and

in its place is sadness. "I understand wanting to protect Peyton, Gavin, but the way you're reacting doesn't match the injury. You talk about Karen sabotaging your relationships, but how much of that is on you for allowing it? You're not treating me like your girlfriend right now, Gavin. You're treating me like I'm still the nanny. We're supposed to be partners here, and while I care deeply about Peyton, and you, it feels a lot like you're conveniently adjusting my role so you can use me as a scapegoat."

"You were supposed to be taking care of her."

She props her hands on her hips. "I think you need to look at this relationship critically and ask yourself what you're doing with me, Gavin. Is this really about wanting a relationship with me, or is this about having someone to take the pressure off parenting? I can't be the former nanny and the girlfriend. Either you let me step into one set of shoes, or you're going to continue to follow old patterns. You can't treat me like this and expect me not to call you on it. I am not twenty years old anymore. I'm an adult in a relationship with a single dad. It's complicated, and sometimes it's messy. But I'm starting to wonder if maybe it's less about Karen and more about you being afraid of dealing with what happened to Marcie."

I shake my head. "How am I ever supposed to let her go when I see her every single day in my daughter?" I don't know how to make her understand, I don't even know if I do.

"I'm not saying you should let her go, at all. But you never talk about her. Ever. Not to me, not to Peyton. I understand that it must hurt, but avoiding all of the feelings that come with that loss aren't going to help you move past it. And I get how hard that is, I really do. Losing my parents was devastating. And I'm sure losing Marcie was more painful than I can fathom, but how can we ever be a real couple when you refuse to deal with all of those old hurts? How can we move forward together when at the slightest sign of trouble, you shut down on me?"

"That's not what's happening." But even as I say it, the truth of what she's saying starts to sink in. Is she right?

Sadness settles behind Harley's eyes. She sighs and looks away, fingers lifting to wipe away a tear. "I can't do this, Gavin. I've tried to be patient and understanding. I know how hard this is for you, and I love you and I love Peyton, but I can't compete with a ghost. If Marcie is the love of your life, then what does that make me?"

"Marcie will always be part of my life."

"And I'm always going to be second. And that isn't enough." And with that, she walks out the door.

Twenty-Six

THIS HURTS

HARLEY

I don't drive home. Instead, I go to Avery's.

Normally with any kind of relationship crisis, I would go to London, but it's after eight and she has a toddler who goes to bed at seven thirty, and I kept her up well past her bedtime last night, so I don't want to do that to her again. She usually goes to bed at nine on non-event evenings because she gets up at a ridiculously early hour so she can have breakfast with her husband while they watch the sun rise.

Yes, it's as sweet as it is gag-worthy.

I use the hands-free to tell Avery I'm on my way over and that I hope that I'm not being a pain in the ass. She's in the final months of her pregnancy, and from what I've witnessed, it's wearing her down. She's used to having full use of her body and being able to do everything, which isn't possible when you have a basketball taking up real estate in your belly.

Thankfully, she's awake. She buzzes me up as soon as I get to their apartment, but it's Declan who answers the door. "Uh-oh," he says when he gets a load of my puffy eyes and blotchy face. "Man troubles?"

"It's that obvious?"

"Ave told me about the failed weekend getaway. Come on in."

He ushers me into the living room where Avery is sitting on the couch, a lap pad perched precariously on her belly, topped with a bowl, presumably containing a snack.

Avery frowns as soon as I enter the room. "What happened? I thought you two were okay."

That's all it takes for the tears to start falling again.

"I'll give you two some privacy." Declan thumbs over his shoulder and kisses Avery on top of the head before he disappears down the hall.

Avery pats the spot beside her. "Tell me what's going on."

Between blowing my nose and wiping my tears, I tell my sister about Peyton's fall and Gavin getting angry and blaming me. And then saying his mother-in-law was right about me being a bad influence. Then I tell her about me confronting him and then breaking it off because I can't compete with a ghost anymore. "Did I do the wrong thing?" I ask, second guessing myself.

Avery shakes her head, her smile sad. "No. You did the right thing. And I know it hurts, but the truth is, you were giving him grace as it is. He needed to hear this, and you needed to do this because you're absolutely right, he can't keep shutting down on you when things get tough, and you can't compete with a ghost. And you shouldn't have to."

"I didn't realize how much he was still holding on to the past. I knew he was struggling to keep boundaries with Karen, but I didn't realize he had a hand in sabotaging his own relationships. I feel awful. I didn't even get to say goodbye to Peyton."

Avery moves the lap pad off her belly and puts an arm around my shoulder. "It's harder when there's a kid involved."

I nod, trying to stifle a sob. "This is so much worse than before."

"You mean when Gavin left when Peyton was a baby?"

"It was awful, but then I was only in love with Peyton and not Gavin too. But this is so much different. This isn't just about his guilt, or letting Karen parent Peyton, or her meddling. It's about him allowing it continue, so he can keep himself safe from the potential for more pain. He said Peyton was all he had left. And he meant of Marcie. It's like he's locked in the past and he won't allow himself to move forward, and Karen is an easy excuse." I rub my temples, trying to sort through it all, to put the pieces of the puzzle together. "And I get that it must be hard to move on from something so traumatic, but we've all managed to cope after the loss of our parents. And it's been years. If he hasn't dealt with those feelings yet, will he ever be able to?"

"I think the difference is that we've had each other to rely on all this time, and that's made it a lot easier for us to process our own loss." Avery motions between us. "But he's had his controlling mother-in-law, who probably helped fuel his guilt train and his memory of Marcie for many years, whether intentionally or not."

"It sure seems like it. What am I going to do?"

"Well, you have two options. You can give him a few days to cool off and hopefully come to his senses, or you can go back over there and try and force him to see that you're right. I think the first option is probably the best, even if it's the hardest. The second is likely to backfire, and you also wouldn't be sticking to your guns and then this has the potential to happen again, but with significantly worse fallout. And as a woman who has dealt with really bad fallout after a relationship crisis, I can say that I would not want to invite option two if at all possible."

"His default move is to bury his head in the sand until he's at risk of suffocating. I can't keep running on this hamster wheel."

"You're right, you can't. And this isn't on you to make things better, Harley. He has to realize he has work to do if he wants you two to succeed as a couple. I think if you can stand your ground, then he'll have to look critically at how he's responding and hopefully see that his reaction did not in any way match the circumstances."

"I wonder if Karen feels a level of guilt for welcoming someone new into their lives who isn't their daughter, just like Gavin feels guilty for what happened to Marcie. Neither of them have had to contend with that before now. It's complicated, and not entirely logical, but emotions rarely are." I let my head fall back. "There are so many more layers to this than I realized."

Avery's expression is sympathetic. "There are. But that doesn't mean it's not fixable. You're a tender soul, and he's been battling with his own feelings. I don't think it's as simple as the accident setting him off, or the influence of his mother-in-law. I think it's everything piled on top of each other, and it was too much for him. Especially with the way he reacted to Peyton getting hurt, and him being fixated on it potentially having been worse. When was the last time he was at a hospital? If it was when his wife died, then would his reaction be more understandable?"

I nod slowly. "Yes, it would make a lot more sense. And Peyton's birthday is soon, which means the anniversary of her death is coming up. Maybe I need to call him." I reach for my phone, but Avery stops me.

"Just because you realize what's going on doesn't mean he does. Give him some time to think. It might take more than a few days for him to get his feelings sorted out, especially since it seems like he's been keeping them buried for a long time."

"How long do you think it will take? A week? More? Less? Do you think it will be months like it was for you and Declan?" I can't imagine hanging in limbo for that long. Although for Avery and Declan, there was ten years of love and friendship as the foundation. They had lots to build on. Gavin and I have a challenging history fraught with loss and guilt. And maybe that's part of the reason why I've been so accommodating. Maybe it isn't just Gavin who needs to do the work; maybe it's me too.

Avery gives my hand a sympathetic squeeze. "It's hard to say. You're the first person he's really let in since Marcie died, and the last time the two of you got close, he ended up moving away. That's a pattern he needs to see on his own. Give him some breathing room. Message in a few days to see how he's doing. If he's receptive, ask if he wants to talk. Then leave the ball in his court."

"Okay. What about Peyton?"

"She's got lots of love in her life. She'll be okay."

I know she's right, but the question is, will I?

The next few days suck. A lot. But while my personal life seems to be imploding, the Spark House franchise is taking off. So I don't have a whole lot of time to wallow in self-pity during my nine-to-five. I save that for when I climb into my bed, struggling to sleep, and wondering if we'll be able to get past this or not.

"I'm sorry I can't be at the grand opening this weekend," Gran says on our biweekly call. Gran's lips are pulled down in a frown which contradicts her sunny-yellow dress and her equally sunny hat covered in a pink flower print.

"It's okay, Gran. We know it's a long trip, and you'll be back soon enough. Besides, these kinds of things are so busy, we wouldn't have time to really visit. It's better for you to wait until the baby is born." Gran is planning a trip around when Avery has the baby, and we decided that was more important.

"I know, but I still would have liked to have been there for this. You girls have worked so hard to get Spark House where it is. Now, tell me how things are going with you and Gavin. I know you were worried about his mother-in-law the last time we talked. Has that gotten any better?"

I purse my lips and tip my chin up, trying to keep my emotions in check.

"Uh-oh. What happened, honey?"

"I broke it off, but not because I wanted to." I fill her in on all the details, from the weekend getaway that started out okay but quickly went downhill, to Peyton's fall and Gavin's overreaction, and me not being able to handle being second to a ghost. "Did I do the right thing?"

She nods slowly, her smile sad. "I think you already know the answer to that. But if it helps, I can confirm what you already know."

"It really hurts, Gran. I don't know what to do or how to make this better."

"That's the hardest part, isn't it? Knowing that you can't make it better, no matter how much you want to. I felt that way after we lost your mom and dad. And then again after I lost your granddad. My heart was so broken. When I met Luciano, I tried so hard not to like him, and falling in love with him was bittersweet. I'd spent years loving your grandad. It was hard to give myself permission to love again. I wonder if it's the same for Gavin."

"What do I do? What can I do?" This is what I need: direction, guidance, a hand to hold, and Gran's wisdom.

"Be strong, be patient, be empathetic, but don't allow him to keep stepping on your feelings in a bid to protect his. All you can do is hope that he's going to be able to let go of the past so he can live in the present. He needs time to sort that out. And you need time to get over the hurt of it all."

"It's not just Gavin I miss, it's Peyton too," I admit.

"Mmm." She adjusts the brim of her hat, her smile soft and knowing. "She's a special little girl, and you have so much in common. I have a feeling she'll be a great ally for you in the coming days."

"I hope you're right about that."

"Neither of you were in a place to be each other's person back when you were Peyton's nanny. Things certainly are different now. I think he's too smart to waste this second chance." Gran was the only one who knew why I struggled after they moved and how responsible I felt.

I ask the question I'm afraid of. "What if they're not different? What if our history won't let us create a future together?"

"You are wise beyond your years, Harley. And the two of you have shared a bond for a long time. I'm a firm believer in fate and destiny. If your grandfather hadn't delivered those flowers all those years ago, I would have ended up with the wrong man, and if I hadn't gone on a trip to Europe with my girlfriends, I wouldn't have met Luciano. Gavin came back into your life exactly when he was supposed to. He needs to come to that realization on his own. And he will. Have faith in the power of true love, my dear. It conquers all."

It's ironic that I'm thankful for the distraction of the first Spark House franchise opening. We were smart enough not to have any events scheduled around the grand opening weekend, so we weren't managing an event at the same time. Two days after the blowout with Gavin, we're scheduled to fly out to California. Before I get on the plane I message to see how he and Peyton are doing.

Gavin: We're managing.

That's the response I get.

I realize I'm the one who broke things off, so in a way it's up to me to try to keep the lines of communication open, especially with what I know of Gavin's challenging past.

Harley: I'm in California for the next few days for the Spark House franchise grand opening, but if you want to talk when I get back, I'm here.

He replies with:

Gavin: That sounds like a hope carrot being dangled. Good luck. I'm sure it will be amazing. Peyton misses you and so do I.
Harley: I miss you both too.

I don't know if this means we'll be able to get past all of this or not, but at least it seems as if he's willing to talk things through.

We fly out to California that afternoon so we can be part of the grand opening ceremony. It's an incredible event and despite my struggle with all the change, I can appreciate what this is going to do for Spark House. On the flip side, I find myself missing Gavin more than I thought possible. I don't know how we're going to get past this, unless he's willing to open up to me about Marcie and his loss. But all I can do is hope that when I get home, we'll be able to figure things out.

It's especially difficult when I'm surrounded by my sisters and their significant others. It's not that I don't want either of them to be happy and in love. It's knowing that for a while it felt like I had that, and I'm not sure if I'll be able to get it back.

So while the grand opening is an amazing distraction from my mess of a life, it also shines a bright, unwelcome light on what I stand to lose. And that breaks my heart.

On Sunday morning we fly back to Colorado Springs. One of the perks of London being married to a seriously rich man whose net worth is close to a billion dollars is that he has his own private jet, which means no waiting at the airport or standing in lines. We just board the plane and head home.

It's a small plane, and the nicest one I've ever been on, with tables set up between the seats that face each other and recline fully to lie-flat beds. Once we're in the air, the flight attendant brings out drinks. Since London has recently stopped breastfeeding, she joins me in a glass of champagne.

We clink our glasses. "Cheers to a successful grand opening of our first franchise!" London says. "I think Mom and Dad would be really proud of how far we've come with Spark House."

"It's amazing that the whole reason behind it was to keep our family close together, and that's exactly what it's done for us," I agree.

"I don't think they ever would have dreamed this would be possible. I know I didn't think we'd be here." Avery motions to the plane and then clinks her orange juice and soda water against our glasses. She waves her hand around in the air as her eyes turn glassy. "Oh my gosh. What is wrong with me?"

"You're pregnant and your emotions are leaking out of your eyes, babe." Declan passes her a tissue.

"I never cry." She dabs at her eyes and gives the damp tissue an annoyed look.

"You rarely cry, but this is a big deal. You're allowed to be emotional about it," Declan reassures her.

"It really is amazing how far you've come in the past few years," Jackson says and winks at London.

"It wouldn't have been possible without you." London kisses his cheek.

He takes her chin between his finger and thumb and brushes his lips over hers before she leans back in her chair.

I turn away, blinking back my own tears, but it's not because of the event. It's seeing both of my sisters with their partners and not knowing what's going to happen with Gavin. I've reached out and left the ball in his court.

Avery reaches over and squeezes my hand, whispering, "It's going to be okay."

"I want you to be right, but I don't know." I squeeze back and slip my hand out from under hers. "I guess we'll see when we're back home."

London gives me a concerned look. "Have you heard from Gavin at all?"

I shake my head. "I messaged him before we left, but I haven't heard from him since then. I'm trying to give him space. I just don't know how much is enough or too much. And honestly, I meant it when I said I can't be in a relationship where I'm second to a ghost. It's not fair to me. Or him. Or Peyton. I've got enough on my plate, especially with my final paper due next week. I can't handle all of these ups and downs."

"Do you want to take some time off so you can focus on that?" Avery asks.

"Honestly? It's not time off that I need. The social media stuff only takes up a fraction of the time it used to. Mostly I'm signing off on things and adding extra content to personalize our feeds, and that's the part I really enjoy. Bringing on a social media liaison and a whole team of people who create content for us has changed the scope of my job." I tap on my armrest and look around at my sisters and their husbands. If ever there was a time to lay it out on the table, it's now. "Can I be totally honest with all of you?"

"Yeah, of course." My sisters nod in tandem.

"I understand why we're growing Spark House. Both of you have families and kids and this all makes sense, and you're both doing an amazing job."

"So are you," Avery says quickly.

I give her a soft smile. "I've tried to find ways to adapt with all the changes, but I can't pretend it's been easy. And I know it's been a lot of change for all of us, but you and London are good at finding ways to keep doing the things you love, and it hasn't been the same for me."

"Do you want more control over the social media stuff? London and I didn't want to overwhelm you since you've been taking classes on top of everything else."

"I appreciate that, but that's not what I mean." I bite the inside of my lip. "When I came on and took over the social media stuff, it was because I wanted to work with both of you, and I needed a break from the nanny gig. Gavin and Peyton moving away was hard on me emotionally. I'd gotten a lot more attached than I'd meant to and my heart needed time to recover." And I didn't trust myself not to get attached like that again. It rocked my confidence and made me question my judgment. How ironic that I'm in the same position I was back then, with the same man. "So I sort of stepped into that role. Don't get me wrong, I love the creative side of things, and taking photos and highlighting our sponsors is definitely something I enjoy. But my role hasn't been defined the same way yours have. When we started hosting those birthday parties, I felt like I was finally finding my groove at Spark House."

"And then we took them away from you," Avery says softly.

"Which I understood. They weren't good for our bottom line."

"But you loved hosting them," London adds.

"It made me happy. For the first time since I started working for Spark House, I felt like I'd found my purpose."

"I didn't even think about the fact that we were canning your baby." Declan rubs the back of his neck. "And not giving you anything in its place."

"It didn't make financial sense and that's what you were looking at. Which, again, I understood. And then there was the franchise. I could see from your perspective why it would be a good thing for Spark House, and for your families, but it reinforced the fact that I don't have a set role. I wasn't on board with the franchise because I was afraid of what it would change."

"Why didn't you tell us?" Avery and London exchange a glance.

"Because it's majority rules, and you and London were excited about it. Why create tension when I wasn't going to win the argument?"

"But you could have told us how you felt," London says softly.

"I know. And maybe I should have. But I didn't want to be the reason that we didn't move forward, and it didn't seem like the hill I wanted to die on. And now that we're here, I think I was right not to put up a fight. In the long run, this is going to be great for us."

"A lot has changed over the past six months," Declan offers. "Now that we've jumped through all the franchise hurdles, we can revisit the birthday parties."

"I appreciate that, Declan." I give him a small smile and turn to my sisters. "When I brought up the idea of in-house daycare before, you two shut me down before we could even discuss it. And I get that maybe the timing hadn't been exactly right, but I felt like I didn't have a voice.

"You're both going to be parents. We have more staff than ever before. Wouldn't it make sense to have something on-site, even if it's a trial basis for weddings, or if we think that's not the best place to start, then we could look at options just for staff? I recognize that it's going to be a lot of work, but I've already come up with a plan and a program, and I'm willing to take that on." Avery opens her mouth to speak, but I hold up my hand, feeling like I need to sell them on this. "Think about the logistics of it. If we started with a part-time program, you could bring your kids to work, even if it's only for a few hours to start. I want to find a way to fit into Spark House, but I also want to do something I love, and that's working with kids again. I want to finish this degree and put it to use, and if I can't find a way to do that at Spark House, then I need to find a place where I can, because it's where my heart is."

"We don't want you to leave, Harley." London drops the star she's been folding.

"I don't want to either, but you and Avery have your thing at Spark House. I need something that's mine. Something that I can nurture and grow, and I think we're in a good position to make that happen now." I bite the inside of my cheek, waiting for someone to throw up another roadblock.

"I think what you're saying makes complete sense. I'd have to take a look at the numbers, but on-site daycare would open things up for a lot of our employees. And us. Especially with a new baby on the way." Declan's eyes are wide, and he glances at Avery and then focuses on me. "We can bring back the birthday parties too. If that's what it takes to keep the three of you together as a team, we can be creative and find ways to make it work. I'm guessing we can probably slot in a couple a month. Sunday afternoons would be the best day since events are usually wrapped up, as long as it's not right after a wedding because the takedown on those is a lot."

"Just throwing out ideas, but what if we renovated one of the outbuildings?" Jackson suggests. "We've got that potting shed behind the atrium."

The potting shed is hardly a shed. It's a large building where we store a lot of random gardening stuff that rarely gets used because we've hired a grounds crew who come in once a week during the summer months to keep everything in order. It looks more like a small cottage.

"Oh! What if we made it into a party palace for kids? It could be called Sparkle House. It could be the place where we host parties for kids, and when we aren't, we can use it as a daycare," I say, thrilled that both Declan and Jackson seem to see this as viable.

"That's a great idea!" London claps her hands. "Do you think the shed would be big enough?"

"I think so. We'd need to clean it out to be sure, but I believe it could work. A reno like that won't be cheap, though," Declan says.

"Think of it like a long-term investment. We're creating new opportunities and ways for Spark House to keep growing," Jackson offers.

"I don't think any of us truly realized how hard this all was for you. We want you to be happy, Harley. And we want you to stay with us." Avery wraps her arm around my shoulder and gives me a side hug.

"I think this is a solid plan. I'll do a cost analysis as soon as we're home and price out the renovation," Declan says.

"I think it would make sense to see what it would cost to set up a full-time daycare center there. I like the idea of Ella being close to you when I have to be away on business and you can't join me," Jackson says to London. "Especially since we'd like to give her a brother or a sister sometime in the near future."

"Maybe we should poll everyone on staff and see how much interest we get," Avery says.

"We have lots of people on staff with kids. Offering on-site daycare could be an amazing perk." My worries over my place at Spark House start to fade as we make this new plan. And I realize that I've been passively sitting back, filling roles as they're handed to me instead of speaking up and asking for what I want.

It's up to me to make my own happiness. And this is one huge step in the right direction.

Twenty-Seven

BREAK YOUR OWN HEART

GAVIN

"Daddy." Poke. "Daddy." Sniffle. "Daddy."

I crack a lid and find Peyton standing beside my bed, her stuffed bunny cradled against her chest. I glance at the clock. It's four in the morning. "It's too early to be up, sweetie."

"I had another accident." Peyton's fingers are in her mouth, eyes wide with worry.

This is the third time in as many days that she's had an accident at night. The only time she ever has accidents now is when she's about to spike a fever. It's how I know she's coming down with something. And I don't think it's happened in more than a year.

I throw the covers off, the fog of sleep too heavy to lift, and scrub my face with my hand. "Did you change your pajamas?"

She nods. "And I used a washcloth to clean myself up. I'm sorry."

"It's okay, sweetie, it's not your fault. Why don't you get in bed with me and I'll toss your sheets in the washing machine."

"Okay." She clambers up into bed and takes the side Harley would normally sleep on. If she and I were still a couple. I lean over and kiss Peyton on the forehead, surreptitiously checking for a temperature before determining she's fine.

I leave her in my room and trudge down the hall. Her bed-side lamp is already on, highlighting the wet spot in the middle of the bed. I put the mattress pad back on her bed after the first time it happened. Which incidentally coincided with her ankle sprain and Harley breaking up with me. All I have to do is strip the bed and drop the sheets in the washing machine.

As I pull them off, a picture frame goes tumbling to the floor. I stoop to pick it up and my heart clenches. It's a photo of me, Peyton, and Harley when we went for a weekend trip to Aspen when Peyton was just a toddler. It was probably taken a couple of months before I decided to move us to Boulder. Karen hadn't loved the fact that I'd taken my twenty-year-old nanny with me on a mini vacation instead of inviting them to join me.

But Harley had been full of life and energy. She'd been great with Peyton and loved every minute of taking Peyton tubing on the bunny hill. And even back then, I wasn't sure what exactly it was that I felt for her. I was grateful to have her as support, be-cause I wouldn't have been able to manage the demands of an infant on my own. The lines had started to blur, and I couldn't get a handle on my emotions. All I knew was that she'd been far too young, and I'd been far too heartbroken to entertain any kind of relationship with anyone, let alone my twenty-year-old nanny.

I'd chalked it up to being alone and needing the emotional support she provided.

I'd moved away and given Peyton a fresh start in a new home. One without the memories of Marcie to keep me teth-ered to the past. But in moving to Boulder, I'd realized that I'd traded one problem for another. There had been a reason we'd moved to Colorado Springs because as much as Marcie loved her mother, she also couldn't handle how suffocating she could be. And I'd experienced it firsthand for a lot of years.

It doesn't matter that I moved back to Colorado Springs and tried for another fresh start. If I can't learn how to manage my feelings about what happened to Marcie, I'll never be able to create a future with Harley, or anyone for that matter.

And I want to.

I place the photo on Peyton's nightstand and gather her sheets, carrying them to the laundry room. I set it on the sanitize cycle and return to bed. Peyton's head rests on Harley's pillow, and I try my best to be quiet and not jostle her, hoping she's fallen back to sleep, but as soon as I slip under the covers, her eyes pop open.

"I'm sorry."

"It's okay, sweetie. I know it didn't happen on purpose. Get some rest, okay?" I lean over and kiss her forehead again. It's still cool, so no fever to explain the bed wetting. I inhale and get a faint whiff of Harley's shampoo, still lingering on her pillow because I haven't washed the sheets since the last time she slept over.

I lie back and close my eyes. Marcie wouldn't want me to live in the past. She would want me to find happiness.

"Daddy?" Peyton whispers. It could be a minute or an hour later.

I make a noise in response.

"I miss Harley." Her voice is tiny and full of tears.

I breathe out the hurt in my chest. This is one of the reasons I've been so careful about bringing someone into our lives like this. I don't want Peyton to get hurt when things don't work out, but in doing that, I've robbed us both of the opportunity to find love. "I know, sweetie."

"When is she coming over again?" she asks on a sniffle.

"I don't know right now," I tell her honestly.

"We're not going to move back to Boulder, are we?" More sniffles.

"No, honey, we're not moving again. Grampy needs me here for work, and I know how much you love being in Colorado Springs," I assure her. "Why would you think we'd be moving back to Boulder?"

"Because Granny doesn't like Harley, and the last time we moved, Harley was taking care of me. And Harley was taking care of me again and Granny wasn't happy about it. Does she not want Harley to be my mom? Is that why Granny doesn't like her?"

I choke back the emotion that comes with these kinds of questions and turn on the bedside lamp before I roll over to face Peyton. "Did Granny say something to you about that?"

Peyton's eyes are watery and tired, and she's chewing on her bottom lip. Hoppy is tucked under her chin and every few seconds she uses one floppy ear to wipe the tears away. "It's not what she says, it's what she does."

"What do you mean?"

"Whenever I talk about Harley, she starts talking about Mommy. And she'll sit me down and tell me lots of stories about her and tell me that it's important that I know all about her even though I didn't get to meet her."

"She's right. It is important for you to know about Mar—your mom," I agree.

"Why don't you ever tell me stories about Mommy?" Peyton asks.

My heart stutters and squeezes. I blow out a breath, trying to figure out how to talk to her about this. "Because it hurts."

"Do you miss her still?" She scooches a little closer.

"Yeah, of course I do." But it's been nearly a decade. And while that space in my heart reserved for Marcie never goes away or gets smaller, I find that I'm able to make more room for new people who can help heal those marred pieces.

She nods and is quiet for a second. "Harley misses her mom too. And I want to be able to miss mine, but I only know about her in stories, so all I can miss is a picture or an idea. I'm sad I didn't get to know her, and I'm sad that I don't have a mom, but I really miss Harley a lot. She's not just an idea or a picture, and I thought that maybe she was going to be my mom again, like when I was little."

"Harley wasn't your mom when you were little."

Her lips twist to the side. "But she did all the things a mom does. She told me all about the things we did together, just like a family would. And we've been like a real family for a while, and now I don't get to see her and I don't like it." Real tears start to flow, and my heart feels as though it's breaking all over again.

I don't know how to make this better, so I hug her and tell her it's going to be all right, even though I'm not sure if that's a lie.

I don't get much sleep after that, but Peyton passes out, and I call my mom first thing in the morning and ask if she can come watch her so Peyton can get some sleep and I can go to work. She shows up at eight with muffins and coffee, her expression reflecting her concern.

"You look exhausted. Is Peyton okay?" Mom kisses me on the cheek and folds my hands around one of the take-out coffees.

"She's fine. Just had a rough night. She's been wetting the bed the past few days, and that hasn't happened in years unless she's sick."

She purses her lips and sets the Tupperware containers on the console table. "Would this be at all related to what happened over the weekend with Karen and Kyle? Or is it because she fell? Maybe you need to take her to the doctor and make sure it's just her ankle that's the problem."

Lying seems pointless. "I don't think it's medical, I think it's stress-related. Harley and I broke up, and Peyton's not taking it well."

"What? When did that happen? Why did that happen, and why didn't you tell me until now?"

"On Monday, after Peyton fell. I said some things I shouldn't have, and I think I pushed her away."

I can tell my mom is about to say something, but I interrupt before she can impart her wisdom. "It's a long story, one I don't have time to tell right now. Can we talk later? Maybe tonight?"

"Of course." She gives me another hug and shoves the smaller muffin container into my hand. "You know your dad and I are always here for you."

"I do. Thank you." I leave for work, feeling more exhausted and miserable than I have in years.

I have a morning meeting, which goes well despite my exhaustion, in part because I cohost it with Ian, who takes one look at me, nabs the file from my hand, and tells me that he's going to run this one.

When it's over, he follows me back to my office and shuts the door behind him. "You look like shit. What the hell is going on?"

"Peyton's been wetting the bed," I tell him.

His eyebrows rise with his surprise. "Since when? Have you taken her to the doctor?"

"Not yet. I thought maybe she was coming down with something, but this morning she asked about Harley, and I honestly didn't know what to tell her, so I said everything would be okay."

"Does that mean you've talked to Harley?"

Ian knows about the blowout after our botched weekend getaway and Peyton's fall. I filled him in, as much as I was willing anyway. I shake my head.

"Are you planning to call her?"

"She was out of town this weekend." But she left the ball in my court, and she should be home by now. And still, I haven't reached out, even though I should.

He crosses his arms and gives me a look. "And now it's Monday, so what the hell is stopping you from fixing things?"

"I don't know." I run a hand through my hair, annoyed with myself and my inability to break this stupid cycle.

"Do you really not know, or are you afraid to face the truth?"

I drop down in my chair and deflate. "Which is what, according to you?"

"You're sabotaging this relationship because you're afraid to lose someone else. You're letting Karen run your life not because you're still carrying around guilt, but because it's convenient and suits your purpose." He takes the seat across from me. "Look, I know how hard losing Marcie was. It was hard on all of us. But you have to move on. Marcie wouldn't want you to live like this, or be alone for the rest of your life. She'd want you and Peyton to be happy. Unless maybe that's not where you see this going with Harley?"

For the first time I really hear him. Really hear what he's saying and how I've been making my own life impossible by allowing Karen to meddle in my relationships. "No." I shake my head. "It's not that I don't want this with Harley. She's exactly who I need, and I'm absolutely in love with her, which is the part I think I'm having a hard time wrapping my head around. Until now, I thought Marcie was the love of my life. But then I lost her and Harley came into my life." I rub my temple, trying to get a grip on my thoughts and feelings, which is a hell of a lot more difficult than I anticipated it would be. "Before Harley left, she said she wouldn't come second to a ghost."

Ian raises an eyebrow. "Wow. I didn't even think about that." He crosses his arms, pensive for a moment. "Do you think you're having a hard time allowing yourself to accept how you feel about Harley because it's stronger than the way you felt about Marcie?"

I shake my head. "It's not that I love her more. It's just different. I'm different. And I feel like I'm burying all those feelings I had for Marcie along with her and letting Harley take her place. With me and with Peyton."

"You have to let it go so you can have a future. Harley's right. She can't compete with a ghost, and more than that, she shouldn't have to. She's someone you love and want to build a future with. And Peyton deserves to have a woman in her life who will love her like a mother would." He rubs the back of his neck. "Maybe you need to talk to someone again. A professional."

"I did that, after Marcie died." And I hated every minute of it. I went for about six weeks and then decided it wasn't for me.

"You should consider giving it another shot. Not just for you, but for Peyton and Harley. If you want this relationship with her to work, and I think you do, despite how scared you are, then you need to work through this stuff."

I lace my hands behind my head, absorbing his words. "I think I tried the therapy route too soon after Marcie died. I don't think I was ready, and then I buried it instead of dealing with it. I don't want to lose Harley because I can't get a handle on my past."

"Losing Marcie was traumatic. You gained a daughter and lost your partner in the same day. No one is expecting you to ever get over it, but you do need to learn how to cope so you can have a healthy relationship with someone else. Whether or not that's Harley is something you need to figure out."

"I think it is Harley. Maybe it always was Harley." I think back to the moment in the kitchen that flipped some kind of switch in me. It might not have been *the* reason I packed my bags and moved myself and my daughter away, but it definitely played a factor. The timing had been all wrong, and I didn't have control of my emotions back then. It seems like that's still the case.

Ian nods. "I see how happy you are with her and how much Peyton adores her and how much she adores Peyton. I'd hate for you to lose that because you're scared and don't know how to deal."

I scrub a hand over my face. "You're right. I know you're right. I really wanted to believe I'd dealt with all this shit."

"Aside from Trista a few years ago, you haven't had a serious relationship in a decade. There are going to be some hiccups. Harley broke it off not because she doesn't want to be with you, but because she doesn't always want to come second to someone who isn't here anymore. It's not a fight she can win. Maybe that's something the two of you should do together, if she's open."

I nod. "That's probably a good idea, and one I wouldn't have entertained until now. Thanks for always being here to keep me on the straight and narrow."

He claps me on the shoulder. "I just want you to be happy, man. You deserve it. More than most."

I call Karen as soon as Ian leaves my office. It goes to voicemail, so I leave a message, telling her we need to talk and that I'd like to come out her way because it's a conversation that would be best in person. My intention is to figure out a time that works for me to drive out to Boulder. Hell, I'd go right now if I could, but I don't want to appear on their doorstep without warning.

So I'm surprised when I pull into the driveway and find not only my parents' car in the driveway, but my in-laws' as well.

"Hello?" I call out as I kick off my shoes.

Peyton comes hobbling down the hall, and she throws her arms around me. "I stayed home from school, and Granny came down for a visit, and we watched a movie and made chocolate chip cookies."

"Well, that's a nice surprise. Was it a good day?" I push down the sudden spike of nerves. I need to get my shit together, and it looks like the universe is giving me a chance to do that.

"It was. But I still feel bad about last night." She twists her hands together and looks up at me with regret in her eyes.

I crouch down in front of her and take her hands in mine. "Don't feel bad, honey. I know there's been a lot going on lately. I want you to know that what's happening with Harley isn't because of you, okay? She still loves you very much, and I still love her, even if we had an argument."

"Does that mean you're going to talk to her and apologize?"

"I'm going to try. And I'm going to see about getting someone for you and me to talk to."

"To talk about what?" She tips her head.

"About our feelings. About the things that scare us and make us happy. Whatever we need to talk about."

"Okay. I can talk about my feelings. I have a lot of them," Peyton says seriously.

"I know you do. And so do I, but I'm not always the best at expressing them."

"It just takes some practice."

"It does." I hold my arms open. "I love you."

"I love you too, Daddy."

I follow her to the kitchen, where I find my mom and Karen sitting at the table with cups of tea.

I tuck a hand in my pocket. "Hey. I guess you got my message."

Karen folds her hands on the table, her smile a little uncertain. "I called the house, and Judith and I had a chat. I thought it might be a good idea for me to come out this way."

My mom gives her hand a reassuring squeeze and pushes her chair away from the table. "Peyton, you and I are going to go pick up some stuff for dinner, okay? Why don't you put your coat on and I'll meet you at the front door?"

"Okay!" Peyton hobbles down the hall, blissfully oblivious to the tension.

My mother gives my forearm a squeeze on her way past me. "We'll give you two some time to talk."

I slide into the empty seat across from Karen, who repeatedly dips her tea bag into her mug. It looks like I'm not the only nervous one here. She waits until the front door closes with a quiet click before she speaks. "Judith told me about you and Harley. I'm very sorry."

"Are you?" I lean back in my chair, trying to read her expression.

She sighs and focuses on the table for a moment before she finally raises her head again and meets my gaze. "Judith told me what's been going on with Peyton, and how hard this has been for you. And I realized that I haven't been fair to Harley, or you and Peyton."

"No, you haven't," I agree. "And I'm trying to understand why."

She swallows thickly. "It was hard for me when you decided to move back to Colorado Springs, and I worried about how that was going to affect my relationship with Peyton. In a way, I felt a lot like I'd been able to take on the role of mother for Peyton, and then suddenly you were gone. It was like losing Marcie all over again. And then you started seeing Harley soon after you moved back. It was a lot of change that I wasn't prepared for, and I didn't know how to deal with it."

"You saw Harley as a threat to your role."

She folds her tissue into a square. "Peyton loves her so much. I felt like I'd been replaced. And I realize that's not her fault, but it's how I felt."

Karen has spent more than half a decade in the role of pseudo-parent, and I took it all away from her. I reach across the table and give her hand a squeeze. "Karen, I can understand better why this has been so difficult for you, but you're Peyton's grandmother. I don't know that it was fair to any of us, and especially not you, to let you take on a parent role in her life."

Karen nods, her smile sad. "At the time it seemed like what I needed, and you needed support. But now, I realize I haven't properly dealt with Marcie's death. So instead of handling it, I tried to mask the loss by taking care of Peyton."

"I get that it's been hard, Karen, but I deserve a partner. I don't want to go through life alone."

"I know, and I agree. And I'm aware I've made this harder on all of us with the way I've managed things, especially where Harley is concerned," she admits.

"Harley is an amazing woman, and I think if you'd give her half a chance, you might find you really like her. She's kind and caring and compassionate."

"I know she's all those things. It felt like I was betraying Marcie's memory if I let someone else who isn't my daughter into my life. I keep going over that day in my head. She'd called the night before and asked me to come down, and I said I couldn't be there until the weekend." She shakes her head. "If I'd canceled my lunch plans, I might have been there . . ." She covers her mouth with her hand and turns her head to the side.

This isn't something I've heard before. And I see with fresh eyes and perspective how all of us have our baggage to contend with when it comes to that loss. "It wasn't your fault."

"I know that. I tell myself that all the time. It was no one's fault. Nothing we could have done would have saved her, but sometimes I wish I'd had those hours with her. Just one more day with my daughter." She puts her head in her hands and her shoulders shake.

I push my chair back and walk around the table so I can take the seat next to her. I put an arm around her. "I've spent a lot of years wondering what I could have done differently and wishing I could change the past. But we can't, Karen. We can only move forward. She wouldn't want you to beat yourself up about this. Not after ten years. And she wouldn't want me to be alone, and she would want Peyton to be loved and to have someone who can be the mother Marcie didn't get to be."

Karen brushes away her tears. "You're right. You're so right.

Marcie would want you to be happy, and she wouldn't want you to be alone, or for Peyton to never know what it's like to have a mom."

"I love Harley, and I want to see if she and I can build a future together. I would love for you to be part of that, but I need you to be on my side here, not fighting against us."

"Do you think she can forgive me for how difficult I've been?"

"If there was ever a person capable of forgiveness, it's definitely Harley. She has a huge heart. All you need to do is give her a reason to let you into hers."

And I realize if I want this to truly work out, I need to take my own advice.

So I get to work on a project that will show Harley how much I care about her.

Twenty-Eight

ANOTHER CHANCE

HARLEY

I'm standing in my kitchen, take-out cup of coffee in hand, ready to leave for Spark House. Contractors are coming in to discuss converting the garden shed into Sparkle House today. We're hoping to use the existing structure because it will mean less hoops to jump through. Every time I think about it, I get excited, and then a pang of sadness hits, because I want to share this elation with Gavin, and I don't know if that will ever happen. I have all these ideas that I want to run by him, including a plan for a play structure, and his input would be invaluable.

Before I can gather my purse, there's a knock on my door. Usually this means that my elderly neighbor has run out of cream for her coffee. It happens once a month or so, and she always makes oatmeal raisin cookies as a thank-you. I leave my coffee on the counter and cross the kitchen, heading down the hall to the front foyer.

But when I open the door, I'm surprised to find not Ms. Wheatly, but Gavin. He's dressed for work in a button-down, black pants, and a tie with a cartoon cinnamon roll pattern on it. Peyton and I were out shopping a while back, and I decided we had to get it for him. I never actually expected him to wear it to anything outside of formal family functions, or maybe to a school production, but it probably makes it into his wardrobe rotation once a week. He's also holding a roll of paper in his hand that looks like it could be a blueprint.

"Hey." I don't know what to do with my hands, so I grip the doorknob like I'm hanging off the edge of a cliff and it's my lifeline.

Gavin gives me a sheepish grin. "Hi. Sorry I'm showing up with no warning, but I wanted to catch you before you left for work. I hoped we could talk, and I didn't want to do it over the phone."

"I guess it depends on what we're talking about." I might have time for a conversation, but I don't know if I have time to redo my makeup if the content is going to make it run off my face.

"I shouldn't have lost it on you about Peyton's ankle. It was unfair, and my anger was misplaced."

"How is she?" Just her name makes my throat tight and my eyes prick with tears.

"Her ankle is healing fast, and she's already off the crutches. We see the doctor again in a couple of days to have it checked out, but she's on the mend."

"That's good. I'm glad to hear that."

He nods and tucks his hands into his pockets, giving me a small, uncertain smile. I swear there's something sparkling on his face, but I refocus on him when he says, "I owe you an apology. More than one, really. And not just for getting upset about Peyton falling off the climber. She knew she shouldn't have been up there, and I was the reason you were distracted."

I step aside and motion him inside. "So why were you so upset?"

Gavin crosses the threshold, and I close the door behind him, moving across the room and putting the kitchen island between us.

"Where do I start?" He sets the roll of paper on the counter, runs a hand through his hair, and tips his chin up, eyes on the light fixture above his head before they drop back to meet mine, his expression pleading. "I was overwhelmed, Harley. By everything. By Peyton getting hurt, by my feelings for you, by the guilt I felt for having those feelings for you. And my own fears and guilt over Marcie. I realize now that my reaction was extreme because I was scared. I *am* scared. I avoid hospitals because the last time I was in one, I lost my wife. I don't know if I can truly ever get over that, but I know that you were right when you said my reaction to Peyton's fall didn't match the injury. It made me realize that I still have a lot to overcome, and some personal work to do, because I don't want that to happen again."

I nod, absorbing his words. All of it makes sense, but it still leaves a lot of questions. "What does that mean for us? I can't walk on eggshells like this, Gavin, or have you shut down on me every time something bad happens."

"I know. I realized that I've allowed Karen to have the control she does, not just because of my guilt, but also because I've been afraid."

"Afraid of what?"

"Of letting myself truly love someone again. Letting someone take the place Marcie has held for so long. But I see that in not dealing with Karen, or my fears, that I'm pushing you away. I've spent a lot of years avoiding falling in love, and I don't want to miss out on all the good parts of it because I'm afraid of the bad parts."

I swallow down my own fears. "But what about Karen? How are you going to manage that?"

"We talked yesterday, and I told her that I needed to be able to move on and move forward with my life. That I deserve a partner, and that Peyton deserves to have someone in her life who loves her like I do."

"And how did she take that?"

"She agreed. She knows she hasn't been fair, and she feels awful, but she also felt like she'd lost Marcie all over again when we moved back here because she'd been so integral in raising Peyton, and she felt guilty for accepting someone who wasn't her daughter into her life."

I nod and press a hand to my heart, aware of how difficult this all must be for Karen, and Gavin, now that he's able to see past the way it affects him and Peyton. "It couldn't have been easy for any of you, and I can see the struggle for Karen, but I don't want to replace her daughter. I just want a chance to be accepted and to not feel like I'm trying to meet expectations that are forever out of reach."

"I know, and she sees that now too. We've all been holding on to the past, not dealing with losing Marcie the way we needed to in order to move forward with our lives. I realize one conversation isn't going to solve that problem, but we know where we stand. She wasn't sure you'd be able to forgive her for making it so difficult."

"There's always room in my heart for forgiveness. Especially since I understand what that kind of loss feels like."

"I'm really glad to hear that." He gives me a small smile and then swallows nervously. "I, uh . . . made you something to show you how important you are. Well, we did."

"We?"

He rubs the back of his neck again and gives me a sheepish smile. "I had help from Peyton and my mom and Karen. It's not a skywritten apology, but uh, well . . . I'll just show you."

He unrolls the piece of paper, and I bite my bottom lip. I wasn't wrong about the sparkle on his face, it seems.

"This is . . ." I press two fingers to my lips, unsure if I want to laugh or cry.

"Very glittery?" he supplies.

I chuckle, and it turns into a choked squeak. It seems like tears are imminent. "Exceptionally glittery," I agree.

In the middle of the banner that spans the entire length of my counter are the words: SORRY MY DAD WAS A TURD. There's a happy poo emoji in brown glitter, something I didn't even know existed. And all over the banner are drawings, some clearly Gavin's handiwork with the neat lines and careful pencil, others Peyton's drawings. There are little captions under each one, cataloguing our adventures together, our trip to Chuck E. Cheese, pizza dinners, our outing to the zoo. Little moments that detail our story. And it shows me exactly how loved I am.

"How much glitter did you go through to make this?"

"A ridiculous amount. And it will totally be worth wearing for the next week or more if it means you can forgive *me*?" I can see the hope and fear written all over his gorgeous face.

I nod once and sweep a tear away. "I can forgive you, Gavin. Love is never easy, and your path has been harder than most. I know Marcie was your best friend and the future you thought you had was ripped away from you. I don't expect or want you to forget her. But what I do want is for you to open up to me about her. If we're going to make this work, I want you to talk to me. She was a huge part of your life, and she gave you Peyton. You can't see her and not think about the person you lost."

"You're right. I can't and shouldn't try to keep those parts of my past to myself," he agrees.

It's the nervous, uncomfortable way he says it, stiffly, like he's still trying to disassociate from the pain, the joy, and the love that he's held so close to his heart for so long that makes me wary.

"My biggest fear though, Gavin, is how you're going to react when things invariably get hard again, or our relationship is tested. The anniversary of Marcie's death is coming up, and I know that's going to be difficult for you. Especially with me in the picture. I'm afraid that I'm going to keep putting my heart on the line for you and that you're just going to run away again. You've done it before—" Before he can interject, I hold my hand up. "It's not the same anymore, I know, because we've both grown a lot since then, but this is your pattern, and it can't keep happening. It's not healthy for me, or Peyton, or you."

He nods. "You're right. But I want this to work, Harley. I want there to be an us, and I understand if maybe you need some time and you need me to prove that I'm not going to cut and run again. I love you, and Peyton loves you. I can see a future with you. Just give me the chance to show you I'm in this."

I close my eyes and tip my head back. I know we're only scratching the surface, that there are more conversations to be had. When I open my eyes, he's chewing nervously on his bottom lip.

"We'll talk to someone regularly? Like couples' counseling? And you have to stick with it even if you hate it and it's hard."

"I know. Especially if the alternative is not having you in my life. This past week . . . it hasn't been good. I've had a lot of time to reflect on how I've handled things, and I don't want to risk losing you again."

I take a step forward, bringing me into his personal space. "I want this to work too, Gavin. But if that's going to happen, we need to have open lines of communication. We have to talk things through, and I need to know when you're struggling and where that's coming from. I can handle all your ghosts. I just don't want to be second to them anymore."

"You were never second. I just didn't know how to let go of the past so I could start living in the present."

"It's not about letting go. It's about giving yourself permission to remember all the good things and the bad, to talk about them, feel the love and the sadness and hurt in equal measure, and relinquish the guilt. You don't need to hold on to things that are going to drag you down, and if you'll let me, I'm going to do my best to be the hand you reach for when you need to be pulled back up."

He takes my hand in his and brings it to his lips, pressing them against my knuckle. "I love you. More than I thought I was capable of. I feel like you've put me back together."

"I love you too. You fill my heart."

He drops his head, eyes on my lips. "Can I kiss you?"

"Please."

He tips my chin up and brushes his lips over mine, one, twice, three times before he presses forward, trapping me between my counter and his body. "I missed you so much." He cups my face between his palms and slants his mouth over mine, showing me with actions and words how much I mean to him.

Twenty-Nine

SNAPSHOTS OF LOVE

HARLEY

"She's going to love it so much, Harley. You've really outdone yourself."

If I was smiling any harder, my face would crack. "I couldn't have done it without your help," I tell Karen and then turn to Judith. "Or yours."

They both put their arms around me and give me an affectionate squeeze. The maternal, warm kind I've missed so much over the past decade and a half. Grandma Spark is an amazing woman, but she wasn't a big hugger.

It turns out that both Gavin's mom and his mother-in-law are big on the squeezes.

There have been some significant changes over the past month when it comes to mine and Karen's relationship. She called me the day after Gavin and I got back together and asked if we could go for coffee.

I warily said yes. If I wanted things to work between Gavin and me, I needed to come to terms with the fact that Karen was always going to be a part of Peyton's life, and if things went the way I hoped they would with Gavin—mine as well. And that meant finding a way to have a relationship that wasn't full of strain and animosity.

The apology was exactly what I needed, and it seemed, so did she.

We cried together, and in the end it felt cathartic and gave us the fresh start we needed.

In the weeks following that talk, I reached out and asked Karen and Judith for their help in putting together a special gift for Peyton. I wanted Karen to understand that I wasn't planning to take her daughter's place, and that more than anything I wanted to celebrate Marcie on Peyton's birthday as much as I wanted to celebrate Peyton herself. More than either of those things, I wanted to give permission to Gavin to talk about Marcie freely, to grieve her loss and embrace her memory and share his love for her with his daughter, and with me. I wanted to normalize discussions about Marcie in the same way my sisters and I embrace the memory of our parents. The love we share outweighs the pain some of the memories bring, and we deal with that as a best we can and keep moving forward.

Karen pulls a tissue from her pocket and dabs at her eyes. "It's always such an emotional day for me."

"You don't have to hold it together on our account. It's okay to be as sad as you are happy," I tell her gently. It's a challenging day, because the day she gained her granddaughter, she also lost her daughter.

"I don't want Peyton to ever see her birthday as anything but a celebration," she says honestly.

"It's a delicate balance. And eventually, when Peyton is old enough, she'll understand how wonderful and difficult this day truly is. But for now we can protect her from that sadness by celebrating Marcie's life and how important she will always be to all of you."

Karen nods and tucks the tissue into her pocket. "You're right. We're so lucky to have you in our lives, always looking at the bright side of things."

"Behind every cloud is a ray of sunshine looking for a place to peek through."

Avery pops into the dining room, where the party is taking place this afternoon. "I thought I'd find you all in here." She waddles into the room, her belly round with the promise of new life. She's due in a few weeks and ready to have her body back and to meet the new addition to her family. "This looks amazing. It feels like we're in a magical wonderland."

"I think Peyton is going to love it," I agree. The room is decorated in a Tinker Bell theme, with green and gold balloons forming an archway. "I went a little overboard with the color scheme."

"It's perfect. The cake was just delivered to the kitchen, and we're all set up for guests to arrive."

"Which should be in just a few minutes." I check my phone as it pings with a message from Gavin. "They're half an hour away, and Peyton keeps trying to convince him to stop for ice cream every five minutes. Apparently there's a lot of pouting." A picture of a pouting Peyton follows.

I laugh and fire back a message to let him know that all the pouting will be worth it, and we don't want to spoil her appetite before the party, but there's a treat for her in the center console. A few minutes later I get another message in the form of a photo with a smiling Peyton, eating a cake pop. Less filling than ice cream and one of her favorite treats.

Guests start arriving a few minutes later, and we usher everyone into the dining hall. Construction has already begun on the
daycare, and normally they'd be working on it right now, but I
asked that they take a few hours off this afternoon so we could
host the party without the sound of machines driving around in
the background.

Peyton's friends from school and some of the parents we've
grown friendly with are here, as well as her aunt, uncle, and
younger cousins. We all gather in the party room and wait for
Gavin to arrive with Peyton. She comes bounding down the hall,
shouting my name, asking where I'm hiding. "Are you sure she's
here? I didn't see her car out front."

"Let's try in here."

"Why would she be in a dark room? That doesn't make
sense."

I flick on the lights, and we shout a collective surprise. She
startles and then her face lights up with absolute joy. Her hands
flutter in the air, and she spins around to look at her dad before
she's swarmed by her friends.

Gavin winks at me from his place in the doorway. When
the commotion dies down, he crosses the room. "This looks like
you're throwing a prom, not a birthday for a ten-year-old." He dips
down and kisses me softly.

"I went a little wild with the decorations."

"It's amazing. She's ecstatic. I can't believe we managed to
keep this a secret until now."

"It sure wasn't easy, but it was totally worth it." I wrap my arm
around his waist and lean into his side, watching the kids as they
head over to the dress-up station and pick out their favorite costume, much like at the party Peyton attended all those months

ago. This one is a little different in that they're all fairy costumes with wings that need to be decorated.

Gavin is quickly reclaimed by Peyton and dressed in a yellow tutu. I'm already in fairy garb, so we go together quite well. We spend the next hour decorating wings with glitter and jewels and whatever the kids think will look good. Gavin tries to make his look like flames, but really it's just a mess of orange and red glitter.

We play games and eat food, sing happy birthday, and bring out an outlandishly large cake that's been decorated in the same green-and-gold fairy theme. There's a lot of green icing which Gavin jokes is going to scare a lot of people coming out the back end.

He's not wrong, even if it's gross.

It isn't until the party is over and we've said goodbye to all of the guests that I give Peyton her birthday present. His parents and in-laws join us in the sitting room, along with my sisters and their husbands, with Gavin and me on either side of Peyton. Even he hasn't seen the finished product, or known exactly what it is I've put together.

Over the past month, he and I have gone through all of his old photo albums. It wasn't easy for him, and a lot of the pictures made him emotional, but it was something I think he needed to do. Not only for himself, but for us as a couple. I had the chance to see what his life looked like before I came into it all those years ago. And the jealousy I first felt at how much space a ghost could take up in his heart disappeared, because what I saw was a man with fond memories of someone he loved very much. But I also get to help him make peace with that loss.

Peyton tears through the paper, and her eyes go wide when she sees the box inside with the inscription THE STORY OF PEY-TON RHODES in beautiful gold script.

Gavin glances over at me, questions in his eyes. I smile and reach across the back of the couch, squeezing his shoulder in reassurance. Peyton carefully lifts the lid from the box to reveal the thick four-inch, twelve-by-twelve book inside. The same inscription adorns the cover, which is decorated in flowers and glitter and all of Peyton's favorite things.

Peyton looks up at me. "You made me a storybook?"

"Not just me, but your dad and your grandparents helped. And some of your friends and their parents too."

"Everyone helped make this?" She flips the cover open and reveals the first page, which is her baby photo. Her little fists curled tight, a pink hat on her head, eyes still puffy and closed, lips parted in sleep.

The next page takes us back in time, to Gavin and Marcie's first date. His eyes widen, and his gaze darts to mine. There's a short, handwritten story about that day from Karen. How he picked her up and stood on the front steps, looking nervous, and how he didn't just bring Marcie flowers, but he brought Karen flowers too.

Each page has a short story attached to the photographs, chronicling Gavin and Marcie's relationship, their wedding, her pregnancy with Peyton, and there's even a page dedicated to her loss. It's decorated with angels and clouds because I wanted Peyton to see all the pieces of her life, but also to see that her mom is always looking out for her, even if from afar.

That's when I begin to appear in the pages, and many of the photos are taken by me. We see first smiles, first words, rolling over, sitting up, solid foods and messy faces, and her first step. That picture was taken by Gavin's parents in their backyard. It was Peyton's first birthday, and it was before guests started to arrive. Gavin had been on the other side of the yard. He'd been struggling that day and had asked if I could attend the birthday party even though it was supposed to be my day off. Peyton had kept crying for him, but he was in the middle of trying to set something up and hold himself together.

When I'd set her down and held her hands, she'd taken a tentative step and let go of my hand, and then she'd taken another and let go of the other one.

Judith had captured all of those moments, including the one when Gavin's face had broken into the most glorious smile, and he'd rushed over and scooped her up and covered her face in kisses.

In another family celebration, there's a picture of me holding Peyton's hand. She and Gavin are looking at each other with complete adoration, and I'm smiling as I watch that love being realized. It's a special moment that I'd been part of. We keep flipping pages, chronicling milestones in Peyton's life until we reach the move back to Colorado Springs and the months since I've been back in their lives.

There are pages already decorated waiting for pictures from today, and more empty pages waiting to be filled.

"There's space for more chapters in your life, and we'll get to write them together," I tell her and motion to our family, still sitting around the room. "All of us get to be part of your story."

"I'm so glad the angels sent you and brought you back." She throws her arms around my neck, and I wrap mine around her small frame, smiling through my tears of joy.

"Me too, sweetie, me too."

"Me three," Gavin whispers.

My heart is so full of love for both of them.

Epilogue

MY FAMILY

PEYTON
TWO YEARS LATER

"Peyton, are you ready to go?" Dad calls out from down the hall.

I check my reflection in the mirror one more time and make sure my dress doesn't have any lint on it. I don't feel any older than I did yesterday, but today is my twelfth birthday.

And it's a big one.

I pat my tummy, hoping to reassure it that there's no need for the butterflies and that everything is going to be fine.

My gaze catches on the picture of my mom and dad on my dresser. Before Dad had crinkles in the corner of his eyes. In it, my mom was pregnant with me. Her smile is wide and her hand rests protectively on her bump. My dad smiles, but he's not looking at the camera, he's looking at my mom. I blow out a breath and accept the pang of sadness that hits me whenever I really stop to look at this photo. I'll never know what my name sounds like on her lips. Not while I'm alive anyway. But one day, a long time from now, I'll meet her. For now I have pictures and stories, and a whole life ahead of me.

And today I get the birthday present I've secretly been wishing for all my life. The other wish will come true in a few months, when I finally get the baby sister I always wanted.

I press my fingertips to my lips and then touch the corner of the frame before I turn away and cross my room. "Coming," I shout on my way down the hall.

When I reach the front foyer, my dad and Harley are waiting for me. Harley's round belly has the phrase SISTER IN THE MAK-ING written across it. My granny and nana and I went shopping as soon as we found out Harley was pregnant and bought her all kinds of fun clothes. I picked this one out. I already took the babysitters' course so I can watch my little sister when Harley and my dad have their date nights. I know twelve years is a big gap, but I love babies the same way Harley does, and being a much older sister is a special relationship.

I've already started babysitting for our neighbors down the street a couple of afternoons a week. They have four-year-old twins, and their mom calls them "holy terrors," but she's always smiling when she says it. I think they're hilarious and so much fun. I can't wait to teach my little sister all kinds of things. Like how to make rainbow glitter flowers and bunny pizzas.

Harley smiles softly at me, and I feel her love like an invisible hug. Last year Dad asked me how I would feel if he asked Harley to move in with us.

I asked him if that meant they were going to get married and if I would have a brother or a sister one day. He laughed and said one thing at a time. But he didn't get sad, or mad, or say no, and I took that as a good sign.

A great sign, actually.

Because a few months after Harley moved in with us, Dad took me out with him on a special trip to a jewelry store, and I got to help him pick out an engagement ring for Harley. We took it with us on our family vacation, and I got to be there with him when he proposed and she said yes. Six months ago they got married. I was a junior bridesmaid and Ella was a flower girl. Even though Aunt Avery's baby, William, was too small to be the official ring bearer, we made him part of the ceremony. Five minutes after it was all over, he exploded the back end of his diaper and needed a full change of clothes. Uncle Declan had fun with that one.

And a month after that, Harley announced I was getting a baby brother or sister. Dad is what Harley calls a nervous mother bird when it comes to her and the baby, but she doesn't mind. He goes to all the doctor appointments and is constantly making sure she's okay. But he's happy and excited, and so am I, and so is Harley.

We went shopping as a family and picked out all the decorations for the nursery as soon as we knew I was getting a baby sister.

And today is another big day for us.

Harley steps forward and takes my chin between her thumb and finger, turning my head from one side and then the other, inspecting me with a stern look on her face. "Yes. You definitely look like a twelve-year-old today."

I grin. "I look the same as I did yesterday."

"Hmm. One day older. But I must tell you, turning twelve does not mean that we're going to stop watching Disney movies or making glitter crafts."

I blow out a dramatic breath. "Phew. I was really worried about that."

Dad rolls his eyes and laughs. "You're only saying that because you're in love with glitter crafts."

"This is absolutely true," Harley agrees with a nod, and then her expression turns serious and her voice soft. "You ready for this?"

I nod and swallow past the nervous lump in my throat.

"Good. Me too." She looks up at Dad.

"Me three." He winks, and then we're out the door and in the car.

My palms are sweaty by the time we get to the big official-looking building. And when we step into the elevator, I take both of their hands and squeeze. I don't know why I'm so nervous. But I keep hold of them both because I don't want them to disappear.

When we reach the fourteenth floor, the elevator opens and we walk down another hall, Dad holding the doors open for me and Harley. I'm surprised all over again when Aunt Avery and Aunt London are sitting in the waiting room, along with Uncle Declan and Uncle Jax. Ella and William are on a blanket on the floor, playing together.

My aunts push out of their chairs. London is pregnant again too. So my little sister and her baby will be close to the same age. It means I'll have lot of babysitting practice.

"I didn't know you guys were going to be here too." I step into their open arms.

"Well, it's kind of a big day." Aunt London gives me a squeeze before she releases me.

"We're meeting up with all the grandparents for lunch after this too. It's going to be an all-day kind of celebration." Harley winks and Dad squeezes my shoulder.

I accept more hugs from my uncles, and then we're being led into a big office with a conference table. It's all a bit overwhelming. An older man named Mr. Rolph with a bald spot on the top of his head and big bushy eyebrows that remind me of caterpillars joins us. He and Uncle Jax must be friends, because they do that thing that guys do where they shake hands and pat each other on the back, like a sort-of-hug. I wipe my hand on my dress before I shake his hand too, because my palms are damp.

"I hear it's your birthday, Peyton. It's a big day today, isn't it?"

"It is. We're going for lunch at my favorite restaurant after this, and then tomorrow we're going to Disney World for a vacation, and I haven't been there before but you're never too old for Disney and princesses," I tell him.

"You're a lucky girl, aren't you? That sounds like it's going to be an amazing birthday week for you!"

I nod in agreement. "I didn't even ask for the trip to Disney World, but Harley loves Disney, and I love Disney, and my grandparents are coming too, and my aunt and uncle and my cousins." I motion to them, realizing how lucky I am that I get to spend a whole week with all of my favorite people. "We're going to swim and ride all the rides, and I think it's going to be the best trip ever. And I get to miss school for a week, which is pretty cool too."

He laughs. "It does sound pretty cool. We should get these papers signed so you can start celebrating, don't you think?"

"That would be great. This is all I wanted for my birthday, so everything else is pretty much a bonus."

Dad chuckles and pulls out a chair for me, and Harley squeezes my hand.

We all sit down, and Mr. Rolph pulls out the papers and explains everything. Uncle Jax and Uncle Declan take William and Ella out when they start to get fussy, which only takes about five minutes. Explaining everything takes longer than I thought it would, but eventually he slides the papers across the table and my dad signs them first, then Harley.

After that we have to wait for it to be given a stamp and a seal, and for copies. But finally, *finally* they hand us the copy of the adoption papers. "That's it?" I ask. "It's official?"

"It's official," Mr. Rolph says.

I turn to Harley whose eyes are heavy and watery. "You're my mom now? For real this time?" I ask.

Two tears track down her cheeks, and she nods, holding her arms wide. "I'm your mom."

I step into her embrace and wrap my arms around her, and Dad engulfs us in a hug with me in the middle.

My aunts are standing a few feet away, hugging each other, smiling and dabbing at their eyes with tissues. I smile back and absorb all the love in the room. It's a gift to have been given not just one mom who lives in my heart, but a second one who's down here with me.

I turn my head, breathing in her familiar shampoo. "I love you, Mom." I smile at the way those words settle in my heart.

"I love you too." She kisses me on the cheek, and I feel the warm wet of tears with it. Happy ones, though.

"I love you, both," Dad says, squeezing us tight.

I send a thank-you up to my mom in heaven for sending Harley to me and Dad, and for giving me a mom to love and take care of me, and the family I always wanted.

Acknowledgments

Hubs and kidlet, you're always my number ones. Thank you for being my biggest cheerleaders.

Deb, you're my favorite friend. Thank you for being the pepper to my salt.

Kimberly, thank you for always helping me polish these stories so they shine brighter. You're an incredible agent and I'm lucky to have you in my corner and on my team.

Eileen, you're an amazing editor and I'm so lucky to have been able to give the Spark Sisters a home with you at SMP. To my team at SMP—Marissa, Sara, Lisa, and Christa—thank you for everything you've done to make the Spark Sisters so much fun.

Jenn and my SBPR team, thank you for being awesome, and for getting my stories into the hands of readers. You're amazing and all deserve Wonder Woman awards.

Sarah and the Hustlers, I can't do this without you. Thank you for being my team.

My ARC crew, my SS girls, and my Beaver Den, I adore you. Thank you for always celebrating with me and for being the most amazing readers.

Kat, Krystin, and Marnie, thank you for being such wonderful friends and amazing women.

To my bloggers, bookstagrammers, and booktokers, thank you for your love of romance and happily ever afters. I couldn't do this without your support.

About the Author

New York Times and *USA Today* bestselling author HELENA HUNTING lives outside of Toronto with her amazing family and her two awesome cats, who think the best place to sleep is on her keyboard. She writes all things romance—contemporary, romantic comedy, sports, and angsty new adult. Some of her books include *Meet Cute, Pucked,* and *Shacking Up.* Helena loves to bake cupcakes and has been known to listen to a song on repeat 1,512 times while writing a book, and if she has to be away from her family, she prefers to be in warm weather with her friends.